Ghosted

Also by Amanda Quain

Accomplished

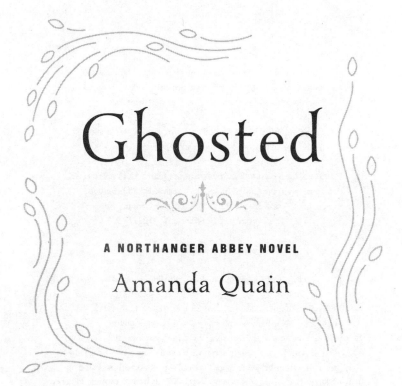

Ghosted

A NORTHANGER ABBEY NOVEL

Amanda Quain

WEDNESDAY BOOKS
NEW YORK

To my parents, Bill and Jeanne Quain,
who taught me to do whatever it takes

First published in the United States by Wednesday Books,
an imprint of St. Martin's Publishing Group

GHOSTED. Copyright © 2023 by Amanda Quain. All rights reserved.
Printed in the United States of America. For information,
address St. Martin's Publishing Group,
120 Broadway, New York, NY 10271.

www.wednesdaybooks.com

Library of Congress Cataloging-in-Publication Data

Names: Quain, Amanda, author. | Northanger Abbey, 1775–1817.
Title: Ghosted : a Northanger Abbey novel / Amanda Quain.
Description: First edition. | New York : Wednesday Books, 2023. |
    Audience: Ages 13–18. | Summary: After her paranormal-loving father dies,
    Hattie Tilney stops believing in ghosts until she works with new student
    Kit Morland on an investigation project and finds herself wanting to believe
    in something.
Identifiers: LCCN 2023004388 | ISBN 9781250865076 (hardcover) |
    ISBN 9781250865083 (ebook)
Subjects: CYAC: Haunted places—Fiction. | Interpersonal relations—Fiction. |
    Family life—Fiction. | High schools—Fiction. | Schools—Fiction. |
    LCGFT: Romance fiction. | Novels.
Classification: LCC PZ7.1.Q254 Gh 2023 | DDC [Fic] —dc23
LC record available at https://lccn.loc.gov/2023004388

Our books may be purchased in bulk for promotional, educational,
or business use. Please contact your local bookseller or the
Macmillan Corporate and Premium Sales Department at
1-800-221-7945, extension 5442, or by email at
MacmillanSpecialMarkets@macmillan.com.

First Edition: 2023

10 9 8 7 6 5 4 3 2 1

The boundaries which divide Life from Death are at best shadowy and vague. Who shall say where the one ends, and where the other begins?

—EDGAR ALLAN POE, "The Premature Burial"

Circumstances change, opinions alter.

—JANE AUSTEN, *Northanger Abbey*

I was eighty-five percent sure there was a ghost in this room, and Kit Morland was grinning at me like it was the best thing that had ever happened to him.

"Maybe we should go," I whispered, as if whatever mysterious entity that was making the small, cramped room so cold wouldn't be able to hear me if I lowered my voice. Around us, the harsh December wind beat against the windows of the abbey, tapping tree branches that offered a warning we hadn't yet heeded. *You're safe from me inside*, the wind seemed to say, *but you're not safe from whoever's in there*. "Kit. Come on."

"Are you kidding?" he whispered back, though whether he was showing deference to the spirit or to the tone of my voice was unclear. It was like he didn't even notice the way the shadows crept along the wall, how the cracks in the old, yellowed plaster looked like they were reaching for us. "Hattie. This is what we've been waiting for. This is why we're here."

I could just barely make him out in the dim moonlight that

forced its way through the age-stained windows: black beanie pulled down low over his forehead, his favorite maroon cable-knit sweater inexplicably tied around his waist, even though it was freezing in here. He had on a black long-sleeved tee underneath, but he'd pushed the sleeves up to his elbows on that, too. *I run warm when I get excited*, he'd said when I'd asked him about it earlier. Typical Kit. An answer to everything, a *reason* for everything.

Including, apparently, a reason we shouldn't run away screaming from what just might be a paranormal entity.

"What if it's dangerous?" I argued. We were currently crouched on the floor in the doorway of the old servants' quarters. Poky little rooms at the top of the old abbey buildings, the servants' quarters came complete with creaky floorboards and dust-covered spiderwebs that would have been spooky even *without* the random cold spots and the half dozen young girls who had died up here over the years. These rooms were used for storage now, but that didn't mean they were abandoned. In fact, I was starting to think they were very much occupied. "What if whatever's in there tries to hurt us?" There were no viable reports of abbey ghosts acting malevolently, but you never knew. This could be the night they made their bone-chilling debut.

I expected Kit to argue, or to roll his eyes and pull me into the room anyway, but instead, a smile spread across his face. Slow. *Delighted*.

"So you *do* think there's something in there."

"That's not what I said." I'd been very careful with my words, in fact. Or at least I thought I had. A chill washed over me, and I shivered in my oversized sweater. When I was with Kit, it was harder to be careful.

"If you didn't think there was something in there, you wouldn't be scared." He nudged his shoulder against mine, and the contact, even through layers of wool, offered me the briefest of distractions from my concerns.

"Maybe I just don't want to fall through the floorboards." My voice cracked, and Kit chuckled, low and quiet. It was a real possibility, with the way each floorboard shuddered under my weight, the long and slow *creaaaaak* that accompanied each shift in our position. But then he turned to me, his eyes serious, and I realized how close we were sitting. How close his face was to mine.

"You really don't want to say it, do you?"

"Say what?" This time, my whisper was not entirely in deference to the ghosts.

"That you believe in something." His tilted his head to the side, and I was mesmerized, and I didn't know if I believed in ghosts, but, God, I believed in Kit Morland. "That the way you think about things may not be a hundred percent right a hundred percent of the time."

"Eighty-five percent."

"What?"

"That's how likely it is that there's a ghost in there." I nodded into the room, lit by the blinking of the EMF detector Kit held in his hand. Its red light cast a bloody shadow against walls that were dappled with age. "Eighty-five percent. Potentially, if the EMF detector's readings from downstairs are to be believed." The light had been so strong, stronger than I'd ever seen it. "And even then. Probably not." Even as I said it, I shivered.

"Right." He smiled, then stood slowly and held his hand out to me. I could only stare at it, his long fingers, the way he held them out like a promise. *Come with me*, they seemed to say, *and for once in your life, allow yourself to be surprised by something.* "You can give it a try, though."

"What?" I asked, though I knew what he was going to say, because it was all he ever talked about; and in anyone else it might have been obnoxious but when Kit did it, he was the sun.

"Believing."

The room was so cold, and there might be a ghost.

I looked at Kit's hand and thought about the question he was asking. It had never been a matter of whether I *could* believe in ghosts. The question was . . .

Did I want to?

Chapter One

THREE MONTHS EARLIER

The sun was shining through the trees, the end-of-summer breeze was light on the back of my neck, and I was deeply, unbelievably over these ghost hunters.

"Hey!" I clapped my hands together as I stepped out my front door onto the postage-stamp lawn that my little brother, Liam, had mowed half of before abandoning the project in favor of *Animal Crossing*. "Can I help you?"

The group, five or six guys strong (in case you were wondering, the proper term for a group of paranormal enthusiasts was "an annoyance") looked up as one from the faded white picket fence that surrounded our cottage. The absolute synchronization would have been creepy, if it wasn't the third time I'd had to deal with this in the last week.

"Are you a student?" The guy who broke free from the hive mind to speak to me might have been tall once, but he had the posture of someone who spent all his time hunched over his computer, reading paranormal encounter reports on Reddit.

That wasn't just conjecture, either—the T-shirt he was wearing literally read *r/Paranormal Investigator* on the front.

"I am, which means I know you're not supposed to be here." The Northanger crest on my blazer was probably already visible, but I tossed my hair back out of the way anyway, just in case. I'd been having a particularly good hair day this morning, turned my usual curly chaos into soft, cooperating waves, and I wanted desperately to get to school while they still had some semblance of their shape, which meant I needed to get moving. The problem was that you could never leave these ghostbusters alone—they'd start with the fence, and then they'd decide that the latch on the gate was just a formality, and then the next thing you knew, I'd be sitting at my desk doing homework and spot one of them crouched in the tree outside my window. I'd scream, and he'd scream, and then he'd fall and break three bones in his wrist and my mother would make me write a get-well note to send to the hospital.

Unfortunately, I was speaking from actual experience.

"I don't care what tour group you wandered away from." I pointed away from the house, back toward the winding path that would lead them to the school. "This is a private residence. If you don't leave, I'll call security, and they'll throw you out of here faster than you can say boo."

"We were just looking for signs of activity," the guy said, glancing back and forth among his friends for reassurance. "There are reports of sightings outside the official school grounds. Chatter online about the twins."

The worst part of all of it was the shiver that went down my spine. You would think, three years into my time at

Northanger, I'd be numb to it. And for the most part, I was, the mention of your average ghost no more concerning to me than a new rotation to the lunch menu. But every time someone talked about the twins, I felt sick to my stomach, like whatever I'd eaten for breakfast had turned on me.

So. Obviously I wasn't going to stand for that.

"I did warn you." I pulled my phone out of the pocket of my uniform skirt, then acted like I was dialing. "Hello? Neil? I've got a disturbance . . ."

"Sorry!" The guy backed up right away, all semblance of color drained from his face. Clearly, he was remembering the part of the tour that the school guides were supposed to emphasize—*anyone caught outside the official tour route will be banned from Northanger Abbey.* It was a death sentence for the paranormal enthusiast. The severity of the punishment was further emphasized as the guy and his buddies took off at a run, away from the house, back toward the school. There was practically a ghost hunter–shaped dust cloud left in their wake.

I should have felt satisfied. But as I leaned against the white, weathered doorframe and watched them disappear into the distance, I just felt tired. Everyone who came through on these tours thought they owned the place, had the right to creep on our private property just because they had the bad sense to believe in ghost stories. It was all so overblown, these grown adults jumping every time the floor creaked. Like the *one* possible explanation was that the floor was possessed by a demon and not that it was just, you know, old. If I started screaming about supernatural forces every time the pipes in our house made a weird noise, I'd be hauled off for questioning.

But instead, these guys just took their shaky-cam footage of my backyard and put it on their YouTube channels with titles like *Spotted: Ghost of Actual Schuyler Sister Haunts Headmistress???*

Such was the burden of living on the campus of Northanger Abbey, America's most notoriously haunted high school.

Well, there'd be no shaky-cam footage today, not unless they called the video something like *Irate Teenager Berates Ghost Hunters for Making Her Late to Her First Day of Senior Year!*

And why, I wondered as I pushed myself off the doorframe to follow them toward the school at a safe distance, did they have to bring up the twins, anyway? They weren't even Northanger's most famous (alleged) haunting. Most people were interested in the Howling Milkmaid, or War-Torn Wilfred. (I didn't choose the names.)

"They keep calling to each other, can you imagine?" My dad pointed toward a faded paragraph in the back of the brochure, well creased from the dozen times he'd read through it. "Just wandering the school. Looking for each other."

Some of us had the good sense not to keep looking.

"Tour group?"

I *definitely* didn't believe in ghosts, but the sudden voice from behind me still made me jump about a mile into the air.

"Mom. Hi." I whipped around to see my mother in the doorway I'd just vacated, watching me with one eyebrow raised as she sipped coffee from a travel mug. Not her first, judging by the mugs that had been in the sink when I'd come downstairs for breakfast. Unsurprising. It wasn't like she ever slept. "Yeah. But they're gone now."

"Good." Already tall and standing even taller in four-inch heels that anyone of lesser poise would find impossible on the uneven terrain of Northanger's campus, my mom cut an impressive figure in a sharp blazer that made my school-issued one look positively casual. My mom—or Dr. Tilney, headmistress of Northanger Abbey, as she was known to the world at large—didn't do soft. "I need to talk to Dr. Wallace about guide training. They should keep better track of their groups."

"Mmm." I straightened my shoulders next to her, tried to emulate her posture. Dr. Wallace, the school's head of outreach, was locked in a perpetual battle with my mother over how much of the school should be open for touring. *I don't care how many servants died of influenza in that wing, Bob!* she'd shout on the phone when she thought she was out of earshot, tucked away in her office at home. *Students* sleep *there!*

"Well," Mom said, looking off toward the now-abandoned gate. "Don't let me keep you. I need to gather my things."

"Right." It didn't matter that Mom and I were going to the same place, walking along the same narrow path that would lead us to the main area of campus. She never walked with me or with Liam. It was part of the agreement we'd all made when she'd first taken this job three years ago. *If students see me as your mother, they won't respect me as their headmistress*, she'd said. *I need their respect.*

I mean, everyone knew. We had the same last name and everything. But we all liked to think it helped to pretend. Besides, she was right to keep us separate. To keep the role of mother from weakening her role as headmistress.

"See you tonight," I said, but Mom was already back inside

the house. Moving slowly, she always said, was a privilege she didn't have.

It would have been weird to have her walk with me on my last first day of school, I reminded myself. A real break from tradition. And anyway, I could use the time to gather my thoughts, to make sure my plan for the year was solid and well formed.

I did this every year—attacked the new season of my life with a plan. If you had plans, you could be prepared for anything. And when you were prepared for anything, nothing could hurt you. If I was prepared enough, I could relax.

Or not. Relaxing had never been my strong suit.

This was my senior year, and it was going to be perfect. Just the right mix of academic achievement and social standing, the sort of thing that would make any parent sit up and take notice. I'd spent three years working toward this, toward tying up my future with a neat little bow and saying to everyone, *See? I did exactly what I set out to do, and it was easy for me. It all came completely naturally.*

As far as they knew, anyway.

And if I'd managed to keep the worst parts of me hidden away for the last three years, I could sure as hell keep them there for one more.

Chapter Two

As the path widened and I emerged out of the woods, stepping onto the long, manicured lawn of the school, my best anchors to normalcy came running toward me, and I felt an instant flush of relief.

"There she is! Miss me?" My best friend, Izzy Thorpe, wrapped me in a tight hug, her cooler-than-thou demeanor betrayed only by the tightness of her embrace. Priya, Izzy's roommate and the third member of our little trio, bounced along behind her, stepping in to give me a quick squeeze once Izzy had moved back. "Ready to take senior year by storm?"

"You know it." I grinned, my rapid-fire heart rate slowing at the sight of my girls. I'd met Izzy early on freshman year, when we were assigned to the same side in gym class volleyball. Already five foot nine at fourteen, with long, shiny blond hair and a constant expression of *I know something you don't know*, Izzy was the polar opposite of sad, lost little me, completely overwhelmed by a new school and a new life. And we'd both known it, too, which was why we had essentially ignored each other until one day, a couple of weeks into the first semester, when I'd walked in on her in the bathroom fighting with her dad on the phone.

"I'll get it done, Dad," she'd hissed, tucked into the corner by the hand dryers. "I told you that you don't have to—No, it's different, okay? I just—"

I'd tried to leave, to back up as fast as I could, but she'd looked up just as I'd reached for the door, and she'd hung up her call, crossed over, and put her hand on my shoulder.

"Dr. Tilney's your mom, right?"

I'd nodded, unsure of what else to say in the face of this blond ball of energy and confidence. Even coming off a vicious fight with her father, she seemed so *sure* of herself. While I was still trying to figure out how to survive high school, Izzy seemed to have it all together.

But I had something she needed, and that made all the difference.

"Oh my God, *perfect*," she'd said, pushing me out of the bathroom and back into the hallway of the school, mostly empty between classes. "Here. Smile." She'd held up her phone and snapped a quick selfie of the two of us, a picture I still had hung up in my room. In it, Izzy is all beaming, megawatt energy, and I look even more lost and scared next to her. A ghost image, almost. It was an objectively terrible picture of me, but that didn't stop Izzy from texting it to her dad. "He loves your mom," she'd explained. "Thinks that she's going to revitalize Northanger education—whatever. And he's been super on my case ever since I got here about not taking my classes seriously, or something, but if you and I are hanging out? Problem one hundred percent solved." She took a breath finally, and then held her hand out in front of her. "I'm Izzy Thorpe."

Together, we'd made something of ourselves. Achieved things at Northanger that we never could have managed alone.

"God, you must have been bored up here without us all summer." Izzy linked her arm in mine as we crossed the lawn to our favorite early-morning hangout, a tall oak tree that grew next to the entrance to the school. Priya took her other side, and we stepped in sync, stretching our legs out left and then right. "What'd you do without us—read in the library all day?"

"We can't all be jet-setting around film festivals." Izzy and I were both Northanger-infamous for different reasons. I was my mother's daughter, which meant that, for better or for worse, basically everyone at school knew who I was. But Izzy's dad was known on an international scale. J.T. Thorpe was the director of *What Cries Beneath*, a found footage nineties horror film that had achieved cult-classic status among fans of the paranormal. They'd filmed it here on campus, and it was one of the things that had catapulted Northanger's noto- riety from "quiet site of local hauntings" to "internationally spooky tourist destination." Mr. Thorpe was rich, famous, and as I discovered quickly, wildly strict toward his daughter. But like Izzy had told me that first day we'd met, he was a huge fan of my mom, and that meant he was a huge fan of me. I was Izzy's shield; and at a school that was literally designed to haunt me with my worst memories, she was mine. High school, at least at Northanger Abbey, was basically war. And in a war, I learned quickly, you needed allies to survive.

"Whatever—the festivals all sucked this year." Izzy let go of my arm briefly to toss her hair back over her shoulder, then linked up with me again. "I did, on the other hand, learn how to pilot a sailboat, so if that comes up this year, we're golden."

"Sounds likely." I let Izzy propel me across the lawn. "What about you, Priya? Learn any more super-marketable skills?"

"Besides how to not die while Izzy's sailing a boat?" Priya asked. She visited Izzy on Martha's Vineyard every summer, and every summer, I did my best not to let it get to me. My mom didn't exactly have "send your daughter on a fancy trip" money. *But you're the one Izzy needs*, I reminded myself. Priya was great, but she was an incidental friend, thrown into our group by constant proximity as Izzy's roommate. I was the one Izzy had sought out.

"Please." Izzy glanced over at me, and I giggled. "Priya did such a bad job the one time we let her drive that the coast guard actually pulled us over. I didn't even know you could *get* pulled over in a boat. It was super annoying."

"That reminds me!" Priya clapped her hands in front of her, making Izzy jump. "Speaking of super annoying. Apparently, Skinner's making us do some giant project this semester, in case we weren't going to be busy enough. Investigative journalism, or something?"

"Really?" That piqued my interest way more than Priya's lack of boating skills. Mrs. Skinner was our journalism teacher, and her filmed assignments were always out of the box. Besides, I loved a good documentary, even if I didn't watch as many as I used to. "Where'd you hear that?"

"Steph Dryden, on our hall. She's an office aide this year."

Priya pulled one of her braids over her shoulder and began to play with the end, like she always did when she was dishing out a particularly good piece of gossip. I scooted in, eager to pick up any scrap of information. Mom never talked about work stuff at home, and I, of course, didn't have Priya and Izzy's access to the amazingly efficient gossip network that was the Northanger dorms. "She overheard Skinner talking about it yesterday, when the teachers were prepping."

"That could be kind of cool." I did my best to temper any excitement in my voice, twisted my (fake) pearl studs around in my ears. "Something different."

"As long as it's an easy enough A, I'll do whatever Skinner wants." Izzy blew away a piece of blond hair that had fallen down in front of her face. "My dad will kill me if my grades dip."

"Yeah, maybe we should all be applying to schools early decision." Priya leaned away from the tree as she waggled her eyebrows in my direction. "Then our grades for the semester will stop mattering, and we can actually *enjoy* ourselves."

I did my best to hide the instant wave of nausea that passed over me. Of the three of us, I was the only one who'd decided to go early decision for a school—Udolpho College, a small, well-respected school with high rates of success for getting its students into graduate programs and a nationally ranked debate team. Mom had first mentioned it a couple of years ago, when she gave a presentation to all the sophomores at Northanger about college applications. It was where she would look if she were applying now, she'd said; so I'd taken the brochure home, pinned it to the corkboard in my bedroom.

Even though we didn't talk about it after, I saw her nod at it approvingly once, which from my mother was basically a symphony of affirmation. It had been the plan ever since.

Of course, planning on attending a college wasn't the same as getting accepted to that college—hence, the nausea. My application was mostly finished, at least, but I'd feel a lot better once I just got in.

"Some of us plan on enjoying ourselves anyway." Izzy smirked, adjusting her skirt to make sure it perfectly covered her knees. "All work and no play makes Jack a dull boy, right? I can think of a few ways to still have fun this year."

"As long as said fun doesn't lead to us getting arrested, I'm down," Priya said, leaning back against the trunk of the oak tree. A breeze passed over us, and I shivered. There was almost always a chill in the air at Northanger Abbey, giving every ghost hunter in a five-mile radius goose bumps that they claimed were *definitely signs of paranormal activity!!!!!!* "We made it this far. I'm not getting kicked out now."

"That'd never happen," Izzy said dismissively, checking her appearance in her phone's camera and adjusting the collar of her shirt. "Hattie could totally get her mom on our side if we ever came close." *That* wasn't a theory I ever planned on testing. Izzy had gotten a lot more confident of my mom's help since we'd first met freshman year, and it was a constant worry in the back of my mind that she would push so far that I couldn't help her. "But let's focus, girls." She nodded toward the front of the school. "If anyone got hot over the summer, I want to be the first to know about it."

"Binocular vision, activate!" Priya said, and I laughed. Our spot under the oak tree wasn't as flashy as the school's front steps where the ultrapopular kids sat—think yacht club, actual pearl earrings—but it gave us the perfect view of what Priya always called the catwalk, aka, the winding paved path that led from the dorms to the front steps of the school. I'd seen more than one freshman cry after making the walk, as the commentary from the A-list crowd ranged from brutal to— well, whatever was worse than brutal.

It could be avoided, of course, by following the unspoken rules of Northanger society. They were mostly the same as the rules in the makeup tutorials Priya loved to watch on YouTube—blend, blend, blend.

But some people never learned.

Some of those people were headed toward the catwalk now, chattering excitedly with one another and completely oblivious to the way the rest of the school stared at them with disdain.

"Dork alert," Izzy announced as a group of whooping, hollering ghost hunters made their way into the school, holding an actual banner above the head of the smallest girl leading the charge with *Northanger Abbey Ghost Brigade* emblazoned across it.

Kill me now.

The Ghost Brigade was, somehow, even worse than any of the tour groups that frequently invaded our campus, because it was an organization made up of actual students, who were therefore allowed full access to the abbey. It was the most notorious club at Northanger, not because they did anything cool but because interacting with them was a clear path to social exile.

"Yikes. Did they make that banner themselves?" Priya tutted, and Izzy's face as she watched them said it all.

"Must we?" She sighed dramatically as Priya giggled. "Like this school doesn't attract enough weirdos with the ghost thing. We have to encourage it in the student population, too?"

"Don't make eye contact." I faked a shiver, and both the girls laughed, even as I felt a weird twinge in my chest. "It's safer that way." Yes, maybe I'd gone to one meeting of the Ghost Brigade, September of my freshman year. It was right before I'd met Izzy, before I'd fully realized how much I was going to have to work to fit in at Northanger. I'd never gone to a second meeting, just fell into her friendship without looking back. Besides, being anti-ghost was an easy thing for the two of us to bond over. She hated what a fuss the world made over her dad's movie, and I hated . . . well, the rest of it.

I turned away from the brigade's garishly decorated banner.

"Do you guys have your meetings set up with Dr. Tilney yet?" Priya asked, scrolling idly through her phone. My stomach swooped. I'd forgotten about senior meetings. Mom always met with every member of the senior class during the fall semester, to make sure they were on track for graduation and whatever came afterward. The meetings were the stuff of legends—some kids left with amazing plans for how they were going to change the world, and some left in tears. "Mine's in like, a week. Which doesn't seem like enough time to mentally prepare."

"Alphabetical order strikes again, Madam Acharya." Izzy smirked. "I'm not until October. Hattie, you must be near the end, too, right? Do you even have an appointment?"

"Um . . . oh, yeah, I do." I pulled out my phone to do a quick scroll through my school email and, yep, there it was at the top: a calendar invite to meet with Dr. Tilney at the beginning of November. I accepted it quickly, then returned my attention to the girls, pushed down the blossoms of excitement at the idea of a full, uninterrupted hour with my mom. Dr. Tilney terrified me, of course, but I'd spent three years making myself into exactly the sort of student she'd admire. Finally, this would be the chance for her to acknowledge that.

"That'll be weird," Izzy said, distilling all the complicated ways my mom and I interacted into a single sentence. "Priya, you'll just have to guinea pig for us."

"So glad my sacrifice will be helpful." Priya dropped her phone back into the pocket of her skirt. "Come on. We should get to homeroom."

As more students started to stream around us into the building, the three of us stood up, dusted off our skirts, and prepared to join the mob moving slowly inward. Northanger wasn't huge, but it was big enough; and as my eyes darted around my fellow students, I reminded myself again how lucky I was to have Izzy and Priya. I could have been alone here so easily.

"Hattie, isn't that your brother?"

Speaking of.

I turned my head to where Priya was pointing. Just at the base of the dark, ivy-edged stairs heading into the school was indeed Liam, staring at the crowd of students with a look of undisguised dread written all over his face. It didn't exactly scream fresh start.

That was my cue. With a reluctant wave goodbye, I let Izzy and Priya carry on without me and pushed against the tide of students until I got to my brother.

"Hey, Hattie." His voice sounded so casual, not at all like he was currently frozen in place, staring at the entrance to the school like it was a death sentence. "How's it going?"

"Oh, not too bad," I said. Liam had gotten tall over the summer, *really* tall, and it was still weird to look up at him. My baby brother, just fifteen, and he was a full head above me. I hopped up a couple of steps, facing him, so we'd at least be closer to eye level. "Just thought I'd go inside and, you know, start the school year."

"Sounds fun." His eyes were distant and glazed over, a bad sign. I knew that look. It meant he was mentally back in his bedroom, trying to beat the high score on whatever game was his current obsession. "I thought maybe I wouldn't."

"I had a feeling." Liam's mood had seemed okay when I'd left him sitting at the dining room table this morning, as our older sister, Freddie—who had graduated from high school five years ago and had no apparent goals now except to ruin her own life and the lives of everyone around her—stared into a cup of coffee. I'd hoped that his mind wouldn't turn to this. But it wouldn't be the first day of school if I didn't have to convince Liam not to abandon the idea of education entirely. "You know you have to, though, right?"

"In theory." Liam shrugged, playing with his green-and-black-striped tie. He'd done a terrible job of tying it, and I resisted the urge to fix it for him. "But I could always run away to Canada."

"They don't have truancy laws in Canada?"

"Don't act like you know all the laws in Canada." Liam cracked a smile, which gave me some relief. When he was in his really bad spells, Liam never smiled. The fact that he was joking around, even a little, meant this was probably going to be okay. "They might not."

"Well, you already did all the summer reading, so it would be a shame to drop out now." Most of the other students were inside by this point, and we were going to be joining the scattered latecomers and oversleepers in an official tardy if we didn't get moving. If there was one thing I didn't want to explain to my mother, it was how two students who lived on campus with the headmistress could possibly be late for the first day of school.

"Besides," I continued, since Liam still seemed pretty skeptical. "It's *high school*. How scary can it be?" I ignored the fact that I frequently compared it to war in my head. War didn't have to be scary if you knew how to fight.

Liam's gaze darted over my shoulder, back toward the school, before he raised one eyebrow at me. Okay, well, fair. I turned to follow his gaze. Northanger Abbey was, objectively, an extremely intimidating-looking place, even if you didn't think it was haunted. The original abbey had been built in the 1700s, a loving homage to all things Gothic and European. When it was turned into a school, they just kept adding new buildings, each one spookier than the last. My personal favorite construction, though I'd never admit it out loud, was the pair of gargoyles that had been added at the entrance to our modest football field in the seventies. When I was feeling particularly overwhelmed by life's pressures, it was fun to figure out which one looked more like Mom.

At exactly the wrong moment, an ominous thunderclap let out a roar overhead.

"Okay, fine," I admitted, turning back toward Liam. "The buildings are horrifying. But school is fine. Come on." I grabbed his arm and gave it a tug. He allowed himself to be pulled through the huge double doors and into the long front hallway of the school, where the Gothic features (huge stained glass window, enormous arched ceiling, stonework for days, etc.) were broken up by such modern amenities as lockers and a PA system. At least we got inside before the rain started. "This year's going to be different. You'll like it."

"You say that every year."

"And have I ever been wrong?" We'd reached the fork in the hall where we'd need to separate, me going right while Liam went left, and his already pale skin had taken on a greenish tinge.

He hadn't always been like this.

"Constantly." He gave me another one of his quick smiles, then raised his hand in a salute. "See you on the other side, I guess."

"Not if I see you first." I wanted to hug him, but even in an empty hallway, I didn't. He already knew I worried about him. I didn't need to make it worse.

Before Dad got sick, Liam knew how to be happy. But a lot of things were different before Dad got sick.

Pushing down memories that would do nothing but hurt me, I ran down the hall until I reached my homeroom, a merciful minute and a half before the bell rang. The rest of my class, unchanged since I'd first started at Northanger, sat scattered on the choir risers, and Izzy and Priya waved to me from the back, indicating the space they'd saved in between them. I couldn't help it—my heart kind of grew three sizes. For all that I had to work for it, I'd nailed this being-a-regular-student-at-Northanger-Abbey thing. I had perfectly functional friendships, a top-notch plan for college, and Liam was adjusted . . . enough. This was going to be a good year.

Before I could make my way back to my friends, my homeroom monitor, Mr. Booth, called me over to him.

"What's up, Mr. Booth?" I asked, stopping at the side of the piles of sheet music he called a desk. Mr. Booth and organization had never gotten along.

"Good morning, Hattie. You're needed in the office." He held an official summons out to me without even looking up, lost in whatever song the choir would be learning for the opening week assembly. "You can take your things—I doubt you'll make it back before first period."

"I—really?" My heart sped up as I glanced back toward Priya and Izzy, who watched me quizzically. It was probably nothing, but I had a strong dislike for anything that deviated from the norm. And who could need me in the office? School had been in session for maybe thirty seconds. "I'm not supposed to go during, like, study hall?"

"It's all in the note. You should go—best not to keep her waiting." Mr. Booth waved me away even as I opened my mouth to ask more questions, which I guessed meant I was very effectively dismissed. Which . . . fine. All right. Maybe my schedule had been printed weird or something. I shrugged at my friends, then stepped back into the empty hallway. I always hated being out here between classes. It was too quiet, too isolated. Before I headed to the office, I opened the note Mr. Booth had handed me, if only so I knew what I was getting myself into.

Unfortunately, the note's contents only confused me further.

Miss Tilney—

Please report to Dr. Tilney's office immediately for an urgent matter. A late pass to your next class will be provided if necessary.

What on earth did my *mother* need to see me for?

Chapter Three

I had never been called to my mom's office before.

I mean, I'd *been* there. Teachers sent me there with notes more often than they sent my classmates, even if I felt confident both Mom and I wished they wouldn't. I'd gone there on behalf of Liam a few times last year, when he was too freaked out by the whole "being a freshman" thing to talk to Mom himself. And I'd heard the stories, naturally, about kids who got sent to see Dr. Tilney and left crying. Like I'd said, the word "soft" didn't come anywhere near my mom, for fear of being destroyed by the laser beams some freshmen worried would shoot out of her eyes.

Which was what made this summons *so* weird. I'd have been worried if it had to do with Liam, but I'd literally seen him less than five minutes ago, and Mom maybe thirty minutes before that. Sure, there were valid, nonscary reasons for a student to be called to Dr. Tilney's office, but I was drawing a blank on all of them at the moment.

For a brief, fleeting second, I wondered if this was Mom

calling me in, not Dr. Tilney. Maybe she'd realized that we hadn't gotten a chance to chat this morning, remembered some words of wisdom for her daughter that she wanted to impart before I started my senior year. Something firm but encouraging.

But that was a silly, useless thought, I told myself as I pulled open the heavy carved wooden door that led to the main office. "Mom" didn't exist inside this building. It was rule number one.

"Hattie!" Mrs. Levenson, the school secretary, beamed at me from behind her desk. It was elaborately carved and excessive in its theme, just like everything else in this school, and she had to sit up as tall as she could in her chair to see me over it. "Are you excited to be a senior?"

"Just a little." I smiled back, the consummate picture of friendliness, as always. "I'm here to see Dr. Tilney."

"Of course! She said you were on your way." Mrs. Levenson tilted her head back over her shoulder, indicating my mother's office, which was flanked by two giant statues of mastiffs whose eyes seemed to follow you around the room. Welcoming. "Go on in, dear. They're waiting for you."

They? I wondered, but just smiled again, then slipped into my mother's office after a quick rap with the door knocker (another mastiff holding a bone, naturally).

She was in there, of course, sitting behind her (regular-size) desk, diplomas behind her, nameplate positioned in front of her. There were two chairs in front of her desk, both tall and straight-backed, their velvet cushions one of the few concessions Mom made to Northanger's aesthetic. And even though,

again, there was literally no way for the timing to work out, I
still half expected to see Liam there, looking scared.

I didn't expect a stranger.

Okay, "stranger" was overdramatic. It was possible I'd
spent a lot of my summer devouring thrillers from the library.
But we didn't get new people at Northanger very often. Besides
freshmen, anyway, and the guy sitting in one of my mother's
chairs, gazing distractedly out the window as rain lashed down
against the glass, didn't look like a freshman.

He *was* a student, that much I could tell, because he was
wearing a Northanger uniform, though he seemed more . . .
casual in it, somehow, than the rest of us. His tie wasn't tightened all the way, part of his shirt already pulling out from his
khakis, wrinkled and rumpled way beyond what Mom would
usually allow. But she probably didn't call me in here to watch
her write up a new student for uniform violations; and anyway,
she wasn't looking at him with the steely-eyed gaze that was a
signature Dr. Tilney, Disciplinarian, look. Instead, she was
watching me, smiling a *lot* more than I was used to seeing, at
school or . . . anywhere else, for that matter.

"Hattie, good. You're here." She held a hand out toward the
free chair and I sat down, keeping my eye on the new kid the
whole time. He was still staring out the window, without even
a hint of acknowledgment that another person had entered
the room. Which was super weird, but it did give me a chance
to get a good view of him without being obvious. Besides his
messy clothes, he was tall and thin, lanky, the kind of build that
was all angles and elbows. His face was narrow, too, with a long
nose, dark eyebrows peeking out from underneath black hair,

longer than most guys around here wore it—just brushing his shoulders—and pale skin that screamed "inside kid."

"Hi," I said, and finally he turned to look at me, just a quick glance, before he turned forward toward my mom. His movements were jumpy, fast, like he'd found himself somewhere he didn't expect. "You wanted to see me?"

"I did. I wanted to introduce you to our newest student." Mom held out her hand as she gestured to the boy, as if there were half a dozen other potential new students in the room she could have been referencing. "Kit Morland. He's transferring in for his junior year." None of this explained why *I* was here, but if there was one thing I knew how to do, especially in front of my mom, it was make a good impression.

I turned in my chair to face Kit, million-watt smile turned up high.

"Hey." I pushed my hand out toward him to shake, and though he hesitated for a second, when he reached back his handshake was strong, firm. Firmer than I would have expected, in fact, considering he looked like he might fall over if he tried to pick up a heavy jug of milk. "I'm Hattie. Welcome to Northanger Abbey."

"Thanks." Now that he'd finally made eye contact, I could see that his gaze was intense, brown eyes—framed under long eyelashes—that seemed to watch me more closely than most people. Slightly unsettled, I broke the handshake first. A point deduction for Tilney hospitality, but my mom didn't seem to notice.

"Hattie's a senior this year." My mom continued to speak,

so I turned my attention back to her. She didn't mention my last name, I noticed. Fair. "I thought she'd be a good fit as your Northanger ambassador."

"Really?" I asked before I could stop myself, then cursed my stupid mouth and its stupid inability to stay quiet. I did *not* ask questions of Dr. Tilney. My question was warranted, though. The thing was, Northanger did have an ambassador program, a small group of our best and brightest who were assigned to show freshmen or the odd transfer around and act as their guide for their first semester. Priya had done it for a year, even. But I'd never joined, precisely because I knew Mom wouldn't want me that close to her headmistress duties.

There was something strange going on, but there was no way to ask about it here, not without violating the headmistress/student relationship we always maintained in this office.

"Yes, Hattie, of course." The new kid probably didn't pick up on the hint of frustration in her voice. For the best. "Is that going to be an issue?"

"No. Of course not." I smiled. Mask *on*, Hattie. Especially here. "Sounds great."

"You'll need to show him where his classes are." My mother handed me a printed-out schedule, with Kit's name in the top right corner. He watched us, quiet. I could only imagine how much more interesting the show would be if he knew the backstories of the players. "And you'll be in journalism together, as he's interested in . . . investigative matters. That's why he transferred here. He's had a scholarship arranged by NPSI."

"The . . . sorry, I don't think I know that one." Inside, I cringed. Admitting I didn't know something in front of my mom was my least-favorite thing. "Nip . . . see?"

Kit answered before my mom could.

"The National Paranormal Society of Investigators." His voice rose with enthusiasm as he turned toward my mom, who nodded encouragingly. Thank goodness he looked away from me, because my mask definitely fell apart, if only for a second.

The—the National Paranormal Society of Investigators? Freaking *ghost hunters*?

And they'd *organized*?

My heart sped up, my vision not as clear as it had been a second ago. What the hell was happening? I'd been called in here out of nowhere, my mom had claimed (falsely) that I was part of the ambassador program, so that I could show around a transfer who was sponsored by *ghost hunters*? Because with the initials spelled out, I realized I had heard of NPSI before. I'd seen their badges all over the tourists who crawled around our house, spotted their T-shirts on every public tour of Northanger. They were another group of lunatics convinced this place was the answer to all their haunted questions, and I had *zero* patience for them. All they ever did was mess around in our business in pursuit of something that had literally no chance of being real.

And now they were sending a student here? And I had to *interact* with him? Absolutely not.

She has a reason, I thought, trying to calm myself, to show less of my panic. Because my mom didn't make choices like this randomly. If she wanted me to be an ambassador for some ghost-loving weirdo . . .

I'd be the best damn ambassador Northanger Abbey had ever seen.

Even if I had to clench every muscle in my body to keep from screaming.

"Well isn't that . . . fun," I managed, and from the way Mom looked at me I could tell I wasn't doing my best work. Frankly, I thought this should be considered a stellar performance, under the circumstances. "And interesting."

"I think so." Kit, at least, had the grace to seem sheepish. Good. "I'm just really excited to be here."

"And we're happy to have you here, Kit." Mom's mask rivaled my own. She couldn't have been happy about this, either—why would she want to do anything to increase the paranormal popularity of Northanger? She and I were on the same page about that sort of thing. Ghost stories were for children and people who didn't know how to face real life. None of this made any sense, and I wished briefly that Dr. Tilney was someone I was allowed to question. "Your first classes are close together, Hattie. Show Kit the way."

The somewhat ominous *or else* echoed at the end of that sentence, but that was how my mother always sounded, so it was impossible to tell if it was specifically related to Kit or not.

I needed to pull it together. Deep breaths, think of a calming wind that starts at your toes and works its way up, all the meditative techniques I'd learned in my short-lived grief counseling sessions. Put the mask back on and for God's sake, keep it there. I was Hattie Tilney, damn it. I was in control.

"Of course, Dr. Tilney." There. Perfect girl reactivated. I smiled, then took a quick peek at the schedule in my hands. "Looks like you've got English Lit with Dr. Kaufman. That's a good one. And Dr. Tilney is right: it's in the same wing as my first class. I'll walk you."

"No need to go back to homeroom." Mom was reading the stacks of paperwork on her desk again, a clear dismissal as she flipped through a folder. "I look forward to hearing how you like it here, Mr. Morland."

"Thanks," he said, unfolding from his chair as he stood. He was *really* tall, which made sense with his frame, even lankier now that he wasn't all bent in on himself. I stood, too, glancing down at my mom's desk as I did. The folder she had open was full of generic school administration nonsense, but that wasn't where my gaze drifted.

My mom didn't believe an office needed to be personal— she was Dr. Tilney here, no one else, and didn't think her students or staff needed to think of her any other way. Consequently, there weren't any photos on her desk of me or Liam or Freddie. (Liam had asked her about it once, and she'd just said, "I know what you look like.")

But she did keep one photo on her desk, tucked in the corner by a cup full of pens. It was small, the size you'd keep in a wallet. A photo of my dad.

He was young in the picture, younger than I ever remembered him being. Probably from when he and my mom were in college, where they'd met, and had Freddie. He had on a worn T-shirt and swim trunks and was posed by the edge of a lake, ready to jump in, arms spread wide.

We didn't have many photos of Dad around the house, so it hit me whenever I saw one. How much I missed him. How different our life was since he'd died.

Sometimes, in my darkest moments, I'd think to myself, *What would Dad do, if he were here?* And sometimes it helped, though not often enough to balance out the extra-sharp pang of missing him I'd feel when I let my mind linger on him for too long.

But whenever I found myself thinking that way, I shook my head and let it go. Because he wasn't here, and he couldn't help me. I had to make my way myself, just like Mom had.

I yanked my gaze away, not wanting to get caught lost in thought with Kit waiting by the door and my mom watching me, expectant. She was always expectant of me. Expecting perfection. Expecting obedience. Expecting . . . I didn't even know, half the time.

Through the window, lightning flashed. Kit jumped. My mom didn't.

Besides, I didn't need to linger on the photo to know exactly what my dad would think about all of this. He'd be excited about it, curious. Have a million questions about NPSI, and what Kit was doing here, and why he was investigating. If he'd seen anything yet, or was still gathering data.

My dad loved ghosts. And that was why I didn't. Not anymore.

As fast as my mom had looked at me, she was looking down again, back at her papers. Like she knew what I was thinking, but couldn't stand to think it herself. Good for her. I often thought how much easier it would be, if I could forget about him like she had.

Ghosts. It just *had* to be ghosts.

"Come on, Kit," I said instead, grabbing my backpack off the floor and leaving Dr. Tilney to her work. I headed out into the hall, with Kit the *freaking ghost hunter* following behind.

Chapter Four

I had a ritual, usually, for when Dad Thoughts took over my mind. Separation was the first step—get away from other people, don't let them see the cracks forming in my walls, because sometimes the illusion of strength was even more important than actual strength. A bathroom usually did the trick, unless my sister, Freddie, was being a jerk and hogging it. Second step, I'd pull up the album on my phone I'd made for this exact purpose, full of pictures from the last three years of the life I'd built at Northanger since he'd died. There were a lot of selfies with Izzy and Priya, obviously. A formal picture from junior prom, posing with wilting corsages underneath a leaning balloon arch. The student council picture that went into the yearbook last year, where I beamed with pride smack-dab in the center. A trip into Manhattan with Izzy's mom, who'd snapped a pic of us looking touristy as anything at the Hard Rock Cafe.

Those moments, those memories, were my prizes for successfully living a normal life. For hiding away the parts of me

that were strange and broken and unusual. The parts that had
gotten me teased even before Dad died, when I at least had
someone to share them with, parts I kept tucked so far inside
me now that they had become unreachable even to me. Videos
filmed on selfie mode where I narrated weird happenings
at my middle school or pictures of my dad standing in the
middle of an antique shop, arm tight around Liam's shoulders,
holding up a doll that he was certain was haunted. (It wasn't.)
I ignored those parts of my life because it hurt too much not
to. Concentrated only on the surface-level, comfortable memories.

Unfortunately, I had nowhere to hide at the moment, not
with Kit Morland talking a mile a minute as we made our way
down the gloomy hallway that connected the administrative
wing to the English department.

"This is so awesome." Despite his long legs, Kit kept pace
with me, which was a small blessing. He turned in circles as we
walked, like we were somewhere cool, and not just the knockoff haunted house that was our high school. "I mean, no matter how much you look at the brochures, it's different to be
here, you know? I never thought I'd see it in person."

"Fascinated by lockers?" I asked wryly, my hands twisting
the straps of my backpack. Mom was right: we didn't have
time to get back to homeroom, but we weren't technically in
class changeover yet either, so it was just the two of us in the
hallway. Said hallway was a perfect example of one of the
school's favorite aesthetics: take a building that looks like a
rejected set from a 1950s Dracula film and stick retro school

fittings on top of it. "I don't want to burst your bubble, but they're not original. Been here since 1978."

"Oh, I know." He glanced over at me, gave a sheepish grin. He had a nice smile, wide and unapologetic. "That probably sounded weirdly stalkeresque. But it's like . . . even though this isn't what people usually think is cool about the building, even though these probably look like every locker in every high school in America . . . they're *Northanger Abbey* lockers. And that's the coolest thing. It's like stepping into a documentary."

He stood up straighter when he was talking about this, I noticed. Like he came into himself more or something. I wondered if I'd ever looked that self-assured.

"We did get all the locks replaced last year, so, you know. That's pretty exciting." I resisted the urge to ask him which documentaries he'd watched—whether it was the same stuff Dad had shown me when Mom was applying for the job, or if new films had come out since I'd shut down that part of my life. We used to make our own documentaries together, my dad and me. *Ghost Hunting with Hattie and Dad!* I called them, like it was the most original title in the world. I'd interview him, have him tell me everything he knew, edit them on an ancient laptop, and then show the videos to him and my siblings on nights my mom had to work late. *When we get to Northanger,* he'd told me, right after Mom got the job, *we'll get you a new computer. Real video equipment. And you can interview everyone there, talk to people in town . . . Oh, Hattie girl. It's going to be amazing.*

We turned again, away from Kit's beloved lockers, continuing down the hallway. The sconces stuck in the wall between each set of lockers actually *were* original, but I was worried that if I told Kit that, his head would explode. "Where did you transfer from?" I shouldn't have even bothered making small talk. As friendly as Kit Morland seemed, there was no way we were going to be friends. I *had* friends, had Izzy and Priya and the small group of acquaintances I'd carefully cultivated. I didn't need another one, especially one like Kit. He was too . . . much, and not just in his stature, though that also made him stand out. He was taller than Liam, even. But Liam had kept himself shrunk down ever since his growth spurt, like he was apologizing for his height. I got the feeling that Kit never had.

Befriending Kit would *not* be a useful chapter in my Northanger Abbey Success Story. I had a very specific plan for how to get through high school, one that didn't involve being distracted by weirdly tall ghost hunters. And I loved my plan. I liked to feed it treats as I tucked it into bed at night. I refused to compromise it.

But I was, apparently, his assigned ambassador, and I *also* refused to let my mom down, even if I didn't understand why she'd put me in this position. I could make small talk for today.

"Middle of nowhere Florida. You haven't heard of it, trust me." He actually stopped and put his hand on the wall, right above the super-gross water fountain I'm pretty sure Liam got pink eye from last year, like it was something to be reverent about. "Okay, but this column is like, *original* original, right? It's definitely older than the seventies."

"Mid–eighteen hundreds." I gave in. As much as I didn't want to engage, my brain had stored up all sorts of useless knowledge about this place over the last few years. May as well put some of it to use. "So, old—and I think it's original to this wing but not technically original to the institution. The school was founded—"

"In 1798." He cut me off, but he did it with so much enthusiasm I couldn't be mad about it. "Come on. You think they would have let me in if I didn't know that?"

"I thought they might just need someone to change the light bulbs," I shot back, and as the bell rang, loud and jarring, making me jump, Kit let out a surprised laugh. Kids began to stream out around us, but he kept watching me.

"This classroom is yours." I had to raise my voice to be heard over the din of the students. Technically the hallways were supposed to be kept to a dull roar, but no one cared about that on the first day; and with all the tall, arched ceilings here, every sound became one long echo. "Second on the left." As he kept his gaze locked on mine, head tilted to the side like I was just as interesting to him as the columns, I felt something . . . unsettle inside me. Kit didn't say anything for a second. Then he smiled again.

"I think we're going to have some fun today, Hattie."

"You know this is high school, right?" I reached up and touched my hair, did my best not to wince at the frizz. Not that there was anyone here I needed to impress. "If they see you having fun, they kick you out."

"Well." He shrugged, adjusted his tie. He didn't, like, make it neater. Just sort of . . . moved it around his neck. "They can try. See you soon."

As Kit Morland ducked into his classroom—literally ducked

slightly, to enter the room, because Lord, again, this boy was *tall*—I felt kind of . . . thrown. And I didn't know that it was bad. But it was definitely something.

⚊⚊⚊

I was, at least, able to put Kit the Friendly Ghost (Hunter) out of my mind for most of the morning. English went off without a hitch, and then I had to practically run across campus to drop him off at his math class in a converted carriage house, so we didn't have time to chat. He had study hall after that, and since it was the one time of day our schedules didn't line up, I'd just given him directions ahead of time. Izzy and Priya, when I met up with them for calc, had questions about where I'd disappeared to during homeroom, but I'd managed to brush it off—"Oh, there's a new kid Dr. Tilney wants me to show around, it's no big deal"—and we'd moved on to other first-day-of-school gossip. Part of me wanted to spill the entire encounter to them, to tell them how weird it had all felt—especially the parts that didn't feel weird at all—but that required a level of vulnerability I didn't have with my friends. "Vulnerability," after all, was just a fancy word for weakness. It was always better to opt for distraction and diversion.

It also helped that Elsa Lewis had come back to school late last night with blue hair, which was expressly forbidden by the dress code, and apparently had tried to bleach it out in the bathroom sink before breakfast this morning. *That* had bought us a lot of conversation. When I'd picked up Kit for journalism, Izzy and Priya had been with me, but they were still so engrossed in the Elsa thing ("You think she'd let it go") that they mostly said hi and then moved on. Good. I'd do the polite ambassador thing and introduce them properly at some point, but the longer I could put off explaining why I'd gained a ghost hunter, the better. Besides, he was probably a huge fan of *What Cries Beneath*, and Izzy *hated* when people brought that movie up, especially once they knew who her dad was.

Luckily, we all made it to journalism without incident. Since this was in an original wing of the school, a small classroom that had been a dormitory for nuns in a previous life, Kit looked like he might explode from joy. When he sat down next to me (taking Izzy's usual seat, which made her raise an eyebrow in my direction before sitting with Priya), his legs extended fully into the aisle, and he almost tripped Mrs. Skinner as she came into the room before she realized the obstacle at the last second and did an impressive duck and weave for someone her age. (Which I was pretty sure was like . . . forty? I didn't know. Old enough.)

"Someone's built to be a camera operator," she said. Kit sheepishly pulled back his legs and the rest of the class giggled. I'd have been mortified by the callout—I was experiencing a nonzero amount of secondhand embarrassment as it was—but Kit didn't seem bothered.

"Sorry. Next class I'll bring in a wider table."

"See that you do. Mr. Morland, is it? Welcome. And welcome back to the rest of the class, as well." Mrs. Skinner perched on the edge of her desk, sneakered feet swinging. She definitely had cooler vibes than most of the other teachers here, with her high-top sneakers and dark pants that Priya swore were jeans, like, half the time. Her hair was the kind of silvery gray that could have been dyed that way, and her glasses took up about half of her face, red-framed to match the jangly bracelets that covered her arms. "Why don't you stand up, Mr. Morland. Tell us a little about yourself."

"Sure." Kit untangled himself from the table as he stood and turned to the class with a wave. "Hey, everyone. Kit Morland. I'm a junior, transferring in, obviously, from a middle-of-nowhere swamp town in Florida, and, yes, everything you read on the internet about my home state is true." He laughed, and a couple of other kids chuckled, but out of the corner of my eye, I saw Izzy smirk, probably because she'd noticed the buttons on his messenger bag that read, among other things, *I like big haunts and I cannot lie.* "Interests include anything paranormal, including but not limited to all of the Northanger Abbey lore. *What Cries Beneath* is a favorite, obviously." Yep, just as I figured. Izzy rolled her eyes. "But, yeah, if you need anyone to talk to about ghost stuff, I'm your guy. Hauntings, possessions, weird green goo coming out of your walls . . ." Personally, I'd have voted to nix the spooky jazz hands that he used as punctuation, but unfortunately I couldn't make that choice for him. Priya was full-on giggling behind her hands now, though Kit didn't seem to notice. Great. "Would love to hear about any experiences you all may have had."

And then, thankfully, he sat. God, he was just making life harder for himself. A standard introduction would have been half as long and spent a lot less time pointing at niche interests, particularly niche interests that alienated him from most of the school.

"Thank you, Mr. Morland," Mrs. Skinner said to Kit, who offered her an air high five—of course he did—before continuing. "This is, of course, the elective highlight of my day and yours, journalism. And if the rumors that have reached back even to my ancient ears are true"—she stared down Priya, who winced—"you've all heard about your big project for the year already. An early journalistic lesson for us all—don't sit on your surprises when there's a chance there could be a leak. And, trust me, there's always a leak."

As she passed out packets of paper, the rest of the class whispered excitedly to one another. Priya and Izzy had their heads together, and Kit leaned over toward me.

"Do you guys not get new assignments very often or something?"

"Welcome to Northanger Abbey, Kit." I grabbed a packet off the top of the pile and passed it to him, allowing myself to feel some gentle excitement. This might be fun, investigating. Izzy and Priya and I could practice our best intense reporter voices and figure out why the dining hall had stopped doing exclusively Meatless Mondays. "Nothing here ever changes. Enjoy this novelty for what it is."

"As it happens," Mrs. Skinner cut in over all of our whispered conversations, "there is a part of the assignment I don't believe you all know about."

"We don't need to investigate to find out, do we?" Izzy called out, and everyone else laughed as Mrs. Skinner shook her head.

"No, but you're not far off. If you turn to the back of your packets"—she paused as we all flipped to the last page— "you'll notice that I've already assigned partners and respective topics for your projects."

I was pretty sure Mrs. Skinner kept talking, but I couldn't hear her. I was too busy staring at my packet in absolute horror. Because it was one thing to have to show the new kid around, then let him fade into the background of Northanger while I went about my business.

It was another thing entirely to be paired up with him on a major project for my favorite class, especially when the subject staring back at me made me want to actually hurl.

Hattie Tilney and Kit Morland: The History of Northanger Abbey's Paranormal Activity—Is There Truth to the Rumors?

Had I offended a beautiful young woman disguised as a very old woman on the way to school this morning without realizing it? Had I been cursed? Because I had a very specific plan for how senior year was supposed to play out, and having to examine the legitimacy of ghost hunters was *not* on the itinerary.

Around me, the rest of the class was similarly—well, not similarly, because I doubted any of them were hanging on by quite as thin a thread as I was, but still—freaking out. Izzy and Priya had both raised their hands way up in the air, waving them around. Kids were whispering; packets were being tossed onto the table; one girl was actively tearing up. It was a whole thing.

About the only person who didn't seem thrown by this news was Kit, who had offered me an encouraging smile. At least, he probably assumed it was encouraging. The only thing I would find encouraging right now was a fire drill long enough for me to flee to a different state.

"I didn't expect quite so much of an uproar, but all right." Mrs. Skinner quirked one side of her mouth into a smile, like she hadn't just tossed a grenade in the middle of our classroom. "I'll just get some of the more obvious questions out of the way, shall I? No, you can't switch partners; no, you can't pick a new assignment; and, yes, I'm serious about the first two parts." Super. "I promise, this assignment and all components of it were chosen carefully. Now." Mrs. Skinner hopped off the desk, made her way over to her computer. "If that's all the unnecessary shouting we have in us for the day, I'd like to go over the timeline for the project. The projects will be filmed, of course, they'll be approximately ten minutes long, and the final presentation will be scheduled for after winter break . . ."

I tuned her out at that point. *Ghosts*. Why did it have to be ghosts? And Kit, of all people? Look, he seemed nice, the sort of person I could have been friends with in my previous life, but it was clear that he was going to have a hard time fitting into Northanger. His enthusiasm was just, like, three notches too high. The class clearly noticed, too, from the way he raised his hand to answer basically every question to the way he laughed when Mrs. Skinner made a joke, just a little too loud. He'd find his place here eventually, but it would be on the fringes. And every interaction I had with him pulled me to the fringes, too. I just couldn't risk it.

This all probably sounded way harsh. But everything about my circumstances pulled me to the edges as it was. When I'd started here three years ago, Izzy helped me realize that there were two ways things could go. I could keep being the weird girl who'd spent more time hanging out with her dad than with kids her own age, who'd loved pushing against the unknown. Who, if you had asked me in middle school, would have thought the Ghost Brigade sounded like a super fun and cool activity, with no regard for how it would affect my social standing. The one who was now missing her partner in crime like a limb that had been torn off and who didn't know how to handle it.

Or I could pretend none of that had ever happened to me, that I was a regular person who happened to be the headmistress's daughter, whose dad had died but it wasn't a big deal. Who rose above all of it and made her own place at Northanger. You tell me which one you would have picked.

My ties to normalcy were desperately important to my survival. But this didn't have to sever those, right? Yes, there was going to be a lot more Kit interaction than I'd bargained for. A lot more ghost-based content than I'd bargained for. But it wouldn't stop me from my student council work, I reminded myself. From putting the final polishes on my Udolpho application before I submitted it, from hanging out with Izzy and Priya and maintaining my status in the school. This was just a group project. I'd dealt with group projects before.

I took a deep, slow breath, felt my heartbeat slow back down to a normal pace. I was Hattie Tilney. I could handle anything.

Skinner wrapped up not long after that. Leaving class, where she had asked Kit to stay behind to chat about his transition into the school, Priya and Izzy had concerns of their own.

"It's such bullshit that we don't get to pick our partners," Izzy complained as she pulled open her locker. "I'm supposed to work with some rando I've never heard of?" Izzy was paired with Lauren Carter, who had been in about a dozen classes with us since freshman year, but when Izzy was on a rant, stopping her was impossible. "No thanks."

"At least you don't have to investigate funding cuts to the bowling team." Priya groaned. "News at eleven! Funding cut because the team kept losing! See, I don't even need to do a project."

"Hattie's got the easiest assignment of all of us." Izzy grabbed a few books from her locker and slammed the door shut, making me jump. "Just like, go to the midnight movies they show in the graveyards in town and call it research. You can interview my dad, if you want."

"Maybe." *What Cries Beneath* had been, for a while, one of my dad's favorite movies—we went to a midnight showing on its December release anniversary every year—and it was one of those things I tried to avoid whenever I could. "I'll let you know."

"That new kid seems like . . . a lot." Izzy wrinkled her nose, and I had to resist the urge to jump in, to say he wasn't that bad. Which was stupid, because I totally agreed with that nose wrinkle. "Hattie's going to need to take naps after every project meeting."

"Fair. Like, calm down, Ghost Boy." Priya laughed, and I joined in, even though it felt weirdly disloyal.

Maybe, I thought, as we made our way to the dining hall, Izzy and Priya still complaining about the project, maybe I could talk to Mom? See about having Kit matched with a different ambassador? Then, at least, we'd only have to deal with the project. It was a long shot, but pairing me with Kit had been a totally weird move in the first place. Maybe if I explained that I didn't really have time for him. Or maybe I could appeal to her sense of motherhood about the ghost thing. Mom knew I wasn't into that stuff anymore, though we'd never talked about it. Still, she had to get my reasons. She was the one who didn't keep photos of Dad around the house.

I was going to make this work, just like I always did.

Chapter Five

Mom missed first-day-of-school dinner.

Which shouldn't have surprised me. After all, it was a big day for her, too, not just for me and Liam. Was it the last first-day-of-school dinner I'd ever have? Sure! Did that fill me with a weird existential dread I couldn't quite explain? It didn't matter!

I'd gotten home after Liam, since I'd had our first student council meeting of the year after school. I'd been elected secretary again, thank goodness, in no small part thanks to Izzy sending out a class-wide email blast over the summer extolling the virtues of electing me. I needed everything to be perfect for my Udolpho application, and losing my streak in student government would *not* have been the look I was going for. After that, the girls and I had gone for our usual postelection coffees at the campus café. They'd both been elected, too—treasurer for Izzy and senior class representative for Priya—and we'd toasted our knockoff Frappuccinos to the start of an amazing senior year.

On the other end of the "doing great" spectrum, Liam

was holed up in his room when I finally made it back, while Freddie was in the living room recliner, sleeping off whatever she'd done the night before.

Ah, yes. Familial bliss.

It took another hour for Freddie to wake up and tell me that Mom wasn't going to be back. Ten minutes later, I realized that meant I was in charge of dinner. Liam tended to get distracted when things were on the stove, and the majority of Freddie's cooking skills were concentrated on Jell-O shot recipes. All of which meant that I was the one to boil the pasta, defrost a bag of meatballs from the freezer (that I'd made over the summer for these very purposes), and get the three of us to the table that Mom was still absent from.

Well, two of us. Liam ate in his room.

It was only when we were cleaning up in the kitchen afterward—a task I did force Freddie into doing, because I wasn't a complete martyr—that she asked me about my day.

"Was it *so* fun?" She leaned back against the counter, blowing at a piece of her bangs that kept falling into her eyes like an overgrown dog's. Freddie was my considerably older sister at twenty-three, the result of Mom and Dad not being as careful in undergrad as Mom always warned us we had to be. (Which. Gross.) She should have graduated college herself by now, but she'd left school with only a semester to go last December and showed zero interest in returning.

"It was fine." Freddie and I were the opposite of close. She'd spent half of my childhood as my babysitter, and now that she'd fallen from grace, it felt like I was babysitting her most of the time. I wasn't about to open up to her.

"You didn't have the best time ever with the Future Step-ford Wives Club?"

"Don't call them that." Neither she nor Liam got why I hung out with Izzy and Priya. You would think my actually well-adjusted life, compared to theirs, would be proof enough, but apparently not. "At least I have friends."

"Totally, I wish *I* had someone to tell me to wear pink every Wednesday and make me practice the latest TikTok dance." She reached out and flicked at my green velvet headband, which perfectly matched my uniform and had been a gift from Priya to celebrate the first day of school. "Is this where you keep the microchip controlling all of your movements? If I take it off, will you short-circuit?"

"Girls." My mom's voice cut through our sniping, and Freddie and I both jumped as I almost dropped the plate I was holding. Mom had taken off her blazer and slung it over her arm, but the stern look of disapproval on her face had "Dr. Tilney" written all over it. "Stop it."

"Why? It's so easy." Another benefit Freddie enjoyed of be-ing older? She and our mom had a way different relationship than I did, the result of a childhood being carted around be-tween classes and thesis defenses and faculty meetings. I didn't know if it was necessarily better, but it meant Freddie got away with a lot more than I did. Did it infuriate me at times? No, of course not—what gave you that idea? "I'm surprised you rec-ognized Hattie at school today. Did you and your little friends all match?"

"It's a uniform," I said through gritted teeth. "Everyone matches." My sister knew exactly how to push every button

I had, which was not at all ideal when I needed to ask Mom for a favor. Sometimes I thought about how it would have been nice to have a big sister who cared about me. But instead, I'd ended up with this.

"Freddie, why don't you let me take over." It wasn't an admonishment from Mom—it rarely was, with Freddie. If I'd dropped out of college and moved back home with no job prospects, she'd have turned me out on the streets. But not Freddie. Never Freddie. "I need to speak to Hattie."

"Knock yourself out. I'm going to Bath Salts." Bath Salts was the seedy townie bar that Freddie had inexplicably decided was her favorite place to hang out since she'd moved home. Again, if *I'd* ever expressed interest in going down there, I'd have been irreversibly grounded. Not Freddie.

"I wanted to speak to you about Mr. Morland," Mom said, once Freddie had grabbed her fake leather jacket and left, the flimsy screen door slamming shut behind her. "I know you're not normally a part of the ambassador program."

"Oh, I—really?" Sure, that was exactly what I'd hoped to talk about tonight, but I thought I'd have to work at it more. The sounds of video game violence permeated the kitchen from upstairs. Liam's homework was going well.

"Yes. NPSI has been a large donor to the school as of late. Mr. Morland is the first student to join Northanger on one of their scholarships, but he won't be the last." She scraped dishes much more efficiently than Freddie, leading me to rush through the rinsing to keep up. "It's crucial he has a good impression of the school."

"Well, that's the thing." My heart sped up. Interrupting my

mother was always a dangerous game, but if I didn't get ahead of her now, I'd have no chance at all. "I'm going to be really busy this year, what with student council and applying to college and everything. I don't know that I have the time to give Kit the attention he deserves."

"That won't be a concern." She didn't even look at me. Her voice was sharp enough that she didn't need to add her gaze to it. "I was under the impression that you did most of your application work over the summer."

"Oh, I did!" Shoot. I was scrambling, and scrambling was rarely an effective defense against Dr. Tilney and her impenetrable logic. Rule number one of talking to my mom was to not show weakness, and what had I done? Acted like I couldn't handle everything she'd thrown at me. And I could. I had to. "I just . . . I want to make sure everything is perfect." My application was *almost* ready, but I needed to spend more time tweaking the essay. It was missing a certain something, a clear answer when it came to questions like *What do you want to do here?* and *What do you hope to get out of this program?*

The truth of the matter was that my only ambition for the last three years had been this. Do well at Northanger, be a credit to my mother, and prove to everyone that I wasn't just surviving—I was thriving. I was applying to a prelaw program because that was something Mom had suggested once, and I didn't have a better idea. I knew that I didn't have her burning ambitions, but I could pretend that I did. Pretend until she was proud of me.

College essays, it turned out, were a difficult place for pretending.

But I could handle it. Of course I could handle it.

If only it wasn't for the . . . well. You know.

"Ghosts, Mom? Really?" I loaded the last plate into the dishwasher, then leaned back against the counter. "That's what we want Northanger to represent?"

"That's what Northanger *does* represent." Her tone had an extra level of sharpness to it, and I drew a quick intake of breath. She placed the plate down carefully and turned to face me. "It doesn't matter if we like it. Ever since *What Cries Beneath*, Northanger Abbey has become synonymous with the paranormal in the minds of the entire community; and while I do whatever I can to stop that from interfering with the academic pursuits of my students, it's ridiculous to pretend we can escape it entirely. I'm not going to bury my head in the sand over . . . personal preference, and neither are you. You *will* show Mr. Morland around, and you'll be the perfect ambassador to Northanger while doing it. I chose you over a more traditional guide because I thought you—"

For a second my mom paused. Like she was stumbling over her words. Which *never* happened to my mom. Honestly, for a second, I thought she might be having a stroke. But she took a deep breath, looked me straight in the eye—I hated when she did that, I felt like I shrunk under her gaze—and continued.

"I won't hear about this again."

"Got it." It was the most I could manage without crying. Which was so stupid. What was there to cry about? In the grand scheme of my life, how was *this* the time my body decided to show external signs of being upset?

If Dad were here, he would have noticed. He was the only

one who could ever speak to Mom. That was when she occasionally *was* Mom at home, when Dr. Tilney didn't take over
her entire personality. But he wasn't here, was he? And Mom
was. This was what I had to work with.

Take care of them, Henrietta. He'd told me that right before
he died, all hooked up to tubes in the hospital room. I'd had a
hard time breathing through my grief and my tears, and he'd
squeezed my hand. *Make your mother proud. You're strong. You can
be strong for them.*

That was me. The strong one. The one who was keeping it
together. *At least you have Hattie,* I'd overheard one of my mother's
friends say to her once, right after we'd come to Northanger.
And she was right. It was my job to be exactly what she needed
me to be. Freddie was a mess. Liam was too young.

I was never going to escape these freaking ghosts.

Chapter Six

Would you believe it if I said I'd devised yet another plan? One that would, if I was lucky (and for once this week, I wanted to be lucky), be the last plan I needed to get my life firmly back on track?

Some people—Freddie being primary among them—might say that I needed to "chill out," to let life take me wherever it wanted to take me. But going with the flow had never been a strength of mine, and I certainly wasn't going to start now.

So, yes, it seemed like I was stuck with Kit Morland. But that didn't mean I'd lost all control over our interactions. What, was I just supposed to accept my fate, get pulled into his weirdly seductive paranormal circles, and completely abandon any hopes of a normal senior year?

Hell no.

That was why, on Friday night, during what *should* have been an awesome celebration of making it through our last first week of school with Izzy and Priya, I was standing by the

front gates of Northanger Abbey, waiting for Kit to join me as
the wind whistled around my ears.

But there was nothing to worry about, because I was going
to make it clear *exactly* where I stood on this whole ghost thing.

That was my best play, I'd decided, as I'd tried my hardest
this week to both make sure Kit knew where stuff was (therefore having nothing to complain about to my mom) and also
made sure it didn't seem like we were, you know, friends. I
didn't want him to get any ideas, and tonight's conversation
would seal the deal.

I'd done my best to conceal my full-on ghost hatred from
the rest of the school these last three years for the sake of fitting in (because a strong hatred of something stood out just as
much as a strong love), but what was Kit going to do—spread
the word that I thought the paranormal was the paraworst?

"Hattie!" I turned to see Kit bounding toward me, making
quick work of the distance with his giant legs. "Hi!"

Kit, I saw, had really embraced the more casual nature of
after-hours Northanger. He'd pulled a dark knit beanie over
his hair, low enough so that only the last few inches of his hair
showed as they hit his shoulders. His T-shirt was black, too; and
in the fading light I could barely make out the name of a band
I'd never heard of. When you added in the dark-wash jeans
and beat-up Converses, the whole look had a real skipping-
class-to-sulk-under-a-tree-somewhere vibe. But somehow, it
didn't seem like as big of a contrast to his beaming grin as it
should have. Something about Kit's attitude made even the
most depressing of clothes look cheerful.

Cheerful or not, I noted as he came up, his look didn't fit

in with our classmates'. Northanger was kind of a preppy wonderland after hours. If there were other people in the world
who listened to Virginia Woolf's Streetcar or had seen them
on their Field of Nightmares tour, they didn't go to my school.

"Hey, Kit." Despite my misgivings, I gave him my best polite smile. "How was your first week?"

"Great, actually." We were right up against the gates of
the school, tall and imposing, all wrought iron and mossy. The
school's motto was spelled out in iron curlicues over the gates—
The Abbey Lives On. Welcoming. He ran his hand over the moss
as he spoke, examining the intricate spoke work instead of
looking at me. I didn't mind. Kit's undivided attention was
kind of intense. "I just—I never thought I'd be somewhere like
this, you know? It's like I fell into a movie."

"Oh. Yeah." It was something, all right. I guessed it would
be amazing, if Gothic everything was your brand, like it obviously was for Kit. As it was, it kind of felt like my life was one
of those big-box stores that had closed and been replaced by a
Spirit Halloween. "Lot of history."

"Should I have brought my laptop?"

"What?"

"To take notes on the history. Since this is the super-official
tour and all."

"Longhand notes will be accepted." I smiled despite myself. "This will, of course, all be on the test at the tour's con-
clusion."

"Naturally." Kit was looking around now, and suddenly he
sucked in his breath quickly. I followed his gaze to a barely
functional water pump about ten feet to the left, dripping with

moss and decay. Nobody I knew would give it a second glance, so of course Kit was staring at it like it was the Holy Grail. "Is that . . ."

I waited, but Kit seemed to have lost all ability to speak as he stared, and I finally gave in. "The alleged site of the Sister Mary Harrington haunting? Yeah." I was worried Kit had stopped breathing entirely. He really was in deep, I thought, allowing myself a bemused smile. Sister Mary wasn't even a particularly interesting haunting. She was a nun here during World War I, when the abbey was turned into a kind of rehabilitation clinic for returning soldiers, who had found herself unable to stomach the wounds and horror stories of the men they treated. She'd run away in the middle of the night and disappeared, and students had since claimed to have spotted her by this pump, begging for water, just like the soldiers she abandoned often had.

Or, you know, a bunch of students got together and made the story up for attention, because *apparently* no one had learned anything from the Salem witch trials.

My dad had pointed it out to me when we'd visited Northanger with my mom for her final job interview, wandering the campus while she convinced the board no one could lead the school better than she could. *If you drink the water, do you get haunted from the inside?* I'd asked. *Only one way to find out,* Dad had said, and then Liam had splashed me and I'd run away, shrieking, while Dad laughed and laughed.

"Have you ever seen her?" Kit asked, his expression locked on the pump.

"You mean heard her. No one sees her. She's an auditory

specter. And also no," I added quickly, as Kit turned toward me, curious. Tamp it down, Tilney. "I haven't."

"Too bad." He shook his head, his smile rueful. As the wind picked up, I wrapped my arms around myself, trying to hold in whatever body heat I could as the leaves on the trees that edged the path rustled. "Have you had any paranormal encounters since you've been here?"

Like I would say anything even if I had. As I was trying to think of a polite way to say *Back off with the questions, dude*, I shifted my weight from one foot to the other. Except I didn't realize that I was, apparently, standing on one of my own shoelaces, so I tripped, stumbling to the side. Kit reached out fast and grabbed me by the elbow, steadying me.

Steadying me physically, anyway.

"You okay?"

"I hate ghosts."

Smooth, Tilney. Super smooth.

Obviously, that wasn't how I'd planned on dropping in that little piece of information. I was going to give him the tour— he'd gotten the official tour when he'd enrolled, but I was going to do the friendly ambassador thing and give him, like, the actual student weekend tour—and then, when the time was right, casually mention that the paranormal wasn't my favorite thing and offer up some alternatives for completing our project that didn't involve us spending time together. Fair and square, and I would have been able to (a) skip out on ghost nonsense and (b) not have to hang out with the new kid.

But Kit Morland continued to unsettle something in me. I

didn't know if it was his unabashed enthusiasm for everything, how we kept getting forced together, or even just how freaking tall he was. But he kept ruining my plans, and now he was looking at me with his head tilted to the side like he didn't understand what I was saying.

And his hand was *still* on my elbow.

"I mean, maybe hate's not the right word," I babbled on, since it seemed like we were doing this. Somehow. "Because I don't believe in them. So, I can't hate them, since I don't think they're real. But the whole haunted high school thing . . . is kind of poppycock, I've always thought. And the world's fascination with it just bothers me and that's probably going to be a problem for our continued relationship because if ghosts are your thing, I think that's great but they're not mine."

Shutting up time.

I snapped my mouth closed, as if that would in any way will the words back into it. Not that any of them were . . . untrue. But when was the last time I'd said that many words to someone in a row? Words that weren't carefully planned out, at least, to someone who wasn't Liam? Kit kept watching me, and although I almost opened my mouth again to apologize, I held firm. It needed to be said, after all. Maybe it wasn't graceful, but if this took care of my problem . . . it wasn't like I needed Kit to like me.

Right?

Then Kit laughed, the sound mingling with the howling of the wind.

"Did you say poppycock?" He let go of my elbow finally,

and took a step back himself, though his was smooth enough that he didn't almost fall on his ass. Lucky him. "Are you sure you don't hate ghosts because you're secretly one yourself? Like, of a nineteenth-century governess? If you are a ghost, legally you have to tell me or else it's entrapment."

"Pretty sure." Unexpected. For someone so passionate about ghosts that he apparently snagged a scholarship based on his love of them, he seemed fairly nonchalant about my attitude. "That seems like something I'd know. That was your big takeaway from that? My vocabulary choices?"

"Well, and that it's weird that you call your mom Dr. Tilney. Also, you should keep a better eye on your laces." He glanced down toward my sneakers, one eyebrow raised, as I dropped down to retie them. "Do you need sensible shoe recommendations? Because I've got half a dozen sisters back home who would love to help you shop, if buying shoes from weird websites that sell untreated alpaca wool is also your thing. It doesn't seem like it is. You're definitely a treated alpaca wool type."

"How did you know about my mom?" I felt disoriented as I stood up again. Talking to Kit was like riding a roller coaster while still trying to take in the view. You could keep up if you worked at it, but it might leave you dizzy.

"The matching last names?" Kit cocked his head to the side. "And, um, my roommate told me. Sorry. Was it supposed to be, like, some big secret? He said that everyone knew."

"No, they do. We just . . ." I trailed off. That was a whole thing I didn't need to go into with Kit. Even if this conversation had taken a million twists and turns I hadn't anticipated, I didn't need to go into that. "It doesn't matter. Does my hatred of the paranormal not turn you off?"

Oh, God. Why did I say *turn you off?* As if there was some insinuation that he'd ever been turned on? My brain was broken. That was the only explanation for this entire conversation. Maybe I'd actually fallen to the ground when I'd tripped earlier and hit my head and everything that happened from the moment Kit Morland had touched my arm to now was some sort of wild hallucination. Maybe I was in the hospital. Maybe I could stay there.

Kit, thank God, didn't seem to notice. Or if he did, he had the good grace not to say anything about it. Either way, he shrugged.

"It would be kind of presumptuous of me to assume everything I enjoy is universally beloved."

"Yeah, but isn't this, like . . . your life's passion?" I should have taken the out, but I kept pushing. Which was *so* not my style, but neither was standing by the gates of the school as the sun set on a Friday night, arguing about ghosts with a guy in ripped jeans. "I saw how excited you got about Skinner's assignment. You can't think it's okay that I don't care about it."

Kit seemed to consider that for a second, then nodded. Well. Good. I deflated a little, though I didn't know why. I *wanted* Kit to admit that I was right. That our partnership was a bad idea.

Maybe part of me had liked, for a second, that he seemed to be okay with a part of me that didn't quite work. But of course, it made sense that he wouldn't be. Who would?

"Just to clarify. You're not *scared* of ghosts." He leaned back against the gate, one foot propped behind him on a decorative curlicue of iron. "Right?"

"Hard to be scared of something that doesn't exist."

"Okay." Kit pushed off from his perch, veered to the left, back toward the dorms. "Come on. Let's walk, and we can figure this out."

"Is there anything to figure out?" Still, I followed. On the wide path back toward the Howe Building—I was pretty sure that was where Kit lived, in Howe—the gravel crunched beneath our feet. "I'm not trying to, like . . . mess with your scholarship or whatever."

"NPSI is fairly hands-off about all of this, actually," Kit said as I fell into step beside him, my apparently much-less-sensible wedge sneakers a contrast to his shabby Converses. "They probably wouldn't love it if I started spouting off about ghosts being made-up, but we haven't found ourselves in a Romeo and Juliet situation here."

"Haven't we?" I asked, although the Shakespearean insinuation—because Romeo and Juliet weren't just, like, casual homework partners—made me gulp. "I've met people like you before. Not always a fan of the nonbeliever."

That made him come to a sudden stop, gravel skidding away beneath his sneakers.

"People like me?"

Foot, mouth, go ahead, get to know each other.

"Paranormal . . . enthusiasts," I managed to get out, as the wind picked up. There was a fog rolling in, I noticed, gathering around our feet as it began to overtake the path. "Sorry. I just . . ."

"You've had some really shitty encounters with ghost people, huh?"

If it was me, if I was in Kit's position, I would have left by now. But Kit still stood there, rocking back and forth on his heels. And for whatever reason . . . I felt relieved.

Most people didn't ask me questions like this. Everyone else in my life was willing to assume my intentions at first glance, ready to accept whatever I told them at face value. *Ghosts just aren't for me! I feel passionate about constantly pushing myself to the brink! I'm happy! I'm okay!*

And Kit not just accepting it was kind of a revelation.

What the hell.

"Would you believe they've tried to break into my house before?" I started moving again, leaning into the wind, and Kit stayed with me. We were approaching Howe, but I turned us to the right at the last moment, following a fork, past the cannons that marked the edge of the residential campus (and that, according to definitely false legend, contained the ghosts of circus acrobats) and toward the old abbey building itself. This was a tour, after all.

"One thousand percent." Kit laughed, and I looked up at him, watched as he pushed up his beanie a little so that he could see me as clearly as possible. "Here's the thing. I think you should give us a second chance."

"Do you?"

"I do." Kit followed as I led us away from Howe, away from Schumacher and Schmidt and the rest of the cluster of residential buildings. "I think I can prove to you that we're not all garbage people. Some of us just have a genuine curiosity about the world around us and haven't closed ourselves off to the possibility that said world involves more than we've previously been able to explain."

"And this isn't self-serving at all." We'd reached the huge brass monument, the Learners' Statue, that marked the center of campus: four people—two women, two men—sitting back-to-back, books in their laps. It had been here since right after the Civil War, and it was, of course, one of the many places on campus the internet insisted was infested with paranormal activity. When the school had been founded, it was a religious institution—hence, abbey—but the board had put this statue up when Northanger had turned its purpose to education, albeit education that was still run by the church until the 1950s. The statue had been featured in a couple of scenes in *What Cries Beneath*, which only added to the haunting rumors.

I probably should have explained some of this to Kit, for tour purposes, but I was caught in his intense gaze again. His eyes were brown, which I'd noticed before, but what I hadn't realized, I noticed as we wandered under one of the old-fashioned hanging lanterns that dotted the campus walkways, was that they were flecked with amber specks. And if I could see that, I must have been standing closer to him than I'd previously realized, but I didn't step back. Not just for fear of tripping again, either.

"Oh, it's definitely self-serving." Kit's hand went up as he pushed a piece of dark hair back behind his ear, and I tracked the movement. "I can't have my ambassador hating me."

"That would be bad for the school's public image."

"And we don't want that." Kit was definitely speaking more quietly now. I wasn't just imagining it. I should have stepped back. I should have explained to him about the statue. I didn't. "What do you think, Hattie Tilney? I promise not to, like, jump scare you or anything. And you can even think of it more as historical research if you want. But I'm legally obligated to ask you to give this whole thing a chance."

"I thought you said NPSI didn't make you do stuff like that."

"Maybe this one's for me."

Kit finally stepped back, and I was weirdly . . . disappointed. But then he stuck his hand between us, held it out for me to shake. The rational part of my brain, the one that was being deeply clouded by whatever *this* was, was starting to scream at me that this was about way more than keeping Kit on the sideline of my life. I avoided ghost stuff for a reason, and it wasn't just because it irritated me. If I went down that road again, it wouldn't exactly be good for my plan. Or my brain. Or my heart.

"Here's the thing." I didn't know what I was saying. I didn't mean to open my mouth and talk at all, but that particular brain malfunction seemed to pop up often around Kit Morland. "I don't know if I can . . . the whole ghost investigation thing. It's a little much for me." When I'd come up with this plan earlier today, I'd thought of it as the perfect way to keep me and Kit apart. Now I was just hoping it would do enough to hold us together without exposing all of my darkest parts. Because I was surprised to realize that I did want to get to know Kit Morland better. I just wasn't sure I wanted him to know me. "What if we took this project in a more . . . untraditional direction?"

"I'm listening." Kit raised one eyebrow. "You're not suggesting a *Blair Witch* remake, are you? Because I know we're better than that."

"Not exactly." I turned and began to pace just a little, filled with a nervous energy I had to burn off somehow. Kit tucked his hands in his pockets as he watched me wear a hole in the ground. "I'm thinking we come at this piece from opposing angles."

"Meaning?"

"You try to prove that ghosts do exist at Northanger." I came to a stop, square in front of Kit again, and this time I was the one who held out my hand. "And I prove that they don't."

I held my breath as I watched Kit, saw him consider the offer. This brilliant idea was my last hope. Not only would it mean that I got Skinner off my back—because I was totally still doing the project—it meant that I could do this my way. The ghost-free way. The way that protected all the parts of me that hurt.

Kit took my hand.

"Okay," he said as we shook. "But we still have to work together, right? I don't know anything or anyone here. You basically owe it to me as my ambassador."

"And as your ambassador, I promise not to disappoint." I let go of his hand, but I still felt its warmth. "But I also promise there will be exactly zero paranormal encounters."

"Don't make promises you can't keep, Tilney." He nodded toward the statue watching over us. "They can hear you, you know."

"How atmospheric of you." I rolled my eyes, and Kit grinned. "Come on. I'll show you the shortcut to the dining hall. Nobody was murdered there, so don't get your hopes up."

I can handle this, I told myself as we headed deeper into campus, deeper into the creeping fog, Kit right behind me. Whatever *this* was. But I could explore the possibility of Kit's . . . friendship, and keep my own baggage out of it. I'd spent the last three years carefully choosing which parts of myself I showed to everyone I met. Who said I couldn't keep doing that with Kit?

Nobody. That was who.

Chapter Seven

When I met up with Izzy and Priya the next morning, I decided not to tell them about the extremely weird, charged-with-something chemistry I was experiencing with the new kid.

It was for the best, I told myself, waiting on the first floor of Schumacher for one of them to come down and get me. Izzy would have had a million questions, questions I didn't want to deal with right now, like *What the hell are you doing?* and *Did you even sleep last night, or did you spend the whole night imagining the dark corners you and Kit might explore over the course of this project?*

The answers to which, for the record, were *I have no idea* and *Most definitely*.

Look, this wasn't my first rodeo. It wasn't like I hadn't dated or anything. I'd experienced the thrill of a guy looking like he wanted to know more about me. But in my (admittedly few) past romantic entanglements, I'd been the master of compartmentalization. When I was with the guy, I was happy to think about him, and when I wasn't . . . I had more important things to worry about.

The fact that Kit hadn't left my mind since he'd left me at the edge of the path back toward my house was slightly worrisome.

It was probably just stress, I reasoned. Senior fall was hard for everyone. I'd been thinking about my grades, which led to thinking about schoolwork, which led to school projects and bam! Kit Morland. It was an easy enough path to follow.

And when Izzy brought him up within five minutes of taking me to her and Priya's room, well, it wasn't like anyone could blame me for talking about him.

"He's like a clone of every intern my dad's ever had," Izzy said, leaning back in her chair with her slipper-clad feet up on her desk. The three of us had settled into our usual study spots in their shared dorm room—Izzy at her desk, Priya sprawled out in the middle of the floor, me watching them both from Priya's lofted bed. "When he told me there was going to be a NPSI scholarship kid here, I figured it would be bad, but I didn't think it would be *that* bad."

"How do you know about NPSI?" We were supposed to be working on college applications, but I wasn't going to complain about the distraction. Priya tossed a bag of Twizzlers up from the floor, and I caught them midair before grabbing one out of the bag.

"Please. My dad's been on the board since *Cries* blew up." Izzy spun in her chair, chewing on her own piece of candy. "He's going to want me to be friends with him but, like, I can't. Not with that hair."

Privately, I kind of liked his hair—liked that it was different from the prep-school haircuts most of the other guys had here—but I wasn't about to say that out loud. Instead, I shrugged, noncommittal. When Izzy had her claws in something, the best course of action was usually to deflect. Luckily, Priya must have wanted to move on, too, since she said, "You finished your application for Udolpho, right, Hattie?"

Okay, well, not my preferred subject change, but sure.

"Basically. Everything's written, I'm just polishing it." Udolpho had rolling applications for their early decision, and my goal was to get the application in by the end of September so I could have a chance to breathe. I probably could have sent it in already, but something kept holding me back. "I want the essay to be perfect, you know?"

"Totally," Priya said, and Izzy shot me a sympathetic smile, properly distracted from ragging on Kit. The two of them may not know anything about my issues with ghosts or with my family, but they got *this*. The need to be perfect. To succeed above all else, even if our measures of success weren't always the same. "Is there anything specific you're worried about? Or is this the kind of generalized concern where we actually need to eat ice cream and say that everything is going to be okay?"

"I wish." I forced myself to laugh, playing with my Twizzler. "I'm probably overthinking it. But it would be good if you guys could read it."

"For sure." Priya nodded, rolling onto her back so she could look up at me without craning her neck. "You wrote about student council, right?"

"Yeah." I laid my head against Priya's comforter. It wasn't

the most original thing in the world, but I'd written a solid essay about how I'd spearheaded a charge to get solar panels installed on the roof of the dining hall. I was proud of that project. Mom had even mentioned it at dinner one night, the sure sign of Tilney success.

"Do you think that's, like . . . raw enough?" Izzy cocked her head to the side, looking at me, and I had the uncomfortable feeling I'd been placed under a microscope. "I mean, obviously everything you've done there is awesome, but you know everyone says you need to really stand out in the application pool."

"I haven't exactly won a MacArthur genius grant, Iz." I resisted the urge to squirm under her gaze. The only reason I even had student council in the first place was because of her, because of the way she charmed everyone in the school into giving her whatever she wanted. Still, I was proud of the work I'd done there, even if it only existed because she needed me by her side in every picture so that Mr. Thorpe would stay off her back. "That solar panel project made a big difference for the school."

"I'm just saying. If you're worried . . ." Izzy drummed her hands against her desk, then shrugged. "You should just write about your dad."

It felt like all the air had been sucked from the room.

Three years of doing everything I could to get away from this, and a single naïve comment still sent me into a tailspin. Even though I probably hadn't even mentioned my dad to them for two years, at least, here was further proof that my dead dad was still the most important thing about me.

Great.

"What?" Izzy continued, glancing down at Priya, who was, from what I could see, giving Izzy some sort of *What the hell?* look. It was a look we both gave Izzy often, even though it rarely made a difference. "It's a good idea."

Izzy was good for so many things. When you needed to blow off steam, to have a fun time, to vent. To have someone in your corner when you had to manipulate your way through the war that was high school.

I'd never claimed she was particularly sensitive.

Logically, of course, I knew there was no way for Izzy to know how much even this suggestion ached. It was my greatest strength, after all—how good I'd gotten at pretending things didn't matter to me. How hard I'd worked to separate myself from his legacy, from letting a single tragedy define my life. How I'd pushed and pushed, taking on every ounce of ambition my mom had thrown at me, so that I would be as far away from him as possible, because the farther away I stayed from my dad, the less it hurt.

Mom and Dad had gotten pregnant with Freddie when they were in college, twenty-one years old with the world ahead of them. They'd made an agreement—Mom would pursue her dreams first. They'd both finished their bachelor's degrees, switching off between who would take Freddie to class their last semester, and then they'd gotten married with Freddie crying in my grandmother's lap.

The deal was supposed to be that Dad would stay home until we were in school, but then we were all in school and Dad just kept staying home. He dedicated his life to making sure Mom could have everything she wanted. While she went on to get her master's, then her PhD, he took care of Freddie, then me, then Liam. He wanted us to have a parent around, he'd say, and that way he could support Mom's career as much as she needed. He'd worked when academia didn't cover the expenses of three kids, but he never went back to school, never pursued a "real" career.

He'd seemed happy to me, but I'd heard Mom arguing with him about it. How he could be more than what he was. How she wanted him to live up to his full potential. As the daughter to the world's greatest dad, I'd taken offense to that. Everything about my dad was clearly designed for parenthood, and he loved it—and us—more than anything. I didn't understand why that wasn't enough for her.

Once he died, though, once everything we'd done together got yanked out from underneath me and I had no one to depend on but myself, I'd realized that Mom was the one I needed to emulate. I didn't understand her blind ambition, but that would have to change. So with Izzy's help, and with Priya's, I'd turned myself into someone she might deign to be proud of. An acceptance from Udolpho would be the final proof of my success; in the meantime, I needed to pretend that this was everything I'd ever wanted. That I'd never dreamed of following in my dad's footsteps.

So really, the fact that Izzy thought bringing up my dad wasn't a big deal was good. To her, it was just another one of her suggestions, just one more way she could help me succeed. I should have felt proud of myself.

Instead, I just felt deeply, incredibly alone.

My heart was beating a mile a minute, and the room was so warm.

But if I ran out of here, ran out of their room and down the endless rows of doors until I broke free of the building entirely and kept running, like I wanted to, they'd know. They'd know that it still hurt; and as far as these girls knew—as far as anyone knew—I never let anything hurt. I was untouchable because I had to be.

So I pushed down the pain, and I laughed.

"It's totally fine. Tragedy isn't unique anymore, Iz. I'd stand out more if I wrote about *your* dad."

"Back off my topic!" She held her laptop against her chest protectively, and Priya giggled, her righteousness on my behalf forgotten. It always was, where Izzy was involved. Neither of us would give up Izzy for the sake of each other. So instead, Priya jumped to her feet, using the whiteboard above her bed to write out ideas that would define our futures while all I could do was try not to think about the past.

It was, objectively speaking, an abject failure.

Eventually, we concluded our prep session, and I left Schumacher, lost in my own thoughts as I sat down hard on a bench in the middle of the quad. Thoughts about how I had gotten so good at hiding the parts of me that hurt. How tired I was of pretending.

Dad had been so excited about coming to Northanger. Because my dad loved ghosts, and since I loved my dad, I'd loved them, too. He'd been fascinated with the idea that there was something more than *this*—that there were hidden depths to the universe we could only begin to fathom. He was an active member of our town's historical society, digging up every possible connection to urban legends or local hauntings he could, even when the rest of the society scoffed at him for it. He'd read hundreds of books on paranormal legends, took me into the city to stand outside the premiere of the *Ghostbusters* remake dressed in matching Jillian Holtzmann costumes when I was eleven. He'd even had a column in our town's tiny newspaper for a while, where he wrote stories about the hauntings people had reported locally. He couldn't wait to get up here, to explore. Even when my mom left brochures for remote master's programs on his bedside table, the ghosts were all he talked about.

The plan was to move onto the Northanger campus in June, after the school year ended, so we'd have time to acclimate to the area before the fall. Sometime around March, Dad got sick. Cancer sick. At first it seemed like he might be able to fight it, and then it became clear that he couldn't. He died the first week of June, and we'd moved up here the second week. Liam cried the whole car ride, and I didn't cry once.

My dad had been my everything. I'd arrived at Northanger Abbey missing an essential piece of myself, determined to not let anyone know how irreversibly broken I was, and armed with a final charge—to take care of the family and to make Mom proud. I got a new computer, but I only used it for school. For googling acceptable colleges and figuring out a career path that would lead to stability and a clear future.

Freddie and Liam could never hide their scars. My mom didn't seem to have any to hide. So I quickly realized that I had to hide my pain for all of us.

The wind rustled around me, and I sighed, feeling as unsettled as I'd ever been. Like it was freshman year all over again, and I was hiding in the library, thinking that I'd never be happy without my dad back. I needed to head home. I'd told my mom I'd spend the rest of the day working on chores and helping Liam with his homework. But I didn't want to go home feeling this way. Didn't want to shove it all back into the Perfect Hattie persona.

Instead, I pulled out my phone, shot off a quick text message to the person I least expected to be contacting.

Hey
Want to see a secret passage?

I watched the screen as I waited for a response, squinting a little against the glare of the sun. And soon, because quickly and with enthusiasm was the only way he did anything, I had my answer.

Abso-freaking-lutely.

And for the first time since Izzy had brought up my dad, I managed a real smile.

Chapter Eight

K it had to finish up some homework, so I killed time at the library for an hour before heading over to pick him up. The courtyard in front of Howe was almost *too* bustling for my taste, guys tossing a Frisbee by the George Howe statue like they were in some kind of targeted Instagram ad for the school, a group of girls who had just come back from field hockey practice crowding the steps, dozens of individuals going about their day like they weren't spiderweb fragile.

It was the sort of scene that threatened to overwhelm me, in my worst moments. But I kept my eyes forward, stared at the huge wooden door that led into Howe until Kit pushed out of it. He was wearing what I was starting to realize was his non-uniform uniform—ripped jeans, a *different* black T-shirt from a band I'd never heard of, a red knit beanie pulled low over his head so that only the last few inches of his hair curled out around the edges. He'd tied a maroon plaid flannel shirt around his waist, since I'd warned him the passage we were headed for got drafty. It was a welcome sight, a breath of fresh air after the stuffy, unair-conditioned dorm room.

But what was he doing talking to Izzy?

She was walking out right next to him, laughing at a joke I couldn't hear, her perfect hair flowing gently around her shoulders in the slight breeze. When she saw me, she raised her hand in a wave, like this was just a super-regular thing for her to be doing. Like she hadn't just basically said she'd rather die than hang out with him.

"Hattie!" She wrapped me up in a hug when she reached me, then stepped back toward Kit, whose grin was smooth and easy. "Hi!"

"Hey, Izzy. Kit." I didn't get it. Izzy and Kit had literally zero reason to interact. "What are you doing?" I'd meant for it to come out as casual, but it sounded accusatory. Kit looked at me quizzically.

"Just wanted to make sure our newest transfer got shown around properly, that's all." I shouldn't have cared that Izzy was standing so close to Kit. But I did. "My dad called after you left. Said he wanted to make sure Kit got the full Thorpe welcome."

Ah. There it was. I doubted Kit could see it, but I recognized the flash of anger around the edge of Izzy's eyes, the look she got whenever her dad called and told her she wasn't living up to the Thorpe name. I would have bet anything that her dad's asking her to show Kit around wasn't nearly as friendly as she made it seem.

What I should have done, at that point, was abandon my secret passage plan entirely. The three of us could have walked around campus, taking in the sights, snapping a couple of self-ies Izzy could send to her dad. I'd keep my mask up the whole time, hope that Izzy's dad-mandated politeness would keep her from being too mean to Kit about the ghost stuff, and then we'd all go our separate ways, the status quo at this school kept entirely the same as it always was. Nothing unexpected. Nothing changed.

But I'd texted Kit because I'd wanted, for at least an hour, to feel the same way I'd felt when we were sitting by the Learners' Statue last night. Like I was someone interesting, not just a cog in the Northanger machine. A reliable component of Izzy Thorpe's senior year. Dr. Tilney's perfect daughter.

Besides, even if she hadn't said it with malice, Izzy's comment about my dad still stung. I didn't really want to play Easygoing Best Friend right now. So even as I pasted on my Perfect Hattie smile, I held my ground.

"I actually already had plans to meet up with Kit." I tilted my head to the side, my expression apologetic, and hoped Izzy didn't see right through me. "We want to get a head start on our journalism project."

"Oh." Izzy's picture-perfect countenance never wavered, but I could feel her stare boring into me. Her eyes narrowed ever so slightly. "You were?" To Kit, this probably seemed like a super-normal conversation, but I could read the message in Izzy's eyes. *What are you doing?*

I almost backed down but managed, just barely, to resist.

"Yep." I turned my smile up to eleven. "We were."

A moment passed between us. Izzy's perfect expression, barely tinged with confusion, turned into a smirk.

"Well." She stepped to the side, ceding Kit to me. He looked back and forth between us, an eyebrow raised. "I don't want to get in the way of anyone's academic achievement. Kit, consider this a rain check." And then she waved and turned away, pulling out her phone as she headed back toward Schumacher. I assumed she was already texting Priya every detail of our interaction, speculating over what it might mean.

Honestly, I didn't know. But I knew that I felt a lot more relieved now that it was just me and Kit. Kit didn't seem quite as settled, from the way he watched Izzy, pulled off his beanie to run his hands through his hair before turning to look back at me.

"What was that?" He looked confused, and I didn't blame him. I was losing control over myself, and I was having a hard time caring. College essays and thinking about my dad and Izzy being Izzy. It was taking everything I had not to just lie down on the ground and give up.

"What was what?" Playing it dumb wasn't the most creative strategy, and from the way Kit kept watching me, it clearly wasn't working. I sighed. "Fine. Izzy and I . . . she's my best friend. One of them."

"Yeah, I can totally tell."

"It's complicated." I shoved my hands down into the pockets of my cardigan, rubbed my fingers against the seam. "But it's nothing you have to worry about. Do you want to go see this passage or not?"

"Not if you're not okay." Kit held his ground, and my heart sank. "And that seemed like one of those things where

people pretend everything is fine but they're super not okay."
Why, exactly, couldn't Kit be like everyone else? Accept my
excuses and move on with his day, so I could move on with
mine without having to examine any of the ways that I felt?
"It didn't seem like you."

"Well, you don't know me very well." I meant it to come
off as flippant, but it felt sharp. A little harsh. Kit eventually
laughed, but it was muted.

I didn't like muting him. Everyone at this stupid school was
so muted already. Kit was the one person who had shown up
in full color.

"I'm sorry." The words tumbled out of me before I could
stop them. "It's been a weird day. I texted you because I
wanted to get away from the weirdness, and then you showed
up with Izzy."

"And that's a problem why?"

"I just . . ." I shook my head, fast. "Izzy and I have been
friends for a long time. And usually she's great. But when stuff
with her dad comes up, she gets weird." *And I didn't know how
long her dad-prescribed friendliness to you would last before she got mean*,
I thought with a wince. I didn't think she was ever purposely
cruel. Just too smart for her own good sometimes.

"She just wanted to talk to me about *What Cries Beneath*."
Kit shrugged. "It didn't seem like she was going to, like, trap
me under the school and re-create scenes from the movie."

"No, of course not." But if she spent time with Kit, and
they talked about *me*, she might realize that I was opening up
to Kit a lot more than I'd ever opened up to her. Maybe that

was what this was about, I realized, with a drop in my stomach. Maybe I wanted to keep Izzy and Kit separate for me, not for him.

Well, whatever. At this point, separation was the key to my Northanger happiness. No one could blame me for wanting to keep that separation intact. "Sorry. Can we pretend this never happened, please? I'm being weird."

"It's okay. I don't mind you being protective of me." Was that what I was doing? Kit grinned, back in full color, and even as I flushed I felt like a weight was lifted off my shoulders. He finally took a step away from Howe as I fell in beside him. "I was starting to worry she was a fellow paranormal enthusiast from the way you were treating her."

"I wasn't *treating* her a particular way!" I protested, falling into the rhythm of Kit again. "I was perfectly cordial."

"Yeah, exactly." Kit feigned a shiver. "It was scary, honestly. Remind me to never make you treat me *cordially*."

"I wouldn't worry yourself about that." I turned left, so that we were headed away from the dorms, back toward the older part of campus. "You don't bring it out in me."

"Good." Kit nodded, like the matter was settled, and I guessed it kind of was. Settled.

What a novel experience.

<hr/>

We walked in companionable silence for a few more minutes before I brought us to a stop in front of the gym.

"Ta-da!" I flung my arms out wide as we stopped in front of smooth metal double doors. "Welcome to the gym, Kit Morland. Technically, the Arthur C. Nebeker Gymnasium for the Pursual of Athletics for Boys. But that's a little long and gendered, so it's easier to call it the gym. Or the Neb, if you're feeling feisty."

"I often am," Kit deadpanned, and I laughed. The trees that flanked the path on either side of us were still lush and green, blocking us off from the sun, but I didn't mind the touch of cooler air.

"Anyway." I nodded toward the building, which definitely had more of an industrial feel than the rest of campus. It had started off as an old barn but had been added to over the years until it was the size of an airplane hangar, albeit an airplane hangar that had the aesthetic of a weirdly misshapen warehouse. They didn't put this one on the brochures, but that was fine with me—it meant that we were safer from the tour groups. "Through those double doors is the secret passage of your dreams."

"I wouldn't be so sure about that." Kit stepped forward and laid his hand on the door, smooth metal with a locked push bar. He tended to do this whenever I took him somewhere new, I'd noticed. Like he was communing with the place. Giving it owed reverence. "My secret passage dreams are all so elaborate they border on concerning. How many rabbits are in this passage? What about blood-sucking Draculas?"

"Do you mean vampires?" I asked, digging my keys out of my backpack.

"I absolutely do not. We will be going over the difference later today. Holy crap," Kit swore as I pulled out a huge skeleton key. "Is that a master key?"

"Perks of being the headmaster's daughter. Or, more specifically, perks of being the younger sister of the headmaster's delinquent daughter." I hadn't used this key in—honestly, I wasn't sure I'd ever used it.

"Oh?"

"My big sister," I explained, inserting the key into the lock hidden on the side of the door. "Freddie. She's kind of a nightmare. Last year, she made a copy of my mom's master. So I made a copy of hers, because I figured if anyone was going to have a master key to the school it should be someone who actually goes here."

Freddie had been so annoyingly pleased with herself when she'd gotten the key, only a few weeks after she came home from school with no plans to go back. She'd bragged about it to me, as if I would care, as if I wanted to be part of her idiocy. But that night, I'd snuck into her room—she was down at Bath Salts, of course, the beginning of her favorite endless pattern—got the key, made a copy in town the next morning, and replaced it by that evening.

I had no idea if she'd noticed it was gone. It wasn't like she could rat me out if she did. But it made me feel like I had some control over something.

"Obviously if you tell anyone about this, I'll have to kill you." The lock clicked beneath my hand, and a rush of adrenaline went through me that I did my best to ignore.

"Naturally." Kit's voice was full of admiration that I wasn't

sure I'd earned, but I liked being this version of myself around
him. Someone who used the key in her bag for interesting
reasons. "So what exactly are we headed toward, here? You
didn't just tell me there was a secret passage to lure me into an
unexpected game of dodgeball or something, right?"

"Kit Morland." I stopped right before I was about to open
the door, turned to face him with the door behind me, hands
tucked up and pressed against its weight. Looked up at him.
"Do you not trust me?"

"Should I?"

It was one of those questions that contained more than
words, and my breath caught in my throat, made my lungs
catch for a second before I nodded. The air was thick with
electricity between us again, I noticed. And we weren't even
in the passageway yet.

Hormones, have mercy.

"Yes." The single word came out as a breath and a promise. One that Kit's nod told me he'd hold me to.

And then I turned back around again, because we had a
secret passageway to get to, and pushed the door open into the
gaping darkness.

Chapter Nine

I pulled the door closed behind me before anyone could see us sneak in, trapping us in the gloom. The gym was off-limits to students when it wasn't being used in an official capacity, and I had worked too hard at Northanger to get written up now.

"Have you been here yet?" I asked Kit as I hugged the wall of the gym, headed left toward one of the equipment closets. With only the emergency lights on high overhead, everything in here was a dark and eerie shadow, and I watched my step as we went, careful not to trip over a wayward basketball.

"Just for class. I didn't expect that there would be other reasons to be in here." Kit's voice was right behind me.

"What kind of paranormal investigator are you?" I asked as we came upon the equipment closet. I pulled the door open with a loud creak that made me jump. "You're losing street cred, Mr. Morland. Did you plan on just never finding the McKinley Tunnels?"

"Of course I— Wait." Kit's voice dropped off, and when

I turned around to face him, his face lit up with excitement. "You're kidding me. We're going into the tunnels? The actual McKinley Tunnels? Where they filmed——"

"The infamous climactic scene from *What Cries Beneath*." I stepped carefully over a bundle of coiled-up jump ropes as I heard Kit exhale.

"But those are——no one can go into those." Kit was basically vibrating, he was so excited. I couldn't help but smile. "In *every* interview the whole crew talks about how they were sealed after filming and, like, detonated shut or something."

"And it surprises you that a bunch of people who got rich for pretending something fake is true lied about that?" One of the reasons *Cries* had become so infamous was the filmmakers claimed it was "adapted from real events" and featured "actual paranormal footage." Complete nonsense, obviously, but it drove modest hype into full-out hysteria. "They did seal the entrance that they used for filming. But that's not the only one."

"Holy shit," Kit breathed. "How do you know about this?"

"It's in the deed listings down in city hall. They scrubbed the connection from all the digital records——that the tunnel also popped up into the Neb——but it's still on the hard copy." It felt weirdly normal, talking to Kit about all of this. It shouldn't have. I'd spent years avoiding any mention of Northanger's ghosts. But I'd absorbed these stories all the same, and Kit was just so damn eager for them.

"Why were you reading the hard copies of deed listings in city hall?" Kit let the door to the closet fall closed behind him, cutting off the little light we had. Shit. I fumbled in my pocket

for my phone as the darkness surrounded me. "Sorry. My bad."
He got his phone out before I did, turned on his flashlight as
I breathed a sigh of relief. Uncontrolled darkness? Believe it
or not, not my idea of a good time. "Didn't think about that."

"An important rule of exploring campus." In a way, I was
grateful for the distraction, hoped that Kit wouldn't ask his
question again. What was I supposed to say? That my dad
had found a file of old school records when we'd come up with
Mom for her interview, records that had missed digitization?
That he'd read every single one, and then read them to me?
That I carried the knowledge around like a glowing ember, the
only thing I had left of my dad; and even though I did my best
to hide every connection I had to this world, there were certain
things I couldn't help but keep coming back to?

Yeah. That would be a great distraction.

This tunnel was one of the places my dad had been most
excited to visit when we got up here. He'd ordered a bunch of
specialized equipment online, scanners that claimed to capture phantom sound and record it at a higher success rate than
anything else on the market.

Maybe we can get in before your classes start, he'd told me, as I
sat in the garage with him and watched him reverently unpack
the equipment from their boxes. *You can film it for one of your videos. It's about time you started coming with me, Hattie girl. High school
in a few months! You're almost a grown-up.*

That was a week before his diagnosis, and those boxes were
all in the basement of our cottage now, covered in dust and
abandoned memories.

I took a few steps back and reached around Kit, testing

the door. Phew. It still gave, pushing open an inch or so to let in light and specks of dust. I grabbed a baseball bat from the corner, used it to wedge the door open. "Don't let doors close behind you, okay? I'm not trying to get stuck down here."

"Right, sorry."

"How much practical ghost-hunting time have you actually put in?" I asked, looking up at Kit. His expression flicked downward, and an inkling of a suspicion crept through me. "Because that's, like, Going Into Old Buildings 101." I hadn't gone on actual ghost explorations with my dad that often, since Mom usually insisted I was too young to spend the night rappeling into abandoned buildings, but I'd watched him plan enough investigations to know that there were a couple of basic, universal tenets.

"I . . . um . . ." Even in the barely there glow from our phones, I could tell that Kit looked concerned. "It's possible my experience has been mostly . . . theoretical?"

Huh. I blinked fast at his admission, surprised. Then again, it wasn't like I'd been a million percent honest with Kit this whole time, either.

"I mean, I've done some stuff," he continued fast, like he didn't want me to stop him. "I did a stakeout with some of my friends last year. This local place, the Flagler Museum, they'd been having weird reports of power outages and cold spots. My friend Enrique's sister worked there, and she let us camp out overnight."

"In a museum?" I did my best to hide it, but my skepticism came through loud and clear. Kit flushed, his hands tapping out an erratic pattern of beats on the leg of his jeans.

"I know. It's not exactly the most . . . Buildings in Florida aren't that old. Not like up here." Kit scratched at the back of his head, shifting the beanie. "And my parents are kind of strict, so I couldn't really explore what old stuff is still around. But I've read everything I could. Watched every movie, every TV show, listened to a million podcasts. *What Cries Beneath* was my gateway to ghosts, and to Northanger." The side of his mouth quirked up into a smile, apologetic, just visible in the gym's dim light. "Have I completely ruined my street cred? Do I not get to present an expert opinion for the project now that I've revealed my ghostly ineptitudes?"

"Ha." I needed to get it together. I didn't need to care that Kit was only half a ghost hunter. *There's nothing real down here to hunt*, I reminded myself. With all of this thinking about my dad, I'd found myself slipping into old habits. Old curiosities. "If anything, this serves my purpose. I need you to look like you don't know anything so my side seems even stronger."

"I wouldn't be so sure about that. I'm a fast learner." Clearly relieved, Kit leaned against the wall of the closet, still smiling. "And I plan on getting a lot of hands-on experience very quickly. So tell me about the tunnels." A subject change. One I'd welcome. "Everything I know is based around the movie. And I'm guessing you don't actually believe that they're haunted by vicious spirits out to pull high school students into hell."

"Do you?"

"Oh, I don't know." In the dim light of my phone's flashlight, I could just barely see Kit shrug. "I know that *Cries* isn't actually found footage. But the screenwriter has always claimed that they pulled the plot from real legends."

"Real *exaggerated* legends, maybe." I ran my hand along the back wall of the closet, feeling for a seam. "Before *Cries* made them infamous, they were used as smugglers' tunnels during Prohibition. And, yes, there are stories about smugglers who died down here. One smuggler was supposed to deliver a case of liquor to one of the students at Northanger, but sampled from his own supply on the way to the drop. He didn't know that the student's dad had some very powerful enemies who were trying to punish him. In the end, the smuggler was the only one punished, poison-style." This was why I'd texted Kit in the first place, I reminded myself. For this exact moment. Because when he looked at me like he was doing now, his head tilted to the side, one hand in a pocket, I felt like I was some-one worth watching.

At one point, *this* was what I'd wanted to do with my life. I'd watched my dad tell stories, listening intently as I curled up next to him, and known, without a doubt, that I'd wanted to do that, too. Make other people feel the way my dad made them feel.

But ghost hunting, as I'd heard my mom hiss to my dad more than once, wasn't exactly a viable career choice.

That was way behind me, obviously. But what was the harm in showing off what I'd learned? Even for an hour, I wanted the feeling of being admired, and not just for my SAT scores.

"I never knew about that." Kit untied his flannel from

around his waist, shrugging into it and buttoning the sleeves over his wrists. "I have the feeling that if you *had* heard about poltergeist-like activity, though, you wouldn't tell me."

"Nothing to tell, Kit Morland." For all that I may have sounded mysterious, it was the truth. My dad had spent a *lot* of time searching, and as far as he knew, there was no evidence that any of the hauntings depicted in *Cries* were based on actual events. It was sensationalism, he'd told me, made-up stories designed to scare people. He'd fallen off the *Cries* bandwagon after that. Said that he only cared about real hauntings.

Well. "Real" hauntings.

I followed the wall to the right, my hand trailing against the plaster, until I came to the corner where a tall shelving unit stood. And then below that by the baseboard . . . I crouched down, let my fingers brush against the wood until I felt something catch. With all my weight, I shoved my shoulder into the wall, pushing down with my fingers as I did . . .

And the wall swung open before us.

"Well?" I turned to Kit, whose jaw was practically on the floor. For the first time, I may have rendered him speechless. "Ready to have your mind blown?"

"Absolutely," he whispered, stepping forward and running his hand over the interior wall of the tunnel, moss covered and dripping with moisture. Watching Kit was like spying on someone at church. It almost felt like a violation. But when he turned to me, his face was lit up in wonder. Open and unafraid. "Absolutely."

And I had a weird moment, a sense of being on the edge of

something myself. Like out there, in the gym, I was Hattie Tilney, who did everything that was expected of her and more.
Who played by every rule and excelled in following them.

And in that tunnel was another girl. The Hattie I had let
go of a long time ago.

"We can go in, right?" Kit was practically bouncing.
"Please?"

"Yeah." I grinned. "And since you're the enthusiast, I'll
even let you go first."

"Best ambassador ever." Kit reached over and squeezed
my hand, like it was nothing, and then he was gone before I
could react, ducking into the tunnel and quickly disappearing into the darkness. He left me no choice but to follow him
(leaving a spare textbook from my backpack next to the secret
door's latch to prop it open, of course). No choice but to feel
the tingling in my hand from where he had touched me and
do my very best to pretend it wasn't there. That I couldn't feel
his touch in every part of my body.

Adrenaline. Hormones. Call it what you want.

Maybe, I thought, as we descended underground, I should
call it Kit Morland.

The tunnel started off narrow, barely wide enough for us to
walk through without turning sideways, but after a little while
it opened up, and it wasn't long before we were at the tunnel's
main attraction—a hollowed-out space the size of a largish
closet filled with abandoned bottles.

"This is awesome," Kit whispered. He'd been whispering ever since we'd walked into the tunnel, like the place deserved it. "It's even better than I imagined."

"Northanger was a popular party spot in the twenties." Even though the ground was damp, I didn't love having my head so close to the dripping ceiling, so I sat, legs crossed beneath me. Kit soon followed. "The school was open, of course, and there were a lot of rich kids here who liked to party."

"So . . . the same as now?"

"Yeah." I laughed, and Kit smiled, lit only by the gentle glow of his phone's flashlight. I'd turned mine off so we didn't drain both of our batteries at once, and the single light cast a glimmer over the abandoned bottles that could be called spooky, if you believed in that sort of thing. "Between them and the folks in town, the smuggling business was extremely profitable. This was how they got onto campus." And where they would occasionally duel, leading to a few reports of phantom gunshots that would echo down the tunnels, but we didn't need to go into that. "And then, you know, the *Cries* team got ahold of it."

"I'm guessing it's not your favorite movie."

"Not exactly." I kept my gaze on the ground, mostly to avoid looking Kit in the eyes. "It kind of . . . sensationalized Northanger. In a way that feels bad, sometimes."

"Isn't it good that it brought attention to the school, though?"

Some ghosts don't want attention, Hattie. My dad's voice echoed around my head, and my chest tightened. *Some ghosts just want to live their stories quietly.*

"The donations definitely went up, according to my mom." I shrugged, noncommittal. "I don't know. It's just . . . Northanger."

"Well, it's awesome." Kit, luckily, didn't interrogate me any further. I was starting to think he saw through my façade and just let me scoot around my emotional minefields because he was . . . what? A good person? "Do you come down here a lot?"

"It's not, like, where I keep all my secret journals." I felt the cold seep in through my jeans, but didn't shift away. "I've been down a few times. Liam—my little brother—he likes it here, but he doesn't like to come alone, so I'll come with him. And it's cool to be somewhere everyone else thinks is gone." When I first took Liam into the tunnels, I didn't tell him it was somewhere Dad knew about, and then afterward it had seemed too hard to bring up. Liam and I never talked about Dad, anyway.

"Damn. I was looking forward to those secret journals." Kit snorted, his legs pulled up against his chest, arms wrapped around his knees. "Find out what's going on inside that mysterious head of yours."

"I'm far from mysterious." That was just about the last word I'd use to describe myself. If I was looking internally, I'd go with "panicked" and "yikes." Externally, the front I presented to the world? There was nothing mysterious about her. That surface girl. "I am, in fact, extremely regular." And I worked damn hard to stay that way.

But Kit shook his head.

"You can pretend all you want." Even though he wasn't

particularly close to me—a couple of feet away, separated by a few bottles abandoned on the floor—I felt that tension shimmering between us again. Like the space that divided us was a rubber band, pulled taut. "And I'll admit, I haven't known you that long. But you've got a lot going on you don't show people. I can already tell. And that"—he reached out across the distance and tapped my knee with his hand—"is what I would call extremely mysterious, Hattie Tilney."

"Yeah, but you see mystery everywhere." I shouldn't be fighting him on this—why bother? What did it matter what Kit thought? But I did anyway. Maybe I needed to know my mask still worked when I needed it to. "That doesn't say anything about me."

"And what's wrong with seeing mystery everywhere?" Kit replied, even as he pulled his hand back from my knee. I ran my fingers over the spot he'd touched. "The world *is* a mystery, Tilney. Do you know how little we know about the universe?" He held his thumb and index finger together, so close they were practically touching. "Basically nothing. We're a speck in the infinity of existence, and to assume we know anything about *anything* is profoundly arrogant. And sure, I'll admit it." He leaned back, his palms pressed against the ground as I watched him. "Humanity is built on arrogance. But that doesn't mean we need to embrace it as our only feature. It's okay to believe, you know."

I felt my heart stir in my chest. Kit Morland watched me, eyes sparkling with fight.

I wasn't going to just *give* him all that.

"And yet you're absolutely certain about the existence of ghosts."

That made him laugh. Broke whatever spell was building between us.

"I never said I wasn't an arrogant ass, too." He flicked the side of one of the empty bottles, the plink echoing around the chamber. "So what are we going to do about our project? Should we be, like, recording while we're down here? Try to dig up some old ghost stories that official records may have missed?"

I blinked, caught off guard enough by the subject change that I needed a second to process. Kit saw my expression, laughed.

"Sorry. Mind jump. But you know, secret tunnels, horror movies, proving ghosts are real . . . it all comes together. I'm guessing we can't actually turn in a project that shows we were in here?"

"Bull's-eye." I smiled, shook my head. "I figured we'd do more like . . . voice-overs of pictures from the archives. That sort of thing." Also, minimizing the amount that I had to hold up a camera and talk about ghosts. That felt a little too close to my past for comfort.

"We can do better than that," Kit said, spinning a bottle idly in front of him. "I mean, that stuff is fine. But it doesn't do anything to take advantage of us being at Northanger. We need to do an actual *investigation*. Do you know anything about the Ghost Brigade?"

"Oh, God. Kit, no." I grimaced. I had to keep up *some*

boundaries, and that boundary was my particular favorite. "The ghost-hunting club? We are not getting involved with them."

"Where is your sense of journalistic curiosity?" Kit pressed his hand to his heart, feigning shock. "Come on, Tilney. We're doing a documentary about ghosts at Northanger Abbey. They're an entire student organization dedicated to the pursuit. Skinner would notice if we just ignored them."

"So? Everyone else does." But as he said it, a sinking feeling in my chest told me he was right. "I don't even know how much investigating they do. I've seen their meetings on the school calendar. It's a lot of movie nights."

"Great. I love a movie night." Satisfied, apparently, Kit stood up, offering his hand to pull me up, too. I took it, let him lift me to my feet, and then suddenly we were standing *way* closer together than I'd expected.

I should, I knew, shut this down. Yes, I'd invited Kit here, but that had been in a moment of temporary weakness. Even if I enjoyed that he made me feel a little less alone, pursuing that feeling was the equivalent of playing with fire. I shut people out for a reason. Just because Kit made me feel a certain way didn't mean those reasons had changed.

If you didn't let people in, they couldn't hurt you. Plain and simple.

Of course, there was no one else who made me feel like Kit did. Like I was worth digging into.

And why, a small, defiant voice in my brain asked, was I holding myself back so much, anyway? My Udolpho app was basically finished. Maybe I could allow myself this small indulgence. A reward for how hard I worked, in the form of dark, smiling eyes that actually wanted to see me.

Kit Morland grinned in my direction, and I made my decision.

"Come on." I cocked my head to the side, indicating the other half of the tunnel, leading past where we had come in. "You want to see the rest?"

"I want to see *everything*." Kit tugged his beanie farther down over his ears, his smile wide enough that it almost took up the entire tunnel. Filled the space between us. "Lead the way."

So I did.

⁓⁓⁓

It was a couple of hours later when we finally emerged from the tunnels, sweaty and dusty and definitely looking the worse for wear. We followed my propped-open doors back out into the gym, then into the sunlight, where I blinked fast from the sudden brightness that hit me like a freight train.

"Is this what outside is always like?" From Kit's expression, the sunshine was a shock to him, too. "Surely the earth secretly moved, like, ten miles closer to the sun since we were last out here. There's no way it was like this before."

"I think—*shit*. Hide!" Panicked, I grabbed Kit and pulled him by the sleeve of his flannel down and into . . . yep, it was the only option. We had to dive into one of the bushes that lined the path to the gym.

Desperate measures? Yes. But I would argue that the sound of my mother approaching qualified as *extremely* desperate times.

"What the—"

"*Shh!*" I admonished Kit, even as I pressed against him in our newfound shrubbery home and tried not to think about all the places we were touching each other. I couldn't make out what my mom was saying, but she was getting closer, talking into her phone to someone. Mostly what I knew was that I didn't want her seeing me out here, poking around in buildings that were firmly off-limits during nonacademic hours.

The sound of heels crunching on gravel got louder as she approached, and finally I could see her coming around from behind the gym. She was still far enough away that I couldn't make out her conversation, only her annoyed expression; but I knew that if we moved, we were still very much within spotting distance.

In the bush, Kit stared at me. Our knees were tangled together, our shoulders pressed side by side into each other, and I wasn't sure whose pulse I felt beating out such a wild rhythm—his or mine. It might have been both. The wind was picking up again, rustling the leaves surrounding us; and for a single, horrifying moment I saw my mom glance over in our direction—but she dismissed the sound, continued forward, and a minute later, she was gone.

Thank God. I (reluctantly) untangled myself from Kit, offering him a hand to help him up. He took it, and I did my best to ignore how warm his skin was, how smooth it felt against mine.

"What was that?" Kit brushed a few wayward leaves off his shoulders, looking at me with interest. "I love subterfuge as much as the next guy, but we hit that bush at a pretty high velocity."

"Are you okay?" I hadn't even thought through what I was doing. I'd seen my mom, and then, bam, pure instinct, into the bush. He nodded, and I breathed a sigh of relief. "Good. Sorry, I just . . . We're not supposed to be over here. And getting caught by, like, security, that's one thing. But Dr. Tilney?" My shiver was only partially feigned. "That's another thing entirely."

"She does kind of have a very appropriate Gothic lord-of-the-castle thing going for her," Kit said, looking in the direction she'd gone off in. "Are you really that scared of her? She's your mom."

"She's Dr. Tilney." No one ever really understood this. Which was fine. I didn't need him to. "That's the role she cares about."

Kit glanced over at me, and for a second it seemed like there was a hint of a storm brewing behind his dark eyes. But an instant later, it was gone, and I wondered if I imagined it.

"Come on," he said, cocking his head back in the direction of the dorms. "I think that's enough ghosts for one day."

I didn't exactly believe him, but I let myself be led.

Chapter Ten

When I finally made it back to the house I found myself, surprisingly, excited to open my computer and dive into research before dinner. Kit had told me on our way back to his dorm that he had already checked out a dozen library books on Northanger's history; and since there was no *way* I was letting him come in with all the research while I looked like some sort of unprepared chump, I needed to get going. I had a ton of knowledge about Northanger legend, of course, but pretty much everything I knew would only serve to help *his* side. I needed information to prove that everything I'd learned was complete horseshit.

It was a challenging task, but research was something I always used to enjoy. I'd loved digging, curling up with my laptop on my bed and diving into the dusty, worn corners of the internet, message boards that had been abandoned in 2006, and articles from small-town newspapers about doors that opened when they weren't supposed to. Surely said corners would also hold testimonies from people who had debunked hauntings in the past—aka, the best primary source for my side of the project.

Unfortunately, all of that rabbit-hole diving would have to wait until after I was done sitting through an excruciating meal at the Tilney dinner table, where my mom was currently ripping Freddie a new one.

"I don't believe I told you that no was an option." My mom had mastered the art of angry chewing years ago, and she was showing it off now, taking vicious bites of enchilada—courtesy of the Trader Joe's freezer aisle—as she pointed her fork at Freddie. Freddie, for her part, didn't seem to even notice. She was playing with a cheese pull that hung from her fork, twisting it around the tines. "Do you know the strings I had to pull to get you this position?"

"Wow, thank you." Freddie's intonation was completely flat, her eyes still on the cheese. Across from her—next to me—Liam held his gaze straight down on his plate of food. He hated when any of us fought, and with Freddie back home, it was basically a guaranteed daily occurrence. "I definitely *want* to get up too early to teach a bunch of prep school brats how to run over hills faster. What an amazing opportunity."

This argument had started when Mom got home, about ten minutes after I did, and had, to my eternal joy, carried into our evening meal. From what I could make out from the shouting, Mom had finally gotten sick of Freddie lying around doing nothing all the time and had gotten her a job at the school, as the assistant coach to the girls' track and cross-country teams. Freddie, it was clear, did not think this development was quite the boon that my mother did. I was still surprised my mom hadn't done this months ago.

Mom stared at Freddie across the table, danger in her face. But instead of yelling, she took a long, slow drink of her water.

"There are rules to living in this house, Freddie. Rules that are *not* to be disobeyed."

"Fine." Freddie practically spat the word out as she pushed her food around her plate. "Whatever."

The room had an unnatural chill to it, like all the air had been sucked out. *See?* I wanted to bring Kit here, show him the unexpected coldness. *Who needs ghosts? We've got all the cold spots and lifelessness you could need right here.*

If Freddie would just go with the flow, like I did, let Mom make her into whoever she needed her to be, life would be way better. It was like Freddie didn't *want* to understand her, to understand that Mom's reputation controlled our entire lives. If she put her neck on the line for Freddie, and Freddie didn't live up to her expectations? If it compromised Mom's job somehow? Then we would have nothing.

God, she was so selfish.

"You'll have to point out all your little friends to me, Hattie." Freddie turned her attention my way, and I wished she hadn't. "Some of them are on the team, right?" Priya had joined last year, and I didn't exactly relish the thought of her spending time around my terrible older sister. "It'll be good for them to learn what a fun Tilney is like."

"I'm fun," I said, which was exactly the sort of thing an incredibly not-fun person would say. Freddie smirked, clearly thinking the same thing.

Liam piped up next to me, our eternal peacemaker. Just trying to keep things smooth. "Maybe I should go out for cross-country this year." He was looking at Mom, who had her head down in her phone. That was a clear sign that it wasn't worth pursuing, but Liam was young. He hadn't learned the signs yet, or if he had, he chose to ignore them. "What do you think, Mom?"

At the sound of the title she frequently rejected, Mom did look up, her head twitching toward Liam as she kept typing with one hand. "What was that, Liam?"

"The cross-country team," he repeated. I wished that I could reach out and stop him. Envelop him in bubble wrap and protect him from his own mistakes. If he wanted approval, bothering Mom while she was working wasn't the way to get it. "I thought . . . I don't know. You always said I needed more activities." He turned to me for backup, but I didn't have any to offer. Our whole family ran, though neither Liam nor I had done it in school—me, since I wasn't good enough to see the point in trying, and Liam because he usually viewed school activities as a waste of time. Clearly, he was feeling the lack of Mom's attention even more than usual.

Mom chewed as one of the lights in the fixture above the table flickered, flickered, flickered, like it always did. Then, just like *she* always did, she turned her attention back to her phone.

"Perhaps you should talk to your guidance counselor about that."

Next to me, Liam visibly deflated. Well, visible to those who were watching him which, again, was not Mom. Freddie had her own phone out and was texting under the table, so I reached over and squeezed Liam's hand. He ignored me. Just pushed back his chair and carried his plate to the kitchen.

Dad would never have let it get this bad.

At the thought of him, my heart raced, and I knew I needed to get out of there, too; so I grabbed my plate, dropped it off in the kitchen, and fled upstairs without another word.

I was pretty sure Mom didn't even notice.

⌇⌇⌇⌇

I knocked on Liam's door when I got upstairs, and when he didn't protest, I let myself in. My brother was sitting in the gaming chair he'd saved up his allowance for all of last year, right in the middle of the room, with a three-monitor setup that I was impressed the electrical circuits in this old cottage could support.

"Hi." I sat on the edge of the bed, pulling the comforter up over me as I did. "How's the game?"

"Terrible," he said, all matter-of-fact, not taking his eyes off the screens. "I'm losing. But what else is new?"

"How can you play a game as often as you play this one and not win all the time?" I meant it as a joke, but from Liam's scoff, he didn't take it like one.

"By being Liam Tilney, that's how." He blinked a couple of times, hard, then put down his controller and swiveled to face me. "Do you want something?"

"I just wanted to talk," I said, hands up in surrender. I hated when Liam got like this. All defensive. I never knew quite how to deal with it—when I was supposed to empathize and when I was supposed to tell him to move on. "Do you really want to try out for the cross-country team? I can help you train if you want." I didn't actually have time for that, but there was a lot I would juggle for Liam. "Go out to the trails with you. Whatever."

"Don't worry about it." Liam sighed, flopping back in his chair. "I wouldn't make the team, anyway. And even if I did, I'd have to hang out with a bunch of jocks who'd, like, shove my head in a locker."

"That stereotype can't possibly hold up."

"I'm not about to find out." He shrugged, and I decided it wasn't worth pushing. I would take him out for more runs, just the two of us, I decided. Then he could try out for the team next year if he wanted.

I tried not to think about me not being here next year to help him. How Liam was possibly going to manage on his own.

"By the way." He looked up at me then, his head cocked to the side. "Did I see you with a new kid by Howe today? Are the GiggleBots finally letting you branch out?"

"Don't call them that," I said, defending Izzy and Priya automatically. "But, yeah, you did. Kit Morland. I've just been, like, showing him around and stuff." And taking him into secret underground tunnels, but Liam didn't need to know that. "He's all right."

"Huh," Liam said, considering, then glanced over at me, a wicked look in his eyes. "He looks like someone that Tumblr would cast as teen Loki. Or that one actor you like. Timothée Chalamet." Instantly, I regretted coming into Liam's room at all. "But, like, stretched out. And slightly less vampiric."

"Don't you slander the great Timothée Chalamet like

that." I lifted my leg to kick at his chair, but he pushed back and out of the way, avoiding my contact.

"I'm just saying. You always like guys who look like poets." Liam glanced at me sideways. "Who was that guy last year?"

"Please don't." Last year was when Priya was briefly going out with a guy from the swim team and decided that we *all* needed matching boyfriends. My extremely short "relationship" was with a guy named Caleb who always smelled like chlorine, and it had ended in the least-dignified way possible—with Liam stumbling across us making out behind the bleachers, before running away at a full sprint shouting, "My eyes! My eyes!" It had been one of the top-ten most-embarrassing moments of my life. "You swore you'd never bring that up again."

"Well, you swore you'd never traumatize me with bleacher make-outs, and here we are." He picked up a weirdly shaped die he had next to his keyboard, began to toss it back and forth between his hands, and I groaned.

"You know, one day you're going to take a girl behind those bleachers, and I'm going to find out about it, and I'll never let you live it down."

Liam's expression shifted briefly, though I couldn't read what it was. Before I could ask, he turned back to his computer, picking up the controller attached to it and restarting the game.

Message received.

"Why don't you and I go out for a run sometime this week?" I offered. "Not for, like, training or whatever. Just to hang."

"Yeah." Liam's voice didn't betray any emotion, but I knew when my little brother was grateful. "That sounds okay."

"Cool." I stood up from the bed, ruffling his hair despite his protests. See? Liam didn't need Mom to take care of him. He had me, just like he always had. "Good luck killing the bad guy or whatever."

"Staking the tower!" Liam called over his shoulder, but I was already slipping out, closing the door softly behind me. I loved Liam, but I didn't want to get sucked into a discussion of whatever this game was.

Besides. I had non-ghosts to investigate.

Chapter Eleven

Once I was firmly ensconced in my room, the latest Top 40 Spotify playlist blasting loud enough that no one would bother me (it was the sort of music that repelled both Liam and Freddie, conveniently), I settled down on my bed, opened my laptop, and started a new Word document.

I stared at the blinking cursor for a good minute and a half before I closed my laptop again.

If I was going to prove to Kit—and to everyone else, of course; Kit was just the most immediate proxy—that ghosts didn't exist, I had an admittedly uphill battle. Was it possible, I wondered as I pushed my laptop to my side and pulled my legs up beneath me, that I'd bitten off more than I could chew here? Kit had somehow ended up with the way easier end of the bargain. He didn't even need to definitively prove ghosts existed—he just needed to show that they could. And I needed to, what, show that they couldn't?

Even if I knew it in my absolute heart of hearts to be true, that wasn't exactly good investigative journalism.

I needed to narrow down my thesis statement, that was all. It wasn't that I was trying to prove the nonexistence of ghosts, something that I knew was, technically, a logical impossibility. But maybe I could prove that all the weird things people thought about Northanger Abbey were based on absolute nonsense. Like how people thought *Cries* was based on actual events, even though there wasn't a single recorded incident of poltergeist-like activity here on campus. Maybe I could start there? No part of me wanted to ask Izzy for a favor, because I never liked owing her anything, but maybe interviewing her dad wouldn't be the worst thing for the project.

I didn't even realize I'd FaceTimed Kit until he'd picked up.

"Hey, stranger." He was in his dorm room, judging by the school-issued bed frame he was leaning against. He didn't seem surprised to hear from me, which was wild, because *I* was surprised to hear from me. But apparently, I would do anything to avoid sitting in my room alone, thinking about my ghosts. "Miss me already?"

"Yeah, right," I scoffed, propping the phone up against my knees. "I was just working on the project and thought we should narrow down the parameters, that's all. They're a little broad at the moment."

"Feeling overwhelmed at your insurmountable task?"

"You're a lot cockier over FaceTime, did you know that?" I shook my head, and Kit grinned. He'd taken his beanie off and was wearing what I assumed were his pajamas. I could only see the top of the shirt, but it was a different one than he'd worn earlier, more worn around the shoulders. "*Obviously* the full breadth of the subject is within my personal grasp. But we're preparing a ten-minute piece here. We need to decrease the scope for both of our sakes."

"Still sounds like an excuse to me, but sure." Kit leaned forward, then back, like he'd propped his own phone up on something. "You're definitely not just calling because you wanted to talk to me again."

"I immediately regret this conversation." I shook my head. "This is a strictly project-related discussion."

"Of course." Kit, I could now see, had his legs crossed beneath him on the floor, his hands tapping out a beat on his knee. Now that he had the phone farther away, I saw that I was right about the pajamas. His pants were a dark maroon plaid, and they looked soft. "I appreciate your dedication to the task."

"That's me. Dedicated." I propped my phone up on the side of my lamp, lay down sideways on my bed. "I'll do whatever it takes to show you that I'm right."

"I don't doubt it." Kit's voice pitched lower, and a shiver passed over me. "I'm mostly hanging out with you for that master key, though."

"Eh, I get it." I laughed, my uneasiness cleared in an instant; and even through the phone screen, warmth radiated off Kit like the comfort of a familiar hug. "Your roommate's not there, is he? I don't want to bother anyone."

"No, I've barely seen him since I moved in." Kit shrugged,

turning the phone so I could see the empty bed across from his. "He's on, like, five sports teams or something. I don't think we're going to stay up all night doing each other's hair, but I'll live. Do you ever wonder . . ." He took a breath, seemed to collect his thoughts. "Do you ever wonder about how we become friends with people? How so much of it is just convenience? Timing?"

What I would have said, if anyone else asked me that, if the mask was up, was no. That I didn't think about that sort of thing, because who had the time for random introspective thoughts? The sort of thoughts I avoided like the plague?

But because it was Kit, I nodded.

"Sure." There was a loose string attached to my comforter, where one of the decorative buttons made a divot in the fabric, and I began to play with it, wrapping it around my forefinger. "I mean, Izzy and Priya and I wouldn't have met if I didn't have gym class with Izzy." Izzy still might have found me. Sometimes it felt like I was an even bigger part of her plan than she was of mine. But she might have found someone else to fill my role, someone else who could give her the protection against her dad she needed. Who could sweet-talk teachers and smile at the edge of every selfie. It felt lonely to think about. "What about it?"

"I just think it's interesting." Kit shrugged. "That so much of our lives is determined by coincidence. That you can go through an entire existence with all of your relationships being entirely circumstantial. In a way, it makes every decision you ever make vitally important, right? But on the other hand, it doesn't matter what you do at all. Because if you just ended up with these people by accident, you'd find the relationships you need no matter where you ended up."

"That's a little depressing."

"Is it?" Kit cocked his head to the side, considering. "I think of it as more . . . hopeful, I guess. That you'll always find someone. No matter what choices you make. There's someone who made the same choice, and they're looking for you just as much as you're looking for them. Like, if I hadn't come to Northanger." Something inside of me squeezed at that idea. "I had friends in Florida. You'd have a different partner for the journalism project, and we wouldn't know we were missing out on each other. So it wouldn't, like, make us sad or anything."

"Yeah, but what if you *don't* have those people?" My gaze drifted to my desk, where I'd framed a picture of Priya and Izzy and me. My incidental friends, our relationship built around what we could do for one another. What would happen if I stopped being useful? "Do you ever feel like you did make a wrong decision? And things didn't work out?"

Kit didn't say anything for a moment, just considered my query.

"Then you have to do what you can to fix it, I guess." He ran one hand over his hair, scattering the dark strands. "But who knows? Maybe there's some cosmic force that makes sure some people end up together whether they make the right decisions or not. That pushes them onto the same path, even when they fight it. Because they're just meant to walk together."

Kit wasn't looking at me, not really, his gaze darting all

over his room as he thought out loud, which was good, because he couldn't see me flush, heat rushing up to my face.

Was that what I felt with Kit? Like we were . . . fated?

No. I didn't believe in that sort of thing, and it was a sign
that I was dealing with *way* too much stress in my life that I'd
even considered it.

"We should get back on task, Kit." I could hear the hint
of reprimand in my tone, and Kit raised one eyebrow slightly,
but then nodded.

"Sorry." That smile again, wry, crooking up one side of his
mouth. "Sometimes I rabbit hole."

"I think we need to focus on a couple of specific legends for
our initial research." I would not get sucked into the charisma
cyclone that was Kit Morland's smile. I had a task to do, the
first of many I'd need to complete tonight. I didn't have time
for wondering. "The big ones would be obvious choices, but
it also means there's a lot of research already done on them.
And we can touch on the story of *Cries*, but I don't want to
make the whole piece about the movie, so we need to discuss
more historically based hauntings as well. The Howling Milkmaid is always a favorite, at least according to the abbey gift
shop." Liam had once purchased one of the shirts available at
the kiosk just outside Northanger's gates that read *Got Milk?*
with a picture of a ghost underneath it, but Mom had given
him such a disapproving look the first time he'd worn it that
he'd donated it immediately.

Kit laughed, and I continued.

"So, we can look into the background of the various phe-
nomena as a whole, how many recorded 'sightings' there are,

and eventually narrow it down to the Milkmaid as our framework for the project." I pursed my lips. The Howling Milkmaid wasn't the most interesting ghost on campus—*alleged* ghost—but I wasn't going for interesting here. "It'll make an easier narrative for the audience to follow. We can pepper in info about how the legends are viewed at the school, toss in B-roll of the grounds. Interview some of the Ghost Brigade kids, if you're still insisting on that. Talk to some ghost enthusiasts for your side, some actual scientists and historians for mine." I'd have to weigh the merits of interviewing Mr. Thorpe on my own before bringing it up to Kit, since I knew he'd get way too excited about the idea.

"I love it when you talk journalistic techniques to me." Kit lowered his voice seductively, chin in his hands, and I would have swatted at him if we were in the same room.

"You can't flirt your way out of doing the project, Kit."

"You think I'm flirting with you?"

Oh, God, there was the flush, and this time Kit could *definitely* see it, because he was looking straight out at me, that stupid eyebrow raised again. I babbled incoherently, trying to cover my tracks.

"I—no, I just—"

"I mean, I definitely am." Kit ducked his head, so that his hair fell in front of his face, and I felt my pulse slow. Well, for a second, before what he had said hit me. "Is that . . . that's okay?"

"I . . . um . . . yes." I kept my tone short, sharp. As if that would disguise the flush. Kit was lucky he had all that hair, where he could hide his face. Mine was pulled back in a businesslike bun and doing absolutely *nothing* to hide my feelings.

But Kit just grinned, big and wide.

"Good." He leaned in close to the camera, lowered his voice. "It'll help cushion the blow when I do a way better job on my side of the project and you're forced to admit that ghosts definitely exist."

"Ha!" I'd take the distraction from actual feelings, even if it was a ghost-related distraction. "As if."

It was amazing how talking to Kit made everything bad in my life fall away. Like it didn't matter at all.

Maybe all the things that were bad *didn't* matter at all.

And as we said our goodbyes and hung up, I made a decision. Grabbing my computer again, I toggled over to the Udolpho application page, uploaded my essay and other materials, and hit Submit before I could question it. Placed my future into their hands.

There. Now I had nothing left on my to-do list. Nothing to do except wait for the acceptance to come in.

And if I had to kill time somehow while I was waiting . . . I could think of worse distractions than Kit and his ghosts.

Chapter Twelve

As I stood outside of the entrance to the dining hall a week later, where Kit and I would be joining the Ghost Brigade for their first getting-to-know-each-other brunch of the semester, I was regretting my choice of distraction.

The K. Strohm Dining Hall was located in one of the original buildings of the abbey (a refectory for the priests), but it had been retrofitted with enough modern finishes that it didn't feel as horror movie–esque as a lot of the buildings on campus. I usually found it comforting, a bastion of modernity in the Gothic nightmare of Northanger Abbey. They did a solid brunch service on the weekends, too. Even the pancakes shaped like ghosts were delicious, if I ignored the shape.

Today's meal was not going to be quite so comforting. But I was a big girl, I reminded myself. I could handle this.

I took a deep breath, pulled open the door, and entered the hall.

The cacophony of a Saturday morning hit me as soon as

I walked in, way different from the low levels of chatter that bounced around Strohm during the week. Even through the chaos, I spotted Kit immediately, waving at me from a table in the far corner of the room where the entirety of the Ghost Brigade—all seven of them—surrounded him. Steeling my resolve, I pushed myself forward.

"Hattie!" Kit pulled his backpack off the seat next to him, and I slid into it, my best Perfect Hattie smile plastered on my face in anticipation of meeting new people. "Glad you could make it. Do you know these guys?"

"Um . . . no." I recognized a few people, of course, but I hadn't bothered to learn names the one time I'd attended a meeting, and besides, that was three years ago. It felt weird, like I was the new kid and not Kit, but of course he'd thrown himself straight into the Ghost Brigade deep end. He probably knew all their greatest fears, hopes, and dreams, too. "Hi, everyone. I'm Hattie."

"You're Dr. Tilney's daughter." One of the Ghost Brigade members (Brigader? Brigaders?), a junior with light brown skin and dark shaggy hair, narrowed their eyes in my direction, and even though I'd gone through this a million times before, I felt myself stiffen. "Right?"

"That's me." I laughed, tried to play it off as no big deal. "I'm also in journalism with Kit. We're looking into the lore surrounding Northanger Abbey's paranormal history for our class project, so. Thanks for letting us join in."

"No problem." They leaned forward on the table, their denim jacket gleaming with dozens of enamel pins. One pin said THEY/THEM; and the rest were ghost themed, ranging from tiny cartoon specters to quotes from *What Cries Beneath*. "I'm Jolie. Club president. I can answer any questions you have."

"We just want to observe, to start," Kit hopped in, his smile infectious. Even Jolie seemed to soften in response to it. "We'll conduct interviews later in the semester and get some footage of meetings, if that's okay with everyone. Mostly we want to see what goes into a paranormal investigation at Northanger."

"Cool." Jolie looked around the table at the other members, who all nodded their agreement. "Well, first, let's go around and introduce ourselves, welcome the new faces into the brigade. Then we need to go over the schedule for this semester's investigations . . ."

An hour later, the brigaders were wrapping up, with most of the group deciding to head over to the common room in Schumacher and watch some Investigation Discovery shows. Overall, I thought, as everyone gathered their bags, the meeting hadn't been too terrible. Once the intros and the schedule were out of the way, they'd spent most of the meeting comparing new T-shirt designs on Jolie's laptop. Nothing particularly spooky.

What did scare me was hearing Priya's voice, shocked and incredulous, from behind me as I stood up.

"Hattie?"

I closed my eyes, turned around slowly. Crap. I knew eating in the dining hall with the Ghost Brigade wasn't exactly subtle, but since Izzy and Priya usually rolled up to brunch service later than this, I was hoping to get away unspotted. And while

Priya just looked surprised, Izzy's expression held something darker.

"What are you doing here? You never eat on campus on the weekends. And with the ghost squad?" Priya checked out the remains of the group with uncertainty. Most of them were on their way out, but Jolie and Kit were still chatting. Kit waved as he glanced over, a gesture my friends didn't return. "Did you, like, fall and hit your head on something?"

"No, nothing like that." It was true that I didn't come here on the weekends much, even though the two of them often invited me to join them. I was usually so exhausted by the end of the week that the idea of keeping up my mask for another hour was too much to even think about. This had been different, I realized. With Kit, I didn't feel worn down by the sheer act of being a person.

But I couldn't go into all of that with Izzy and Priya. This didn't have to be a big deal if I just kept my cool. "It's for Skinner's project. You know—we have to investigate all the hauntings and stuff? This is for research."

"Right." Izzy finally spoke, exchanging an expression that wasn't my favorite with Priya. "And this club doesn't offer something . . . more than research?" From the way she looked over at Kit, I knew exactly what she was implying. And the deep flush that covered my neck and cheeks at that exact moment? Definitely didn't help my case. Because, yes, maybe things with Kit had felt . . . friendly, lately. But even though I could talk to Izzy and Priya about anything related to Northanger or college, actual feelings? Those were kept way off the table.

So instead, I backpedaled.

"Oh my gosh, no!" I laughed, though even to me it sounded brittle. "Kit's just my project partner. And I'm his ambassador. I have to show him around."

"That's it?" Priya sounded skeptical.

"Obviously." I faked a shudder. "Come on, guys. Don't be ridiculous."

"Ridiculous?" Izzy lifted an eyebrow. "We're not the ones having secret ghost brunches in the dining hall with a bunch of dorks while dodging meal invites from your *actual* friends." The look she gave me was pointed. "We've barely seen you this week, Hattie. Is this why?"

"Come on, Iz." I had to salvage this while I could, had to throw the girls off my trail so I could figure out whatever this was on my own. "You think I'd hang out with Dork Patrol on *purpose?*"

"Hattie."

Oh, shit.

Izzy smirked and Priya's eyes widened as I turned around to see Kit, standing right behind me with a completely neutral expression on his face.

"I'm going to walk back to the dorms with Jolie." His voice was lifeless. "I'll email you about the project, okay?"

"Yeah, totally." Oh, God. He'd heard everything we'd said, hadn't he? Priya's face said that he definitely had. "I'll . . . I'll talk to you later." What was I supposed to do? Throw myself to the sticky linoleum and start apologizing? He knew that my relationship with Izzy and Priya was complicated.

But there was deflection, and there was saying something

that couldn't be unsaid, and I was suddenly and extraordinarily worried I'd just done the latter.

As soon as he was fully out of earshot (for real this time), Izzy let out a low hiss.

"Nice one, Hats."

"I can't believe he heard that. I can't believe you made me say that." I felt anger begin to rise as Izzy cocked her head to the side, her hair falling over her shoulder.

"Made you? Excuse you, I didn't realize I had the power of puppetry over the great Hattie Tilney. I'm just looking out for you. Like I always have," Izzy said, and my heart pounded. Like I could ever forget. How alone I'd felt, with only my ghosts for company. How Izzy, and later Priya, had pulled me from the depths of my despair. "You know all this ghost shit is the worst part of Northanger."

"Hey." Priya stepped forward, her hands out in front of her as she stood between Izzy and me. "We're all probably just hungry. Come on. They have booberry pancakes."

"I ate already." I owed Izzy and Priya so much. Yes, I'd done my part in our relationship. I was the one who'd gotten Izzy a redo on her Spanish midterm last year by telling her teacher how much my mom appreciated her contribution to the school. I'd gotten on the phone with Mr. Thorpe at the end of sophomore year, told him that *of course* I was going to the class's Six Flags trip, and I would *definitely* keep an eye on Izzy. But she—and Priya—had been there for me a dozen times over. Last year, Izzy had told off a group of seniors who kept posting on my Instagram, asking me if the stick up my mom's ass was genetic. Priya had rounded up dates for all of us for every single school dance since freshman year and was the main reason any of us had passed AP Bio. Plus, every time Izzy's dad sent over her allowance, she would order takeout for all three of us, putting together a giant feast on her dorm room floor. Our relationship may have been transactional, but all of those transactions had to add up to something.

And yet I owed Kit something, too. Something real.

I glanced over my shoulder toward the door, where Kit and the rest of the brigade were long gone. I had to fix this some-how. "I just . . . I have to go, okay? I'll text you guys later."

Izzy looked like she was about to say something else, but I was already gone, dodging students and trays as I ran toward the door, toward my latest mistake. I was so good at pushing people away, sometimes it came too naturally. Sometimes I pushed too hard.

Sometimes I pushed away the people I didn't want to.

※

"I'm sorry."

"Is that all?" Kit stood on the front steps of Howe with his arms crossed over his chest, the most standoffish I'd ever seen him.

I'd texted him when I'd made it to his dorm, asking if we could talk, and he'd responded with a single syllable, "k," the most devastating texted letter in the English language. I knew he was mad. I didn't blame him. If I was being honest, I was mad at myself.

Now I was here, standing in front of a boy I'd been a real asshole to, and "sorry" wasn't going to be enough to cover it.

"This ghost stuff is complicated for me, okay?" There was no way I could go into the full details with Kit, not without falling apart, but I knew I had to give him something. "I tried to get into it, when I first got to Northanger. I didn't have any friends yet and I didn't know how to be . . . all of this." I waved my hand over my body self-consciously, my preppy plaid skirt and the fitted gray sweater I'd pulled on over my T-shirt. "Izzy, and Priya, too . . . they pulled me out of it. They helped me find my place here. And Izzy's got her own issues with ghost stuff, with her dad, and I overcorrected, to reassure them. But I was still a jerk." I shifted from one foot to another. It was a shitty explanation, and I could tell Kit thought so, too, from the roll of his eyes. "I didn't know how to explain to them that we're friends."

"Does it require that wild of an explanation, Hattie?" Kit leaned against the brick wall of the building, tucked into the archway that marked the entrance to Howe. Ivy crept up the mortar, like the building was being overtaken by the woods. There was a storm rolling in, the sky darkening around us, adding an extra level of ominous to our conversation. "When I tell people about one of my friends, I don't usually see a need to justify them. People just accept it as part of the human experience."

"Yeah, but you're . . ."

"Some kind of ghost-obsessed freak, right?" Kit's laugh was short, pointed, as he kicked his scuffed-up Converse against the worn concrete of the stairs. "The paranormal-loving loser someone like Hattie Tilney could never be friends with? A member of the . . . what was it? Dork patrol?"

"No. You're confident. You know who you are." The words tumbled out of me, fast and stumbling. "I'm not, okay? I'm just, like, a carefully cultivated shell of a person whose only purpose is to succeed." Horrifyingly, I felt tears prickle at the corners of my eyes, but luckily, they didn't fall. "I barely have real friends. I don't know how. You're the first person to— God, this is embarrassing." I looked up at the darkened sky and blinked fast. "I like you, Kit. And letting myself hang out with someone just because I like them is new for me. You're the first person in forever I've wanted to seek out." I took a deep breath, looked him straight in the eyes. "I feel like that means something."

Kit leaned back against the wall again as he looked out over my shoulder. Eons passed.

Finally, he spoke.

"I think it does, too. But you can't— One of the reasons I was so excited to come to Northanger was because I was tired of being the ghost-obsessed freak in my high school. I figured here, people would be into the Northanger legends. And some of them are, but it's clearly not doing anything for my social standing." He chuckled, though there was no humor in it. "That doesn't bother me. But if it bothers you, maybe we should end this now. Before it becomes harder to disentangle ourselves. I'm not interested in forcing you to hang out with me."

"You're not," I said quickly. "Honestly, Kit. If I didn't want to be here, I wouldn't have followed you."

"Yeah." Finally, Kit stopped his fidgeting. His smile was small, but it was there, and I let myself have a moment to enjoy the triumph of it. "Wow. I didn't think I was coming to Northanger Abbey to start ruining people's reputations."

"Maybe my reputation isn't that important to me."

"No, it is." Kit's words were still accompanied by a smile, but they stung nevertheless. Not that he was wrong. "It's fine, Tilney. I'm not exactly looking to be indoctrinated into the cult of Northanger Abbey popularity here. I just want to do my thing, and whoever wants to come along on that ride . . . cool. Are you actually in for that?"

"Yeah. I am." I should have felt relieved. Kit wasn't asking me to make some big dramatic gesture for him, or anything, which was good, because I didn't know anything about big dramatic gestures. I knew about big dramatic keeping your head downs. Big dramatic ignore all the bad things that have ever happened to you.

Kit was giving me an out, and I was glad to take it.

But for whatever reason, I still felt the gnawing of guilt inside of me.

That's probably why I did what I did next.

"Why don't you come over for dinner?" I said, before I knew what I was doing, before I considered the magnitude of my offer. That I'd never even had Izzy or Priya over to my house, because once anyone saw the way my family interacted with one another, it would be a lot harder to hide how bad things were. "Come hang out at my place this afternoon, and then stay for dinner."

"You sure?" Kit asked, scratching at his head, hesitant.

"Because the last time we saw your mom, you full-on jumped into shrubbery to escape her. She isn't going to, like, roast me up and eat me, is she?"

"She's the headmistress, not the gingerbread-house witch from 'Hansel and Gretel.'" Though the metaphor wasn't that far off. "You don't believe in fairy-tale witches, too, do you? Because if so, I'd rather know up front."

"You're funny." Kit pushed off from the archway, bumping my shoulder with his as he came down beside me, and I felt relief wash over me. Whatever else was going wrong, I hadn't ruined this. Not this time. "I remember you."

I laughed.

"Come on." I reached out and grabbed his elbow, tugged on it until he started walking. To an outside observer, we'd look completely out of place side by side. Him in his ripped jeans and yet another black concert T-shirt, covered by a dark plaid flannel with the sleeves rolled up. Me in my plaid miniskirt, practically matching the weekday uniform, with a tucked-in sweater and my hair perfectly waved.

But we maybe still matched, in our own way. Being with Kit felt like more of a fit than being with Izzy or Priya ever did.

And he wasn't asking me to abandon them or anything. To choose him.

Would I, though?

Shouldn't I?

Chapter Thirteen

As we hit the edge of campus and stepped onto the path that led through the woods to my house, my heart started beating approximately ten million times a minute.

Which was ridiculous. It was just my *house*. It wasn't like Kit was going to walk in and immediately be confronted by members of my family screaming about their dysfunctional lives.

Well. It was unlikely, anyway.

Kit must have heard my quick intake of breath, because he looked over at me, stopping right in the middle of a story about a paranormal-themed scavenger hunt he'd attempted back in Florida with some of his friends that had gone hilariously wrong. (Or so he'd said. I hadn't really been listening.)

"Hey." He paused, fallen leaves crumbling under his sneakers. The storm seemed to be holding off for now, but the clouds still made the woods unnaturally dark, unnaturally ominous. The little light that made its way through the trees picked up every angle of his face, casting it in garish shadow. "You okay?"

"Totally fine!" I kept moving, pushing through the woods, because if I stopped, too, there was a good chance I'd never get up the courage to start again. "This is a completely regular thing to do, right? Having you come over. You're the one who has experience at a normal high school. Are you expecting ants on a log or something?"

"I mean, I'd never turn down ants on a log." Kit had to half run to catch up to me. "Do you freak out every time you have friends over?"

"I've never had anyone over before." I said the words so fast that they almost got swallowed up by one another, stumbling over and over like they were in a race to make their way out of my mouth.

Finally, I stopped, and Kit came to a halt behind me, watching me with one eyebrow raised as he leaned on the nearest tree trunk. The wind picked up around him, lifting the ends of his hair off his shoulders.

"I told you that you were different from Izzy and Priya." I tried to make it sound casual, throwaway, but from the way Kit looked at me, he didn't buy it.

"Yeah, that's been made pretty clear to me at this school."

"No, Kit." Without thinking, I reached out, grabbed his hand—long, pale fingers, the skin cool—and held it between us. He stared down at it like he'd never seen it before. "That's not an insult, okay? It's good that you're different. I *like* that you're different. It makes me feel less alone because I am also deeply, wildly different from any of them. I've just gotten really good at not letting them see." I took a deep breath, inhaling the incoming storm, exhaling slow. Letting my breathing follow the pulse I could feel in Kit's fingers, even if it was picking up in pace a little. Our own private hurricane. "You're the first person who ever bothered to look past the outside. So I'm showing you more. Okay? As a . . . I don't know. A gesture. Or whatever."

"Or whatever," Kit echoed. The wind hit my legs, brushing against my tights like it was pushing me to Kit. He glanced up toward the sky, at what little he could see through the thick canopy of the leaves. "This is quite the dinner invitation."

"We're all about the grand gesture over here." I dropped his hand, albeit a little reluctantly, then tried to rearrange my features into at-least-a-little-bit-together mode. It probably wasn't successful, but it was something. "Just let me like you, okay? And feed you meatballs, I guess. You like meatballs?"

"I do." Kit fell into step beside me as we kept going down the path, at a slightly more manageable pace this time. Part of me was worried about the rain, but it hadn't started yet. Maybe I didn't need to worry about it until it did. "They're my third favorite ball."

"That's a loaded ranking."

"You have no idea."

I laughed, and Kit did, too; and even though we were literally walking into the world's strangest situation, with Kit, it didn't feel too bad.

"I'm home!" I called as soon as I pushed open the front door
of the cottage, giving it an extra shove when it stuck in the
frame. Normally, I didn't announce myself, but under the circumstances, I wanted to know exactly who was here and what
I was walking into. "I have a friend with me!"

"So, this is your house." Kit stepped in behind me and
pulled the door closed before he bent over to shed his shoes
and jacket. "Did you text someone to hide all of the embarrassing photos as soon as you invited me over?"

"We're not really a photo family. Sorry." We used to be,
with Dad, but we'd never had pictures up here. "And while
we're on a roll with disappointments, the house isn't haunted,
either." I tapped on the wall next to me, and Kit groaned, a
sound I hadn't expected to like. "So if you need to go back to
campus, I get it."

"When I was promised meatballs? Not a chance." Kit
peeked his head through the doorway off the foyer, which led
to our living room, messy as always. I did my best to swallow
down embarrassment. No matter how much I tried to keep it
in order, Hurricane Freddie could undo my work in an instant.
Liam was too checked out to fix it, and Mom never seemed
to notice. "Besides, I'm not going to accept your word as to
what's haunted and what's not when you don't even believe in
ghosts. You don't think *anywhere* is haunted."

"Ghosts?"

Interaction, incoming. I braced myself as I turned to the
stairs, where Liam had appeared, looking like he'd just woken
up. He'd only made it a few steps down before he'd noticed us,

and now he was suspended in limbo, in between floors. "Who doesn't believe in ghosts?"

"Anyone with a rational brain," I answered, as Kit rolled his eyes. "Liam, this is Kit Morland. The new kid at school I'm showing around. Kit, this is my little brother, Liam. He's a sophomore."

"Hey." Kit waved, while Liam stared, jaw slightly agape, presumably in sheer disbelief that I had someone over.

Which, yes, was completely justified, but he could have done a better job of hiding it. I especially didn't like the way his face turned to astonishment when he looked at me, how I *knew* he was thinking of what he'd said the other day about Timothée Chalamet.

Kit didn't even look that much like my favorite actor. Not more than a passing resemblance, anyway. Stunt double, at best.

"Oh, you're Kit," Liam finally said, which was about the worst thing you could say to someone when you didn't want them to know they'd been mentioned before. Kit grinned. "Hi. You're at our house?"

"I'm as surprised as you are." Kit held up his hands in front of him in surrender. "Trust me. I find it easier not to try and predict your sister's actions."

"Ha. Yeah." Liam looked over at me through the balusters, and I shrugged. I was just as much at a loss as to how this was supposed to go as he was. "Mom went into town for a couple of hours." He stretched his long arms up into the air, yawning. "She said she'll be back for dinner."

"Cool." I wouldn't have minded if she missed tonight's

meal, but I was just going to have to be brave. Maybe everything would be chill, for once. "I'm going to show Kit around.
Okay?"

"You got it." Liam saluted before scurrying back up the
stairs, presumably to hide in his room and definitely *not* do
homework. I let out a long, slow breath. That hadn't been
nearly as bad as it could've been.

"So that was your brother." Kit watched the spot where
he had been, head cocked to one side. "You guys look alike."

"Yeah, I guess." Liam had the same dirty blond hair as
me, the same dark eyebrows, and freckles across similar noses.
Freddie did, too. It always perplexed me how much the three
of us looked like a set when we hardly ever felt like it. "Do you
want to go into the backyard? It's not raining yet. We can hang
out on the deck." "Deck" was generous, but it was big enough
for a couple of chairs, and we were less likely to be bothered
out there.

"Sure." Kit smiled down at me, encouraging, and I tried to
absorb that encouragement the best I could. I was trying, but
I knew if I looked down at my fists they'd be clenched, white-
knuckled as I tried to anticipate all the ways this visit could
go wrong. Freddie could roll in, plastered. Mom could be in a
terrible mood and take it out on Kit.

But I was trying. I owed Kit trying.

I led Kit into the backyard with a quick stop in the kitchen
for mugs of tea that I heated up in the microwave, an extra
layer of protection against the still-rushing wind. As we settled
into the Adirondack chairs that had come with the house, I
watched Kit to see his reaction to the view.

As expected, he gasped. Our backyard led down into the woods, but peeking out over the trees was the spire of the abbey, rising tall and foreboding. With the sky still blocked by thick gray clouds and the sun starting to set behind us, the dusky hour made the towers even more Gothic than usual.

Dad would have loved this view.

"Wow," Kit said finally, once he got his words back. "You're so lucky—you know that?"

"That's what they tell me." I'd have traded this view, this life, in an instant to get back even a fraction of what I'd lost. "I thought you'd like it out here."

"I love it." Kit's voice was overwhelmed with earnestness, his hands wrapped around his mug as he stared out into the distance. "This . . . being at Northanger. This is all I ever wanted. You know, I used to watch student tour videos on YouTube? For hours." He laughed, the sound captured by the wind and spirited away into the trees. "Especially this spring, when I was waiting to see if I got the scholarship. The day I found out I did . . . it was the best day ever." He smiled, lost in a memory. "My parents took me out for ice cream. *Just* me. Which, like, never happened, with all my sisters around. And they told me how proud of me they were."

"Do you miss them?"

"Sure." Kit's gaze was still on the spire, long fingers tapping the pale green mug. I didn't even know where we'd gotten these mugs. Maybe they'd come with the house, with the life we'd slotted into. "But this is where I'm meant to be. That makes it easier. You must be getting ready for that, too, right? With college? Do you know what you're doing yet?"

"Yeah." I tried to imbue some unearned confidence into my voice. My tea was still too hot to drink, but I attempted to sip it anyway, pulling the scalding liquid into my mouth like a punishment. "I applied early decision to Udolpho. Prelaw."

"Really?" The surprise in Kit's voice was clear as he set his mug down on the arm of his chair. I raised an eyebrow in his direction. "No, I mean—sorry. That's a good school, right? You'll definitely get in. The prelaw thing just kind of surprised me."

"It's a stable track." I sounded more defensive than I needed to. Another too-hot sip of tea. Kit wasn't attacking me. Not everyone who asked me questions was attacking me. "A good career. That's important."

"Definitely." Kit's smile was reassuring as he turned his gaze back to the school, though I didn't feel particularly reassured. With his beanie and flannel, sprawled casually in the Adirondack chair, he seemed to belong here in a way I never could. "I bet *Dr. Tilney* is a big help with that. College." I didn't miss the emphasis on her title.

"Well, she's pretty busy." I kept my voice light, even as the sky continued to darken. We weren't going to escape the storm forever. "It would be unfair of me to ask for extra attention, when she has all these students to take care of. I'm not the only one she has to worry about."

"Yeah, but you're her daughter."

"And she's the headmistress." Finally, my tea was a more manageable temperature, and I sipped lightly at it, warming from the inside out. "I've got my senior meeting with her scheduled for right after Halloween. We'll talk then."

Kit watched me. The sun had almost entirely set, and I hadn't turned on the porch light before we came out, so his face was once again cloaked in shadows. He seemed like he wanted to speak, and when he started to open his mouth, the shadows seemed to move with him.

He paused again. But then he shook his head, smiled at me.

"Come on. If we stay out here much longer, the ghosts of the abbey are going to come after us."

"They'd have to be real first." I stood up from my chair, grabbed our mugs, and headed back inside, glad that Kit hadn't pushed any further. I wouldn't expect him to understand my relationship with my mom. I didn't expect that of anyone. But Kit was the only person who might have been interested in trying. And it just . . . it wasn't worth it.

The wind whistled in my ears, low and menacing.

Chapter Fourteen

S ince we were creeping up on dinnertime, I led Kit into the kitchen. It was small, a remnant from when the house was in full-on cottage mode, with little woodland animals painted all over the backsplash (a detail my mom *hated*). Kit pulled out a stool in front of the counter, sat down, and leaned forward on his elbows, watching me. His height was even more apparent in this kitchen, built for times when people were generally shorter and someone like Kit would have been a circus act.

"So I met your brother." It wasn't a subject change, exactly, but it was close enough that I welcomed it. "And you said you had a sister. The one with the key?"

"That's Freddie," I said, rummaging around in the freezer until I pulled out a bag of meatballs. Our last one, which sucked, because I *thought* that I'd made enough to at least get us to Thanksgiving. Clearly, this semester had us all wrapped up in even less domestic bliss than usual. "I don't think we'll see her tonight."

"Why? Does she turn into a bat during daylight hours?"

"For someone who loves ghosts, you have kind of a vampire fixation." I grabbed the box of pasta next, placing it on the counter in front of me.

"You can avoid my question all you want. I'll figure out the truth eventually. What other deep, dark secrets are you hiding?" Kit's voice had the cadence of a joke, but I suspected that he was just doing that to mask the real question. Which was fair, I guessed. I'd brought him here. Told him that it meant something. I probably owed him at least a minimal breakdown of who he might see wandering the halls like one of his ghosts.

"Do those chipmunks look like they could live in a house with deep dark secrets to you?" I nodded toward the painted animals that were frozen in a permanent run behind the sink, and Kit laughed. "I just don't talk about my family much. It's weird at school, right? With my mom. I'm basically in an eternal quest to be as normal as possible."

"Hence, Izzy and Priya?"

"Yeah. I mean, we're friends. But they don't, like . . ."

"Hunt for ghosts in the hallways?"

"Don't worry," I offered, with a small smile that Kit matched. "I'm starting to find the endless ghost hunting kind of endearing." But I knew I couldn't deflect that easily. "Izzy and Priya are invested in their places in the social hierarchy for their own reasons."

"Especially Izzy?"

"Yeah." I dumped the meatballs into a bowl, placing them in the microwave to defrost. "They're not used to people threatening to disrupt it."

"People like me." Kit put his chin in his hands, elbows on the counter. If Mom was here, she'd be tossing him a signature Headmistress Tilney glare, and I was glad that she wasn't. Glad that someone was sprawling all over her precious counters.

I shrugged. "Isn't disrupting the system, like, your whole thing?" I nodded at—well, *him*. He smirked. "You don't care what anyone else thinks. You love ghosts, which are, like, the ultimate disruption to the status quo. The idea that our dead can come back to haunt us is an idea that fundamentally turns what we know about the universe on its end. You love that."

"Man. Am I that easy to figure out?" Kit sat up, shaking his head as he laughed. "I'd argue that for a lot of people, the idea of the dead still being part of our lives is *exactly* in line with what they know about the universe, but point taken. With a caveat." He glanced down at his hands, long fingers intertwining, thumbs twiddling. "I care what *some* people think."

He looked up at me, and his dark eyes were pools of night I could drown in.

If I were braver, I would have reached across the counter and grabbed him. Stopped his twiddling hands, stood on my tiptoes so I could reach his face, press my mouth against his, and let him know exactly what I thought.

I was a lot of things. I was a master of hiding myself, I was a decent student, I was a Tilney. I was determined to keep my family moving forward, even when all they ever seemed to want to do was claw themselves into a stop.

But I was not brave.

So instead, I pivoted away from the counter, opening a jar

of sauce and dumping it into a pot that I'd placed on the stove, turning the burner on and watching the flame catch.

"Tell me more about Liam." Kit let me get away with it, with my cowardice. "He seems cool. But . . ."

"Different from me?" I finished, and he nodded. "Yeah, well, Liam's not as committed to presenting a front of normalcy as I am." After the microwave beeped, I pulled out the meatballs and began to drop them in the sauce, standing back a little ways so they didn't splatter on me. "He's a good kid, though. Smart. Funny. Kind."

"You two are close."

"We are." I lowered the heat a little so that the sauce could come to a simmer before I finally turned back to Kit. He'd put his chin in his hand again. "We look out for each other." Kit pushed off the stool, coming around to my side of the counter.

"Here. Let me help."

"It's okay," I said, but Kit had already grabbed the pot I'd placed on the other side of the stove top, filling it up with water at the sink. "You really don't have to."

"Please. My parents would kill me if I didn't put all my hard-earned kitchen skills to good use." He opened the box of dried pasta I'd taken out, set it down with care next to the pot. "I can do more than just boil water, you know."

"Really?" I smirked, giving the sauce a stir. "Tell me more."

"I don't want to brag . . ." Kit glanced around conspiratorially, then leaned in, his breath a whisper in my ear that made me shiver. "But I've been known to make rice *without* a rice cooker."

"What do we have here?"

Oh my God. At the sudden intrusion of my sister's voice, Kit and I sprang apart like we'd been repelled by a magnetic force. I jumped, causing the wooden spoon I was holding to splatter tomato sauce all over the counter and—oh, good—Kit, too, who had jumped about halfway across the room, but apparently not so far that he was out of the line of fire. Instead, a spray of tomato sauce covered the front of his shirt, like he was an extra in a low-budget slasher movie. The look of horror on his face had studio potential, though.

When I turned around to face Freddie, she was leaning forward with her forearms on the countertop, grinning. I hated her for it.

"Freddie." I just barely managed to get her name out through gritted teeth. "You're home."

"Sure am. Who's this tall drink of water?" I couldn't see Kit behind me, but I could guess at his facial expressions. "What's your name, kid?"

"K-Kit," he stammered, and I briefly considered just throwing myself through a window to release myself from this situation. "Kit Morland. I go to Northanger."

"And here I thought you'd just snuck onto campus and brainwashed my baby sis into making you meatballs." Freddie looked like she was going to explode with happiness. This level of humiliation for me was basically Christmas and her birthday all rolled up into one. "I'm Freddie. Hattie's older, better sister."

"Nice to meet you." When I turned around, Kit was

smiling again, all traces of embarrassment gone from his face. It was a talent I envied. "I should probably— Do you think your brother has a shirt I could borrow, Hattie? I should soak this before it stains too badly."

"Oh my gosh, yes, of course." I should have offered that immediately, but, in my defense, I was dying. "I can take you up—Freddie, can you keep an eye on the sauce? Please?"

"Wow, you'd trust me with such an important task?" She gasped, hand pressed over her heart. Come *on*, Freddie. "It's a small house. You can find your own way, can't you, Kit?"

"Um . . . sure?" Kit, ever-polite, held up a palm when I started to protest. Clearly, he sensed the tension simmering like the sauce between Freddie and me. "I'll be fine. Be right back." With a small twitch of his mouth in my direction, which didn't do anything to reassure me, he was gone.

And then it was just me and my sister, all five feet four inches of pure smugness.

"Henrietta Tilney." She hopped up on the counter, even though Mom would kill her if she came home and saw her like that. "You brought a boy home."

"Please don't say it that way." If I just paid attention to the food, maybe I could manage to ignore Freddie entirely. "He's my partner for the journalism project."

"Oh, right. The ghost thing."

"How did you know about that?" My voice was sharp.

"Chill, Hen." God, I hated that nickname. Freddie only called me that when she *really* wanted to push my buttons. Hen, short for Henrietta, but more specifically, like a mother hen. Or a chicken, depending on what type of insult she was trying to levy. "Your friend Priya is on my team. She told me. She thinks I'm really easy to talk to, you know that? A great listener."

"You shouldn't be talking to her." This was not the best I'd ever been at ignoring Freddie. If I had the power of time travel, I would—well, admittedly, there were about ten billion things I would change. But if it was restricted to the last fifteen minutes only, I'd spray tomato sauce all over *her* instead, an acidic blaze of red across her tight white tank top and baggy sweatpants that somehow made her look like a Hollywood backup dancer getting a Starbucks after rehearsal, especially with her tight curls pulled up into an artfully messy knot on top of her head.

"And yet, I am. Funny how that works, isn't it?" Freddie crossed past me and pulled open the door to the refrigerator, pulling out a Diet Coke and leaving the door half open behind her as she twisted off the bottle cap. "You know what's weird? She didn't even know you had a sister."

"Yeah, I can't imagine why I'd want to hide you," I muttered, and Freddie's eyes narrowed.

"God, Hattie." Freddie's voice dropped from gleeful to spite in an instant. "Does it ever get old? Feeling so superior to everyone else all the time?"

"I don't do that." I stirred the sauce with a lot more force than I needed to, narrowly missing splattering myself, too. I didn't even know what we were fighting about anymore. But if there was one thing I hated, it was letting Freddie win. No matter how low a blow I had to use to beat her. "I can't believe they even let you work at the school."

"Some of your classmates like my leadership, Hen." She laughed humorlessly as she hopped back up onto the counter, her feet swinging. "That Thorpe girl sure seems to."

"Izzy?" It was like my stomach had dropped down to my feet. If I could think of one combination that would only lead to absolute disaster, it would be Freddie and Izzy. "How do you even know her?"

"She comes to watch Priya practice. You know, like a good friend." I wanted to wipe the smirk off Freddie's face, but I'd never figured out how. "She's an interesting one, that Izzy. Just a little too smart for her own good. Asked a *lot* of questions about you and this Kit kid."

"Leave her alone, Freddie."

"Or what? You're going to tell on me?" Before I could respond, I heard footsteps pounding down the stairs, and a second later, both Liam and Kit appeared in the doorway. I took only a second more to glare at Freddie—she wasn't worth more than that—before turning my attention to them. I'd have to talk to Izzy later, even if it would probably involve a nonzero amount of groveling over the Kit situation. There was no way that her getting involved with Freddie ended well.

But in the meantime . . . Kit. Just take a deep breath and think of Kit.

Liam had lent Kit one of his shirts, I saw as he came into the room, something bright and colorful from a Japanese show I'd never watched. It was weird to see Kit in a shirt that was neither black nor part of the school uniform. Not that the light faded green of Liam's shirt was *bad* or anything. It was just different.

It was a welcome distraction from Freddie, anyway.

"Can we eat?" Liam, as always, was completely immune to the tension bubbling between Freddie and me. That was always my main goal, after all. Protect Liam, the way I wished Freddie had protected me. "Or should we wait for Mom?"

"That's a losing battle," Freddie muttered, hopping off the counter and dumping rigatoni into the pot in one smooth motion. I stepped back, half to avoid getting splashed by boiling water and half out of shock that Freddie was doing anything remotely helpful. "Anyway, I'm not joining you."

"Two-for-one night at your favorite local hellhole?" The words came out before I could stop them, before I could remember that Kit was here, that *Liam* was here, as Freddie paused in her tracks. Kit and Liam both turned to stare at me. Liam's mouth was agape.

It wasn't worse than anything Freddie had ever said to me, but I usually kept it more civil in front of Liam. He didn't see her like I did, didn't see all the ways she'd failed us, because I did everything I could to make up for her. If I had one goal at home, it was protecting Liam from seeing the worst of our family.

As for Kit, well . . . I'd wanted him to know me. Apparently, this was part of knowing me. And when I looked over at him, his expression wasn't one of surprise. I didn't know what to make of it.

After the world's longest pause, Freddie spoke.

"I'm eating with Coach Grill, actually." Coach Grill was the head of the cross-country team, someone I only knew from gym class and her commitment to getting the entire school to love weight lifting. It hadn't worked out so far. "But thanks for that."

Part of me knew I should apologize, but she left before I got the chance, the flimsy screen door swinging shut behind her. Besides, it wasn't like she'd want an apology, anyway. She was *Freddie*. She didn't have feelings. That was her main inheritance from Mom.

I turned my attention back to Liam and Kit, my face bright and smiling, my mask firmly secured.

"Come on." I opened the cabinet above me, grabbed a stack of bowls. "Let's set the table, okay?"

"Sure." Liam jumped in, eager to be past the discomfort, as always; and eventually Kit did, too, though his smile was quizzical. This was why I didn't have people over, I reminded myself. Because no one needed to see this. To see all the cracks in our family. In me.

But I pushed that feeling down, and I kept moving forward, because that was all I could do.

※

The rest of the night, somehow, went well. Mom never showed up for dinner—shocker—but Kit and Liam got along famously, talking about their favorite video games for the entire meal. Liam had even given Kit his phone number, so they could text each other their high scores. It made my chest ache, in a good way, to see Liam open up like that.

Before Dad died, Liam was—still quiet. Still reserved. But

he wasn't sullen. He wasn't a loner, like he was now. He had a small group of friends, guys who he ran with, who would come out bowling with us for his birthday every year.

Dad and I were close, of course. But he and Liam were, too. Their favorite thing to do together was to go out to thrift stores and garage sales on the weekends, sort through piles of junk until they found things that they deemed treasures. Sometimes it was a novelty mug commemorating the two hundredth birthday of some English author. Sometimes it was a miniature cannon (nonfunctional, I was mostly sure) that came to our house covered in rust and scrapes. They cleaned up each and every treasure, made them functional again if they could, and loved them for their stories if they couldn't.

Before we moved, after Dad died, Liam threw most of it away. And it was like he threw all of his stories away with them. He clammed up, shut down, seemed determined to retreat completely inside himself. He went to the local middle school for our first year here, and as far as I could tell, got bullied pretty bad, though he refused to ever talk about it. I thought things might be better when he got to Northanger—hardly anyone from his middle school was there, it would be a brand-new start—but he didn't make any effort to fit in. To try.

All I wanted to do was find the bright, fun kid who Liam had been before Dad died. I'd worried he was gone entirely.

But maybe Kit had found him.

Later that night, I went up to my room after Kit had gone back to the dorms, after Liam had gone to bed, after the storm finally started. I went into the back of my closet, the way, way back, and pulled out a shoebox I'd shoved in there when we first moved in. Dust filled the air when I opened it, and I did my best not to cough too loudly. I didn't want to wake anyone up. Didn't want anyone to ask what I was doing.

There was a stack of photos in there, some ticket stubs. A single floppy paperback, worn and yellowed.

I didn't take anything out. But I looked at the top picture, examined it at its haphazard angle. It was the entire family. *Actually* the entire family—me, Freddie, Liam, Mom, and . . . Dad. All wearing matching Northanger Abbey hoodies. The photo had been taken just days after Mom accepted the job here. We were smiling, all of us, even Mom, her face almost unrecognizable. Dad was laughing. We looked happy. Maybe that was the last time we'd all been happy.

I didn't take the photo out of the box. But I didn't put it back in the closet, either.

Chapter Fifteen

Ever since Kit had come over for dinner, things had been good between us—easy and comfortable, aka two feelings I'd never associated with Northanger before.

We spent a lot of time together in the library after school, often joined by Liam, which marked the most time he'd ever willingly stayed on campus . . . ever. And even though there were parts of me that wouldn't have minded some more Kit-based alone time—not that it mattered, because we weren't going to *do* anything, I reminded myself—hanging out with the two of them felt right. I felt more at home at Northanger than I'd felt in a long time.

Admittedly, I probably could have done without the day my mother stumbled across us in the library, sitting shoulder to shoulder as we shared a dusty old book that Kit had sweet-talked the librarian into digging out of the back. I'd forgotten to keep my guard up—I knew my mom liked to do rounds after school, but we'd managed to avoid each other for a while, or at least, she'd managed to avoid me. So seeing her in full Dr.

Tilney attire, her stiffness the exact opposite of Kit's relaxed slouch, had thrown me.

"Hattie." She'd nodded at me, her expression as neutral as ever, Dr. Tilney perfection. Light streamed through one of the library's endlessly tall windows behind her, casting her in a glow like an avenging angel. "Mr. Morland. I trust your partnership is going well?"

"Yes?" The question startled me, if only because it had been a few weeks now and she'd never asked me about Kit at home. But here, of course, it made more sense. Dr. Tilney always checked in on her students. "Right?" I turned my attention to Kit, who had been watching my mother, not quite smiling. But as soon as I shifted in his direction, his face transformed.

"Best ambassador ever," he said jovially, and I did my best not to blush. If I did, my mother had the decency not to mention it. "Ten out of ten. Two enthusiastic thumbs up."

"Good." Her expression flickered down to the book between us. *Milkmaids, Acrobats, and Other Oddities: A History of Northanger Abbey.* She didn't comment on it. "I'll leave you to it."

As soon as she was gone, vacating the light to move on to the next table of students, I let out a long, slow breath. Kit watched me.

"You know," he said, once she was safely out of earshot, just before I returned to the book (which was absolutely ridiculous, by the way, but I was trying to be nice about it), "if you had asked me if it would be cool to have my mom be the headmistress of Northanger, I would have said yes. But it mostly seems terrifying."

"Hey." I frowned. "She's just setting a good example."

"That's— Okay." Whatever Kit was going to say, he seemed to think better of it. And judging by the uneasy feeling in my chest, that was the right call.

I could have pressed him, probably. But things between us had been working. Why mess with a good thing?

Instead, we returned to our book, taking notes and jostling elbows and not talking about my mom again. And after that, things kept being good.

Even things with Izzy and Priya seemed . . . if not perfect, at least stable. Priya was gearing up for her first cross-country meet of the year—every time she mentioned my sister's name, I did my best not to grind my jaw audibly—and Izzy was leading the student council committee to plan Cry Fest, the annual December on-campus festival that celebrated the anniversary of *What Cries Beneath*'s release with a giant fundraiser carnival. When I'd tried to apologize to her about the ghost brunch thing, she'd brushed me off, told me with a smile not to worry about it.

"Trust me. I know all about parental-based ghost obligations," Izzy had said as we sat under our tree before school one day, basking in some short-lived fall sunshine. She put on a *Cries*-loving front for the rest of the school, but Priya and I knew that she found the whole business insufferable. "You owe me, that's all. You know I need some extra-good letters of recommendation to make sure I get into Northwestern, right? Maybe you can get your mom to write me one."

"Really?" I didn't usually mind doing stuff for Izzy—it was part of the deal, after all—but she'd never asked me to actually get something from my mom before. My mom didn't mind Izzy, but I didn't even ask her for things for *me*. "I thought you got Skinner to write you a letter. And isn't your dad dating that reporter?"

"I'm not depending on my dad's connections to get me into college, thanks." Izzy's voice was sharp, short, and both Priya and I looked at her with surprise. But her next words were softer. "Come on, Hattie. For me?"

It didn't seem like I had much of a choice, so I just said, "Yeah. I'll see what I can do."

Okay, so maybe things weren't a hundred percent perfect there. But it was just Izzy being Izzy. Nothing I hadn't dealt with before.

Besides. I had Kit now, and having someone who actually seemed to like me—the real me, not the perfect Northanger me—felt like it strengthened all of my defenses.

So when Kit told me he'd set up an interview for us with a member of NPSI for our project, it hadn't seemed like a big deal when he'd asked if we could do it at my house. The library's internet wasn't always good enough for video, especially after class when the whole school was trying to use it.

It all made sense. And he'd been to our house before.

But I was still scrubbing down the kitchen counter like he was going to inspect it with a microscope.

"Timothée is going to be so hurt by all of this." Liam was sitting at the counter, head propped up on his hands, watching me clean without a single offer of help. *Brothers.* "Does he know about Kit yet? Because once the tabloids latch on, there's no way he'll miss it."

"First of all, there's nothing going on with me and Kit." Friendship was one thing. But I'd read enough romance novels to know that actually *being* with someone involved exposing yourself (metaphorically) a lot more than I was comfortable doing. "Second of all, even if there was, I'd choose Timothée over literally anyone, so that isn't a concern. And third of all, do you want to help?"

"Just so you can tell me all the ways I'm doing it wrong? Pass." Liam pushed himself back from the counter, hopping off his stool. Fair. I did have a higher standard for kitchen cleanliness than either of my siblings. "I'll be in my room if you need me. I have a group project I need to work on for English."

"Oh, that's . . . cool?" I said, but Liam was already gone, scurried up the stairs before I could ask any more questions. And then the doorbell rang, and Kit was here.

Swooping feeling in my stomach, calm thyself.

"Hey, Tilney," Kit said as I opened the door for him. He brushed the dirt off his boots before leaving them by the entrance. "Ready to have your skepticism completely demolished? Because you won't believe who I got to talk to us today."

"I'm holding out hope for Casper, and I'll officially be disappointed if it's anyone else." I stepped back so that Kit could squeeze past me in the narrow hallway, though his hips still brushed against my side and, yes, I felt it like an electric shock. Pretty sure it wasn't just the static, either. "Come on. I've got a ring light set up in my room for the recording."

"Your room?" Kit glanced down at me quickly, and it was hard to tell, with the length of his hair, but it seemed like the tips of his ears had gone pink. "That's okay? Like, with your mom?"

"Please. My mom isn't home enough to make those kinds of rules for us." I waved my hand dismissively, ignoring the flip in my own stomach. "And it's the only room in the house where we won't be interrupted." Oh, God, the more I spoke the worse it got. "For the recording."

"Right." I heard Kit swallow a laugh. "For the recording."

I led him up the stairs, past Liam's and Freddie's closed doors and toward my room, down at the end of the hall. I'd spent an embarrassingly long time cleaning up in here, too. "Here it is. Is it the studio you always dreamed of?"

"Something like that." Kit had to duck down a little to come through my doorway—old house, tall boy—and when he crossed the threshold, he looked . . . out of place. My bedroom was about as generic as you could get, considering we'd moved in post-tragedy and I'd never bothered to decorate. I had a corkboard over my desk where I'd pinned up a few pictures of me with the girls; but other than that, it was like a picture from a not particularly interesting magazine spread. "Didn't you say you'd never brought anyone else from school here? Why'd you bother hiding your personality?"

"Ouch." Not that I had any right to be offended.

"No, I mean . . ." Kit sighed, dropped his messenger bag at his side, and ran his fingers through his hair. "I know you've got this whole hide-who-you-are thing at school. I feel like you'd want *somewhere* you can let yourself be you."

"Highly overrated, my good sir." I forced myself to smile

before changing the subject. This wasn't therapy hour. "You can plug in your computer at my desk, and I'll make sure the rest of the setup looks good. So who's this big fancy surprise guest?"

I doubted Kit bought my redirection. But I appreciated that he let me distract him anyway. Besides, from the way his eyes lit up, he was just happy for the chance to tell me his big surprise.

"Drumroll, please?" He looked at me long enough that I actually started to drum my hands against my thighs, and grinned. "Waverley Rodriguez! Screenwriter of *What Cries Beneath*!"

"You—what? How?" Waverley Rodriguez was notoriously reclusive. He came out for an interview approximately once every five years, and our school project wasn't important enough to warrant that level of celebrity.

"Izzy hooked us up," Kit answered, and a flutter of nerves coursed through me. Not that I had any reason to worry. But Izzy didn't do random favors without reason. Maybe she'd wanted to apologize for being weird last week? Stranger things had happened. Or maybe she was just trying to remind me about her recommendation letter for Northwestern. I still hadn't figured out a way to ask my mom about it, even though Izzy had already texted me to check on my progress earlier today. "It's going to be awesome; we can talk all about the Northanger legends that inspired *Cries*!"

"Yeah. Totally," I muttered, wrapping my head around this new piece of information. Maybe Izzy thought Kit would tell her dad how helpful she'd been? That was probably it. Either way, I was nervous. It was one thing to ask questions of some random ghost expert. Interrogating Waverley Rodriguez wasn't my idea of a good time. "Can't wait."

"That's the spirit." Kit sat down in my desk chair, adjusted the ring light I'd set up in front of him. "Let's do this thing."

"Let's," I agreed, hoping that my voice didn't betray my deep, *deep* level of concern.

⁓⚡⁓

"Now, tell me about this project one more time." Waverley Rodriguez's voice (excuse me, *Dr.* Waverley Rodriguez, as he'd corrected Kit twice already) was scratchy from years of smoking and, presumably, screaming during false ghost sightings. We'd been on Zoom with the good doctor—who had exactly as much of a mad scientist vibe as I'd expected—for twenty minutes now, and he'd spent the whole time telling Northanger and *Cries* stories, much to Kit's delight. It wasn't anything I hadn't heard before, of course. In fact, I was pretty sure he'd gotten a couple of facts wrong along the way, but I wasn't about to correct him. Besides, I was in camerawoman and producer mode, making sure that both Kit and Dr. Rodriguez stayed in frame, adjusting audio levels, trying not to feel like I was twelve years old again, setting up a camera to interview my dad.

What did it feel like, I'd asked, watching my dad through the screen of my phone, trying to keep my expression appropriately serious, *when you knew they were real?*

There wasn't one moment that I knew, Hattie girl, he'd said, even though I'd told him time and time again not to use that nickname on camera, that this was *professional. Belief is a series of small moments that add up to a big conviction.*

His voice still echoed around my head sometimes. *Hattie girl.* Just another ghost.

Nope, time to shut that memory back down. I returned my attention to Kit and Dr. Rodriguez. This was the second time he'd asked us to describe the project; at this rate, we'd never get through all the questions Kit had for him, and we *definitely* wouldn't have time for me to talk to him. Kit, at least, didn't seem to mind explaining it again.

"It's for our journalism class," he said, glancing at me and smiling. "A ten-minute investigative piece exploring whether the legends of Northanger are real or not. We thought *Cries* would be a great lens to examine at least a portion of the project through, since so much of the lore around the movie debates whether it's real or not."

"Ten minutes?" Dr. Rodriguez mumbled something else under his breath that I couldn't make out. If I squinted, I was pretty sure I could see a full-on conspiracy board on the wall behind him. "That's not nearly enough time."

"Maybe if all goes well, we can expand the piece later." Kit beamed charisma out of every pore. I didn't know how he managed it. "Do you have a favorite haunting, Dr. Rodriguez? Besides the *Cries* poltergeist, of course." You know, the one he'd definitely made up. "Something you'd focus on if you were us?"

"Oh, well, it's so hard to pick a favorite." Dr. Rodriguez was clearly milking this attention for all it was worth. I was starting to suspect that the reason there were so few public interviews with him was not because he was reclusive, but because he was insufferable. "The Walks of Rebecca O'Connor is high on the list, of course."

I couldn't help it. I scoffed, half choking on the sound as Kit looked at me with one eyebrow raised. It wasn't my best moment of professionalism, but, come on, the Walks of Rebecca O'Connor? Talk about the most basic (and sexist) ghost story Northanger Abbey had to offer. Rebecca had been a servant at the school in the 1920s and had apparently been spurned by every boy who lived in Howe at the time. They said she still roamed the halls every night, knocking on the doors of freshman boys in hopes of finding someone, *anyone*, who would love her.

It was the worst type of ghost story—the type that took a real-life person (because Rebecca O'Connor *was* real—Dad had found her in the school records) and made her into some sort of . . . insipid teenage-boy fantasy. I didn't know much about the real Rebecca, but I suspected she had more interesting things to do than try and seduce a bunch of fourteen-year-olds.

So yeah, I scoffed. From the look in Kit's eye, he knew why. But from the way Dr. Rodriguez was clearing his throat, he was not going to brush the slight aside so easily.

"What was that?" He pulled off his glasses, gave them a quick and decisive polish. "Is that your associate?"

"Oh, yeah, sorry." Kit waved me over, and before I could stop him, he'd pulled me down into the frame, in full view of Dr. Rodriguez. "This is Hattie."

"Hi there." I tried to give him the full power of the Tilney Mask, but from his expression, he would not be easily dismissed. "Sorry. Something in my throat."

"Is there a reason you're so disdainful of poor Rebecca, Hattie?" I didn't like the way Dr. Rodriguez said my name. Like I was just some kid. "Girls like you can learn a lot from her." That was patently untrue, but it wasn't like I could say that, so I just looked to Kit for guidance. He turned back to Dr. Rodriguez.

"I wouldn't worry about Hattie, Dr. R. She's our resident skeptic." Kit said it in a way that was clearly meant to smooth things over, but from the thunderous look that appeared on Dr. Rodriguez's face, it had the opposite effect. "I mentioned her, in our email? After I finish my questions we're going to switch, so that she can talk to you, too."

"She doesn't believe?" Ironically, now *he* was the one who sounded disbelieving. "A member of NPSI should never associate with someone that pathetically blind to the truth." What the hell? My jaw dropped, and I felt Kit tense next to me. "How could someone walk the halls of Northanger Abbey daily and *not* see what lies beyond? Who dares not to believe, to look at the universe and claim to know all of its secrets? The paranormal exists because the normal doesn't, and nonbelievers are to be dismissed out of hand and thrown out with the garbage."

Neither Kit nor I spoke, both of us staring at the video screen at this old man who didn't seem to realize he was talking to an actual person.

Or maybe he did, and he just didn't care.

"You're wrong."

I almost didn't hear Kit at first, so wrapped up in my in-
dignation.

"Excuse me?" Dr. Rodriguez clearly did, though, from the
way he stared at Kit, leaning so far forward that his nose was
almost brushing against the camera on his computer. "What
did you say?"

"You can't just . . . that's just as bad as skeptics who think
we're all crazy. No one *has* to believe anything. And if you're
going to insult Hattie like that you can just . . ." Kit paused for
a second, like he was trying to figure out an appropriate level
of insult. But then with a shake of his head, he leaned forward
and clicked End Meeting.

Oh my God.

Once Dr. Rodriguez had disappeared off the screen, Kit
turned to me.

"I'm so sorry. I had no idea—"

"Kit." His face was so close to mine. If I leaned forward,
if I *breathed* forward, our mouths would be touching, and I
could do something with this overwhelming feeling inside of
me, this pressure valve that craved for Kit to release it. I didn't.
"It's okay."

"It's really not." He burst up from his chair and began to
pace around the room, hands on top of his head. "He can't
talk to you that way, you know? That's disrespectful bullshit. Just
because he wrote *one* semi-successful movie about, like, blood
coming out of the walls or whatever. And who picks Rebecca
O'Connor as their favorite haunting? Full-on red flag."

"Is he going to mess with your scholarship?" I did my best

to keep my tone even, because Kit was worked up enough for both of us, and I was feeling a lot of feelings.

"I don't know. I don't care." Kit kept pacing, his long legs making quick work of my small room. "Obviously he's an important person to the society, but it's not like he's on the board."

"Maybe I can ask Izzy to vouch for you." My mind was racing, whirring, because suddenly I was imagining Northanger Abbey without Kit and it was the worst kind of imagining. "Her dad's worked with Dr. Rodriguez for years. He must know what he's like. He can protect your scholarship."

"Maybe." Kit was still moving, still going. "I'm so sorry, Hattie, I had no idea he was going to be like that."

"It's really okay." I shrugged, leaned back against my desk for support. I didn't like relying on Izzy for favors, but she would take care of this for me. She had to. "It's Northanger, isn't it? I'm kind of used to it."

"You shouldn't have to be." His pacing was picking up speed. "You're amazing, Hattie, and however you feel about all of this, that's your business, and I shouldn't have tried to—"

I reached out and grabbed his hand, stopping him in his tracks.

"Hey," I said. His hand was cool against my palm, and his fingers wrapped around mine like an instinct. "Thank you. I don't care what that dude said. But I appreciated what you said."

"Oh." He stared down at our hands, locked together like

puzzle pieces. "Of course. You matter. No one should make you feel like you don't."

What a novel concept.

"We can still use the first part of the interview." I pushed myself off from the desk and turned back toward the computer, and as Kit walked to stand behind me, he didn't drop my hand. I didn't pull away. "It's decent background. And he's a big get. I can just find someone else to interview for the skeptic half."

"We're not giving him the satisfaction." Kit squeezed my fingers, an acknowledgment that we were still connected. "We can cut most of the *Cries* stuff. It'll give us more time to focus on the actual hauntings of Northanger."

"If you're sure."

Kit sat down at the desk again. Let out a long, slow breath.

And then we were just there next to each other, holding hands in my bedroom.

"Have you thought any more about which of those stories to focus on?" Kit leaned back in his chair a little, his tone sounding more . . . normal again as I shrugged and he grinned. "That's fine. I definitely think about them enough for both of us. Anyway, I know we'd mentioned the Howling Milkmaid, and I guess we could do something associated with *Cries*, but . . . I keep coming back to the twins. Have you heard about them?"

It was a good thing I was holding his hand, because I needed the lifeline.

"I think so," I managed.

Kit nodded. "Cool. It's not one of the most popular stories, but that will make it more interesting to investigate, right? We can do a stakeout or something."

"Can we talk about this later?" I could tell my voice sounded weird, tight, and from the way Kit looked at me, he could tell, too. But I couldn't do this right now. I couldn't have my emotions bounced around like a Ping-Pong ball and then hear a boy tell me about the twins like they weren't woven into the fabric of my trauma. "I have a lot of other homework."

"Oh. Sure?" Kit stood up, finally letting go of my hand, and I felt his absence right away. "You feeling okay, Tilney? I don't want what that guy said to get in your head."

"Already forgotten about it." My mask still had its purpose, even around Kit. I put on my best and brightest smile as I herded him out of my room, down the stairs and toward the front door. "I'll see you tomorrow?"

"Okay." Kit hovered in the doorway for a second, like he was considering something. Then he bent down and kissed me on the cheek, his lips just as soft against my skin as I'd imagined. "See you."

And then he was gone. Out into the darkness, down the winding path back toward the school, the academic buildings providing a beacon of light in the distance.

I waited exactly five minutes, so that he wouldn't think I was following him, and then I slipped out the front door as quietly as I could.

Chapter Sixteen

To say that I didn't spend much time wandering the old abbey building would have been putting it lightly. I *never* came here if I could help it. It was the epitome of Gothic spookiness, with its huge arched ceilings and stained glass windows that were currently being pummeled with rain, rain that had started shortly after I left my house. The storm lashed against the intricate designs—disciples and miracles and all manner of things that anyone today would call supernatural. It was a question I never knew the answer to: the difference between paranormal and religion. The school didn't bother to address it, having shaken off its religious affiliation years ago. Nowadays, the only mention of worship here was in the rituals ghost hunters would sometimes attempt.

My dad had treated them as one and the same. It was spirituality, he said, and he believed in it all.

There wasn't a lot of the original nave left—the entire back half had been turned into classrooms—but I had snuck in through a side entrance, into the half that still felt like the set of a Brontë novel. It was preserved in its original 1800s glory, and was technically off-limits to unaccompanied students, but I was already breaking a lot of my own rules tonight just by coming here. May as well add some school rules to the list.

I slid into one of the pews, the wood beneath me cool and smoothed with age. I shivered, pulling my jacket around me, not quite willing to admit what I was doing here. Telling myself I'd just needed to get out of the house. To process what Dr. Rodriguez had said. Ignoring the fact that my current emotional state had a lot more to do with what Kit had said.

The twins.

When Dad first saw photos of the nave, he'd gotten teary-eyed.

This is the sort of place where special things happen, Hattie. He'd run a hand over his computer screen, full of reverence. *And we're going to be a part of it.*

The twins were the one legend of Northanger that my dad loved more than anything. I hadn't thought of them fully in years; I'd gotten pretty good at redirecting that train of thought whenever it threatened to come into the station. But this time, I let myself think it. I let myself remember how he used to tell it.

"Come on, Hattie girl." I was nine, almost ten, too old to cuddle up next to my dad and let him tell me stories, but I still came over when he called me, curled up next to him on the couch as he scrolled through the laptop that was balanced precariously on one leg. "Have I told you about the twins yet?"

I shook my head, and he smiled, tucked me in closer under his arm.

"Some ghost stories, Hattie, are so intricate it seems hard for them to be real." He was watching our fireplace as he spoke, like he was reading from the flames. "Blood dripping from walls, runes, that sort of thing. The sort of story that's so far-fetched you can't help but wonder if someone made it up."

"Is this one of those stories?" I asked.

Dad shook his head and pushed his wire-rimmed glasses back up on his nose. "No. This is one of the other ones. The ones that are so simple, so commonplace, that they feel like they could happen to you."

"Your favorite."

"Yes, Hattie girl. You see, the twins were just like you, or your brother or your sister. They lived in an old church—an abbey, they call it. Just a few hours from here. They used to play among the pews, the two of them. Hide-and-seek, mostly, though they would play pranks on the nuns, too."

"I like that." I let my head rest on my dad's chest, and he laughed.

"I thought you might. This was just around the time of the Civil War—the late 1860s. The twins were orphans, like so many children back then, but they weren't lonely, because they had each other. Even when they were playing games, even when they were hiding, they knew they'd always find the other, so there was nothing to be afraid of."

Dad always waited for me to ask the next part. That way, if I got scared, if I didn't want to hear what was coming, I didn't have to.

I always asked, though.

"What happened to them?"

"It was a terrible snowstorm." His eyes were still on the fire. "They were outside playing, and the storm came upon them too fast. They were separated by the snow, and the nuns from the abbey found them days later. Adelaide, the girl, had drowned in the river—probably fell through the ice. And Lawrence, her brother, was in the woods. The cold got him."

"They weren't together?" My voice was small, and Dad squeezed his arm around my shoulders.

"That's the thing, Hattie. A few months later, one of the nuns was cleaning up after services in the abbey when she heard a voice. A child's voice, one she recognized."

"One of the twins." I had goose bumps.

"Exactly. She could hear Adelaide calling for Lawrence, just like they used to when they played. She assumed her mind was playing tricks on her—she was tired, it was late, you know the excuses people make. But the next day, another sister heard Lawrence, calling back for Adelaide. And ever since, there have been stories about the twins in the abbey. Still looking for each other after all these years."

Dad gave me another squeeze, an indication that the story was finished. I leaned back on the couch, unsatisfied.

"I don't like that one."

"You don't?" Dad looked down at me, surprised.

"It's too sad." I shook my head. "They can't find each other."

"Oh, Hattie, no!" Dad closed his laptop and turned to me. "No, my darling, that's not it at all."

"It's not?"

"The point isn't that they're lost." He was staring at me intensely, willing me to understand. "The point is that they never stopped looking."

I tilted my head to the side, considered it. Dad kept talking.

"You see, when you love someone, when they're your whole heart . . . you'll do anything to find them. You'll keep calling for them, even when they're gone. Even when you're gone. That's what we like so much about ghosts, isn't it? That even when someone's gone, their hope and their love can be powerful enough to keep them here."

I nodded. I still wasn't sure I quite understood, but I grasped at the *edges of it. Dad pulled me in close for another hug, his chin resting on my head.*

"I love you, Hattie girl. I'll always find you."

"So why haven't you?" I asked the empty nave, the pews echoing silence back to me. There were no whispers in the room, no twins searching for each other. It was just a story. Just like everything else. "If love is powerful enough to keep someone here, how come you've never come to find me?"

Dad didn't answer. He never had. Not the first night, when I tried to call for him in the hospital room after he died. Not every night after that for a year. Not at Northanger, not at home, not anywhere.

Because ghosts weren't real. They couldn't be.

I stayed in the nave for a while after that, anyway. Not really listening. Not really looking. It was easier that way. Easier to not look than it was to look and come up short, again and again.

Chapter Seventeen

Ultimately, I decided on the healthiest coping strategy of all—ignorance. After all, I reasoned, it wasn't like the entirety of our project was focused on the twins. They were just one small aspect of the piece, a brief note at the end to show a specific example of a Northanger legend. Maybe I wouldn't even interact with it. We still had the Ghost Brigade footage to shoot, and that was going to eat up some airtime. If I really tried, I could just push down this very broken part of myself until it disappeared entirely.

Healthy? Never claimed it was. Some choices were just about getting by.

I'd at least managed to ask Izzy about Kit's scholarship, painted her the absolutely broadest picture I could of how the interview with Dr. Rodriguez had gone down.

"Can you talk to your dad? I don't want Kit to lose his scholarship," I'd asked, feeling uneasy at the request. But it was worth feeling uneasy to help him. "It'll be good for you anyway, right? Your dad would want you to help Kit."

"Yeah, he loves all that NPSI shit." Izzy had been looking past me, lost in her own thoughts. "I can talk to him, I guess. He's been calling constantly anyway, asking about college applications. It's so annoying."

"He still wants you to go to California?"

"UCLA." Izzy's tone had turned bitter. "'Keep the family legacy alive, Isabella!' Like he'd even pay attention to me if I did come out there." She'd glanced back at me again finally, her eyebrows furrowed. "Did you get a chance to talk to your mom yet? About my Northwestern letter?"

"I—no, I haven't." Shit. I'd barely seen my mom recently, and when I had, there definitely hadn't been an opportunity to bring up Izzy. "Maybe you should just email her? It might sound better coming from you anyway."

Izzy watched me for a second, her expression unreadable. Then she'd shrugged.

"Right. Well, whatever, I'll take care of Kit." She'd squeezed my shoulder for reassurance, even if her grip felt unnecessarily strong. "Don't stress."

I was going to have to take her word for it. Besides, I didn't need anything new to worry about. Some of the other seniors were starting to hear from the colleges they'd applied to, and it was stirring up anxiety in all of us.

Izzy was mostly unaffected, but Priya was starting to freak out. Apparently, during Priya's senior meeting with my mom, she'd gotten the impression that better cross-country times in her senior year would really boost her chances of college acceptance. Since then, she'd spent every day after class out here on the track, and today she'd recruited Izzy and me to join her.

"Is this really the best training for cross-country?" I asked Priya as we stretched against the side of the bleachers. Izzy had commandeered a golf cart from somewhere and was currently driving laps around the track, whooping as she went. No way that was going to end badly. "I can always go into the woods and get a bunch of sticks and dirt to lay in front of you."

"Funny." Priya stood up straight and began to stretch out her shoulders, pulling her arms across her body. "But Freddie said she wanted me doing track intervals." At the sound of my sister's name, my stomach dropped. "And, trust me, you'd rather be out here. It's been raining so much this month that the woods are a disaster."

"Incoming!" Izzy shouted, and Priya and I both threw ourselves against the stands to avoid getting hit by her cart. Her face was all wild recklessness; and for a second I felt a fondness for her, for Priya, for the life I'd built here with them. Sure, things had been weird this semester, with me hanging out with Kit, but it wasn't like they were the only friends I could have, right? Me spending time with Kit didn't negate our friendship. Didn't undo what we had done for each other.

"How did you even get that thing?" I asked, as Izzy finally came to a stop ten feet ahead of us. I was pretty sure the golf cart had started smoking.

"Your sister gave me the keys." Izzy's hair was pulled up in the highest ponytail I'd ever seen, and she tossed it over her shoulder as she stepped out of the cart. Oh, good. What could go wrong there? "She's super cool, Hattie. How come we've never hung out with her before?" *Because she sucks*, I thought, but I wasn't about to say that out loud.

"She's not around much." It wasn't even a lie. "Freddie just *gave* you the keys to the cart?" God, I hated this. I'd kept Freddie away from my friends for a reason. As far as they knew, I had the perfect, well-behaved, and relatively boring family. Freddie didn't fit into that equation.

"Yeah. She trusts me." Izzy shrugged, zipping up her sweat-shirt against the cool October fog. "It's a fun little novelty, isn't it? An actual adult with power who thinks I can handle some-thing."

"What do you mean?"

"Oh, nothing." Another hair toss, as Izzy gave Priya a quick glance. Priya looked down at the ground, then moved to take her place at our starting positions. Whatever they'd just signaled to each other, I hadn't gotten it, and I felt a rush of loneliness wash over me. "Just a nice change of pace, to be around an authority figure who thinks I have merit beyond being friends with you."

Ouch.

"Izzy . . ." I began, but she pulled a whistle from around her neck, held it up to her mouth, and gave a sharp, piercing tweet.

"To your starting line, athletes!" she shouted, and I winced from the volume and the change in subject before lining up next to Priya to pace her for her intervals. When Izzy was done talking about something, she was *done* talking about something. And yet, as she blew the whistle once again and Priya and I took off, racing down the length of the track, I had the sinking feeling that Izzy actually had quite a lot more to say.

An hour later, Izzy shouted from the golf cart that we were finished, and Priya and I collapsed onto the grass next to the track, breathing hard. If I'd ever had thoughts about joining organized sports, this workout had thrown those ideas out the window, along with my dignity and my pride. As I lay in the soft grass, trying to get my heart rate back to normal, Izzy walked over from the cart and tossed down a couple of water bottles.

"That's one way to forget about school for an hour," Priya managed to say in between gulps from her bottle as she wiped sweat from her hairline. She wasn't wrong. "Iz, are you sure you didn't modify that workout to make it way worse? That was brutal."

"Don't shoot the messenger; I literally just read out the instructions." Izzy waved around her phone. "You killed it though, Pree. Totally going to crush it in the meet next week."

"Thanks." Priya sighed, sitting up on the grass and wincing. "I need the distraction. You know that some of the schools that do rolling admission are announcing acceptances already? I even heard of a couple of kids who got their Udolpho acceptances, Hats."

"Excitement!" Izzy shouted with way more enthusiasm than the situation called for, considering how my stomach dropped to my shoes at the mention of Udolpho. "You haven't heard yet, have you? If you got in and you didn't tell us, I'll kill you."

"I—I haven't heard anything." Honestly, Udolpho had been about a thousand miles away from my thoughts recently. *Because you'll get in, so you don't have to worry about it,* I reminded myself. "Sorry."

"You will," Priya said with certainty that I did my best to emulate. "God, senior year is flying by! Izzy's already like, deep in Cry Fest planning."

"Oh, right." I sat up, slowly, trying to minimize the head rush I was sure to experience. The last couple of years, Izzy had dragged me into working on Cry Fest with her—you know, my worst nightmare—but this year, she'd been remarkably chill about the whole thing. I'd only gotten *one* late-night text about flyer colors, which was pretty good for Izzy. For all that she pretended not to care about school or anything related to it, Cry Fest was important to her, because it was important to her dad. She'd never say as much, but I knew she wanted to make him proud.

There were some parts of Izzy that I innately understood.

"How's it going, Iz?" Maybe I should have volunteered to help again, but the temporary absence of *What Cries Beneath* in my life was not something I was complaining about. After the Dr. Rodriguez thing, even Kit had stopped bringing it up. "Everything coming together?"

"Obviously." Izzy took a long pull of water herself, even though all she'd done for the last hour was follow Priya and me around in the golf cart while yelling instructions our way.

"*And* I figured out the perfect way to keep Ghost Boy in NPSI's good graces. Guess who's going to be the special guest of honor at this year's festival?"

Before I could answer, she pulled out her phone, unlocked it, and held it out in front of me. There, zoomed in so I could *definitely* see his face, was a flyer for Cry Fest with a picture of Kit in the upper right corner, with the heading *Guest of Honor: Kit Morland, NPSI Scholarship Recipient!* written in the spookiest font available on Canva.

I glanced sharply up at Izzy, confusion all over my face.

"I talked to my dad, and he thinks it's a great idea." Izzy shrugged as she pulled the phone back. "Ghost Boy needs the NPSI board to love him, right? So he'll stand up at the festival and be crowned Mr. Teen Ghost, or whatever, and Dad can give a speech about all the good NPSI is doing for Northanger. It's a slam dunk."

"And Kit . . . is into this?" Something about this whole situation struck me as off. Yes, Izzy had stopped outright mocking Kit when I was around, but this level of altruism was beyond what she usually went for. *But it's for her dad*, I reminded myself. "That's a lot of attention."

"You've *met* Kit, right?" Izzy giggled, dropping her phone back into her pocket. "He's here on a *ghost scholarship*, Hattie. I think he can handle a little attention. Besides, you wanted me to take care of things. That's what I did." Her voice shifted quickly to sharp, which was almost comforting, because that at least was the Izzy I knew how to deal with. "What else did you want me to do?"

"No, you're right." I shook my head. I was just overreacting, stressed out, anxious about Udolpho and everything else that senior year was throwing at me. I'd asked Izzy for help, and she'd helped. That was all. "Thanks, Iz."

"Anytime." She reached out two hands to pull both Priya and me to our feet, then grimaced and wiped her hands on her leggings. "Gross. You guys are all sweaty."

"You love it," Priya joked, and then with energy I didn't know she had left, began to chase Izzy down, arms outstretched for a hug. Izzy shrieked and ran away, taking off down the track at a speed impressive enough that *she* should have been the one pacing Priya, not me.

And as I watched them chase each other around, my two best friends, I tried to pretend that everything felt normal. That I didn't have a weird, uneasy feeling sitting right in the center of my chest.

You'll feel better once you hear from Udolpho, I reminded myself. *Once everything is settled.*

In the meantime, I grabbed our water bottles and ran after Izzy and Priya, trying to act like nothing had changed between us.

Chapter Eighteen

By the time Halloween hit a few weeks later, my rising anxiety was becoming harder to ignore. I was going to hear from Udolpho any day now, and even though I *knew* I'd get in, knowing it and feeling confident in it were two different things. Izzy and Priya weren't helping—Priya, who had started running twice a day, both before and after school, looked on the verge of tears at least 75 percent of the time, and Izzy was dividing her attention fully between Cry Fest planning and her Northwestern portfolio, which she refused to let me or Priya look at even when we (well, Priya) asked. Said it was a "surprise," as if reading a bunch of articles she wrote for the school website about uniform sourcing was something thrilling for us to look forward to.

Who was it, again, that said senior year was fun?

But as I headed toward the front gates of the school, I was determined to put all of that out of my mind. I usually avoided Northanger's Halloween celebrations like the plague, preferring the comfort of my comfortless room to shrieking

costumed students and fake cobwebs that covered every ancient sconce, but when Kit learned about the Ghost Brigade's
annual haunted cemetery tour on Halloween night he insisted
that we *had* to go, for the sake of the project. Since I needed
to take my mind off Udolpho even more than I needed to
avoid Halloween . . . here I was, dressed all in black in a small
concession to the evening ahead of us. It may not have been a
costume, but it was as close as I'd get.

The more surprising part was that Liam had decided to
join me.

He was wearing what I was pretty sure was a Jedi robe,
talking a mile a minute about the English project he was working on, where they were comparing old King Arthur legends
to modern interpretations. It was possible I zoned out a little,
but it was great to hear Liam engaging with school. Engaging
with anything, really.

We reached the gates, where most of the Ghost Brigade
gang had already gathered. Kit stood off to the side, one of
the big cameras we'd checked out from Mrs. Skinner's room
balanced carefully on his shoulder as he filmed the group. As
soon as he saw us, though, he lowered it, waving at me with a
big, cheesy grin.

I grinned right back and walked over to him, pulling my
own camera out of my bag. Liam stayed back talking to one of
the brigaders—another boy, also dressed as a Jedi.

"Hey." I wrinkled my nose as I checked out Kit's outfit: a
bright Hawaiian shirt with baggy shorts and a wide-brimmed
hat. "Is there a reason today is the *one* day you're not automatically dressed for Halloween?"

"Um, excuse you." He gestured down at his ensemble with his free hand. "Halloween is about costumes. I'm Florida Man! Ready to terrorize Northanger Abbey with my love of approaching alligators on the side of the road. And you are . . ."

"A journalist, trying to blend in." Any hint of admonishment in my voice was drowned out by my smile. I couldn't help it. Kit just made me want to be happy. "Liam came with me, but we lost him to one of the ghost hunters."

"Oh, yeah. Erik, right?" Kit nodded in Liam's direction, where he and the other boy were watching something on Liam's phone, laughing as their shoulders bumped together. "He's in some of Liam's classes."

Before I could ask any more questions, like about when Liam had managed to make a friend, Jolie clapped their hands, capturing our attention. They were dressed like a video game character I vaguely recognized from the internet, complete with full cosplay armor, and I was starting to feel underdressed in my dark jeans and black jacket.

"Brigaders!" they announced, waving armored hands above their head. "We're walking down to town, where we'll hit the nine o'clock cemetery tour. Mr. Nguyen is our chaperone, so let's make sure he doesn't get lost again, please." The young, sleepy-looking teacher at the back of the group sheepishly raised a hand, and the group tittered. "Hot chocolate back at Schumacher after we're done. Roll out!"

"That was a lot more declaratory than spooky," I whispered to Kit as we did, indeed, roll out, crossing through the gates of the school and stretching out onto the narrow sidewalk that led toward the center of town. It was about a mile walk down to the cemetery, so we had some time before we needed to start filming. "Not a single 'hear ye' or 'avast.'"

"That's more pirates than ghosts," Kit said, pushing his shoulder against mine, a movement I felt in my chest. "Speaking of hear ye. . . . Here." He passed me the camera so he could rummage through his cross-body bag, emerging with a small cat-ears headband. As he handed it over to me, his expression was triumphant. "Thought you might want to get in the spirit."

"Oh . . . thanks." An hour ago, I would have pushed these away, but now I had only a second of hesitation before I put them on, tucking my hair behind the ends. "How'd you know?"

"That you wouldn't have a costume, or that you'd want one?"

"Both, I guess."

At that, he looked from side the side, then leaned down to me, his whisper suddenly conspiratorial.

"I'm starting to figure out your mysteries, Hattie Tilney."

When we finally made it down to the cemetery, a thick fog had rolled in, so atmospherically perfect that I barely believed it was real. Kit, for his part, was giddy. He was grabbing footage everywhere he could, getting shots of gravestones lurking in gloom and Jolie and Molly, the vice president, shining flashlights onto reverent inscriptions. *Beloved mother, departed brother, wife and partner* . . . I panned my camera over all of them, only skipping anything that said *father*. We'd decided that the Ghost

Brigade would be the second-act focus of our investigative piece, the connective tissue between Northanger's history and its current paranormal activity, with both of us offering our own takes on how accurate said history and activity actually were. In the background of my shots, a group of children, who had come to the cemetery tour with their unenthusiastic parents, darted between the markers, shrieking.

As I followed them with my camera, my attention was caught by the girl who would be leading the tour, who didn't look as enthusiastically spooky as I'd expected a ghostly tour guide to look. Like me, she wasn't dressed in a costume, and she lacked that glazed-over "indoor kid" quality that most of the ghost hunters I'd encountered over the years so often had. She probably didn't really care about this stuff, I told myself as I grabbed a smaller, handheld camera from Kit's bag and made my way to her. It was probably just a job. *Good*, I thought. She might even be helpful for my anti-ghost side of the doc.

"Hey," I said as I reached the girl, who turned her attention toward me. She was probably a few years older than me—somewhere in college, I'd guess—Black, with a short Afro that puffed out around her head and a purple T-shirt from the Northanger Abbey Historical Society. "I'm Hattie Tilney. Do you mind if my friend and I film on the tour tonight? We're doing a project about local paranormal legends for our journalism class."

"Sure." The girl's smile was bright. "Cool class. I'd have loved studying that sort of thing when I was in high school."

"You're into journalism?" I asked, but she shook her head.

"No—I mean, it's interesting, it's just not my thing. But

studying ghost stories?" She let out a whistle that seemed to bounce around the stones. "That's awesome." My heart sank. Another ghost fan, after all.

"Got it." I moved to step away, but the girl reached out and stopped me.

"What? You have something against ghost stories?" She was probably teasing, but my expression must have given me away. "Why?"

"Oh, you know." She seemed nice, but I wasn't about to unpack my childhood trauma in front of her, not while my little brother was just a few feet away discussing kyber crystals in the most serious tone I'd ever heard. "Like, logic and science and stuff?"

"Come on." She gave me a small smile, and I got the feeling she'd had this discussion before. "Ghost stories can be just that—stories. They don't have to negate scientific observation. But they *are* a way of keeping our history alive. Of remembering people who would be forgotten otherwise. The best ghost stories aren't about the rich and the famous, after all. They're about ordinary people who lived ordinary lives whose stories get to become extraordinary in death. What does science have to do with that?"

Her eyes were bright, and I wanted to argue, but . . . she had a point.

"So you're into history as opposed to, like, reports of blood coming out of walls?" I asked, deflecting a little, and she laughed.

"I'm not just a *What Cries Beneath* super fan, if that's what you're asking. I'm majoring in history and anthropology, which is a roundabout way of saying that I want to study the history of the individual and how they relate to society more than I want to learn about Henry the Eighth. I'm Mara, by the way."

"Hattie." I stuck out my hand, and she shook it, still smiling. "And ghost stories help you do that?"

"*Stories* help me do that," she corrected. Behind me, I could sense the brigaders getting restless, but Mara didn't seem to be in any rush. "And ghost stories are just one way people tell them." Finally, she glanced down at her phone, making a tsk sound with her tongue. "Shoot. We should probably get started."

"I hope you weren't waiting for me," a new voice interrupted, and the hairs on the back of my neck stood up as I turned around slowly. It couldn't be. . . . But it was.

My mother was at the entrance to the cemetery, and she was headed straight toward us.

"Dr. Tilney!" Mr. Nguyen, who had definitely been texting, shoved his phone down into his pocket and tried to look as awake as possible. "You made it."

"Of course I did. It's tradition." If this was tradition, it was the first time I'd heard about it, even as the brigaders around me nodded their heads in agreement. It made sense that my mom wouldn't advertise it to me, though. If there was one person who hated the paranormal more than I did, it was her. This must have been something the last headmaster had started, something my mom simply couldn't get out of. "Mara? Are we ready?" Of course she already knew the tour guide. Mara gave me a small wave goodbye before heading to the front of the pack.

A memory flashed into my mind, unbidden.

"It's your turn to tell me a story, Hattie girl." My dad and I were walking through the tiny Main Street that sat in the middle of our town, a block we'd strode a thousand times before. "You know them all."

"I don't tell them like you do, though." I was eleven then, old enough to realize that not everyone loved the things Dad and I loved, but young enough that I still loved them, too. "You're way better than me."

"And how do you think I got that way? Practice." He waved at the woman standing behind the counter of the bookstore as we passed it, and she smiled back. Everyone in town loved my dad. That was what he was best at—making everyone he was with feel like the most special person in the world. "You could tell them, too, Hattie. That's how we keep stories alive, in the telling and the retelling. So tell me a story."

I'd done a terrible job that first time, but Dad had been so encouraging. And after that, every time he told me a story, I'd have to tell him one back, an even exchange that could have lasted forever.

I'd really thought, back then, that it would. That I'd keep making my little videos and that people would like them, and I'd figure out a way for my dad and me to keep telling stories. But once he'd died, I'd stopped entirely, because there wasn't anyone to listen to them. Even at Northanger people didn't talk about ghosts that way—didn't treat them like people who had lived full and interesting lives, instead of just jump scares and phantom sounds. For a second, I wondered if I should grab Mara after the tour was over. Interview her from that perspective, talk about how ghosts weren't real but the stories could still be important, and reconcile my side of the project with Kit's.

But my mom was here, since apparently she did this *every* year, as I heard Jolie whisper to some of the freshmen. Dr. Tilney walked next to Mara as she led us through the cemetery, her smile small and her eyes empty. Going through the motions. And I wasn't going to show an interest in this stuff in front of her. I wasn't going to do her the injury of reminding her of Dad.

Mara launched into her first story, of a cat who lived in the cemetery at the turn of the century and could still be heard scratching outside the groundskeeper's door, looking for treats. Kit stood beside me, fascinated. Up ahead, Liam was locked in a whispered conversation with his friend, and Mom was leading us all, though I could tell she'd rather be anywhere but here.

"Hey," Kit whispered in my ear, and I shivered, only partially from the cold. "Are you okay? I didn't know your mom would be here. If you need to go . . ."

"I can handle her, Kit." And I could. I could handle all of this, as long as I kept my memories pushed way down. Even if they kept wanting to force their way to the surface, like a weed from a grave. "I'm going to fall back, okay? Get some shots of the whole crowd."

"Sure." He tucked a stray piece of hair behind his ear, and even though he seemed like he wanted to follow me, he didn't. I appreciated the space.

You don't need this, I reminded myself as I began to trail behind the group, filming. *Soon you'll be at Udolpho; and when you're not hit with constant reminders about ghosts, it'll be easier to forget about them. Just hold out a little longer until you can forget.*

I was holding on for dear life these days. But soon, so soon, I'd be able to let go.

Chapter Nineteen

The day after Halloween was a Wednesday, a fact that I absolutely hated as I snoozed my third alarm of the morning. This was Northanger Abbey, for crying out loud. Surely we could declare the day after Halloween a school holiday.

Okay, we did have a half day, because it always took the school a few extra hours to clear up the detritus, and years ago the administration had decided it was worth just letting us have the few hours off. Between the gym turning into a haunted house and the sheer amount of broken pumpkin, this was the easiest solution for everyone.

Still. I could have used a few hours more.

The tour hadn't gone particularly late, but Liam and I had joined Kit and the brigaders at Schumacher for hot chocolate afterward (Dr. Tilney hadn't joined us for that part, thank God); and even though we'd gotten back home before my eleven o'clock curfew, I'd ended up texting with Kit for two hours after that. It had felt worth it at the time, worth giving up a few hours of sleep for the swoopy feeling in my stomach; but now that the bright light of morning was glaring through my window, I had about a thousand regrets and no time to deal with them. With a groan, I pulled myself from the bed, staggered toward the bathroom to get ready for the day.

"Hattie?"

I looked up, startled, to see Liam in the doorway of his room, running shoes in his hand and a concerned expression knitting his brows together.

"Hey." I rubbed my hands over my eyes, tried to conjure some semblance of being awake. "What's up?" I needed to get it together. Get my remaining homework done, make sure Liam did, too. *Take care of them, Hattie.* That was what I needed to do.

"Want to go for a run?" He nodded back toward his window. "It's nice out."

"I—uh—sure," I sputtered, because I didn't know the last time *Liam* had asked me to go outside. Liam, leave the house willingly? A novel concept. Sure, I'd tossed out the idea of us running together a while back, but I didn't expect him to take me up on it. My homework could wait. Pretty much anything could wait, where Liam was concerned. "Let me change, okay? Ten minutes." Liam nodded, and I headed back toward my room to grab my running stuff, allowing myself to be glad for the time spent with my brother.

***

I didn't know what to expect as we ran past the boundaries of the school and into town. Liam was silent for the first mile or so, and I fell back into my own head, thinking about Udolpho, about how relieved I'd feel when the acceptance came in, when Liam stopped suddenly at the edge of the sidewalk. We were just outside downtown, about to cross into a small park where we sometimes ran laps around the perimeter.

"Hey." He gasped out the word as his breath, long and ragged, returned to him; and I took deep breaths, too, feeling my heart rate slow. I hadn't realized how fast we'd been going, our legs pounding underneath us like we both wanted to get away from the school as quickly as we could. "I need to talk to you about something."

"Of course." God, I hoped he wasn't failing. I really didn't have it in me to take care of Liam any more than I already was.

"I'm dating someone." The words tumbled out of Liam fast, and my train of thought jarred to a sudden stop as I whipped my head around to look at him. *Liam? Dating?* That was, like . . . how? Who did he even know who he could date?

"You are?" I'd blame my shortness of breath on the run, and not on this revelation about my brother's life, except who was I kidding, it was totally about Liam. "That's— Who?"

"That's kind of the thing I wanted to talk to you about." Liam shifted from foot to foot, looking about as uncomfortable as a person could look. "It's, um . . . it's Erik. From the Ghost Brigade?"

"You—oh. Yeah?" About a thousand pieces fell into place at once. The way Erik had been hovering around Liam last night. The whispering. Liam's general improved mood.

"Is that okay?" Liam's eyes were wide and nervous, and this time I didn't hesitate, because I knew what he was asking.

"Oh my God, Liam, of course." Sweat or no sweat, I pulled my brother into a hug, ignoring his protests. "Come here. Of course that's okay."

"You're squishing me."

"With love." I released him, if only because my face had been buried right around armpit level and that wasn't the most pleasant experience. "That's great, Liam. Seriously. I'm really happy for you. And I love you so much."

"Yeah, yeah." Liam brushed my comment off, but I saw a small smile creep over his face. "Whatever." He started jogging again, and I followed him, my mind whirring with this new revelation. In the entire time he'd been at Northanger, Liam had barely talked to *anyone*, let alone gotten close to someone in a romantic way. I didn't know what had changed, but I liked it. Liked anything that brought Liam out of his shell.

"So how did this happen? What's your big romantic story?" I asked as we came to a stoplight, taking a second to stretch my calves out in front of me. I was tight all over—whether that was from falling off my regular running routine or my extremely high levels of stress, I couldn't say. "Did you meet in an online game and then realize you'd been attending the same high school all along? Was there some sort of speed dating at the comic book store that you stumbled into by accident? Or did you randomly get assigned the same locker this year, forcing you to share your space and eventually, your hearts?"

"You've thought about this a lot." Liam rolled his eyes, but I assumed it was with affection. As the light changed and we took off again, he fell into step beside me, our strides matching as our sneakers pounded against the sidewalk. "We have some classes together. That's all. I kind of knew him from last year, but this year, I don't know—we just started talking?" As Liam reached up to wipe the sweat off his forehead, I didn't know if his flush was from exertion or embarrassment. "Things kind of . . . evolved from there."

"Look at you, though! Talking to people." I grinned as we turned a corner, taking an extra-long stride to avoid the puddles that lined this stretch of sidewalk, fresh from the morning's rain. "I'm proud of you."

"Thanks." Liam shrugged, and from the way red was spreading up his neck and into his ears, I suspected that *this* flush was, indeed, embarrassment. "Kit may have . . . told me to?"

"*What?*" I skidded to a halt, nearly taking Liam down with me, but this wasn't the sort of conversation I could have while actively moving. Liam let out a curse as he grabbed my arm for support, righting himself at the last second before he could trip over his own feet and land in a nearby bush. Liam may have shot up into the aggressively tall category over the summer, but coordinated he was not. "*Kit* told you to open up to people? And you listened to him?"

"I mean, not in so many words. Also, you need to signal when you're going to stop like that—I almost died." He shot me a dirty look as he bent down to retie his shoe, and this time, I was the one who rolled my eyes.

"I'll get my brake lights checked before the next time we go out. Don't avoid the question."

"I don't know, Hattie." Liam stood up, brushing his hands

off on his shorts. "We'd just been texting, and I mentioned that I needed to figure out my partner for a group project in my English class, and Kit told me to just ask the person who I thought was the most interesting. And that I shouldn't be scared they'd say no." The sides of his mouth quirked into a smile. "It didn't sound as terrifying when he put it like that. So I asked Erik and . . . you know."

"Now you have a behind-the-bleachers buddy?"

"Oh my God." Liam was so red that he was practically purple. "Come on." He took off at what could only be described as a sprint, and I launched myself after him, shouting at him to slow down as warmth filled my chest.

I'd wanted Liam to step outside his comfort zone for years but had filed it away as an impossible task. And within a couple of weeks of meeting him, Kit Morland had him talking to boys and falling in love.

Are you surprised? I thought as Liam finally slowed down, though it was more in deference to the uphill climb back toward campus than it was to answer my shouts. *Look what he's done to you.*

Whatever it was. Whatever he was doing to me, to Liam, to our family. I liked it—and him—so much.

And that scared the hell out of me.

"Have you told him, by the way?" I asked, as we finally hit the edge of campus and began a cooldown walk back toward our cottage, both of us breathing hard. "Kit, I mean. About you and Erik."

"You're the first person I've told about . . . any of this." Liam wiped his face with the bottom of his shirt, though I suspected

that was partially to hide his face. "I mean, except Erik, obviously. I do want to tell Kit. And Mom and Freddie, too." I
didn't envy him that conversation. Not that Mom or Freddie
would have a problem with Liam dating a boy, but the idea
of having a conversation with either of them about romance
made me want to curl up and die. "But I wanted to tell you
first. You're . . . you're my best friend."

He may have purposely mumbled the end of that into his
T-shirt, but there was no way he could mumble that sentence
quietly enough for me to miss it. I put my hand over my heart,
genuinely touched.

"Aww, Liam." He let out a deep sigh before taking off at
high speed away from me, apparently deciding that cooling
down wasn't worth any more emotional conversations. "Run
as fast as you want!" I shouted behind him, bursting out to
catch him. "You can't outrun my love!"

"Watch me!" he called back over his shoulder; and for a
second, just a brief second, I felt free.

Chapter Twenty

I t had been a few days since Liam told me about Erik, and in those few days, I'd seen him happier than I ever had before. He'd invited me to (officially) meet Erik during lunch; the three of us had sat on the grassy quad, enjoying a brief spot of unseasonably warm weather, while I did my best not to actively squeal over my brother's romance and he'd smiled proudly while Erik spent most of the period describing his theories for the next *Star Wars* limited series. (He had a lot of them.) The day after that, he'd invited Kit to join us, too, and even though the warmth of the sun disappeared as quickly as it had come, forcing us to eat in a quiet(er) corner of the dining hall while the weather doomed and gloomed, the warmth I felt inside from seeing Liam so happy more than made up for it.

Every now and then, during that lunch, Kit would glance over at me with a smile, proud. And when I smiled back, it was with butterflies in my stomach unmatched by anything I'd ever felt. Turns out that the one thing more attractive than Kit

Morland on an average day was Kit Morland helping my little brother, the other half of my heart, find fulfillment and self-actualization. It was the emotional equivalent of a shirtless slow-motion run down the beach.

Not that I could picture Kit at a beach. Or that I'd pictured him shirtless. Obviously.

Every interaction with Kit felt charged with electricity, with the knowledge that *something* was happening. And even though I hadn't been brave enough to give in to the crackling static yet . . . every grin, every wink, every brush of his arm against mine while we sat next to each other in the dining hall, picking fries off each other's plates, pushed me further toward that next step.

But whatever we were barreling toward would have to wait. Because as Monday approached—the day that Skinner wanted to get progress reports on our projects and, more importantly, the day of my senior meeting with my mom—I did my best to turn my attention back toward school. I did *okay* at it. Yes, I picked up my phone every five minutes to check if Kit had texted me (he usually had), and, yes, I'd taken more than one break to scroll through his barely used social media, looking at his life in Florida and wondering if everyone there missed him as much as I would, if he were gone.

I got *some* schoolwork done, anyway.

And now Monday had arrived. The day of reckoning.

Skinner was hearing our presentations individually, so all eighteen of us were hanging out in the classroom while she took pairs into her office one at a time. As you might imagine, chaos was nigh. I was sitting on top of one of the desks near the back of the class, Priya and Izzy's backpacks gathered on the floor beneath me. Priya was currently presenting, and Izzy had commandeered the storage closet, going over note cards with her partner.

Kit was with me, of course, but he mostly kept to himself, scrolling on his laptop through the slides he'd prepared. We had a rough outline and a few clips of footage from the Ghost Brigade and *Cries* mixed in with some B-roll from around the school. The incident with Dr. Rodriguez had taken a chunk out of our plan, but I was hoping Kit's enthusiasm for the subject matter would carry us through the rest of the way. *We'll have to nail the twins segment,* I thought, ignoring the pit in my stomach. I'd let Kit handle all the preliminary research, begging off for other homework or prior obligations whenever he suggested we dig into them. But I wasn't going to be able to avoid them forever.

In an effort to distract myself, I pulled out my phone, toggled over to my email. Nothing interesting ever came my way but, hey, maybe today would be the day I'd get a coupon I could really use.

What I didn't expect was to see an email right at the very top with the subject line: "Udolpho College: Early Action Decision."

Oh my God. Here it was, then. The moment of truth. I hovered over the message with shaking fingers, wondering if I should wait for Izzy and Priya, to read it together so they could celebrate with me. I thought about getting Kit's attention, but he was lost in his computer.

Alone, then. I'd tell them all afterward, get to hear them

shout with excitement and see them jump for joy and all the things I'd dreamed about when I was picturing this moment.

I clicked the email.

Dear Miss Tilney,
We regret to inform you . . .

What?

No. No, no, no.

Shock spread through my veins like ice, freezing me from the inside out. This couldn't be happening. It wasn't possible. I'd been so sure I'd get in, so sure that, even if this wasn't a path that I was thrilled about, it was the one I'd be on.

But I hadn't gotten in.

And I didn't have a backup plan. Oh, God. I didn't have anything besides Udolpho. And now I didn't even have that.

I crashed off the desk and onto the floor, stumbling over Priya and Izzy's bags as I grabbed my own. Kit looked up with a start.

"You okay?" he asked, but I needed to get out of here, to run and run until I was as far away from this nightmare scenario as possible. I had, somehow, ruined my future, and I didn't know how to fix it. I pushed past desks and legs and backpacks until I was out of the classroom, then out of the hall, then out of the building.

And I ran.

I burst through the doors of the (thankfully empty) nave, midmorning light streaming through the stained glass windows. I wasn't sure why, exactly, my feet had carried me here, but I needed to go *somewhere*; and for all that this wasn't my favorite place on campus, it had the highest likelihood of being empty.

In that regard, at least, I'd been correct.

I strode down the center aisle. Most of the religious iconography had been removed, since it wasn't a functioning chapel, but there were still stairs leading up to what used to be the altar. I collapsed onto them, my head in my hands.

God, I was so tired. Tired of everything stuck inside of me.

And I'd thought things were *okay*.

"What am I supposed to do now?" I didn't know who I was asking. I barely knew *what* I was asking.

"Hattie?"

Holy hell.

I screamed as I looked up, shocked, but it was just Kit, sweat dripping down his face. He stood at the entrance to the nave, breathing hard.

"What?" I managed once my heart rate lowered. Not a ghost. Of course. It was never a ghost. "Did you follow me?"

"Yes?" Kit wiped some of the sweat off his brow. "What happened? Is it the presentation?"

"No." Shit, the presentation. Though that was admittedly low on my list of worries now. "You know I used to be good at all this?"

As I spoke, Kit made his way down the aisle toward me,

albeit slowly, as if he was worried I might start screaming again. It was a valid concern.

"Before you came along, Kit Morland. I used to be good at school. At being a Northanger student and a friend and a daughter. But then you showed up and I started getting everything wrong."

"Hattie." Kit was a few feet in front of me now, and he came to a stop, his hand on the back of the first row of benches. "You need to tell me what happened."

"I didn't get into Udolpho, that's what happened," I said, on the verge of tears. Great. Just what I didn't need. Beside me, I heard Kit's sharp intake of breath. You and me both, pal. "You remember Udolpho. My entire plan for the future? Completely up in smoke."

"There are other schools . . ."

"I didn't *apply* anywhere else." I didn't mean to shout, but it happened, and Kit winced. "I was supposed to. I was supposed to do a lot of things this semester, but instead I got all wrapped up in you and your stories and I thought, it'll be fine, I don't need a backup plan, but it turned out I super did and now I'm completely and irreversibly screwed."

Kit was silent, and so was I. The light from the windows shone down at our feet.

"So we just need to figure out other places for you to apply," he said, coming around to sit next to me. "You've got time before applications are due, right?"

"What if I don't want that?" My voice was small, so small I could barely hear myself. Kit furrowed his brow. "I don't know what I want, Kit. Maybe this isn't what I'm meant to do."

"What do you mean?"

"All of this." I waved my hands around. "The overachiever super student. Law school or whatever. I'm starting to think that isn't my path."

"That's not a bad thing."

"It is when you have no idea how to find another path, and when changing said path will lead to your mother absolutely flipping out." I pressed my hands against my face, willing back the tears. "She's going to be so disappointed in me."

The words were sand in my mouth.

We sat together in silence for a minute. Kit didn't touch me, but I felt his presence, and it was as close to comforting as anything could be right now.

"Your mom's kind of a lot."

"Hey." I looked up fast, my words sharp. "Don't—she's my mom. She wants me to be successful."

"Right." Kit's voice was neutral, but he didn't push the issue any further. "We need to figure out what you want to do. Not just what your—not just what anyone else thinks you should do." His correction was too little, too late, but I appreciated the gesture. "This isn't over. We'll find some new colleges you can apply to—colleges you're excited about, even—and we'll get things on track. This is a setback. It sucks that Udolpho didn't let you in, and I think they're giant idiots for not seeing how great you are." I snorted. "But it's not the end. We're go-ing to work together to make sure it's not the end."

I took a deep breath. Let it out slowly as I concentrated on the wood grain of the stairs beneath me. Swirling and infinite.

Tilneys didn't give up. And even if Udolpho had been the

dream, I'd just have to make a new one. Kit was right. This wasn't over.

"Okay." I nodded as I stood. "And I've got . . . my senior meeting with my mom is today." I hadn't expected to start that meeting with an Udolpho rejection, but maybe it was good timing. The whole point of the senior meeting was to make sure students were on the right track for the future. We could figure it out together. "Maybe she'll have some new ideas?"

"Those are the ideas you want?"

"She knows what's she's doing, Kit." My tone was sharp, an indication for him to stop pushing; to his credit, Kit backed down.

"Okay." Kit stood up, almost tripping over his own feet as he did, though he caught himself on the side of the pulpit at the last second. "Let's get back to class. We can still do the presentation for Skinner. And then after class, after your meeting, we can figure this out."

Figure it out. Right. I followed Kit back down the aisle and out into the world. Ready to try . . . anything, frankly, if it would stop this overwhelming feeling of *you ruined everything* from rising inside of me and taking me over from the inside out.

Mom would help. Even if Kit didn't believe it. The only reason she hadn't helped before was because I'd never asked. But the senior meeting was all about asking, about helping, and with her steering my ship . . . I'd get back on track in no time.

I had to.

Chapter Twenty-One

Our presentation to Skinner was mediocre at best, but I was in such a haze that I barely registered it. She gave us some notes, Kit wrote them down to email to me—good, because I hadn't heard a single thing she'd said—and we separated, Kit promising to meet me in the library after my meeting.

Izzy and Priya, obviously, had questions about where I'd run off to. Just stress, I'd explained to them. Nerves. It upset my stomach, and Kit came to check on me. But I was fine now, nothing to worry about, how did *their* presentations go?

I didn't think they believed me (Izzy definitely didn't), but the excuse would buy me some time. I could have told them about Udolpho. Priya would be horrified on my behalf, and Izzy would be—well, it was hard to predict Izzy's actions sometimes, but she would want to help. Start planning to break into the admissions office and change my acceptance or something. But I wanted to talk to my mom first, before I talked to anyone else. Wanted her to put me on a new track so that when I told Izzy and Priya about it, I already had my next steps in place, steps that didn't involve breaking and entering. I didn't need them to see me stumbling. They only needed to see me get up again.

Finally, the last bell of the day rang, and it was time for my meeting. I made a quick stop in the bathroom to make sure I seemed as collected as possible, and once I'd determined that my headband was level and my socks were pulled up straight, I headed toward my mom's office, ready to let her take over for me. To let myself breathe, knowing that she was in charge.

Mrs. Levenson smiled at me quizzically when I opened the door.

"Hattie!" She stood up from behind her desk, polishing her glasses on her sleeve. The last time I'd been in here was when I'd met Kit, I realized with a start. And yet it looked exactly the same, even though it felt like so much of my world had changed. "I didn't expect to see you here today. What can I help you with?" The question took me by surprise. Mrs. Levenson was in charge of my mom's schedule, so she should know I had my meeting today. But it was Monday, I reasoned. Maybe her mind was still caught up in the weekend.

"Hi, Mrs. Levenson. I'm here for my senior meeting with my—with Dr. Tilney." I'd almost slipped there, but caught it at the last second.

Mrs. Levenson's feelings, on the other hand, were not so easily disguised.

"Didn't you see my email?" Her face was twisted into concern, her glasses framing wide eyes. "These old servers are always eating my messages."

"I haven't checked my email." Not since I'd seen the Udolpho news. I didn't need to look at the subject line of that one ever again, but it wasn't like I could delete it, either. "Did you— Is something wrong?" I glanced over toward the door of my mom's office, which was firmly closed.

No light coming out from under the door, though.

"Unfortunately, Dr. Tilney is no longer available to meet today." Mrs. Levenson pursed her lips, and my heart sank. "She's had meetings with the board all afternoon. There's been— It's funding issues, you know."

I felt totally and completely numb. There was always funding to be dealt with at Northanger, and it was the cause of constant headaches for my mom. But I still thought . . .

"Can we reschedule?" I asked, my voice as even as possible even as my heart raced. "I'm flexible. And I really wanted to—it would be good to meet." There was a portrait of my mother framed next to Mrs. Levenson's desk, four feet tall at least, an actual oil painting that the board of trustees had commissioned when she took over the school. I'd heard other students whisper about it, how terrifying it was, the gilded and ornate frame surrounding my mom's dagger stare. I'd never minded it when I'd been in here before. Having my mom keep an eye on me was a welcome change.

Now her expression was blank, distant. And this painting was still the closest thing I had to my mother.

Mrs. Levenson reached across the desk, like she wanted to put her hand on my shoulder, but I flinched and she reconsidered, pulling her hand back. Still, when she spoke, her voice was soft. Apologetic.

"Her schedule is full, Hattie."

"Right." I was drowning. This was as bad as getting rejected from Udolpho. They had no obligation to me; rejecting most of their applicants was their express purpose. I didn't realize it was also my mother's. "Thanks, Mrs. Levenson."

"Maybe you two can chat at home?" Her words were kind but meaningless. Like that would ever happen. School talk was for school, Mom had always made that clear, but when she didn't want to meet at school either, I had to assume she just didn't want to talk to me at all. She didn't want *me* at all.

"Maybe." I raised my hand to wave goodbye, already half backing out of the office. "Thanks again." Mrs. Levenson was nice, but if she thought there was even a chance Dr. Tilney would talk to me at home, then it only showed that she didn't know her at all.

The halls were empty as I rushed through them toward my locker to grab my stuff and then out into the quad, where the dark gray clouds only served to emphasize my mood. Around me, students stood chatting in clumps, completely unaware of what was happening to me right next to them. And that was good, right? That was what I'd always wanted. For no one to see my vulnerabilities. To have no one to turn to because I didn't *need* anyone to turn to.

"Hattie?" Izzy's voice cut through the din behind me, and when I turned around, I saw that it wasn't just her—she was standing with Priya and, of all people, Freddie, aka, the last person I wanted to see. "Going somewhere?"

"Apparently not," I managed, and if I had a list of people

I wanted to fall apart in front of, Izzy would be on the bottom and Freddie wouldn't even be allowed to read the list. I didn't let my friends see my emotions, and I sure as hell didn't let Freddie. "What are you doing?" My gaze shifted to Freddie. "Why are you even with her? You don't have practice today."

"Suddenly you've got our schedule memorized?" Izzy matched my sharpness beat for beat, crossing her arms over her chest as she stared me down. "Are you going to tell us what's going on, or are you just going to run away again? Tell Ghost Boy everything and leave us out of it?"

I didn't answer. I *couldn't* answer. Freddie glanced between the two of us, one eyebrow raised, before she put her hand on Priya's shoulder, who had been watching Izzy and me with confusion.

"Priya, Izzy, why don't you head toward the gym. I'll catch up with you there."

"Fine," Izzy muttered, and I was going to have to pay for this later, pay with groveling to Izzy and to Priya, too, probably, by extension, but I had a hard time forcing myself to care. As the girls hurried away, Freddie turned toward me. She was in her responsible coach outfit, a fitted Northanger hoodie and leggings, her curly hair pulled up in a perfect ponytail, and I hated her for it. Hated her for blending in so seamlessly when it had taken me years of work to even pretend.

"Who pissed in your cornflakes this morning?" Freddie asked, once the girls were out of earshot. That was my sister. Ever the delight. Around us, the wind was starting to pick up, the sky growing darker. "Didn't you have your senior meeting with Mom today? You should be over the moon with all that personalized Dr. Tilney attention. Isn't that basically your drug of choice?"

"You're a jerk, Freddie."

"Yeah, well." She shrugged, her ponytail whipping against her face from the wind. "We all have our talents. Did Mom not praise every single one of your accomplishments or something? Was her criticism just a little too constructive?"

"She wasn't there, okay?" The words came out as a shout before I knew I was saying them, and Freddie stopped talking, finally. "She canceled the appointment. And we're not rescheduling. Even though I needed—" I stopped myself, but it didn't matter. Freddie knew what I meant.

The rain started to spit at us, the sort of short, sharp drops that meant a lot more rain was coming. Neither of us moved.

"It doesn't matter what you needed, Hen." Her voice softened, and I would have called it kind if it wasn't Freddie. "Mom isn't going to give it to you. Because she doesn't care about us. Okay? I know you've spent the whole time since—you know—like, hero-worshipping her. But here's the hard truth, because you're seventeen, and it's about time you learned this one." She leaned in, close, and the rain was pouring down on both of us but neither of us budged, neither of us took the opportunity for shelter from the weather or the truth. "As long as it doesn't interfere with her precious career, Mom could care less about what we do. She doesn't pay any attention to us."

Even though I'd seen the proof hardened into reality all day, I still shook my head.

"She's just . . ." But I couldn't figure out how to say it this time. How to reconcile someone who treated me the way my mom did with someone who cared about me.

Freddie's smile was cruel.

"Welcome to the club, little sister." She clapped her hand on my shoulder, and I stumbled backward from the impact. "It sucks here. But you'll learn to numb the pain. Now if you'll excuse me." And she walked away at a leisurely pace, like she didn't even feel the rain. Like she didn't even feel anything.

I envied her.

And then I turned and ran for Howe, the rain pelting down on me as everything I'd thought to be true poured away with it.

Mom *didn't* care. I put so much time and effort into doing things she'd care about. But would she have even been proud if I'd gotten into Udolpho? She'd probably have given me a firm nod, then gone back into her office. I'd pictured her being so *proud* of me. But that picture was a lie that I'd made up.

By the time I made it to Howe a few minutes later, texted Kit that I was outside, I'd made a decision.

"How'd it go? I thought we were meeting at the library," he said when he got downstairs, a raincoat pulled on over his clothes, concern flashing in his eyes when he saw me. "God, you're soaked."

"It didn't. I'm not going home tonight." It felt good to say. I grabbed my backpack off the ground, ran up the concrete steps toward the door while Kit stared at me, slack-jawed. "I'm basically an adult and I've never done anything reckless in my entire life, you know that? So I'm not going home tonight."

"Where will you—what?"

"I was hoping I could crash in your room." I pushed into the ornate and intricately carved entranceway to the dorm and headed into the lobby, Kit jogging to catch up. "Not for anything . . . inappropriate," I hastened to add, because there was reckless and then there was stupid and I was aiming for the former. "We can even watch ghost movies, if that's what you want. You in?"

I spun around to face Kit, arms crossed over my chest. He skidded to a halt in front of me, looked down in confusion. Then he nodded.

"Good." I pushed past him, headed toward the front desk. Toward a different type of decision. "Let's do it."

Chapter Twenty-Two

We didn't end up going to Kit's room.

We tried, but Kit's dorm monitor was in rare form and wouldn't even let me go upstairs because it was "too close to the end of visitor hours." There was clearly no chance he'd "forget" I was up there, like some of the monitors did, so Kit just ran upstairs to grab some dry clothes for me—Florida State sweatpants that I had to roll up five or six times so they wouldn't drag in the mud, plus a faded black T-shirt and a second rain jacket, changing in the common room's bathroom and shoving everything wet into my backpack—before we headed back to the main campus, where we settled in front of the Learners' Statue I'd shown him way back during his very first week. Well, I say settled. Kit was settled, sitting up on the base of the statue with his feet swinging above the ground. I was pacing furiously in front of it. The rain had mostly stopped, blown through like everything did at Northanger, though every surface was still soaked.

"I can't believe she canceled the meeting." I shook my head. I'd filled Kit in on the way over here, and he'd kept quiet, let me rant. "I mean, the evidence for how she felt about her children has been in front of me for years. I just thought things were different with me."

"That's not your fault."

"No, it is." I sighed, stepping straight into a puddle that soaked through my white sneakers instantly. Kit winced. "So what do you want to do? We can go down into town, get some pizza or something."

"Yeah, I'm going to need to sign back into my dorm sooner than that." Kit shifted, uncomfortable. "But I can see what you're doing, Tilney. Your whole avoidance thing. This isn't just about a canceled meeting."

Damn Kit Morland and his insightful nature.

"It's just . . ." I hated even talking about this. "Freddie was talking about how Mom doesn't care what we do. And she wasn't wrong." I tried to keep my voice as even-keeled as possible, even as my throat thickened with tears. This was so stupid. It wasn't like Mom and I were close. What did it matter? It shouldn't. "Everything I've done here, I've been trying to hold myself together as this, like, perfect specimen of a daughter, you know? Like if I live out some sort of Northanger wish fulfillment for her, she'll pay attention to me." I was barely processing the words as I spoke, the thoughts spilling out of me. "She's living her dream. Headmistress of an elite institution. It's everything she ever wanted. And I thought that she also wanted, like . . . a matching set." I pressed the toe of my sneaker into a nearby puddle, testing the waters. "The perfect child to go along with her perfect life. So I tried to be that for her, because it seemed like . . ." I ran out of words, my breathing ragged.

Kit didn't shift from his spot, just watched me pace as he spoke. "Is that your job?"

"Dad told me to make her proud. To take care of them." I'd never admitted it out loud before. Who would I have admitted it to? No one in my family. None of my friends. Just Kit, who looked at me like he knew me in a way no one else ever had. "Right before he died. So that's what I tried to do. I tried to take care of Liam, and to minimize any damage caused by Freddie, and to be the perfect student for Mom. But she never even noticed. So what am I trying for?" I tossed my hands in the air, looked up toward the darkening sky. "This isn't what I want. I don't care about getting into, like, the most elite college ever."

"What do you want?"

I shook my head. "Honestly?" I gave Kit a half-hearted smile. "I'm so tired, Kit. I just want to stop."

He seemed to consider that for a second, the wind lifting his hair from his shoulders and ruffling it around his ears, before he spoke again. "Do you know why I transferred here?"

"Because of the NPSI scholarship, obviously. But don't worry, I've stopped holding it against you."

"Thanks," he said dryly. "But it wasn't just that. I mean, Northanger has always been this incredible dream. But that was all it felt like—a dream. It didn't feel like something I could do. It's far from Florida, and it's expensive, and I'd have to leave my family. But one day last fall I was in my boring, regular, non-haunted classroom, and I just thought . . . I know what it is I want to be doing with my life. And it isn't this. So what can I do to get to where I want to be? And I found the NPSI scholarship, and here I am."

"I'm glad you did." I smiled at him, possibly the first genuine smile I'd managed in hours.

"Thanks." He smiled back, lit up my whole chest. "I knew what I wanted, and I went after it. And you just . . . I don't think that stopping is what you really want, Tilney," he said, and my heart sank just a little. "There's something else out there you want. Something you know you love. Why can't that be the thing you go after?"

Because you couldn't go after people who were dead, and the dreams that had died with them.

"I don't really have that, Kit." There was vulnerability and there was stupidity, and telling Kit my history with ghosts—with stories, with the dreams I'd thought I'd had— was a prime example of the latter. I gave up on my pacing and sat down next to him at the edge of the Learners' Statue, tucking the bottom of Kit's rain jacket underneath me so the water wouldn't soak through his sweatpants. "I'm sorry."

From his look, I didn't know if he believed me. But either way, he nodded.

"Okay." He stood up, offering me his hand as he pulled me to my feet. I let myself be pulled. "Then we just need to find some chiller schools for you, right? They don't need to be the dream. They just need to be forward motion. Maybe we go full-on to the other end of the spectrum, one of those schools where they don't even have majors or barely have grades. Something that'll really show your mom that you don't care about what she thinks."

"Yeah. Maybe." Good, this was good. I was buzzing with adrenaline, with our decision, with staying out late and making choices that weren't Perfect Hattie Tilney 101. A school like that sounded like exactly the sort of place Dr. Tilney would *hate*, which made me suddenly very interested in it. "Great. Thanks."

"You got it," Kit said. "So . . . what do we do now? It's kind of freezing out here."

"I'm not sure." I clenched and released my fists at my side. "I told you, I don't want to go home. Not that she's even going to notice, but it feels like I have to do *something*. I guess I could sleep in the gym."

Kit considered, his mouth a thin line. Then he jumped up from the statue, his hand held out to me.

"Come on," he said, as I looked at his hand. "I'm taking you back to Howe."

"You can't." I gestured around at the quickly emptying quad. "That power-hungry dorm monitor's not going to let me in your room."

"Don't worry." Kit's grin was as infectious as it was, indeed, worrying. "I've got a plan."

<hr />

Let the record show that I was right to be worried about Kit's plan.

In fact, as I was climbing as carefully as I could up the rope

ladder Kit had tossed down to me from his third-story window
("Why do you *have* this?" I'd asked, to which he'd just shrugged
and answered "Florida," as if it was a reasonable explanation),
I couldn't help but feel that it was maybe safer to be a perfect
Northanger student than . . . whatever this was.

But when I finally made it up to his window, and he pulled
me inside, I had to admit that the rush of adrenaline I felt was
the sort of thing you could get hooked on.

"Told you it was safe." Kit pulled the rope ladder up behind me, rolling it up and depositing it in a canvas bag with
"Miscellaneous" scrawled on the side, like that was a helpful
organization system. "Come on. It's a lot warmer in here than
it is out there."

"And a lot less likely to end in a free fall," I muttered, but
I stepped farther into the room, letting him close the window.
As expected, neither Kit nor his perpetually absent roommate
had done much with the decorations in here. Kit had a *What
Cries Beneath* poster above his bed, of course. When I nodded
toward it with a raised eyebrow, Kit shrugged.

"What can I say? My brand is strong. Don't worry—I got
it used from an old movie theater, so Dr. Rodriguez didn't get
any of the money."

"Glad to hear it." I laughed, running my hand over the
bottom of the poster, where Izzy's dad's name was bigger than
all the others. "You're still excited about Cry Fest, right? Mr.
Guest of Honor over here."

"If it's what it takes to keep my scholarship, I can make
anything work. Izzy wants to get together a couple of times

before the festival, too, so that I seem involved in the planning. Said it'll look good to the board." He shrugged, and I felt a sharp pang in my chest at the mention of Izzy. At how I'd treated her earlier. If she was emailing Kit, though, maybe she really did want to help him. Maybe she did really want to help me.

"Well, if you end up covered in glitter from making posters all day, don't ask me to help you take it off." I shuddered. "I hate that stuff."

"Seems like you'd be even more eager to help me take it off, then."

I shook my head, then continued to examine the room. Besides the *Cries* poster, the only other decoration on the wall was a *Ghostbusters* poster from the remake.

"Oh, yeah," Kit said, when he noticed my gaze. "I know. Continuing the walking stereotype over here. But it's a great movie. Well, not great. But I love it."

"Technically, the walking stereotype would be the original." I hadn't seen this poster in forever, but it instantly transported me back to the premiere my dad had taken me to when I was a kid. Kate McKinnon had waved at me, and I'd just about died. "You like this one better?"

"I mean, the original one is a classic. But it's kind of misogynistic. And this one isn't perfect or anything, but it makes me happy." He turned back toward me, his full attention like a thousand-watt bulb. "So, yeah. What do you want to do? We could play a game, or—"

"I want to watch it." Screw messing up college. Screw

staying out all night in a boy's dorm room. This was the bravest I'd ever been. "Lady Ghostbusters. You have it, don't you? Or we can stream it."

"Really?" Kit's eyebrows shot up high enough that I worried they might go through the ceiling and into the room above us. "You do know what it's about, right?"

"Do you want to watch it or not?" I crossed my arms over my chest, the challenge in my voice clear. After a second, Kit nodded.

"Yeah. I—yeah." He grabbed his laptop from his backpack, opening it and setting it on the desk behind him. "I've got it downloaded. Make yourself comfortable."

"Cool." I grabbed a few pillows off his bed and made myself a nest on the floor. "*Ghostbusters*. Let's go."

"Let's go," Kit echoed, before pressing Play and settling down beside me. Not pushed up against me or anything, but still close.

And as the movie flickered to life, and I could feel Kit breathing against me . . . everything seemed like it might just be okay.

⁓⁓⁓⁓

"It's morning." I turned toward the window, where the sun had started streaming in between the blinds. After *Ghostbusters*, we'd gone down a YouTube rabbit hole of shaky-cam ghost footage, critiquing everything we saw and booing at the obvious CGI. It was the most ghost-related fun I'd had in a long time. "I should probably . . . I should go."

"You sure?" Kit cocked his head to the side. Over the

course of the last few movies, we'd settled into each other more fully, and his face was only a few inches from mine. I did my best not to think about it. "If you want . . . you said you wanted to stay, before. You still could."

His invitation hovered between us, and I knew what was implied. Could hear the way his voice caught, quivered on the last words.

I wanted to. I wanted to grab Kit's arms and wrap them around me, let him hold me close until everything else went away. Kiss him finally, until we were both senseless, like the world was reduced to just the two of us.

But the world wasn't just the two of us, and I still wasn't ready to pretend.

"It's okay." I smiled, hoping he understood my rejection. "I think I got my rebellion out of my system for now. And I don't want anyone to see me leaving and get you in trouble."

"You're sure you trust the rope ladder for your descent?"

"Should I?" I countered, and Kit laughed.

"Yeah. It'll be fine. I just don't want you to go."

The raw honesty of this boy was beautiful and terrifying all at the same time.

I didn't say anything, just watched him unroll the ladder again, toss it out over the windowsill. I climbed carefully, lowering a few rungs until just my eyes were peeking into his room. Kit stood with his hands leaning on the sill, watching me.

"Thanks for letting me in, Juliet," I said, and he laughed. I wanted to squeeze his hand, but I was too afraid to let go of the ladder, so I stuck with a smile.

"Anytime, Romeo. And if the Tilney name is getting to

you . . . remember that a rose by any other name smells just as sweet." He leaned out, cupped my cheek in his hand for a quick second, then leaned back. "Text me when you get home, okay?"

"Okay," I promised. And as I descended the ladder, it was impossible to tell what was making my heart thump at an increasing speed—the slow and cautious descent to the ground, or the way that Kit was still looking at me when I made it there. Serious. Like he felt seriously about me.

Who was I kidding? I knew exactly what that boy was doing to my heart.

Chapter Twenty-Three

No one had noticed that I'd spent the entire night out of the house.

Well, maybe Liam had from the way he looked at me when I stumbled down to breakfast, all bleary-eyed and yawning, but he went right back to texting Erik without asking any questions. Freddie wasn't even there, and although Dr. Tilney was sipping her coffee at the dining room table when I came downstairs, she didn't say anything more than good morning. Nothing about our meeting. Nothing about missing it.

So, fine. Suspicions confirmed. Dr. Tilney didn't care about me. Freddie was out God knew where, and Liam was wrapped up in the thralls of first love, which meant that I was totally and completely on my own.

Good.

⁓⁓⁓

As the Halloween decorations came down and the Thanksgiving decorations went up, I spent most days after school in the library with Kit, looking at the colleges he'd picked out for me to consider. I'd seen Izzy and Priya a couple of times, offered them the best apology I could muster without revealing any of my inner turmoil, but things had been off with us. Izzy hadn't texted me in days, and even though Priya still sent me memes and new track workouts she wanted to try, my replies had gotten a lot less inspired. It was a lot of *you can do this!* and *crushing it!* instead of my usual supply of relevant GIFs from old NBC comedies.

But we'd get through this, I reminded myself. Once I figured out my next steps, I'd fill them in on the broad strokes of everything that had been going on, and we'd be right back to normal. No one was asking me to choose between Kit and my friends. I just needed to figure out how to balance them.

After I figured out literally everything else.

Through it all, Kit kept trying to figure out my secret passion. Trying to trick me into realizing that I actually loved . . . fill in the blank here. I played it clueless every time, let my newfound aimlessness take center stage, because it was easier than explaining how much my actual passion hurt. It was bad enough that we were spending more and more time working on our journalism project. I'd been trying to write the script for my portion—the there-is-no-evidence-of-ghosts part—for days, but everything I pulled together felt flat and uninspired. The project wasn't due until after winter break, but we still needed to record voice-overs and edit all of it. I had to put *something* together.

My latest assignment from Kit definitely didn't help matters. Because it was the Monday before Thanksgiving, I had a meeting with the Ghost Brigade, and Kit wasn't coming with me.

You'll be fine! he'd said after texting me that he had to skip this meeting to work on a group project for another class. *They trust you. Just follow them, observe what they do, and record it. What, are you worried they're going to find something real?*

I hadn't responded to that last part, just shoved my phone back down into my skirt pocket, fuming as I made my way to the meeting. As we'd previously established, I didn't exactly have a lot of free time on my hands, what with trying to figure out my entire future and everything. Now I had to join the Ghost Brigade on a hunt, and I didn't even have Kit with me? Absolute garbage.

"Hattie!" Jolie waved me over when I met them at the Learners' Statue at 8 p.m., the evening full dark around us. I gave them a tight smile in response, my hands deep in the pockets of my blue peacoat. They were surrounded by to-night's chosen few of the Ghost Brigade, who all stared at me like I was an alien. Which wasn't even fair. I'd *met* them all before. Just . . . with Kit.

"Hey, team," I said cautiously, as the rest of the brigade waved hello. "Everyone still cool with being recorded?" I'd be filming on one of the school GoPros tonight, recording everything they *wouldn't* find on their ghost-based expedi-tion. Kit had gotten everyone to sign waivers, but Skinner always said that when we were working with minors, it was good to remind them that they were going to be filmed. They looked nervous, but nodded. "Great." I started the camera, pointed it toward Jolie. Of the group, they were the one who seemed most visibly excited, smile beaming. "What are we doing tonight?"

"Okay." Jolie clapped their hands together, and the rest of the group gathered around them, instantly captivated. "So tonight, we're going to explore the gym, talk about a few of the sightings that have happened there over the school's history, and see if we can detect anything ourselves."

"Hattie!" We all turned at the shout to see Liam, running down the path with Erik jogging behind him. Great. When I hadn't seen Erik, I'd figured both he and Liam would be out of the picture tonight. "Don't start the ghost hunt without us!"

"What are you doing here?" It wasn't that I didn't love my little brother and his adorable romance, but tonight already had me on edge. I didn't need to be worried about Liam on top of that, constantly glancing at him whenever Jolie mentioned something Dad used to talk about to make sure it hadn't dragged up some long-repressed memory. He wasn't nearly as good at shoving those down as I was.

"We're brigaders?" Liam skidded to a halt in front of me, breathing hard—clearly, we needed to work on keeping our running more consistent—as Erik caught up behind him. "I mean, Erik already was, but I officially joined this week." He waved at the brigade, who waved back at him with a lot more enthusiasm than they'd given me. Traitors. "First ghost hunt! That's okay, right?"

"Of course!" Jolie held their hands out toward Liam and Erik. "The more the merrier!"

"Great," I muttered, then, louder, "I'll get waivers for you two to sign when we get back. You're fine with being filmed?"

"Oh—um, yeah, sure." Erik looked over at Liam, who gave him a small nod. I made a mental note to keep them out of my shots as much as possible, just in case. "Hi, Hattie."

"Hey, Erik." Polite, polite, mask, mask. Yes, I was annoyed that Liam was here, because I was annoyed that *I* was here. But I didn't want Erik to think I didn't approve of him. I liked Erik. Mostly, I liked how much he liked my brother. Liam deserved to be liked. "So. Ghosts, huh?"

He shrugged. "Better than homework, right?"

"New T-shirt idea!" one of the girls called out, and the rest of the brigade laughed. I laughed, too, half a second behind; and even if I was the only one who noticed, I still felt the discomfort.

"Let's walk and talk." Jolie pointed toward the gym, where the Arthur C. Nebeker Gymnasium for the Pursual of Athletics for Boys sign had been dismantled over the years, chipped away at by both nature and students with ill intentions, until only "Neb" remained. As we all followed Jolie, I did my best to stay up front so I could record everything. "The Neb has been host to thousands of reported sightings over the years. Stories range from the innocuous—cold spots, hot spots, any kind of spot you can imagine, really—to the more intense. In fact, some say that the ghosts who inspired *What Cries Beneath* were spotted right here in the Neb." They had no idea we were standing over the tunnels where they filmed *Cries*, but I sure as hell wasn't about to say anything. "Though admittedly, all of the more nefarious energy could have been from the laps we've been forced to run over the years." They grinned at the camera, and I could tell this, right here, was what they loved.

Jolie could have been a killer school tour guide if they wanted to be. "And some of the stories are a lot more specific. In both world wars, the Neb was annexed as a training ground for nurses and other medical practitioners preparing to go overseas. In World War Two, it was also a rehabilitation center for returning soldiers."

"What ghost stories came out of the training side?" Liam asked, and Jolie smiled.

"Let's just say that not everyone should be a nurse. But that's not what we're looking for tonight!" We reached the Neb, the entrance bathed in the glow from one of the school's strategically placed campus lights, and Jolie pulled out their phone, held it up for the group. It was open to a picture of a woman, dressed in what looked like a military uniform. "Rosie McDowell was one of the women placed at the Neb for rehabilitation. Records show that she died of an infection while she was here, and over the years, students have reported several sightings of her. A woman in a 1940s military uniform is fairly specific—she's the only death on campus that matches the description." Jolie tucked their phone back into their pocket, stared straight into the camera. "Earlier this week, Rob spotted her."

Erik and Liam both gasped, and I swung the camera over to where one of the brigaders, evidently Rob, stood, looking nervous.

"Can you tell us what you saw?" I asked, doing my best to keep my voice professional. This would have been Kit's bread and butter. But I could handle one little false ghost sighting.

Rob nodded. "I'm on the basketball team, and I was

practicing free throws." Exactly how all the best ghost stories started. "It was just me in there. I had my eye on the net, threw the ball, sank it—and as it bounced to the floor, I realized it went through *a woman*." Rob leaned into the last two words with all the emphasis of a carnival barker, and I resisted the urge to roll my eyes. "Right there! Under the net! And then the next second . . . she was gone."

The rest of the brigade gasped, right on cue, while Rob seemed extremely satisfied with himself. And why wouldn't he be? I'd be satisfied if I made up a story like that, too.

"Rob is the first person we have on record to spot her by the hoop, so we're going to examine that area and see if we can find any signs of supernatural activity," Jolie explained directly to the camera as they pushed in the door to the gym, which had been left unlocked for our purposes. Because the Ghost Brigade was an officially sponsored campus club, this whole expedition was a lot more aboveboard than the times I'd snuck in.

"That's awesome," Erik breathed, as we all filed inside. "Do you think we're actually going to see her?"

"We can hope, but with a group this size, it's unlikely," Jolie said, turning on their phone's flashlight and shutting off the gym's overhead lights. How convenient. "Most of our paranormal explorations look for more subtle signs of activity. It may not be as flashy, but, trust me, it's still exciting." Jolie and I had different definitions of the word "exciting." But whatever. I wasn't here to judge; I was here to get the footage we needed for our project. I panned the camera over the dimly lit faces of the rest of the brigade. They were nervous, excited, whispering to one another too quietly for me to hear. I wondered what it felt like to get so excited about something. These days, I mostly got tired.

"How often are these expeditions successful?" There was perhaps slightly more bite in my voice than was strictly and professionally necessary; but, in my defense, when I looked at the giggling brigade, I only saw myself when I was younger, staring at my dad in awe as he pulled out his latest ghost-hunting gadget to show me. If any of these people had actually experienced loss, they wouldn't be nearly as excited about all of this.

"What are we counting as useful?" Jolie asked, pulling EMF readers from their backpack and handing them out to the rest of the brigade.

"Actual evidence of paranormal activity?" I raised an eyebrow. "Seems kind of self-explanatory."

"'Evidence' is a hard word to use around the paranormal." Jolie passed their last reader to Liam, who turned it over and over in his hands with interest. We had half a dozen of them in the basement, but he still examined it like he'd never seen one before. "What do you count as actual evidence? We observe changes in the environment, and we draw conclusions based on what we know and what we've seen before. Nothing lights up on our EMF readers—that stands for electromagnetic field, it basically means unexplained energy—and says 'It's a ghost!' It's not a pregnancy test." Jolie smirked, and the brigade tittered. I felt my face flush. "Every paranormal expedition is successful, Hattie. It brings us one step closer to understanding the other side."

"Right," I muttered. Clearly, I wasn't going to get a straight answer out of them. As we headed toward the hoop on the opposite side of the gym, I tugged on Liam's shirt, pulling him back. "Hey. Sorry this is such a mess."

"What do you mean?" His expression was perplexed. Erik had gone on ahead, chatting with Rob with animated hands. "It's cool."

"Really? You think so?" I grimaced. "I guess when you compare it to your video games . . ."

"Shut up." Liam pushed his shoulder into mine. "I think it's kind of interesting. Not, like, the searching for hot spots or cold spots or whatever it is we're trying to do here. But everyone believes in this stuff so much that they'll risk everyone at school making fun of them just for the chance to catch a glimpse of what they believe in."

"You've been talking to Kit."

"Maybe." Liam looked at me sideways. "I feel like you should get it, though. You used to be into this stuff, too."

"That's different." My chest tightened. Liam and I didn't talk about this. I didn't talk about this with anyone. "That was just because . . . that was just because it was what I did with Dad. It wasn't like I was looking for this stuff on my own."

"Does Kit know?"

"Does Kit know what?" I should have been concentrating on filming—Jolie was walking in circles under the hoop now, EMF reader held out in front of them—but I owed it to Liam not to walk away.

"That you were so into ghosts, before."

My breath hitched on the intake and I forgot, for a second, to let it go again.

What's your passion, Tilney?

"I just think it might be good for you to talk to him about it," Liam continued, like this was easy, like I could just *talk*. "It would be good for your project, too, right? So that he knows where you're coming from."

"I don't believe in ghosts, Liam."

"Anymore." Liam shrugged. "I don't know."

"Do you tell Erik everything?" I meant it as a distraction, a diversion, but Liam grinned when I said it, and I realized my mistake.

"So you're saying you and Kit have the same relationship Erik and I do?"

"Oh my God." I groaned, covering my face with my free hand. "I—obviously not. Forget I said anything."

"Do I need to start staying clear of the bleachers again?"

"*Go*, Liam." I shooed him away, back toward the group, where everyone was now spinning around with their EMF detectors, Erik included. Liam laughed but ran toward him obligingly, and I breathed a sigh of relief. Now that was a line of questioning I did *not* want to go down.

Back by the hoop, Jolie was talking to the rest of the brigade about some of the other ghost encounters (*alleged* ghost encounters) that had taken place in the Neb. I drew closer, making sure to record their face, as well as the reactions of the brigade around them.

"Sarah Bright came through here when she was on her way to Canada," Jolie explained. "She was trying to flee from her husband, who was *not* a good dude. But he followed her here and she was killed on this very site."

"No she wasn't." At the interruption Jolie looked up, startled, and it took me a second to realize that the interrupter was me. "Sarah escaped. It was her husband who was killed on the grounds."

The entire Ghost Brigade, plus Erik and my brother, turned to stare at me. I wanted to stare at me, too. What the hell was I doing? One, this was terrible reporting—I needed to observe the story, not insert myself into it. And two, I'd spent years hiding any remnants of my ghost knowledge from the world. Sure, Jolie was dead wrong about Sarah, but what did it matter?

"Sorry," I said, shaking my head, as the brigade stared. "Never mind."

"No, go on." Jolie watched me with a furrowed brow. "What do you mean, Sarah didn't die? Of course she did."

"You're probably right." I gave my blandest smile, tried to yield to Jolie. "Go on."

"Is that not true?" Liam prodded me, because Liam didn't know how to leave well enough alone. "Hattie?"

"Yeah, Hattie." Jolie raised one eyebrow. "Tell us."

That was the last thing I wanted to do, but the entire brigade was waiting for me, and I didn't know how to back out of this one any further.

So I told them.

"The school tours say that Sarah died." I did my best not to shrink under their undivided attention, new as it was for me. "But that's not how it really went down. Sarah and her husband were both staying at the local inn. Separately, of course—Sarah didn't know he'd followed her there. But one of the cooks tipped her off, and she realized she couldn't get away from him forever. So she worked with a group of women in town who officially didn't even exist—there's no historical record of any of their names or anything, just articles about how the Snakes had struck again. That's what they called them," I explained as the group looked at me, rapt. "The Snakes. There's no direct proof of their involvement, of course; but one night Sarah lured her husband out here, to the grounds of the abbey, and the next morning he was found dead. Poisoned. And Sarah was gone."

"Sick," one of the brigade members breathed. She wasn't wrong. I felt an unexpected warmth, a rush of adrenaline, just from telling the story.

"So why does the school say Sarah died?" Erik asked.

"Because she basically did historically," I said. "A death certificate showed up in town with her name on it. Planted by the Snakes, of course, and everyone must have known that, but it still worked. Sarah needed to become a ghost to escape her past—even with her husband dead, he had family that would have come for her. So the story that lived on was of Sarah's death."

"And you know about this . . ." Liam must have known the answer, but he asked anyway. I kept it vague.

"It's pretty clear from the historical records what actually happened. Newspaper interviews, that sort of thing. You just have to know where to look."

"Okay." Jolie jumped in. I'd almost forgot they were there, I was so wrapped up in my story, in the way it felt to dip into that part of my brain again. "Well. The number one rule of ghost hunting is to respect the wishes of the spirit, as long as they don't cause any harm to living creatures. It sounds like Sarah wanted to be dead. So officially, we leave her dead. But thanks, Hattie." They smiled at me, and I couldn't help but smile back. "That was very . . . enlightening. Now, who's found an interesting reading?"

"*Very* enlightening." Liam leaned over and whispered in my ear as the brigade crowded around Jolie, waving their EMF readers through the air as they tried to compare results. "Dad?"

I nodded.

"Cool." Liam turned to Erik, leaving me alone with my thoughts. With the realization that for all of the trauma I'd been keeping to myself, maybe Liam was going to be fine. If he could bring up Dad without retreating into himself . . . maybe he'd be okay. Maybe he'd be able to go into antique shops again one day, like he and Dad used to, and be able to find treasures on his own without Dad helping him do it.

Maybe he was stronger than I was.

Chapter Twenty-Four

A few days after the ghost hunt, I woke up with a pit in my stomach and an overwhelming sense of nausea that could mean only one thing—it was Thanksgiving.

I did not, historically, look forward to this holiday. None of us were particularly passionate about cooking a giant meal, for starters. Even when Dad had been alive, and in charge of things like cooking, he didn't enjoy the elaborate dance that went into pulling a meal like Thanksgiving together. In fact, when he was alive, he used to make our Thanksgiving meal entirely out of different types of takeout from local restaurants. And not, like, ordering a turkey dinner or something. No, we'd have orange chicken next to naan, a huge platter of nachos in the center of the table with pupusas at every plate. One year, he'd ordered a hundred crunchy-shell tacos from Taco Bell for a Thanksgiving meal that had definitely lived in infamy.

The year after he died, Mom had ordered a turkey from

the grocery store deli section, precooked. We had that with a couple of standard sides I'm pretty sure were just defrosted sympathy casseroles from well-meaning neighbors, and there was absolutely zero joy in it.

So, yeah. Not my favorite big, celebratory tradition, Thanksgiving.

But I just had to get through it. Get through it, and then Monday would come, and I could go back to hiding out with Kit in the library.

In the meantime, he was enjoying his vacation by visiting an aunt in New Jersey, and I was standing in the kitchen at 7:00 a.m. on Thanksgiving morning, staring at a turkey that was *just* starting to drip with melted ice.

"I told Mom I'd take care of the turkey this year." There was a nonzero amount of panic in Liam's voice, just as there had been since he'd shaken me out of sleep fifteen minutes earlier. "I bought it last night. Why is it still frozen?"

"Turkeys take, like, famously long to defrost." Already, this day was off to a banner start. I was getting a headache, too, a tightness growing between my eyebrows.

"This isn't helpful information." Liam was holding a hair dryer, which didn't inspire any confidence from me. "Not at this stage of the game, anyway. You don't have a more powerful hair dryer than this one, do you?"

"Liam." I shook my head. "We can't blow-dry a turkey."

"What the hell are you two up to?" Great. Leaning in the doorframe of the kitchen was Freddie, her hair all scrunched up with last night's hairspray and her voice bleary with sleep. We'd barely talked since her fun little bombshell that Mom couldn't care less about the family, and I'd been hoping to keep it that way. "Liam, why are you giving that bird a blowout?"

"It's frozen." He nodded toward the obvious, while I did my best to avoid eye contact with my sister. "I thought this would help."

"It definitely won't." Freddie yawned, then pushed off from the door. "Follow me. I have an idea."

"You do?" Liam sounded understandably skeptical, and Freddie barked out a laugh.

"Yeah, kiddo. It's my one for the year, so let's not waste it. Both of you, get your shoes on and take the turkey out back. I'll meet you there."

"Why?" I hadn't meant to speak, to acknowledge Freddie's existence, but I couldn't help myself.

She just grinned. "You'll see."

〰〰〰

This was the worst idea anyone had ever had.

"Stand back!" Freddie shouted to us, even though both Liam and I were a good fifteen feet from her already, tucked behind the big bare tree that marked the corner of our cottage's backyard. She had to shout, because otherwise we wouldn't have heard her over the revving of the chain saw she was holding out in front of her, ready to descend onto the turkey.

That's right. *A chain saw.*

I still wasn't sure how we'd gotten here, but in the blur of the last ten minutes, Freddie had given us all safety glasses, pulled a chain saw out of our shed, and set the frozen turkey down on an exposed tree trunk in the yard, where we usually took turns splitting wood for the winter.

"Wait!" Liam shouted before Freddie could lower the chain saw. "Should we like . . . say a few words?"

"It's already dead, Liam." I watched Freddie nervously. She seemed way too competent with that chain saw, and I couldn't help but think that if one of the campus tour groups spotted us now, we'd spawn an entirely new Northanger legend. "Isn't it a little late for that?"

"I'm not trying to pardon it or anything." Liam rocked back and forth on the balls of his feet, and as Freddie and I made eye contact across the yard for one brief second, she flashed me a grin that seemed to say, *our brother, right?*

It disappeared as quickly as it came, but it was still a surprise, coming from Freddie.

"Maybe I could read a poem?" Liam offered.

"How about a moment of silence instead?" I wrapped my arm around Liam's shoulders—or tried to, at least. His growth spurt was still catching me by surprise. I settled for one arm up on his shoulder as I pressed my face against his shirt sleeve. "For this turkey, who is going to nourish our bodies."

"For the turkey," Freddie repeated solemnly, even if the chain saw soured the image slightly.

Liam nodded. "For the turkey."

After the appropriate ten seconds had passed, Freddie revved up the chain saw again, and I turned Liam around quickly, because whatever was about to happen, he didn't need to see it, growth spurt or no. But after a minute of slicing and dicing, it was, mercifully, done.

"There." Freddie moved her safety glasses to the top of her head, wiping her forehead with the end of her sleeve. "Now you put the pieces in a cold-water bath—not the actual bathtub, Liam, like a bucket or something—and change the water every half an hour. It should defrost a lot sooner that way."

"How did you know how to do all of this?" I asked. As Liam scurried forward to collect the pieces of turkey (wearing gloves that Freddie tossed him before he started), she rolled her eyes.

"Surprised your big sister has a competent bone in her body?"

The sharp left turn back into combative Freddie caught me by surprise. Not that it should. Clearly, whatever we'd shared during the Great Turkey Dismantling was over. But nevertheless, I stumbled.

"That's not what I said."

"Right." She turned toward the house. "You two take care of that. Once I clean up out here, I'm headed out."

"It's Thanksgiving."

"Wow, is it? I had no idea." She smirked. "I'll be back. If only to see how the turkey ends up."

"It's going to be perfect!" Liam shouted back from across the yard. I didn't even realize he could hear us. "I watched a whole YouTube series about basting!"

"And none of those mentioned defrosting the turkey?" I muttered to myself, but Freddie must have heard me, because unexpectedly she grinned.

"This is can't-miss TV, Hen. You don't have to worry about me skipping it."

We'd pulled the meal together the best we could, Liam and I, puttering around the kitchen all day just the two of us, mashing potatoes and opening a can of cranberry sauce, microwaving gravy and green beans before he popped a frozen pie in the oven. (Freddie reappeared right as the sun was setting, with wild eyes and alcohol on her breath.) It wasn't exactly a feast, but Liam looked pleased. Even the turkey—in pieces as it was—had at least cooked through, which was about all you could ask for.

And Mom was nowhere to be seen.

"Come on, Leems." I used my fork to grab some turkey, dropped it onto Liam's plate. Across from me, Freddie began to scoop out mashed potatoes. "If she said not to wait, then we shouldn't wait." Mom had sent the three of us an email—an *email*—several hours before, saying that there had been a pipe burst in one of the dorms and she'd need to be on campus all day to deal with it. I couldn't help but wonder if she'd burst that pipe herself, just to avoid us.

"Fine." He deflated, and I felt like shit, but he should have known better than to put expectations on Mom. Therein lay the way to madness.

The three of us ate in silence, punctuated only by our chewing and the clinking of ice in our glasses. A few times, Liam looked like he wanted to speak, but thought better of it. Good. The sooner we were through all of this, the better.

Across from me, Freddie held a slice of turkey out in front of her, examining it like she'd placed it under a microscope.

"It's cooked, right?" Liam asked, his voice tinged with nerves. I cut my eyes over to Freddie, willing her to be easy on him. She didn't need to be nice to me. But if she was anything less than kind to our little brother, I'd chase her out of here with the carving fork.

But she nodded, saving both of us from confrontation.

"Yeah. You nailed it, kid." She cut into her piece, popped a bite into her mouth, and chewed. "It's juicy, too. That's hard with turkey. Dad never got it right."

"Dad never made a turkey." I looked up toward my sister, fast. I wasn't one to bring up old Dad anecdotes—obviously—but I wasn't going to let her make up new ones. "He did the international smorgasbord every year."

"Yeah, because of how bad he used to mess up the turkey the few times he tried it." Freddie shrugged, continuing to pick at her plate as if talking about Dad, the three of us, was the most normal thing in the world. "You were too young to remember, Hen. But he only started doing the whole takeout thing because Mom begged him to stop ruining birds. Where do you think I learned my chain saw technique?" Freddie's gaze was far away, like she was watching a memory unfold. A memory Liam and I weren't privileged enough to share. But then she shook her head, seeming to snap out of it. "Anyway. It's good, Liam."

"Thanks." Liam looked over at me, grinning. I knew what he was thinking. That for once, we were actually managing to play at being a happy family. That Freddie was opening up, sharing stuff about Dad. That we were *bonding*.

But all I could feel was the deep, stirring hurt of jealousy deep inside of me. I was supposed to be the one who knew everything about Dad. Not Freddie.

"Maybe Mom will make it down for dessert? Should we wait?" Liam asked, clearly getting swept up *way* too far into his domestic bliss dreams. Freddie and I caught each other's eyes again, but this time, I was the one who broke contact, looking back down at my plate. "She has to come home eventually."

"I wouldn't bother," Freddie answered before I could, and maybe there was something to be said for Freddie, who threw out the words bluntly so I didn't have to. Who handled hurting Liam on Mom's behalf.

"Right," Liam said. For another couple of minutes, we picked at our food in silence, before Liam spoke again, asking the room at large:

"Do you think Dad would like it here?"

God, the hits just kept coming.

"What do you mean, Leems?" I kept my voice steady. Freddie's eyes were back on her turkey. Two mentions of Dad in one meal: it had to be some kind of record.

"I've just been wondering." Liam's eyes were cast down toward his plate. "I remember he was—excited about coming here. I was wondering if he'd like it. Freddie, what do you think?"

Freddie looked up at the same time that Liam did, and for the second the two of them locked eyes, I saw something pass across her face. Something like sadness.

But it was Freddie, and she didn't *have* feelings, so it disappeared immediately.

"Probably, Liam. I don't know. I guess."

"Yeah, but you remember him better than any of us." Go ahead and chainsaw my emotions, why don't you. "Would he be happy here?" I felt what Liam was asking. *Could we have been happy?*

I doubted Freddie had an answer. I sure as hell didn't.

"Well, as fun as this has been"—Freddie pushed herself back from the table, picked up her plate as she moved toward the kitchen—"I think I'll take my dessert to go." Before either Liam or I could say anything—although I had no idea what I would say—she was gone, dropping her plate in the kitchen sink with a clatter just before I heard the screen door slam shut behind her.

That, at least, fit the Freddie I knew.

"Come on." I grabbed my plate, and Liam's, too, carried them into the kitchen where the store-bought pumpkin pie was slowly separating from its too-dense crust. "Pull up that video again, okay? The whipped cream one."

That was how Liam and I moved through the rest of the night. Slowly, going through the motions of Thanksgiving. Like projections in a haunted house that looped the same ghosts again and again and again.

And Mom, of course, never showed up.

Chapter Twenty-Five

The next few weeks passed in fits and starts. When I was with Kit, the time flew. We were mostly in the library, alternating between work on our project and my application to Wieland College, a small school Kit had found for me because I hadn't thought of anything else. Each brush of Kit's elbow against mine, sitting too close together at beat-up wooden tables, felt like a million volts of instant power into my system.

I did consider asking him if he wanted to take a walk that just happened to end behind the bleachers, but decided against it. Whatever we were building toward deserved more than Northanger's favorite make-out spot, even if Kit would probably look hot as hell pushed up against the back of it.

Focus, Tilney. Focus.

But focus was a losing battle. My classes, for one, seemed to have slowed to a near stop. At least in Skinner's we were mostly spending the entire period working with our partners, but in every other class, my attention was completely out the window. A few times, Priya had hung around outside the door into journalism, trying to grab me to catch up, to ask if I'd checked my spam folder for my Udolpho answer, but I always made up excuses not to talk. "Okay," she'd said each time, giving me a half wave that would have made me feel terrible if I wasn't already feeling terrible about everything else. "I'll text you!" And she would, and I'd answer, but not in a way that kept a conversation going, because if I let her in, I was too fragile not to break. I didn't want her—or Izzy, especially not Izzy—to see all the cracks that had formed in my armor, all the ways my mask of perfection had become undeniably permeable.

Izzy had texted me a few times, too, always about Kit or Cry Fest. *He's ready to give his speech, right? You're still going, aren't you? You better not leave early this year! I've got some amazing surprises planned!* Clearly, it was the only thing she could concentrate on these days, which was fine with me, because I didn't need Izzy turning her concentration ray gun in my direction. It was bad enough that she was pointing it at Kit—she had, as promised, made him come to a few Cry Fest planning sessions, and he'd texted me selfies of all the glitter that had ended up in his hair. It sounded like she was being polite to him, at least? Mostly asking him questions about NPSI, about how he'd gotten into ghosts. Which was weird, but whatever. She was probably just trying to impress her dad again. As long as she wasn't being outright cruel to him, Izzy's strange turnaround on Kit was the least of my worries.

Once I got my Wieland app in, I told myself, I'd catch them up on what was going on. But for now, why worry about my friendships with Izzy and Priya when Kit was right there, offering me everything I needed?

Speaking of.

We had our first snowfall in early December, unusually late for the area, and I was mostly happy to be done with the endless rain that had coated Northanger for the last two months. All day, Liam had been texting me screenshots of weather forecasts, hand-drawn arrows pointing at percentages and predicted snowfall. Liam loved snow.

So that Tuesday night, when the first fat flakes of snow fell outside my bedroom window as I was editing my script for Skinner's project, I was mostly thinking about how happy Liam was going to be.

I was *not* expecting a clattering of rocks against my window, echoing through the silence.

"What the hell?" I jumped to my feet to investigate, half afraid it was going to be some lost late-night ghost tour that wanted after-hours access to the headmistress's house. But when I flung my window open, wincing at the sudden rush of cold air, I had a much more pleasant surprise waiting for me.

Kit Morland, bundled in the puffiest jacket I'd ever seen, standing in the snow-dusted garden just below my window, grinning up at me through the flurries.

"What are you doing?" I whispered, my heart racing in my chest, half from the surprise and half because it was Kit. "It's almost curfew."

"Everyone knows curfew doesn't count when there's snow. Did I tell you I've never seen snow before?" His cheeks were bright red, his grin massive, and I couldn't keep myself from smiling back. "And since you're my official Northanger Abbey guide, I thought it was only right that you be part of my first snow-based experience."

"So you, what, came all the way down here?" No one had ever broken a rule for me before Kit, and I was starting to realize how much I liked it. "You're going to get locked out of your dorm."

"Maybe. But it's worth the risk to see you."

Sometimes I wondered if Kit Morland was specifically designed to capture my heart.

"Be right there." I closed the window again, grabbed a coat to pull over my pajamas. Downstairs, I added boots and a pom-pomed hat, then stepped out into the whirling snow, closing the door behind me as quietly as possible. The rest of the house was dark, either asleep or still out, but either way, we were alone.

When I crossed into the garden, Kit's grin hadn't faded.

"This is way cooler than the fake snow they pump out at Disney World." He held his hand out to me, and I took it without thinking, letting him pull me toward him as the snow fell heavily around us. As first snows went, this was a good one, thick without being too wet, beautiful without being obstructive. Tomorrow, the entire campus would be coated in a heavy layer of white, and Kit was going to flip.

"You've really only seen fake snow?" It felt like we were outside of time out here, away from consequences and tomorrows in our own quiet pocket universe. "I hope this lives up to your expectations."

"How could it not?" He looked straight at me as he said it, and my heart fluttered. Even as snow gathered on his knit cap, settled on his shoulders, danced around his face, he just kept looking at me. Seeing me. "All of this is so much more—so much better—than I ever expected."

Maybe it was the snow. Maybe it was the quiet. Maybe it was the feeling that it was just the two of us, that maybe it had always been just the two of us, that to keep holding myself back from this boy was a mistake I didn't need to keep making.

Either way. Something about the snow made me brave, as I finally—*finally*—reached up, laid my free hand on the back of his head, let it tangle in his hair. Let myself look back at him just as hard. Let my eyes ask the question I'd known the answer to for weeks.

He answered anyway.

"Hattie," he said, his voice quiet. "You have no idea how much I want to kiss you right now."

"Yeah?" Our faces were drifting closer together, our breath mingling. "Show me."

Kit's lips crashed against mine, and even in the freezing cold air he was the sun. My other hand went up into his hair, pressing against his neck to pull him closer to me. He responded with hands on my waist, tugging me closer so that I was flush against his body or at least, flush against his puffer coat. Our mouths moved together as we searched for warmth, for each other.

Everything felt better when I was holding Kit, when he was holding me. When was the last time I'd felt protected? Taken care of? Like I could find safety in anyone's arms but my own, like there was anyone standing between me and the brink of total collapse, ready to pull me back from the edge.

Or even better, someone who would jump over the brink with me. Who made the unknown feel a hell of a lot less terrifying than it did otherwise.

We broke apart finally, dusted with snow. Kit was beaming.

"I was worried you'd make me wait forever." His arms were still around my waist, his hands connected at the small of my back, and I cradled him in return, my hands around his neck like we were dancing. "I would have, of course. But I'm glad I don't have to."

"Can you believe you kissed a nonbeliever?" I was drunk on him. On this night, on the snow and the cold. "This is just one more thing you're going to have to hide from the scholarship committee, you know."

"I can make it work." He bent down and kissed me again, less urgently this time, as the snow kept falling around us. "You're the one who kissed a ghost hunter."

"Yeah, well." Something bubbled up in my chest, a feeling like nerves, like anxiety, but it wasn't a feeling I wanted to explore at the moment. "I have to warn you. This sort of thing doesn't happen every time it snows." I dropped my hands from around Kit's neck and stepped back, putting some distance between us. He let me, even as he watched me curiously. "You've gotten kind of spoiled."

"What if it could?" While my voice had been light, joking, Kit's was suddenly all serious, and my chest tightened. "What are you running from, Hattie?"

Before I could answer (thank God, because I didn't know how to answer), the garden was suddenly flooded with light.

"Hattie?" My heart sank in my chest as the back door to the house creaked open, revealing my mother on the other side, dressed in a bathrobe and looking confused. "What are you doing out here? And—Mr. Morland?"

Kit looked stricken. I didn't blame him.

"Kit was just dropping off some recording equipment I needed!" The lie flew out fast, my brain working double time to make up for my actions. Mom raised one eyebrow, but didn't stop me. "I needed a file that was on one of his cameras. For our project. And the file was too big to email, and Dropbox wasn't working, and—"

"Stop." Mom waved her hand in front of her, her eyes closing for just a second. She seemed more tired than I'd seen her in . . . a while. "It's almost curfew, Mr. Morland."

"Yes, ma'am." Kit's voice was small, and all I wanted to do was take his hand, but there was no way I was going to do that in front of Dr. Tilney.

"Well, then." She looked pointedly toward the path that led back to campus. "I suggest you get moving."

"Of course. I—" He glanced down at me, then back to the doorway where my mom was still standing. "I'll talk to you later, Hattie." And then he was gone, taking off at a light jog back to campus, away from my mom, away from me.

When I turned around, she was still watching me.

"I better get back to work." I clearly wasn't holding any equipment, but it didn't seem like she was going to mention it. "Lots to do."

"Of course." Mom watched me for a moment longer before she stepped aside to let me back in. Turning the light off in the garden, where I had been, for a brief moment, perfectly and completely happy. "Good night, Hattie."

"Night, Mom," I said, but she was gone, the door to her office closing behind her.

And I was left standing in the hallway, wondering what I had done.

Chapter Twenty-Six

The morning dawned bright and clear, and the campus of Northanger was, in fact, covered in snow. I would have enjoyed it more if I wasn't filled with nerves over what my mom would say to me today. Of course, she could easily ignore the situation like she ignored everything else in my life, but that didn't make the waiting any better.

I was helped, at least, by a text from Kit, the first thing I saw on my phone when I woke up.

Is it bad that I miss you already?
This is the first time in my life I'm not excited for
winter break.

Yeah, that'd helped, as I held the phone against my chest and tried to breathe like a person. I could manage my mom's reaction. I had Kit.

Besides, it turned out that I wasn't going to have to wait very long to see what Dr. Tilney's reaction was, since my mom was sitting at the dining room table with breakfast laid out in front of her when I came downstairs.

"Mom." She gave me a small smile as I walked in, which managed to throw me even more. "You're still here."

"Yes. I thought we should talk about last night." She leaned back in her chair, sipped at her coffee as she watched me. Dr. Tilney always looked tired, but today it was even more pronounced than usual. "About Mr. Morland."

"Oh." It figured that *now* was the time she chose to care about something to do with me. She couldn't have been there when I got the Udolpho rejection, or when we were supposed to have my senior meeting. No, she just had to stumble across my snowy, sexually charged rendezvous. "What . . . what about him?"

"Hattie." The look she gave me was stern. "I know you two have been growing . . . closer." Oh, God. This wasn't the birds and the bees talk, was it? Mom had avoided ever giving that to me, enlisting Freddie instead when I turned eleven, which was one of the more traumatic experiences of my young life. "Is that a fair assessment?"

"He—I—um." So articulate. "I'm just trying to be a good ambassador," I finally managed, although I was pretty sure there was nothing in the ambassador guidebook about late-night wonder at the first snow.

"Right." If it had been anyone else, I would have called my mom's tone sarcastic. "Well. Don't let it distract you from your studies." As if. Yes, I was pretty wildly distracted from my studies at this point, but that wasn't Kit's fault. Most days, it felt like Kit was the only thing tethering me to the ground.

Is it bad that I miss you already?

Suddenly, I had an absolutely wild idea, one that had almost zero chance of working, but what the hell, right? Why not try to be happy for once in my life? All I'd ever done was go along with what the people around me wanted. Mom. My teachers. Izzy. Kit was the only person who'd never asked anything of me. And I didn't want to let him go, even for a second.

"Actually, I wanted to ask you something." I sat down in the chair across from my mother, hard, and she looked at me with surprise. "Kit and I really need more time to work on our journalism project, and his parents are traveling over the holidays, so he doesn't really have anywhere to go." An absolute lie, but if I was going to ask for something so huge, I needed more than *I want it* to get anything from my mom. "I thought maybe he could stay here. With us."

The silence that followed was so long that, if I wasn't talking to my mom in person, I would assume our connection had broken. Words were building up in me, threatening to spill out, but I knew I needed to hold my ground. Stay quiet.

Finally, Mom spoke. "There are dorms open during winter break for students who aren't able to go home."

"Yeah, but is that really in the ambassador spirit?" I tried my best to look as earnest as possible. "Please, Mom. He's Liam's friend, too. I just think it would be really nice to have him around. And I bet he'd tell the NPSI board, and they'd be extra eager to up their donations."

"I don't think it's a good idea, Hattie." Mom began to stand up, the issue clearly settled, and I couldn't let her walk away from this, I just couldn't.

"Dad would let him stay."

The words were out before I could stop myself, and my mom froze in her tracks, one hand on the back of her chair, the other one clutching her to-go mug of coffee like it was a lifeline. I shouldn't have said it. I knew that, but it was too late now to take it back.

"Fine."

The word was short and clipped out of my mother's mouth, and it took everything in me not to audibly gasp.

"Just—fine. He sleeps in Liam's room." And before I could say anything else, before I could say thank you or I'm sorry (not that there was anything to be sorry about, I told myself, because if Mom was that affected by me even mentioning Dad it would be proof she had emotions, and that was clearly out of the question), she was gone. Slipped into her office with the door closed firmly behind her.

Oh my God. I'd done it. I'd actually done it.

Well, except for the part where I *asked* Kit if he, in fact, wanted to stay. But compared to facing my mom, that would be a complete walk in the park.

⁂

"What do you think?" I was in my room, sitting cross-legged on the bed as I FaceTimed Kit. I'd called him as soon as I could, not even wanting to wait until I saw him on campus, so that I'd at least know one way or another if I should get excited or not. "Do you want to stay?"

"Your mom wants me there?" Kit sounded skeptical, and I guessed I couldn't blame him. I wasn't about to tell him that she had been about to say no, until I mentioned Dad. I didn't need to drag Kit into any more of my weird family trauma than he was already involved with.

"She said it was okay." I shifted as I leaned back, resting my head against the wall.

"I guess. And . . . you want me?"

"Yes." I saw Kit flush just a little, and felt my heart pound.

I should just say it. Say what I'd been thinking ever since I'd issued this invitation, what I'd been thinking for a long time before that.

"I've been scared of . . . this. From the first time I saw you, honestly. And every time after that." Kit smirked as I kept going. "I know last night I— I don't want to run away again. I'm not scared anymore." I took a deep breath. No going back now. Screw Northanger and its expectations. Screw my future. This was the only thing I'd felt certain about in months. Wanting Kit was the only instinct I had. "So. Yes. If yesterday was not the full implication you needed. I want you."

Kit let out a deep whoosh of breath.

Same.

But I tried to keep it casual, to act like I hadn't just given into an urge that felt like jumping off a cliff.

"Come on," I added. There was no way my tone was actually light or casual enough to disguise my nerves. "Don't you want to experience real winter? More snow? Not that Florida nonsense."

"You haven't experienced Christmas until you've seen an alligator in a Santa hat, thank you very much." The corners of his mouth quirked up into a smile. "I have to talk to my parents, but they'll probably be cool with it? Maybe I can convince them to use the money they save on flights to buy me a really good present."

"Hope springs eternal." Just like it did in me. "You want to stay?"

"On one condition."

"I'm afraid sharing a room with Liam is nonnegotiable." I grinned as Kit flushed again. "Dr. Tilney has insisted."

"That's not— You're the worst." Kit half coughed, half laughed. "No. If I'm going to stay at Northanger over winter break, I want us to do a stakeout. A real one."

And suddenly, all that excitement was replaced with dread.

"You're sure?" It wasn't that I was worried about ghosts. Because how could I be? But that seemed . . . logistically challenging. Emotionally challenging. "I thought we decided to just use voice-over and still photos for the third act. Plus the footage we get from Cry Fest. If we add more content now, it'll mean more work in edits."

"Yeah, but if we have the chance to get some *actual* footage related to the twins . . ." Kit's voice pitched lower, and a shiver went down my spine. "Besides, I wouldn't mind wandering the abbey after dark with you."

I'd spent three years being so safe. Being so careful.

Screw it.

"Okay," I whispered, and Kit fist-pumped triumphantly on his end of the call. "Deal."

Chapter Twenty-Seven

T he week before winter break was always useless at Northanger, especially with Cry Fest taking over the last day of classes. Some schools might throw a big holiday dance or give out candy canes in the halls, but not Northanger. No, instead the campus was flooded with *What Cries Beneath* enthusiasts, pushing through crowds and screaming in glee whenever they saw a plot-relevant statue. We had a half day of classes in the morning, and then the festivities began: a full afternoon and evening of carnival games, activities, and shenanigans to raise money for the school.

It was a lot. It also meant that, because it was a uniform-free day, I was currently dressed in a short black skirt with red tights, a bright red tank top, and a black cardigan dripping with red pom-poms and rhinestones.

"This seems aggressive, guys." I had Izzy and Priya on speaker phone as I got dressed that morning, staring the cardigan down in my room. If Izzy hadn't ordered these back in

September, I'd have a better excuse not to wear it. As it was, there didn't seem to be a way out. "You're sure it's meant to have this many pom-poms? It looks like a craft store exploded onto a Hot Topic."

"It's *distinctive*," Izzy said, and I heard Priya agree in the background. Their voices seemed too loud for my room, tinny and unfamiliar. "Come on, Hattie. This is the first Cry Fest I'm actually in charge of. I need my girls to present a united front with me."

"The alternative outfit involved wigs, if that helps," Priya chimed in, and I shook my head. But Izzy was right. This was important to her, which meant it had to be important to me, too. *One more day,* I reminded myself. *One more day, and then you won't have to worry about any of this.* And at least Kit would be at Cry Fest this year, automatically making it significantly more bearable than usual. I'd felt antsy, ever since Kit had agreed to stay for winter break. Like the school version of me was a suit a size too small I was itching to get out of.

We hadn't kissed again since that night a week ago. Partially because we hadn't been alone together, always surrounded by other students or, at the very least, Liam and Erik, who had taken to joining us for our library study sessions. We *definitely* hadn't discussed what the kiss meant for us, for our friendship. And while the idea of adding some sort of label to whatever we were made me wildly anxious, it might be worth dealing with that discussion if it meant I got to feel his lips on mine again.

Yikes, this cardigan was warm.

"Fine," I said with a dramatic sigh, and through the phone,

Priya cheered. "What's today's schedule of events, Iz? I don't want to miss anything important."

"Of course you don't." I could hear Izzy moving around the room, probably gathering up last-minute supplies and piling them into Priya's arms. The thought felt almost nostalgic. "The festival is pretty basic. Rides, games, blood-colored hot chocolate, blah-blah-blah. Dad'll talk, introduce Ghost Boy, you're welcome. And I've got a special surprise planned that you'll *love*, Hats."

"Sounds good." I was a little distracted, trying to find my one pair of black boots, so I was only half listening, but Priya could steer me in the right direction later. "I'll see you soon, okay?"

After we said our goodbyes, I added a layer of black lipstick and some complicated eye makeup, per Izzy's *very* specific instructions, then took a deep breath. This was never my favorite day. But with Kit by my side, I was going to get through it, and then I wouldn't have anything to worry about for two whole glorious weeks.

One more day. I could do this.

I didn't see Kit until after class let out early that afternoon, but when he *did* finally see me, his jaw absolutely dropped.

"Oh my God." He'd met me by my locker, planning to walk down to the carnival on the quad together, but from the way he was looking at me, it seemed more likely that he was going to drag me into the nearest closet instead. Score one for the cardigan. "You look—Hattie. Did you break into my dream journal? Is this my Christmas gift?"

"Black lipstick's your thing, huh?" I blushed, but I didn't mind the attention. Not from Kit. I tucked a strand of hair behind my ear—Izzy had insisted I straighten it, and it hung low and long around my shoulders—and struck a dramatic pose, leaning back against my locker with one hand on my hip. "Did you always have crushes on girls who worked at haunted houses?"

"Absolutely." He stepped forward, his arm coming up beside my head so that I was boxed in completely, and my heart skipped a beat before he seemed to remember where we were. "Um. Anyway. You look great." He stepped back, held out a hand for me to shake, and I took it, laughing. "Well done. Send my regards to the costuming department."

"You look nice, too, you know." He wasn't a Gothic wonderland like I was, but I far from minded. His suit and tie, which he'd put on to impress the NPSI board members who would be in full attendance today, wasn't *that* different from our regular uniform, but it fit him well, even given his height. "Sharp."

"We look like a rookie detective and a moody teenager who paired up to solve a crime, and I wouldn't have it any other way." Kit held his hand out to me, and even though we were surrounded by hundreds of other people streaming out of the school and toward the festival, I had eyes only for him. I put on my peacoat, took his hand in mine, squeezed once, and followed him out.

Wow. Izzy had really outdone herself this year.

Our quad had been transformed basically into a haunted carnival. Tents striped in black and red formed rows in front of us, beckoning us with the smells of fried foods and cara-mel apples. Stilt walkers with ghastly makeup leered over the festivalgoers, a mix of students, people from town, and the die-hard *Cries* fans who came out every year in hopes of meet-ing J.T. Thorpe. (Izzy's dad was always way too busy for a dedicated meet and greet, but she *had* set up a tent where you could meet one of the actors, and the line for that already wrapped around half the school.) Spooky music was being piped in from somewhere; and next to me, Kit's face split into a broad grin.

"This is officially the best high school in the world," he declared, and I laughed, because even though I suspected he couldn't be further from the truth, it was nice to see him so happy. A little preview, almost, of what I hoped the next few weeks would hold for us. Sure, I was looking forward to the campus clearing out . . . but seeing Kit like this, caught up in the Northanger hullabaloo, was pretty nice, too.

"Come on," he said, grabbing my hand and tugging me to-ward the festival. From the other end of the quad, a huge Ferris wheel loomed over us (with black and red spokes, of course), just starting its operation. "I've got a little time before I need to start schmoozing all the NPSI people, and I want to spend that time eating as many corn dogs as I can physically handle and winning you a stuffed animal from a rigged car-nival game."

"You know I can win my own stuffed animals, right?" I laughed, letting him pull me into the madness, past face-painting booths and squirt gun games, jugglers with painted-on smiles and a woman selling haunted flower crowns.

"I know." He stopped us in front of the flower crown woman, who I recognized, now that we were closer, as my sophomore-year science teacher, Ms. McGervey. I gave her a half-hearted wave while Kit reached for a crown of red and black roses, woven together with gold ribbons that hung down across the back. I didn't know what, exactly, made it haunted, but knowing Izzy, she had just thrown as many scary-sounding adjectives onto the festival booths as she could and called it a day. "But just because you can doesn't mean you can't let me do it anyway."

As he placed the crown carefully on my head, Ms. McGervey oohing and aahing in the background, I felt something I hadn't felt for a long time. Settled. Safe. And I was at school! At a major school event surrounded by everyone and everything that usually made me an anxious mess!

"I can pay for it," I protested as Kit pulled out his phone and tapped it against the iPad that Ms. McGervey held up in front of him.

"Too late," he said, and before I could push back again, I was hit by a stroke of inspiration.

"Fine." I grabbed a matching crown, reached up high, and placed it on Kit's head, settling it gently so it wouldn't get all tangled in his hair. He'd forgone his usual beanie in deference to his suit, and honestly, he looked a lot more like himself with something on his head. "Then I'm getting this one for you."

"Who would ever turn down a gift like that?" Kit grinned as he adjusted the crown, and as I paid Ms. McGervey that settled feeling, that safe feeling, only grew stronger.

And I owed it all to this marvelous, magnificent, ridiculous ghost hunter.

Chapter Twenty-Eight

Alas, after about forty-five minutes of corn dogs and ring toss games (none of which we won), Izzy popped up out of nowhere, effectively ending our spooky carnival fun.

"There you are!" Izzy looked the picture of goth perfection. She had a coat on over her cardigan and skirt, too, but it was made entirely of black lace and embroidered flowers, which was way more on-theme than my blue peacoat. "Kit, we needed you at the stage, like, ten minutes ago. It's almost time for your speech."

"Oops." Kit grinned down at me, sheepish, and even though I could *feel* Izzy rolling her eyes in our direction, I flushed anyway. "Guess I lost track of time."

"It's a great carnival, Iz," I added, even as she waved her hand in my direction to dismiss me. "You crushed it."

"I did, didn't I?" She looked around, self-satisfaction written all over her face. The expression flickered for only a second as she said, "Dad doesn't appreciate it, of course.

Said he didn't understand why I didn't just hire an event planner."

"I'm sorry."

"Don't be. I obviously don't care." Izzy rolled her eyes as she deflected, just like she always did. "Luckily, the fun is just beginning." She threw a wink in my direction, then grabbed Kit by the elbow and pulled him toward her. "Come on. My dad wants to talk to you before the speech. Hattie, Priya's over by the gates already; you can go hang out with her."

"Okay, thanks, I— Good luck!" I shouted, because Izzy hadn't even let me finish my sentence before she'd pulled Kit away, marching him determinedly to the small stage set up back by the gates to the school. He waved over his shoulder to me, and then they were both gone, leaving me standing alone in the middle of the world's most haunted carnival.

Great.

Without my protective shields of either Kit or Izzy, I darted toward the school gates as fast as I could, keeping my head down so I didn't have to talk to anyone I might pass along the way. Another hour, maybe two, and I'd be out of here. We didn't have to stay too long after Kit's speech, I reasoned. Let him schmooze, let me get some face time in with Izzy and Priya, and then . . . winter break bliss.

Priya was, as promised, standing in the small crowd that had formed in front of the stage, which was set just in front of the part of the gates that read *The Abbey Lives On*. She waved when she caught my eye, dressed in our matching outfits but with her Northanger track jacket tossed on over the cardigan.

"Hattie!" She pulled me into a hug as soon as I made it over. "There you are. I've barely seen you in weeks." A pang of guilt coursed through me.

"I've been doing a lot of recording. For Skinner's project." And a lot of panicked college application work, and a lot of staring at Kit and thinking about his mouth, but she didn't need to know that. I could work on being a decent friend to Priya again next semester, I reminded myself, once I got my own life in order.

"I can't believe you've spent so much time around ghost stuff." Priya shook her head. "But at least it's almost over, right?"

"I guess." That was *not* a path I was going to go down with Priya, thank you very much. "How are your applications going?" It was a guaranteed way to distract her, and sure enough, Priya's eyes widened before she launched into a monologue about the short answer questions she was currently working on.

"And, like, they need to have a cohesive theme, but they need to still be different answers, and I just—" Before Priya could go any further, the crowd (which had grown bigger at this point, a mix of students and *Cries* enthusiasts) broke out into applause as J.T. Thorpe, Izzy's dad, took the stage.

Mr. Thorpe looked a lot like his daughter—blond hair, high cheekbones, piercing eyes. Their most common shared attribute, though, was the way they commanded a crowd. The applause only got louder as he stepped up to a small podium, and his wide smile seemed to welcome all of us without words.

"Thank you, thank you!" he finally said, once the cheering quieted down. "I'm J.T. Thorpe"—more cheers—"and I'm so excited to be back at Northanger Abbey for this year's Cry Fest. Before we really kick off the festivities, I want to take a moment to acknowledge the students responsible for putting all of this together—led, naturally, by my daughter, Isabella Thorpe. Belle, why don't you come on up?"

The cheers continued as I watched Izzy step onto the stage, her face a careful mask of feigned surprise. But she should be happy, right? Her dad being proud of her—this was what she wanted.

Mr. Thorpe continued.

"I'm just so thrilled to have my daughter continuing the family legacy of spooktacular celebrations." He squeezed his arm around Izzy's shoulders, and for a second, I thought I saw a flash of annoyance pass over her face—but it was gone so quickly I figured I had to be mistaken. Mr. Thorpe gave her a nod and she stepped back, waving to the crowd as she hopped back off the stage. "And speaking of students . . . some of you know that this year, the board has partnered with NPSI—that's the National Paranormal Society of Investigators, for those of you more new to the field—to enroll our first student here at Northanger through their scholarship program. I believe that NPSI has found one of the brightest young paranormal enthusiasts that these United States have to offer, and I'm just so thrilled to hear how well he's doing here at Northanger Abbey. Now, if you don't mind, I'd like to have him up to say just a few words. Please put your hands together for Kit Morland!"

Kit ran up to the stage with so much enthusiasm that he almost tripped over the top stair, catching himself just in time. He grinned, shaking Mr. Thorpe's hand, before stepping up to the podium. He'd left on the flower crown, I realized, and my stomach flipped.

But as he started talking, going on about how he'd always dreamed about coming to Northanger Abbey, I started to notice murmurs spreading through the audience. People—and it was almost entirely students, I realized—were pulling out their phones, reading something on the screens, and then leaning in close to whisper to one another, eyes wide. When I glanced over at Priya, her eyes were still on Kit, so I pulled out my phone to check it, just in case.

What I saw made my stomach drop out of my body entirely.

It was an email notification, sent to my school account, from some sort of anonymous email address that was all scrambled letters and numbers. The subject line read: "GHOSTED: Northanger Abbey's 'Ghost Hunter Scholarship' Prime Example of School That's Lost Its Way."

As I clicked through to the email, which led me to a Substack account, a picture of Kit in his uniform appeared next to a block of text. I skimmed it quickly, and it seemed to be just what it said—a takedown of Northanger's obsession with the paranormal. That might have been all well and good, but whoever wrote this had clearly talked to Kit and done their best to make him sound like some sort of ghost-crazed lunatic who didn't deserve to be at Northanger.

"There's ghosts all around us, you know?" Morland runs his hands through his hair again, just a few steps away from becoming a full-on meme. "Every hallway you turn down. Every door that

doesn't quite close. They're everywhere." From the way his eyes
dart back and forth as he speaks, one has to wonder if he's seeing
ghosts right now.

The article went on from there, littering in as many out-
of-context Kit quotes as possible to frame him—and the
school—in the worst possible light. And the worst part was,
even though the article was signed *Anonymous*, I had a sinking
suspicion that I knew exactly who had written it.

Kit must have finished his speech while I was reading the
post, because when I looked up, he was being ushered to a
VIP tent by some of the *Cries* team, Mr. Thorpe was telling
everyone to have an amazing festival, and Izzy was strolling
toward me and Priya, her eyes gleaming.

When she stopped in front of us, I didn't bother to say anything. Just held up my phone to her. And while I didn't really
expect her to deny it, I didn't expect her to look so gleeful,
either.

"Surprise!" Even though she was holding cotton candy, she
clapped her hands in front of her as Priya looked over at us
with confusion. "Told you, Hats. Do you like it?"

"Do I *like* it?" My anger was rising, my blood starting to
boil. Out of the corner of my eye, I saw Priya pull out her
phone, let out a little yelp of surprise when she saw her notification. "Why would you do something like this, Iz?"

"Um, because I needed a scathing piece of journalism for
my Northwestern portfolio, duh." Izzy tossed her hair over
her shoulder, looked at me like I was an idiot. "Maybe if
I had a letter of recommendation from Dr. Tilney I could

have gotten away with my portfolio as it was, but without it I needed *something*." As if that was an excuse. As if anything could be an excuse for this.

"And that something needed to tear down Kit?"

"Oh my God, Hats." She rolled her eyes. "It takes down the *ghosts*. All of this stupid paranormal nonsense. Kit was just, like, a journalistic example. An exposé needs to actually expose something, you know. Otherwise it's just a rant. If the board happens to realize what a dumb idea a ghost-hunting scholarship is, that's just an extra added bonus."

"Your dad's going to kill you." Priya was scrolling through the article, her eyes wide.

"No, he's not." Izzy sighed, like she was explaining this to children. "That's why it's *anonymous*. I'm untraceable. It's the best of both worlds, right? Dad can still think I'm all on board with ghost shit, and Northwestern can appreciate my awesome writing. Bonus, maybe people actually wake up and realize that their high school shouldn't also operate as a haunted house."

"That's still not an excuse to drag Kit into this." I kept picturing him up on the stage, looking so thrilled to be there. How crushed he was going to be when he saw this, if he hadn't already. "You were supposed to be helping him."

"Oh, please," Izzy hissed, her eyes flashing. For a second, she looked like she'd been caught in something. But then her smirk returned, except this time, there was a layer of viciousness beneath it. "What did I do that's so bad, exactly? I got your stupid little boyfriend his forgiveness from the board. It's not like they're going to hold this against him; if anything, they'll probably rally around him and give him extra money to buy a ghost detector or something."

"That doesn't make it right."

"Suddenly we're concerned about what's *right?*" She glared at me, her expression made even more menacing by all the black lace. "The whole reason we've ever hung out is so that I could manipulate things around you to make your life easier. I got you friends, I got you a place at this school. Now I finally do something for me, instead of waiting for you to deliver on something you were *never* going to do, and I'm this huge villain?"

"That's not what I meant."

"All I know is that you spent this whole semester with Ghost Boy instead of with us." Izzy's voice was sharp, and when I glanced over at Priya, she looked down at the ground, quick. Priya never got involved when Izzy turned on me, and I never stood by her, either. I was starting to think that had been a mistake. "You used to want to help me, too. Just like I've always helped you. But suddenly you've got *Kit* and that all goes out the window. I saw you two earlier, you know. Saw the way you were with him. And I don't actually care if you want to hide how you're really feeling all the time and pretend everything is fine with your family—and it's clearly not, because we've met Freddie, and it's obvious things aren't all hunky-dory there. But showing him who you really are, when you've *never* done that for us, that sucks, Hattie." If I didn't know Izzy better, I'd think that she looked hurt. But this was Izzy Thorpe. She'd never been hurt in her life.

She kept going.

"So, yeah, maybe I took things into my own hands." She shrugged. "Sue me."

I'd learned, over the years, the best way to navigate an argument with Izzy. Back down, let her get it out of her system, wait three days for her to decide she was over whatever you apparently did. I'd done it a dozen times before—so had Priya, who was watching all of this go down with wide eyes—and I'd never thought it was a problem. This was the price I had to pay, I'd told myself, for having a place at Northanger Abbey. For the reputation Izzy had gained me, as someone who was at least casually fun, who was more than just Dr. Tilney's daughter. It was what I had agreed to, back in freshman year. What I'd always accepted.

But after spending this semester by Kit's side instead of hers . . . I didn't want to be treated like that anymore.

"You know what?" I stepped forward, pressing into Izzy's space, so much so that she half stumbled back, not expecting me. No one ever did. "*Screw* you, Izzy."

"Excuse me?"

"You can't hate me because I found someone who actually likes me." My voice was rising, and the festivalgoers around us were starting to look in our direction, but I no longer had it in me to care. "Who doesn't just see me as something useful."

"Guys." Priya stepped forward, then, hands held out between us, entirely too late to stop what was happening. "Come on."

"I'm not going to 'come on,' Priya," I snapped, and I *never* snapped at Priya. From the way she stepped back, that was what she was thinking, too. But Priya and I were only friends through the connective tissue of Izzy. Without her, there was nothing holding the two of us together. "And, Izzy, I'm sorry if me being friends with Kit has sent you into some sort of, like, existential tailspin. But I'm actually happy, for once in my life, and you know what? I think you can tell, and I think that's what you hate the most."

I stepped back. Izzy stared at me, while Priya stared at anything *but* me.

"Whatever, Hattie." Izzy dropped her cotton candy in the nearest trash can, like she was too disgusted by me to eat anything. "I hope you and Ghost Boy have a nice life."

And then she turned and walked away, shoulders back, like they always were. Tall and proud.

If she was hurting, if the sting I was feeling from my best friend of three and a half years walking away from me was something she felt, too . . . she didn't show it.

Typical.

Priya still stood in front of me, shifted from foot to foot for a second before she spoke up. "She's just being Izzy, you know. She'll probably take the post down in, like, a day. She's been really stressed out, with her dad and—"

"I'm tired of her excuses." I was tired of my so-called friends, of this school, of this year. I'd thought I could have both Kit and Northanger. Keep both my reputation and the guy who saw through it. But if I was being forced to pick— and that was what Izzy was making me do—I'd pick Kit. "And

I've forgiven her a million times already. You think I'm not stressed out?"

"How would I know? You never tell us anything." That was *not* like Priya. But I was starting to think I didn't really know either of my so-called friends.

"Yeah, well." I was over this, over Izzy and over Priya, over these stupid Northanger games. I just wanted it to be winter break, wanted to have Kit 24–7 and to let my guard down for, like, a second. I didn't think that was too much to ask. "Sorry."

Priya closed her eyes for a second, frustrated. Fine. Let her be frustrated. She opened her mouth, looked like she was about to say something, but thought better of it. Instead, she turned and left, too, following Izzy into the crowd.

That was that, then.

Just then, Kit came up, his tie loose around his neck, the top button of his shirt unbuttoned. He looked exhausted, but happy. Maybe he hadn't seen the post yet.

"Hey." His smile faded when he saw the look on my face. "Everything okay?"

"Not really." I sighed, because it was probably better to get this over with, and people were starting to stare at Kit, now. "Look."

Kit took my offered phone, scrolled through the post with an unreadable expression. Once he reached the end, he glanced back at me.

"Anonymous, huh?"

"It was Izzy." I shook my head. "I'm sorry, Kit."

"Is that why she just stormed off all Valkyrie-like?"

"I mean, unless someone else called her out on her bullshit between when I did two seconds ago and just now." I sighed. "How are you?"

"Oh, I'm fine. You should have seen some of the stuff kids said about me in Florida. This is the fate of the paranormal enthusiast." He handed my phone back to me with a shrug. "It'll blow over."

"Yeah." Kit was probably right, I told myself. It would pass. And in the meantime . . . I now had an extremely good excuse to leave the festival. "What do you say we get out of here?"

"I'd say . . . that sounds like an excellent idea. Come on." He tilted his head toward the woods behind the dorms. "I ran into Liam earlier. He's convinced he and Erik found a previously undocumented haunted tree or something at the edge of campus."

"Oh God, this again?" I shook my head as Kit looked at me quizzically. "There's a weird tree behind Schumacher that he's been obsessed with since he started here. He used to say it was a portal to Narnia; I guess now that he's a full-on brigader, he's decided ghosts are the most likely answer."

"Sounds like you know where to go."

"That I do. Come on, Morland." And I didn't look around, didn't check to see who might be watching us. Just took his hand, tugged him away from the crowds. Toward me.

Chapter Twenty-Nine

When Kit appeared on our doorstep the next afternoon, Liam and I were both waiting for him on the front steps.

"What ho, weary traveler!" Liam called out, and I rolled my eyes even as Kit grinned, his suitcase bumping along the gravel of our front path. It had snowed again overnight, but though it had mostly melted in the morning sun, he still had to step carefully to avoid slush puddles. "Welcome to our humble abode!"

"Hail and well met, my dudes." Kit's smile only widened as he got up to us, eyes sparkling with his absolute favorite thing—adventure. "I didn't realize I was getting the full Tolkien welcome here."

"Expect the unexpected during your stay at Tilney cottage." I reached out and grabbed his suitcase, pulling it through the doorway. "But not that unexpected, because Liam made a schedule for every single day of our vacation."

"I didn't want us to miss out on anything!" Liam protested

once we were all crowded inside the warm hallway, Kit closing the door behind him. Liam had been even more (visibly) excited than I was when he'd heard Kit was coming to stay with us. It was cute, even if it was going to get in the way of, you know, *me* spending time with Kit. In a one-on-one, meaningful sort of way. "Kit hasn't done a Northanger Abbey Christmas before."

"Is it different from a regular Christmas?"

"For you? More snow, less palm trees," I said, as we all removed our muddy shoes and hung up our jackets by the doorway. The sight of Kit's jacket next to mine did something to me.

"Right," Kit said, with a smirk. "Sure."

"I can take your bag up to my room," Liam offered, grabbing Kit's suitcase. I didn't argue. "You're staying with me. If that's cool?"

"Hell, yeah," Kit said, holding his fist out to bump against Liam's. "How else are we going to stay up all night talking about embarrassing stories from your sister's childhood?"

"Not allowed!" I called, but Liam was already gone, halfway up the stairs and laughing. It was good to hear him laugh.

Then it was just me and Kit, in the hallway, and he was smiling at me, his dark hair messy from the hat he'd worn outside.

"So." He stepped in toward me, not so close that it would be suspicious if someone saw us, but close enough so that I felt the tension between us like it was a physical thing. "How's Liam as a roommate?"

"Terrible," I informed him, trying not to think about how good he smelled. Like outside, like the forest. "I assume, anyway.

He's never actually shared a room with anyone." Kit stepped just a little closer, leaning down, his mouth inches from mine.

"Maybe I can hide out in your room, if things get bad."

Gulp. So we were doing this.

"Maybe," I said, but then Liam was running back down the stairs, and Kit backed away, following Liam into the living room at his request, tossing a wink back over his shoulder at me when Liam wasn't looking.

Yeah. This was going to be *some* winter break.

⸻⸻

Liam's schedule was—in a word—extensive. Determined to give Kit "the true Northanger Christmas experience," he'd filled the days so thoroughly that I barely had time to breathe. Not that I minded—the more time I had for myself, the more I would have to think about the college applications that were due in just a couple of weeks or the texts Izzy kept sending me, asking me to just call her so she could explain. I ignored all of them, deleting them as they came in. NPSI had made a statement in favor of their scholarship program—and by extension, Kit—so if Izzy had been trying to ruin his life with her email blast, it clearly hadn't worked. Still, if she wanted to absolve herself of blame now, I wasn't interested in hearing it.

The first day of break, Liam had made pancakes, terribly, then insisted we take a long walk through the campus, enjoying how quiet it was, empty of students. He'd pointed to different buildings and statues and challenged Kit and me to tell the stories of the ghosts who lived there, and we'd obliged.

While the stories had been foggy at first, they came back to me quickly, as clearly as if I could hear my dad telling them.

"What was the one with the cats?" Liam asked, running his hand over the base of the Learners' Statue.

"Oh." I glanced at Kit, a smile dancing on both of our faces, like we were sharing it. I'd stuck to safe stories, stories I could have conceivably learned just from being a student at Northanger Abbey, but this was one of my favorites. "Northanger had a terrible mouse problem when it first transitioned to education, probably because so many students were hiding food in their rooms when they weren't supposed to."

"Man. The more things change, the more they really do stay the same." Kit shook his head, and I laughed.

"Apparently. But anyway, they started bringing in cats to deal with the mice, but they didn't realize they'd then have, well . . . cats. Tons of cats. Unfixed cats who had kittens who, if you can believe it, grow up to be even more cats. The abbey was basically flooded with them."

"That's awesome." Liam grinned. He'd always wanted a pet, but Mom had never gone for it. Probably the idea of pretending to love one more thing was too much for her. "What happened to them?"

"Not much, honestly." I kicked gravel from beneath my feet, careful to avoid Kit's path. "They eventually brought in a vet to do a bunch of spays and neuters. But the cats that were here were allowed to stay. And so the story goes . . ." I lowered my voice and allowed it to become *slightly* more spooky. Normally, I wouldn't go for the added drama, but the rules were different for Liam. "That if a student leaves food in their room to this day, you can hear phantom meowing coming from under the beds, where the cats would always hide out."

"That has to be a record for least-scary ghost story attributed to Northanger Abbey," Kit said, once Liam nodded, satisfied, and ran up ahead of us. "They only meow? They don't, like, claw at people?"

"Not everything has to be scary, Kit," I told him, a statement I was even starting to believe. "Even at Northanger Abbey."

⁓⁓⁓

On the third day, it *really* snowed, thick blankets of white that enveloped Northanger in soft sheets. Within a few minutes of waking up, Liam was pounding on my door—seriously, whenever it snowed, he reverted to eight years old.

"Hattie!" Pound, pound, pound, as I did my best to put my pillow over my head. "Snow! Come on!"

I didn't want to drag myself out of bed, but once I did, there was Kit, bleary-eyed but smiling. And as we traipsed out into the fresh new world, Liam running ahead of us, Kit took my hand, held it tightly in his.

It was the best reason to get up early I'd had in a long time.

For the most part, I hadn't seen Freddie since break started, which was a welcome relief. I didn't need to hear her snide comments about Kit and his presence here. Mom was around sometimes, but it was still rare, so for the most part it was just Liam, Kit, and me. No terrible family members, no so-called friends . . . it was basically heaven. Sure, I had a brief twinge of something in my gut when I saw the thick layer of snow, thinking of the first big snow we'd had on campus freshman year, when Izzy had organized her entire hall into an epic snowball fight and made sure I was included, too. But a relationship couldn't be held together by nostalgia, I reminded myself. I couldn't let vaguely pleasant memories weaken my resolve, so I pushed the girls out of my head again and got back to Liam- and Kit-based snow adventures.

⁓₩₩⁓

On the fifth day of the break, Liam announced we were going for "a good old-fashioned tromp."

"And what, exactly, is a tromp?" I asked, stirring my bowl of oatmeal. Next to me, Kit was adding brown sugar and berries to his. I relished this new side of Kit, sleepy morning Kit, who didn't wake up properly until after he had his breakfast and was adorably fuzzy in the meantime.

"An aggressive snow walk. Duh." Liam rolled his eyes, his own breakfast basically already finished. "Campus always looks so cool when it's all packed in with snow like this. And then maybe we can go downtown? Check out the game store? I've got a gift card from my birthday."

"And we're sure we don't want to spend a quiet day in the house? Reading next to a fire or something?" We'd basically spent every day outside since vacation started, and I was getting cold just thinking about it.

"We don't even have a fireplace," Liam pointed out, admittedly correct. "Come on. Kit wants to."

When I looked over at Kit, he held up his hands in surrender.

"I have zero opinions. But Liam said if I agreed with him, he'd let me sleep for another ten minutes. I took it."

"Fair enough." I sighed. "I can respect that. But bundle up, okay? It's cold out there."

"Whatever, *Mom*." Liam stuck his tongue at me—wow, wildly mature, great job, Liam—before clearing his bowl to the kitchen.

I had to admit, once we got outside, it was kind of fun. The huge Gothic architecture of Northanger was extra cozy when it was covered in snow, spires and gargoyles barely peeking out among the white. And when we finally made our way downtown to Mazes and More, Liam's favorite indie board game store, he disappeared among the shelves, finally giving me and Kit a second alone.

Kit, who seemed to realize this at the same time I did, leaned back against a shelf and smiled at me.

"Hi."

"Hi." It was cozy here, tucked in the back of the store among the overstock and the secondhand games, as Kit and I stood close together. "How's your day been going?"

"Oh, you know." Kit laughed. "Another day, another chance to get dragged all over creation by your extremely enthusiastic brother."

"He's not normally like this." My chest squeezed. For all that Liam's deep attachment to Kit veered toward the annoying side, it was still the most I'd seen him come out of his shell in . . . years. Kit made him better, just like he did me. "But he really likes you."

"Tilneys have good taste." Kit leaned into me, and my breath caught in my throat; but then he kept reaching, up and back over my shoulder, to check out one of the games there. I did my best to will my heart rate back to normal. "How many games do you think we could combine before we completely lost any chance of playability? Three? Four?"

"I think that depends on what your qualifications for playability are." I turned around, grabbing another game off the shelf. "Really? Must we bring the paranormal into every part of our lives?" I held a game titled, creatively, The Haunting of Bill House. "Is this, like, a knockoff of that Netflix show? Isn't the book public domain?"

"Um, pretty sure this is original content." Kit took the box from me, turned it over to look at the back. "Obviously we're buying this. Get a few more, too—the more dissonant the game experience, the better. We're going to invent a megagame."

"You're sure your true passion isn't game design?" But I perused the shelves anyway, trying to figure out what the worst possible game to combine with Bill House was. "If this works out, you may need to give up the ghost. Literally."

"That was a terrible joke, and I'm mad at you for it." Kit pulled a small game off the shelf with care, doing his best not to dislodge all the others piled around it. "Look, this one's perfect. Pirate Unicorn Shell Attack, Part Two: Revenge of the Shellicorns. It plays six to eight. That means lots of pieces."

"You are the most chaotic person I've ever met in my entire life—you know that?" Obliging, I pulled down a third game. "This one's just called Town. Good sign or bad sign?"

"I don't believe in bad signs, Tilney. Only opportunities."
He grabbed the box from me and added it to the pile at his
feet. "Once we get these home, I'll teach you the true wonders
of Ultimate Board Game Mash-Up."

"Is that a threat?"

"Let's call it a promise." Kit glanced around the aisle,
where we were, in fact, very much alone. Then he leaned forward and kissed me, his mouth pressed up against mine, pushing me back into the shelf so that I could feel the various boxes
jabbing into my back. *Worth it*, I thought, as my hands drifted
up to his neck, his hair soft beneath my fingers. Kit's breath
hitched, and I grinned as he pulled away.

"This is my favorite game mash-up," I said, his ragged breath
warm against my face as he pressed his forehead into mine. "I
call it 'see how long we can stay back here before an employee
finds out and kicks us out of the store.' Do you like it?"

"It has potential." He kissed me again before stepping
back, even as my body protested the distance. "Not sure how
marketable it is, though."

"It's definitely just for us," I agreed, and Kit's smile lit up
my whole world. He reached forward and squeezed my hand,
and the fact that even *that* sent butterflies careening around my
stomach really spoke to just how far gone I was.

As we wandered to the front of the store, where Liam was
deciding between two different sets of D&D dice for the new
campaign he was gearing up to start with Erik—not that I
asked, this was just told to me without warning—I realized I
was having fun.

Fun. Who knew, right?

Chapter Thirty

I'm going into the city overnight."

On a top ten list of things I never expected to hear my mother say, that one would have been deemed too outlandish to even be on it.

We actually had the entire family gathered around the table that morning—well, minus Freddie, plus Kit. But Mom was eating with us for once, and I should have suspected it wasn't just to hang out with the fam. As soon as she made her announcement, Liam and I stared at each other, spoons full of cereal halfway to our mouths.

"Is it for an academic conference or something?" I asked. Mom *never* went anywhere. Sure, she was hardly ever home, but it wasn't because she was gallivanting around the country. She just liked being in her office way more than she liked being with us.

"No, actually." Mom dabbed the side of her mouth with a napkin and took a long sip of her coffee before she spoke again. "A few of my friends from undergrad are getting together, and they asked if I wanted to join them."

"And you said *yes*?" Again, not to put too fine a point on it, but this was not the sort of thing my mom did. Between this and allowing Kit to stay with us in the first place, I was starting to suspect a body-snatching situation.

"I didn't realize I was going to find myself in the middle of the Spanish Inquisition when I told you about this." Mom furrowed her brow.

"I mean, nobody expects—" Kit started to say, but I bumped my knee against his under the table to stop him. Mom didn't do jokes.

"It's just kind of a surprise," Liam choked out, coughing on his Cheerios. Kit gave him a pat on the back and he managed to clear his throat. "That's all."

"No matter." Mom dismissed him, turning to her toast. "The relevant information is that I'll be leaving Saturday morning." Tomorrow. "And I'll be back Sunday around midday. I trust you all can behave yourselves while I'm gone?"

I did my best not to look over at Kit.

"Freddie will be here all weekend, of course." Okay, maybe a little more supervised than I'd hoped, but it was *Freddie*. She'd never cared what I did before, and I doubted she'd start now. "Kit, I hope that will be all right with your parents."

"Sure," he said hastily. "They'll be fine with whatever you think."

"Good." She nodded, firm. "Then it's settled."

I felt anything but settled as we returned to our breakfast, the dining room falling into the same unnatural silence it always did when Mom was eating with us. This was good, right? That was a full twenty-four-hour period where Mom would be gone. Leaving me in the house, with Kit. Basically alone. Liam would be here, obviously. And Freddie, allegedly. But still. I should have been thrilled.

But I didn't know. Something about the way she'd said "it's settled." Something about the texts from Izzy that were *still* appearing on my phone, though less frequently now. I'd had moments of bliss this winter break, sure, but I still kept getting hit by reminders that things weren't quite right. That I wasn't actually living the perfect happy-family mirage that Liam and I had constructed for Kit. That my moments of happiness were a temporary reprieve from my life, not a part of it.

But I had to shake it off. A whole overnight without any (real) adult supervision. That could offer me one hell of a reprieve.

Kit must have had similar ideas, because he cornered me in the upstairs hallway after breakfast, one arm against the wall as he leaned next to me with a devilish smile.

"So your mom is going to be gone, huh?"

"Looks like it." Infuriatingly, I blushed. *Come on, Tilney*, I urged myself. I was a senior in high school, for goodness' sake. Practically an adult. "Have you been making plans?"

"Maybe." His smile only grew wider, and my heartbeat sped up, thump, thump, thumping in my chest. "I was thinking it could be the perfect opportunity for that ghost-hunting stakeout you promised."

That was *not* the plan I was hoping for. All of a sudden,

that Kit-focused escape I was looking forward to? Just gained a whole lot of extra emotional baggage.

"Right. Of course!" I tried to keep my voice casual, like *of course* I was also thinking about a stakeout, and not how long Kit could be in my room with the door closed before Liam got suspicious. "Our stakeout. Sure."

"Hattie Tilney." Kit pressed his hand against his chest in mock horror, and I felt the blush spread over my neck and face. "You didn't think I was insinuating something else, did you?"

"Definitely not." My laugh came out strangled. "Why would I think that? Obviously I'm team ghost, all the time. Let's go find some. Or not. Because they aren't real." My head was spinning, and Kit was still grinning. "But, stakeout. Yes. For sure."

"You really should have joined the speech and debate team. Your talent for extemporaneous speaking? Inspiring." I knew he was joking, but it didn't help the heat flooding my cheeks. "Let me plan it, okay? I've got some ideas."

"Like almost letting locked doors close behind us?"

"*One* time." He shook his head. "Come on. I'll let you double-check all of our work once we're out there. But let me do this for you. It might even be . . . fun."

"Like a date? A ghost date?" My flush slowly subsided as we fell into our familiar pattern, the banter the only thing holding me together. Maybe this would be fine. Maybe the ghost part of our overnight would be more like . . . set dressing to a romantic interlude. A girl could dream. "Kit, I've seen that Hallmark movie. If you take me somewhere haunted over Christmas and there's a ghost there, I *will* fall in love with it."

"Which means you'd have to admit they're real, which is a risk I'm willing to take." He pushed himself off from the wall, finally, turning toward Liam's room, then stopped to look back at me. "It'll be good. Really."

"Okay." I held my hands up, surrendering, as I laughed. "I'll hold you to that, Morland."

"You do that, Tilney." It was half threat, half promise, and as he slipped into Liam's room, I had to lean back against the wall myself, take a few deep breaths until my heart rate had slowed.

That boy.

Chapter Thirty-One

The last time I'd packed this many snacks in one bag, I'd been nine years old, on my way to my one (and only) attempt at a Girl Scout camping trip.

It hadn't gone well. Yes, I'd had enough snacks to last me for three to four weeks, but I'd gotten scared and homesick about an hour into the trip; my troop leader had to call Dad, who came and picked me up before the sun even got a chance to set. I was worried Mom would be mad, but if she was, Dad hid it from me entirely. He set up a tent in the backyard and slept out there with me all night, and we ate so many of our snacks that we both had terrible stomachaches the next day.

I had a stomachache right now, thinking of it.

The hormonal fog that had gotten me to agree to this stakeout in the first place had faded by this point, leaving me with residual panic about a whole night spent searching for the twins. You know, the twins, the one ghost story at Northanger Abbey I'd done my best to avoid ever since I'd gotten here?

But I had to put them out of my mind. I was with Kit now. Kit, who had appeared at the door to my bedroom—less than an hour after Mom left that morning—with a printed list of supplies I needed to pack. (When I'd asked why he hadn't just texted it to me, he'd said, "This way no one can track our intentions." I didn't ask further questions.)

Before Mom left, she'd looked me dead in the eyes and said, "Be good." Even though good was the only thing I'd ever been, and it still hadn't been enough for her. I'd felt my blood begin to boil, my hands clench into fists. An entire lifetime of being her perfect daughter, and it had gotten me approximately nowhere.

So. We were going to see what the opposite approach felt like, and we were going to do *that* with a little unauthorized ghost hunt. Twins be damned. I could handle one little traumatic ghost story. Probably.

I'd told Liam where we were going, of course. With Kit staying in his room, there was no way he wouldn't notice us sneaking out. Freddie was theoretically home, too—she'd been here to see Mom off this morning, and I'd heard music coming from her room ever since—but I wasn't worried about getting past her. It wasn't like she hadn't snuck out constantly in high school.

I spent most of the day failing to read in the living room, pretending I wasn't thinking about all the ways tonight could go wrong until, just after sunset, Kit knocked on my door.

It was time.

We were mostly quiet as we slipped out of the house, leaving behind the sounds of Liam's video games. Freddie's room was dark, as predicted. Outside, we crunched through a thick layer of snow into the woods, the lights from our cottage soon disappearing behind us.

Once we couldn't see the house anymore, once I finally felt alone with Kit, I spoke.

"So will you tell me the plan now?" I hiked my backpack up on my shoulders, adjusting to the weight. Kit's list of supplies for our stakeout had been, in a word, *extensive*. We had food, water, recording equipment, extra layers of clothes, flashlights . . . I was grateful that I'd been able to dig up a couple of old hiking backpacks in the attic, because my school bag wasn't big enough (or supportive enough) to manage all this stuff. "Are we secretly hiking the Appalachian Trail? We've got enough supplies."

"Oh, man, I'd love to do that one day." His quick turn down a rabbit hole didn't surprise me anymore. "What do you think the hardest part of that is? It has to be the mental game, right? Like, the hiking part is hard, obviously. But the actual hardest part must be convincing yourself to get up each day and do it all again."

"Sounds like high school." I laughed, meaning it as a joke, but from the way Kit looked at me, it maybe had come off a little too dark. "Sorry. I mean, I guess I feel like I'd get bored. Who wants to spend that long walking?"

"Depends on the company." Kit's mouth twitched up in the corners. "I'd try it, though. I like the idea of pushing myself. Of finding out what I'm capable of."

"And what if you find out you're not capable of it? What if you fail?"

Kit shrugged.

"I don't think you really can fail, if you try."

"Okay, Yoda." We'd come to the end of the wooded path, emerging into the main part of the campus. I gulped. I didn't think I'd ever been here at night when the school was closed. It was . . . eerie. *Not* spooky, of course, because for something to be spooky, you had to acknowledge the existence of paranormally caused spookiness, and I wasn't about to do that. But eerie, I'd allow.

"This is weird," Kit said, managing to sum up everything I was thinking in a much less complicated way. He was good at that. "I mean, obviously it's super cool and haunted all the time. But it looks a lot more haunted now, all empty."

"Schumacher isn't." I pointed at the one lit-up building at the edge of our vision, tucked behind the old abbey. The dorm building's lights were blazing through the first floor of windows. "That's where everyone who doesn't go home for break stays."

"Hattie Tilney." Kit shook his head as he laughed, and I smiled. "You have no sense for the dramatic." We had made it to the Learners' Statue now, a familiar landmark for our strolls. I felt a surprising fondness as I looked at it, the statues bent over books. I'd never expected to develop any positive memories associated with Northanger, not really. I had Kit to thank for that.

"So." I hopped up to sit on the base of the statue, my legs swinging beneath me. "We're here. Now will you tell me what you have planned?"

"Fine." Kit stepped up in front of me, so that my knees

were bumping against his chest. He put his hands on them, the warmth from his palms seeping through my jeans. "The twins are usually heard in the old abbey building, sometimes outside, sometimes inside. But the strongest signals for them . . . they always come from the altar. So that's where we're staking out tonight. We're going to the nave, and we're going to see if we can spot them."

Romantic part of the night over; grin and bear it part of the night activated. *Breathe in and out, Tilney*, I told myself, even as my heart immediately began to race. I'd known this would be something to do with the twins, but I'd thought we were just going to film B-roll of the woods where they'd died. Maybe wander through an abandoned dorm or something. Spending that much time in the nave, in direct confrontation of all my greatest hurts? That wasn't something I was prepared to deal with.

"It's going to be the perfect ending note for the doc," Kit went on, completely unaware of my impending panic. "I don't think we're going to, like, get a recording of them standing in full corporeal form explaining how they died or anything. But if we get *something* . . . it'll be amazing. The nave is the oldest spot on campus. The perfect place for our big, climactic moment."

Great.

"It was a terrible snowstorm." Dad shook his head, eyes still on the fire. "They were outside playing, and the storm came upon them too fast. They were separated by the snow, and the nuns from the abbey found them days later. Adelaide, the girl, had drowned in the river—probably fell through the ice. And Lawrence, her brother, was in the woods. The cold got him."

"They weren't together?" My voice was small, and Dad squeezed his arm around my shoulders.

No. I wasn't going to get caught up in memories of my dad now. I was here for Kit, and for our project; and if Kit wanted to go looking for Lawrence and Adelaide, it wasn't going to bother me. I would go along with it because Kit was all I had left. If I pushed him away, too . . . I'd be left with nothing and no one. I'd broken what I had with Priya and with Izzy, who'd sent me one last *Whatever, Hattie, enjoy Ghost Boy* this morning with a promise to never talk to me again, since that was apparently what I wanted. I'd stopped being what my mother wanted me to be, and I'd rejected the last wish of my father. I needed Kit. I couldn't be alone again. I needed him.

I had to keep it together.

"Fun!" My voice sounded unnaturally high, at least to me, but hopefully Kit didn't notice. "I mean, not fun, because ghosts. Or the lack thereof. But you're right. It'll look good for the doc. We can get B-roll of the empty nave. Let you do a spooky voice-over about how cool it would be if we *had* seen a ghost down there."

"Because we definitely won't?"

"Because we definitely won't," I repeated, and Kit rolled his eyes before taking my hand to help me down from the statue's base. As he held it, I had to hope he didn't realize how unnaturally cold it was.

But he didn't say anything, even as he kept my hand in his on our walk toward the abbey. For someone whose entire hobby basically depended on noticing cold spots in rooms, he was weirdly immune to temperature changes when it came to me.

The door to the nave was locked, of course. But Kit had been prepared for that, too, putting *School key!!!!* on my packing list.

"Key, please," Kit said now; and I dug it out of my backpack, shifting aside water bottles and bags full of gorp before I finally found it and handed it over.

And then we were inside, the door closed softly behind us (which Kit only did once I confirmed that we could, indeed, open it again, so at least he was learning), the nave and the night stretching out before us, like a too-long dream that was starting to slip into a nightmare.

My panic rose, chilled my bones until I began to shiver. It was one thing to pretend that the twins meant nothing to me. It was another thing entirely to go searching for them.

Kit, too wrapped up in his own plans for the evening to notice my fast deterioration, bounded down the center aisle of the nave, leaving me standing by the entrance. Bathed in only the light of my flashlight, he looked like a changeling, or something equally ethereal. He kind of felt that way, too. Something magical, with hopes and dreams and intentions bigger than anyone else's at Northanger Abbey. Well, not bigger, exactly. My graduating class was full of Ivy League hopefuls, future doctors, aspiring politicians. Wider, maybe? Broader. Or maybe they were bigger. Maybe it was bigger to dream about a fulfilled life.

But no matter how much I had pretended over the last few days that we were the perfect pair, that being together would be all flirting and stolen kisses and long walks in the snow, this was what kept us separate. As I stood there staring into the nave, at the optimistic boy who was my opposite in so many ways, I couldn't figure out how to shake the baggage of my past, of my dad, of my mother's expectations. It was ironic. He spent all his time looking for ghosts, and I was just trying to escape mine. When I looked at Kit, I saw someone who had ascended past the stupid, basic problems of being a person that I was still stuck in. Kit was already the best version of himself, while I was still figuring out how to get by at all.

No matter how much I liked Kit, no matter how much he liked me . . . that difference ached between us, a gnawing growth.

I told you not to stop looking, Hattie girl. My dad's voice echoed in my head, the closest to a ghost I'd ever managed to find. But it was exhausting. I was exhausted from searching and searching and searching, from looking for myself and never finding her, from keeping my gaze behind me instead of ahead of me, from being the person everyone turned to as some sort of beacon of responsibility. How were you supposed to find the energy to keep looking when you were so incredibly lost? How was I supposed to bother with my search when I was standing next to Kit Morland, the epitome of found?

This was what it meant to be haunted.

Kit stopped halfway down the aisle, turned and looked at me.

"Come on, Tilney." He tilted his head back, indicating I should follow him, and I did, albeit slowly. "I know you've been in here before. It doesn't bite."

"You're full of mixed messages, Morland." I tried to keep

my voice light as I made my way in his direction, even as my dad's stories filled my head. "There are ghosts in here! But it's definitely not scary! You need a communications director."

"You volunteering?"

"Maybe." I'd finally reached Kit, and he took my hand again like it was a completely natural motion. "So what's the plan, O captain my captain? Do we hold a séance? Break out a Ouija board?"

"God, no." Kit shivered. "Those things freak me out. But we'll set up readers around the nave, get a few cameras going . . . and then hang. Is that okay? At least for the first few hours. Then we can explore more of the building while we leave the detectors here to see if they catch anything. But I want to stay with them for a bit at first. Just in case anything happens."

"Like a dragon appearing and knocking the cameras over?"

"Please." Kit set his backpack down on one of the pews, began to pull out all sorts of equipment. "Dragons aren't real."

"Real as ghosts." If I kept it light, I could keep the anxiety from crushing me under its weight. I sat on the pew across from Kit, watched him set up with muted interest. This was all a lot more complicated than anything my dad had ever invested in, but then again, my dad wasn't working with a scholarship from NPSI. "That sounds fine."

"Fine?" Kit looked up at me with a smirk, an EMF detector blinking in his hand. "I'm hoping we can manage more than fine."

"Don't get your hopes up." I felt myself shutting down, but that didn't mean I could stop it. It was inevitable. The sun would rise in the east; the tides would fall with the moon; and I, Hattie Tilney, would reject any attempt at emotional intimacy at the first available opportunity.

I was going to ruin things with Kit. I could just feel it.

"You okay?" Kit asked from the front of the nave. I didn't know where to begin to answer a question like that, as the cold pressed in around me and I could hear my dad's voice like a chorus, *never stop looking, never stop looking*, like that wasn't an impossible task to place on a fourteen-year-old, like *take care of them, Hattie* wasn't the hardest thing you could ask a kid to do. "I know this isn't your top choice of an activity, but I promise, it's going to be fun. Do you want me to tell you more about the twins? It's a good story. Heartbreaking. But, like, in a cool way."

Heartbreaking. In a cool way.

Like my dad dying. Like my mom leaving us to fend for ourselves while still holding us to impossibly high standards. Like the way Freddie had folded in on herself like a collapsed star and Liam had shrunk himself down until he could hide in every shadow and I had become so brittle and hardened that I had no choice but to shatter.

There was an old legend of Northanger Abbey, one that didn't get talked about very much. It was about the first nuns who lived here, in the abbey's earliest days. They gave themselves to their work so thoroughly that they forgot even to serve God, so absorbed were they in their tasks. Scrub the abbey. Sweep the abbey. Don't let anything happen to the abbey. And they never stopped, even when their bodies turned to stone from lack of feeling, even when their bones collapsed and muscles failed and they were nothing more than a collection of thoughts. You can still hear them, the legends said, if a student or a visitor tracks in too much dirt from outside. You can hear their hiss of admonishment as their beloved abbey is marred by an outsider.

In the end, it was just another story about women who lost themselves in service to something else. Who became a story for people like Kit to pass around a campfire.

Heartbreaking. In a cool way.

That, it turned out, was the end of my rope.

"I don't want to hear about them, Kit." My voice cracked like a twig, like a heart, like a promise. "I know the story of the twins, okay? I could tell it better than you could, I bet. But I don't *want* to."

"Hattie?" He blinked, or at least I thought he did, because I could barely see, the edges of my vision blurring.

"I know all these stories." I waved my arms around, like I was indicating the entirety of Northanger Abbey. "Not just a few that I've picked up over the years. I know every single one. Every single story you've ever told me, and every one you didn't."

Kit stared at me. Whether it was with hurt or shock or what, I didn't know. I was breathing heavily, my voice ragged.

"I wish I didn't." This was where Kit would leave me, probably. Everyone else had. But at least if I was alone again, no one would expect anything from me. "But I do."

"Hattie." Kit came over to me, grabbed my hand, and guided me to sit in the pew. The wood was hard beneath me, but it was grounding, too. "Talk to me."

"I've been talking."

"Yeah, you're talking, but you're not making any sense," Kit said, and I snorted despite myself. He tightened his grip on my hand in response. "Hattie. You need to just . . . to tell me what's going on. Okay? I can't help you if you don't tell me. I know you're weird about ghost stuff. Do you want to tell me why?"

I didn't.

And I did.

"I'm not sure you actually want to know." I managed a shaky laugh. Kit's hand wrapped around mine was even more grounding than the bench, and the stories in my head were finally getting quieter. "You're sure you want a lesson in Hattie Tilney's Trauma 101?"

"Hattie, I don't know how I can make it clearer to you that I want to know you." Kit reached out and brushed a strand of hair out of my face, tucking it behind my ear. "Tell me."

Telling ghost stories was what had gotten me in trouble in the first place. But maybe this one, the story of my own ghosts, could be my last. Could finally quiet the shouting in my head.

So I took a deep breath, and I told Kit my story.

"My dad loved this sort of thing. He taught me all about it." The rhythm of storytelling found me so easily. "Besides our family, it was his entire world."

Kit nodded. "You mean . . . ghosts?"

"Yeah. You two would have gotten along great." A smile played at the edge of my mouth as I pictured how *that* meeting would have gone. It would have been a lot more effusive than any of the times Kit had met Mom, that was for sure.

"It wasn't just him, though. I was, too. I mean, it was probably just because I wanted to spend time with my dad, but I was all-in on the paranormal. I read the stories right alongside him."

"You did?" Kit looked at me, perplexed, but I barreled on.

"We moved to Northanger right before my freshman year. Mom got the job in the spring—everyone was so excited. My dad, especially." I felt a lump form in my throat, but pushed past it, determined to get this out. If I stopped, I doubted I'd ever start again. "But that was when Dad got sick. He died a week before we moved onto campus."

"I'm sorry, Hattie." Kit put his hand on my shoulder. I felt like I could only half hear him.

"That's the thing, though." My voice thickened with held-back tears. "I was devastated, of course. Who wouldn't be? He was my dad. We were best friends. We had all these plans for Northanger, for going on tours and doing research—he'd even set up an appointment with an archivist at the historical society downtown, because the school's records weren't particularly well tied to the town's and he thought that was, like, this huge oversight, something where he could figure out links between some of the stories and historical things that happened here." I shook my head. "He had so many plans. When he died, they just all . . . stopped. But there was still a part of me that didn't feel sad."

"What do you mean?" Kit's voice was hesitant. I wondered if he'd figured it out.

"He was dead, of course." I shrugged. "But he wasn't gone. He couldn't be gone. Because we believed in people coming back, him and me. We never talked about it—he got sick too fast to talk about it—but I knew he was going to come back. I knew he was going to come back because I needed him, and he knew I needed him, and he had all this unfinished business, which is, like, *prime* ghost incentive." I laughed, even as Kit watched me with rising realization. "So I didn't need to be entirely sad. Because he was going to come back to me."

"Hattie."

"I waited for him every night, Kit." I couldn't look at him anymore. "I stayed up every night as late as I could so I wouldn't miss him. I set up EMF detectors all over the house, wherever Mom wouldn't notice them. I wasn't necessarily even expecting a full-blown specter, but I knew he'd show up. Somehow."

"How long did you wait?"

"Three months," I said, and Kit let out a long, slow breath. "Not long after school started, I realized it was pointless. I had to move on. Abandon all the paranormal shit I'd clung to. So, I reinvented myself. Became the daughter my mom wanted me to be, instead of the one I'd been with Dad. I felt guilty all the time, but I didn't have a choice."

"And you stopped believing in ghosts after that?" Kit's voice had a hint of confusion in it, and I realized he still didn't get it. He still didn't see.

"Kit." I said his name slow. Said all of it slow. "I *can't* believe in ghosts anymore."

"I mean, I know it's all tied up in your dad and every-thing—"

"Kit." I said his name again. "Ghosts aren't real. They can't

be. Because if they are . . ." I wasn't going to be able to hold in
the tears after this. But I needed him to understand. Needed
to say it out loud. "If they are, it means my dad didn't come
back for me. He could have come back, and he didn't love
me enough to do it. If ghosts were real, Kit, I wouldn't be so
lonely."

I'd finally found a way to get Kit to stop talking.

I had tears in my eyes, but to my surprise, managed not to
actively cry. I guessed it made sense. I'd spent so much time
crying about it freshman year. Before I shoved it way, way into
the back of my mind, where it couldn't hurt me as much.

It was snowing again. I could just barely make it out
through the stained glass over the altar, lit by moonlight as it
fell in gentle drifts outside the abbey.

This probably wasn't how Kit had imagined our stakeout
was going to go.

"I'm so sorry, Hattie." Finally, he spoke, his voice soft as
the snow. "That's . . . I can't begin to imagine going through
what you've been through. It's enough to shake anyone's belief system."

"Yeah, well." I shrugged, the tears held in, everything held
in. "Sometimes it's better not to believe."

Kit fell silent again, let go of my hand as he ran his through
his hair. The snow was picking up now—getting home was
going to be its own adventure. On the altar in front of us, the
EMF detectors blinked slowly, sensing nothing.

"I think the thing about belief is that it's supposed to be
hard," he said eventually, leaning back against the pew, his
hands wrapped around his knees. "If it wasn't, you wouldn't

have to believe in it, right? It would just be fact. If you're believing in something, it's because there's a chance that you're
wrong. But you hope beyond all hope that you're not. And
that hope is what keeps you moving forward. It keeps you
pushing, looking for answers. And the way that I believe . . . it
should be different from the way you believe. It's different for
everyone. But I can't think it's not important."

"My belief is pretty broken, Kit."

"I'm not saying that you have to believe in the same things
as me," he said quickly. "The stuff with your dad . . . that's not
for me to decide for you. For what it's worth, I think belief—
the sort you can live with, the sort you have to reckon with—
isn't binary. The idea that I'm a hundred percent right or
you're a hundred percent wrong isn't . . . it's not just that it's
not correct. It's not *interesting*. Belief leaves room for nuance. It
has to, if you're going to live your life by it."

"I guess." I could see Kit working his way toward something, the way he always did. By talking his way into it. For all
that this brought out intense trauma for me, I loved to see him
do it. Loved to see the way he worked his way into an answer.

Maybe there was something to that. How both of those
feelings existed at the same time.

"Here's what I believe." Kit took a deep breath. "I believe
that you can believe whatever you want. Anyone can. And that
if you believe in something strongly enough, hell, if even *two*
people believe in something strongly enough . . . sometimes
you can make it true." He bumped his shoulder into mine. "I
don't know whether your dad could come back or not, Hattie.

But I know that I believe in the process of searching for the people we've lost. And I don't know that cutting off everything he loved is the best way to keep him around."

"That's a little harsh."

"I'm sorry." Kit winced. "I'm messing this up, probably. But you said you were lonely. I guess what I want to know is— how about now?"

I closed my eyes. Considered the question.

I thought of the girl I was freshman year. Who shut down everything she had been, determined to create a whole new person out of nothing. A person without any of the baggage that actual Hattie Tilney carried. And I thought about how I had inadvertently dragged that baggage around the entire time I'd been at Northanger, weighing myself down even further in my attempts to hide it.

I thought about who I'd become since I'd met Kit. Since I started to let a little bit of that weirdness back into my life. About how he made me smile, how he hadn't left me every time I thought he was about to. How I'd occasionally enjoyed the antics of the Ghost Brigade, about how Liam was the happiest I'd seen him since Dad died. How I suspected I was starting to figure out who Hattie Tilney actually was.

Maybe I'd surprised myself.

"I guess . . . I'm not." It was a revelation as I said it. All this time, and I'd maybe been getting better. Slowly but surely, I'd been becoming a person again, not just a mask. "I guess I'm not as lonely anymore."

That sort of revelation required a punctuation, so I turned

to the side and kissed Kit, my hand on the side of his face as I pressed my lips against his, drinking in the feeling of being connected to this other person. He let out a little breath of surprise before he kissed me back, one hand in my hair, the other on my waist, holding me as tight as he could. As his grip tightened, the kiss deepened, and I shifted myself so that my whole body was leaning toward him, leaning onto him, leaning into him.

And then, out of the corner of my eye, I saw it.

The EMF detector, blinking fast.

"Kit." I barely got his name out, and when he caught my eye, I darted my gaze to the altar, where the light was now glowing a steady red. "Look."

I didn't know what I believed. But I did know what I saw.

"Holy shit," Kit breathed, his eye catching it. "Um. Should we—"

"Go!" I pushed him, and he jumped up, rushing forward to the reader. I felt a thrill in my chest I hadn't felt since . . . well. Years. The thrill of possibility.

Kit grabbed the reader as soon as he got to it, pulled it up close to check the signal.

"There's definitely something messing with the frequency," he said, his voice betraying his excitement. "I mean, it could be nothing, of course." He glanced back at me, his expression concerned. "That definitely happens. These things are notoriously spotty."

"Yeah." I rummaged through my backpack, pulled out the GoPro, and pointed it at Kit as I turned it on. "Or it could be something. Go. Explain."

Kit's face broke into a wide grin, and I knew it wasn't just about the ghosts (or the possibility of ghosts, at least). It was, at least partially, because of me.

And I believed in that. I believed in Kit Morland.

Chapter Thirty-Two

I was eighty-five percent sure there was a ghost in this room, and Kit Morland was grinning at me like it was the best thing that'd ever happened to him.

Okay: eighty-five percent was an exaggeration, particularly given the low reliability of EMF detectors. It wasn't like a single talk with Kit was going to turn me back into a believer overnight. But the room was cold, and Kit's smile was warm, and my capacity for belief had just increased, if not quite to a normal human level, to a level I hadn't thought was possible since I'd lost Dad.

As we stared into the garret room tucked away at the top of the abbey—because Kit had insisted, once the nave's detector had gone off and we'd filmed a quick explanation for what might be happening, that we explore the rest of the building immediately, in case there were similar energy signatures anywhere else—I felt a sense of . . . trepidation? Not quite. Not quite excitement, either. But something.

Maybe it was belief. I had no way to know.

But I knew Kit was excited. I was willing to allow myself some excitement, too.

"Just go in," I urged him, staring at the center of the room. The cold spot was undeniable, and the EMF detector in Kit's hands would tell us if it was . . . well, if it was more than just a cold spot.

Kit nodded, his eyes locked forward. He took a deep breath and stepped into the room, the EMF detector held in front of him like a weapon. As he reached the center, we both stared at the detector, waiting for a sign.

And it showed . . . nothing.

Kit burst out laughing, cutting the tension like a knife.

"I think it's just a draft, Tilney." He pointed at one of the windows where, sure enough, I could just barely make out a hole in the glass, snow blowing in. I let out a raggedy sigh, and Kit chuckled again, watching me. "But it was totally worth it."

"How?" I shivered, not from an unnatural ghostly cold apparently but from regular earth cold. "Were you aiming for frostbite?"

"Not exactly." He crossed back to me, grabbed my hand in his. It was cold but not unwelcome. "But you thought there might be a ghost."

"I didn't . . . emotions were high." I blustered, even as Kit smiled, then leaned down and kissed me again. I let him.

After a second, he broke away.

"What are we doing?"

"What do you mean?"

"I mean what are we, Tilney?" He dropped my hand, pointed between us. "I know things are different in the northeast than they are in Florida. But this feels like we've moved beyond ambassador duties."

"Is that—is that okay?" My voice cracked. Cute. "I know we're— I'm not trying to mess with a good thing."

"Hattie, *this* is a good thing. You and me." Kit reached forward and ran his hand over my hair. "I just want to be more than, pardon the pun, what you do in the shadows."

"What, like, be your girlfriend?" I'd meant it as a joke, but it didn't come out sounding like one, and Kit kept looking at me. "Is that really what you want, Kit? I'm a mess."

"Yeah, but you're the kind of mess I understand." Kit smiled, and I snorted. "I'm a mess, too, Tilney. Let's be messy together."

An hour ago, I still would have said no. I wouldn't have believed it was possible, Kit and me. Wouldn't have believed we could work, that we could be anything more than stolen kisses and secret smiles.

I still didn't know if we would. But I was willing to take a leap of faith.

"Okay," I said, and a smile spread across Kit's face, slow and wonderful. "Yes. I'll be your girlfriend."

Kit's arms were around me in an instant, and even though we'd been kissing all night, all week, this felt different. Better. Surer.

Like I believed in it.

⁓⁓⁓

We snuck back into the house just before sunrise. The amount of evidence we'd been able to collect for the doc was minimal, but we'd still gotten some fun footage, and my happiness was pretty much at its max. I felt warmer than I had in months, and it wasn't just because Kit's arm was wrapped around my shoulders. I felt warm from the inside out.

Upstairs, Freddie's light was off, her door ajar. She wasn't home, either. Liam's light was still on, but when I peeked into his room, he was sound asleep.

Kit and I stopped in the hallway, holding hands and watching each other. We couldn't *stop* looking at each other. If it was anyone else, I'd have been disgusted by us. As it was, I was kind of deliriously happy.

"Thanks for the stakeout," Kit said, his voice low. His hair was tousled around his neck, tangled from how often my hands had gotten lost in it. I resisted the urge to do it again.

"Did you find what you were looking for?"

"Yeah." Kit grinned, leaned down and kissed me one more time. "Good night, Tilney."

"Good night, Kit."

As he slipped into Liam's room, and I headed to mine, I felt like I was floating. Lighter than I'd ever felt, like nothing could touch me.

I'd finally, *finally*, figured out how to be happy, and no one was going to take that away.

Chapter Thirty-Three

D r. Tilney was all smiles when she got home that afternoon, which I would have taken as a warning sign earlier if I wasn't so distracted by Kit.

"We really have to go down to the city as a family," she told us ("us" being me, Kit, and Liam, since Freddie was still MIA). "I know it's cliché, but the Christmas decorations are spectacular. Have you been to New York, Kit?"

"Just the airport on the way here," Kit answered. We were sprawled out around the living room, warming ourselves with mugs of hot chocolate after a vigorous snowball fight. Kit and I were both slouched on the floor in front of the couch, legs pressed together, while Liam was curled up like a cat, as close to the heating vents as possible. A month ago, I would have sat up straight the second Dr. Tilney came into the room, pushed myself away from Kit, and thrown my shoulders back. Now, I didn't care what she thought of my posture. Of how close Kit and I were sitting. "Not the best example."

"Maybe next year we'll all go." She was humming to herself, *humming*, as she unwrapped her scarf and hung it on the rack next to the front door.

"Right." I glanced over at Liam with confusion, and he helpfully shrugged before laying his head back down on the rug. *Thanks, bud.* Though I probably should have just been glad he hadn't asked me a million questions about where Kit and I had been last night. "Glad you liked it."

I'd expected her good mood to wear off quickly, but Mom didn't stop talking about New York for the rest of the afternoon. It was weird enough that she was so *present*—sitting with us in the living room while Liam, Kit, and I played board games, offering to make tea for everyone when she got up to make some for herself. Even at dinner, when we sat down to Chinese takeout, she was going on about how nice it had been to get away.

Gee, thanks, Mom. We get it: you hate being with us.

But, I reminded myself as Mom went on and on and I picked at my sesame chicken, it didn't matter. I had Kit now, didn't I? Thoroughly and officially. I'd given up on Dr. Tilney and her plan for me, because she'd clearly written me off years ago. It didn't need to bother me that she'd had such an amazing time with other people. I had my own people now, and I was better off without her.

Still, I wasn't prepared for when Mom turned her attentions my way after the meal.

"You know, Hattie, some of these women have children right around your age." We were doing the dishes together, Liam excused to his room, Kit clearing plates in the dining room while we stood in the kitchen, cleaning them off before loading them into the dishwasher. "Jennifer's daughter is a junior, I believe. Olivia's son is a senior."

"Cool." And I was sure they were way more successful than I'd ever be, I told myself, taking a plate Mom handed to me. Perfect children for their perfect parents. Whatever. As soon as this was done, I'd disappear upstairs, too. Spend time with the people who *actually* valued me.

"It was funny." Mom laughed—*laughed*—as she rinsed off her sponge. "They both complained about them the whole time we were together. The stress they put them through. All the ways they failed to live up to their expectations."

"Huh." That must have been extra fun for her. Plenty of room for her to insert all the ways in which her own children had failed her, too.

"And it made me think." Mom hummed to herself as she scrubbed orange sauce off a bowl, then rinsed it and handed it to me. "I don't tell you enough, Hattie, how glad I am that you've stuck to your path. Your sister is . . . well. We both know she's chosen her own direction. But you've always done what you've needed to do to succeed. And while everyone else was complaining about their children, I didn't have to. I just thought of my Henrietta, who never let me down." She was looking out the window over the sink, her eyes a little out of focus. "You're going to do great things. Just like we always wanted for you."

I couldn't breathe, holding the bowl in my hands like a lifeline.

When I was little, eight or nine, I'd been in a bounce house at a birthday party. There had been too many kids inside of it, and they'd started bouncing all over the place, and I'd fallen, and then other kids had fallen on top of me, and I'd been trapped, pinned at the bottom of the pile, facedown into the vinyl. And I couldn't breathe. I'd tried to, but there was someone lying across my back, crushing me; and with my mouth against the floor I couldn't even turn my head to try and drink in some air from the side. I'd felt panicked. Hopeless. Utterly and completely done for.

Dad had noticed the pileup and pulled the other kids off me, picking me up and holding me tight against him until I could catch my breath again.

Now I still couldn't breathe, and there was no one to help me.

I'd been so sure, so certain, that Mom didn't care about what I did. That she'd ditched my senior meeting because I was more of an annoyance than a daughter, a task to be checked off a list rather than a person to be valued. That no matter how hard I tried, I'd never be good enough to break through to her, to make her see me.

But according to her, I *was* part of her reputation. Her list of accomplishments to show off to the world. It hadn't occurred to me that she'd thought I was doing *well*. That maybe, I realized, she'd canceled our meeting because she didn't think we needed to have one. That I was just so good, so successful, that she could file me away and move on with her day.

What would she do when she found out all the ways I'd failed her this semester? When she found out that my plans for next year had changed, deviated from the path she'd expected of me?

Take care of them, Henrietta. Make your mother proud.

I didn't think she'd even notice when I started making different choices.

I'd tried to throw away my legacy. My responsibilities. Because they'd seemed hopeless, unattainable. There was no reason to try to *take care of them, Henrietta* when failure was guaranteed. But if my mom was saying that she valued the mask, the work I'd put in over the years to be the best . . .

She was *proud* of me. Well, not me, I corrected myself. She was proud of the person I'd pretended to be. Dr. Tilney wanted the perfect daughter and thought she'd gotten her. Thought that I was still her academic wunderkind, about to head off to an elite college and then an elite graduate school and an elite career. The person I actually was—the one who snuck out with Kit, who got rejected from Udolpho and decided that academic achievement wasn't important, who chased ghosts instead of legacy—she would be nothing to my mother. A disappointment, just like Dad was. I hadn't minded, because it had made me feel closer to Dad again. Let me relive the memories I had of him without breaking.

But Dad was gone, and Mom was here. And maybe I still had a chance, a quickly closing window of opportunity where I could make her happy. Where the last three years of my life wouldn't be wasted.

"Can I go upstairs?" My voice forced its way out in a squeak as I placed the bowl I was holding carefully into the nearly full dishwasher, doing my best not to drop it from my sweating palms. "I don't feel great."

"Oh. Of course." Mom nodded, her brows furrowed in what might have been concern. "Go lie down."

Lie down, panic—it was all the same. I ran from the room, ignoring Kit's questioning look as I passed through the dining room to book it up the stairs and into my room, slamming the door hard behind me.

I had to undo my mistake.

Throw myself at my desk, open my laptop, pull up window after window. I'd had one job, one responsibility, and that was to be the best version of myself I could be. The path had been clear, it had been right there, and it was the one thing my dad had asked me to do: to take care of them, to be the me that Mom could be proud of.

I'd tried to throw that version away, find a different path, but there *was* no other path for me. I didn't have Udolpho but there were other places, other schools, that would be acceptable to Mom. Places I could still make her proud.

I pulled up the Wieland application on my computer. Finished, basically. Ready to be sent in, a firm step in a new direction. A direction my mother would hate.

"Hattie? What are you doing?" I hadn't heard him come up, too lost in the buzzing of my own thoughts, but Kit was in the doorway, his face wrinkled in concern. "Are you okay? What did your mom say to you?"

"I know you said that I could take my own path, Kit." I had turned around to face him, but I wasn't looking at him, not really. I was looking past him, at the vision of what I could have been, if that version of me was allowed to exist. But she couldn't. That version of my life was the ghost now. Maybe he'd pick her up on his EMF detector one day, find the energy signature of a happy Hattie Tilney. "But I can't."

"Because your mom will be mad?" He stepped into the room, crossed to my desk, and dropped to his knees beside me. "Who cares?"

"*I* care." I shook my head. Even this near-empty room was starting to feel claustrophobic. "It's the one thing I'm supposed to do! It's not like I even have this clear vision of what I'd rather do instead. I can't throw away everything on a whim."

"Being happy isn't a whim."

"Neither are my mother's plans for me."

"Your mother . . ." Kit let out a growl of frustration, and as I swiveled my chair back around to face my computer again, he put a hand on my knee, stopping me from completing the rotation. "How do you not see it, Hattie? Your mom is *ruining* you. She doesn't care about what makes you happy. She just wants you as, like, a trophy, to show off to her friends and to the school what a perfect daughter she's produced and put in a cage."

"Come on, Kit." I wanted to knock the buzzing out of my brain, like water trapped in my ear. "I have responsibilities here. To my family. You may have made me forget them for a while, but they didn't go away. I can't throw away everything I worked for to chase a pointless dream."

"What does that mean?"

"It means this."

And with a click, I deleted the Wieland application.

I didn't feel sad, oddly enough. Just empty. Just like before.

Kit stared at me, open-mouthed. Then slowly he stood, backing away from me, his eyes narrowing.

"I can't believe you let her brainwash you like this. You're so much more than what your mom wants you to be."

"You don't understand owing someone." My voice was hollow.

"What I understand," Kit spat, "is that you shouldn't owe anything to someone who ruins you. You don't believe in ghosts but you're a ghost around her, you know? You just become this projection of everything she wants. That's not being a person. She's a monster, Hattie. And you had a chance to escape her, to stop her from sucking the life out of you, and you just, what, deleted it? What other options do you have? You haven't applied anywhere else. You don't have a backup plan."

"Excuse me, Mr. Morland? Would you care to repeat that?"

No.

My mother had appeared in my doorway, her eyes furious.

I didn't know how long she had been standing there, but apparently it had been long enough, from the way she turned on Kit, every ounce of her quivering with rage.

Still, I was the first one she addressed.

"What does he mean, you haven't applied anywhere? I signed off on your application for Udolpho."

A beat. But it wasn't like I could lie.

"I didn't get into Udolpho."

Dr. Tilney let out a long breath. Her gaze was sharp, her posture straight and proud. I winced, afraid of what she would say to me.

Then she whipped toward Kit.

"I don't know what you've done to my daughter." She stepped forward, almost imperceptibly, and Kit stumbled back, tripping over my gray carpeting. "I don't know how you've steered her from the path she's been on since she was born, but I do know that I won't stand for it. I won't stand for you speaking about me that way, and I won't stand for you helping my daughter ruin her life." She pointed at the door as Kit's mouth opened and shut, as he stared at me in horror. "I clearly misjudged you. Get out."

"I—what?"

"Get. Out." Mom spoke the words like they were knives. "It's time for you to leave. I want you to go to Schumacher and wait there until I can arrange for your transportation, because you're not welcome here."

Kit didn't say anything. Just watched me. I knew what he was doing. He was waiting for me to jump in, to say something, to defend him. I'd done it with my friends, after all. Stood up to Izzy and Priya and chosen Kit.

But neither of them was my mother, who held me as a prisoner of my own obligations.

He'd never liked her, anyway. Never understood why she did the things she did.

I turned my attention down toward the floor and closed my eyes.

Kit barked out a laugh.

"Fine." Footsteps as he approached the doorway. "I'll get my bag and go."

"See that you do," Mom hissed.

And then Kit was gone. My mother closed the door behind

him (slammed it, more like) and crossed over to me, and I knew I was done for, too. But I had to look at her. I had to see what was coming next, so I opened my eyes and tilted my chin back up.

"You didn't get in?" she said. I shook my head. She sighed. "I can't believe you let this happen."

"I . . ."

"Even *if* you didn't get in, you were supposed to apply to other schools. We had a list, Hattie, a plan that we prepared for this eventuality." She began to pace around the room. "And you just threw it all away because—what? Laziness? Getting distracted by a boy?"

"I tried so hard, Mom."

"I thought I could get away without babysitting you." Her pacing continued, hard and furious. "I thought that I could trust you to handle this. I've sacrificed *everything* for this family, Hattie. For you to succeed."

I'd been so hopeful just a few minutes before, when I thought she could still be proud of me. But I'd been wrong, and in that moment of weakness, I'd lost more than her respect. I'd lost Kit. I'd lost him *for* her, let him go willingly because the way she saw me was still the most important thing to me. And yet she was still beating me down, again and again and again. No matter what I did. No matter what sacrifices *I* made. I didn't want to fight, but I didn't want to just lie down and take it, either. Not when I already felt so low.

"If you wanted me to succeed so badly, why didn't I have my senior meeting?" The words came out before I realized I was saying them. Mom stopped in her tracks, turned to stare at me, her face as pale as the blank walls that surrounded her. "You canceled on me. I know you don't want to—to babysit me—but that's something every senior gets. Except me."

"I . . ." For once in my life, my mom seemed unsure. "It was a busy day. I *thought* you were on track. We didn't need to talk about it."

"We never need to talk about anything." My heart beat faster, pounding against my ribs. "You just assume I'll do everything perfectly. But I didn't, okay? I messed up. I'm not like you. I don't have your ambition, the need to get a dream job where I can spend all my time, just to get away from my family." My words were gaining bite, and Mom's expression darkened.

"You think I spend all of my time working because it's, what, fun for me?"

"I mean, yes." This was absurd. Did she honestly believe that she did a single thing for us? Everything my mom had ever done was for her. "You love work. Even when Dad was alive, all you cared about was work. Not us."

"How dare you."

"It's true." I had fight coming back into me, because if I was a huge disappointment anyway, I may as well go out with a bang. "When he was alive you pushed him just like you pushed me. He didn't want some hugely ambitious life. Why is it so hard to believe that I don't, either?"

"Kit Morland got into your head." Mom's hair was coming out from her picture-perfect bun, frizzing around her face. "I never should have paired the two of you together."

"Kit was the only person at this school who ever wanted me to be happy." And, yes, I'd irreversibly ruined our relationship, but that was neither here nor there. "And he was right. You *are* a monster. Dad was the only parent who ever cared about us, and as much as you pretend to, you can't manage to do it. So just stop pretending, Mom. For all of our sakes."

Mom stopped her pacing finally. When she looked at me, something in her eyes was like . . . no. It couldn't be hurt. I couldn't hurt my mother. She would need to love me first.

But she did, at least, listen to me. Without another word she turned and left the room, closing the door tight behind her.

That was when I fell onto the bed and finally let myself cry.

Chapter Thirty-Four

For the next two hours, I lay on my bed completely alone, just thinking about all the ways I'd irrevocably ruined my life.

First, the Kit thing. He'd never forgive me, probably. Then, the combination of college stuff and Mom stuff. I'd deleted the Wieland application with the idea that I'd . . . I didn't know. Beg some Mom-approved school for an application extension? I hadn't, admittedly, thought that far ahead. If she hadn't overheard Kit, it might have worked.

But once she knew all the ways I'd failed, there was no going back. It didn't matter, at this point, if I went to Yale on a "My Mom Respects Me" scholarship. She was never going to look at me the same way again.

I didn't know that I wanted her to. The things I'd said to her were . . . harsh. But were they untrue? If she loved me, she'd never managed to show it. Maybe it was time I'd said it out loud.

A better time to have said it out loud would have been,

perhaps, right before I got on a train speeding toward Alaska, since I still lived in her house and was going to have to deal with the fallout from my actions. But that was Tomorrow Hattie's problem. Maybe even the day after that. That would be a fun game. See how long I could survive in my room so that I didn't have to cross Mom's path.

When the knock on my door came, close to midnight, it wasn't exactly welcome, but I wasn't mad about the break from my own thoughts, either. Besides, it had to be Liam. He'd presumably heard the shouting—or heard from Kit—and was checking in on me after an appropriate amount of alone time.

"Come in," I called, fully expecting my little brother. I was understandably surprised when the door opened to reveal Freddie standing in the doorway. Liam darted in in front of her, looking apologetic.

"Some party, huh?" Freddie smirked.

"No. No way." I sat up in bed, dropped my feet to the floor. I wasn't dealing with *her*, on top of everything else. It turned out I had a line, and this was where I was drawing it. "Get out of here, Freddie."

"Oh, come on, Hen." Freddie rolled her eyes and didn't leave, because of course she didn't, because when had she ever respected a single thing that I had wanted? Honestly, I felt more betrayed by Liam. He should have known better. "What are you going to do, stay holed up in here forever? You're going to have to interact with another person eventually."

"*Eventually* being the operative word, and when I *do* choose to interact with another person again, it's not going to be *you*." I pulled my pillow over my face and leaned down over my knees, like I could block out whatever weird gloating power play my sister was clearly here to pull. "Can you just stay out of my life, please? Like, forever?"

The silence that followed was long enough that I actually pushed away the pillow, checked to see if maybe my siblings had left. But they hadn't. Liam had sat down in my desk chair, watching me with a sad expression. And Freddie had moved back into the doorframe, not looking at me, just frowning into the distance.

Finally, she spoke. "You know, you're a real asshole, Hattie."

"Excuse me?" That made me sit up, aghast, as my pillow fell to the floor. "*I'm* the asshole? Who's been the one keeping this family together, Freddie? Who's been the one cooking and cleaning and showing up for everyone? Who takes care of Liam? You know, jobs that if Mom refused to do them, would make the most sense to go to the oldest sibling? Was it you? Or were you too busy dropping out of college and getting drunk with strangers?"

"At least I didn't develop some holier-than-thou savior complex at the age of fourteen," Freddie snapped, and before I could open my mouth to bite back, Liam stood up, my desk chair pushed back beneath him.

"Can you both stop? Please?" He clenched his fists at his waist, knuckles white, and I reeled back, shocked. After all I had done for my brother, the idea that he wouldn't be entirely on my side in this had never crossed my mind. "Can we just admit that everything has been terrible since Dad died? For everyone?" I sucked in a quick breath. We never talked about this. "Freddie, Hattie's right—she stepped up and she took care of me. I know you were away at school, but you still could have helped. But, Hattie, sometimes you forget you're not the only one who's hurting." He spoke fast, and when I looked over, his eyes were damp. "We all lost Dad."

He grabbed the chair and sat back down again, stared at his hands. My heart cracked a little at my brother, my baby brother. I hated that he had to go through this. I hated that any of us had to go through this.

While I was trying to process what he'd said, Freddie spoke up. Still standing in the doorway, like she didn't know how to breach any farther. Like she was protecting herself from an earthquake.

"I know I'm a shitty person." She laughed, and the sound was hollow. "You think I'm proud of that? I'm not. And I would love to have finished school, but I just . . . I couldn't. Sometimes you just can't do things." *You know what that's like*, I thought, my mind betraying my resolve. I scooted back on the bed, tucking my legs underneath me as I leaned against the pale eggshell wall of my bedroom. "Then when I came back, you guys didn't need me. You had your little routine, the three of you, that you'd built since you got here. There was no place in it for me."

"Of course there was." This couldn't be my fault. This couldn't be one more thing that was my fault. "You think I wouldn't have liked having my big sister around more? I know we were never close, but it didn't seem like you ever wanted to be. You had Mom."

"Please." Freddie scuffed her foot against the carpet, gray

and lifeless, like the rest of this room. Like our family. "Mom's the only person in this family more closed off than you are, Hattie."

"I'm not closed off." Okay, I definitely was. But I didn't like the idea that Freddie could be right about anything.

"You kind of are," Liam said, spinning the desk chair. "Or you were, anyway. You were so sure you had to be perfect that you forgot to be, like . . . a person."

"That's not fair."

"Isn't it?" Liam asked, stopping his spin once he faced me. "You didn't even let Izzy and Priya know the real you, and they're supposed to be your best friends." *Yeah, right.* "And then Kit showed up, and you actually did let your guard down, and you might have been happy if you hadn't thrown it all away."

"Um, hello?" I leaned forward to grab the pillow off the floor, held it against my chest like a shield. I needed extra protection here. Was Liam speaking from an alternate dimension or something? "Did you not hear what happened? Mom ruined things, not me. You want to hold some stupid emotional intervention for someone, do it for her. She's the one who kicked Kit out."

"Yeah. And she's the one who's hurting the most," Freddie said, and I scoffed, clutching the pillow tighter.

"Mom doesn't have emotions."

"Are you listening to yourself?" Freddie kicked her foot against the doorframe now. *Don't,* I wanted to say, but, really, what was one more scuff in a family full of them? "I could have said the same thing about you, Hattie. You think just because she threw herself into her work, because she doesn't talk about Dad, she doesn't miss him? You don't talk about him, either. Do you not miss him?"

The question hit like a cannonball on the side of a ship, sending a splintering impact through my chest. Even my emotional support pillow couldn't cover the wound.

"That's not fair."

"No shit." Freddie shrugged. "None of this is fair. It's not fair that Dad died. It's not fair that we all had to keep living afterward like things got better. And Mom isn't . . . I'm not saying the way any of us coped was the right way to cope. Or, like, the healthy way. My way sure as hell isn't." A smirk as she tossed her ponytail over her shoulder. "And I don't think the way you used to hero-worship Mom's work ethic was good, either. But she can be wrong and still not be the huge villain you're suddenly determined to make her. I know it's shitty of me to say that you don't remember the way things used to be as much as I do, but it's the truth, okay? You don't. And you and Dad . . . you had your own thing, the two of you. And I'm sorry you lost that. But Mom and Dad were in love. Really and truly. I saw it my whole life." Her smile saddened. "Yeah, they clashed sometimes, but all they ever wanted was for the other person to be happy. Mom worked so hard so that all of us—Dad included—could have whatever we wanted. And Dad died right on the brink of coming here." As she spoke, Freddie was still watching me and Liam from the doorway, like an observer instead of a member of the family. Maybe that was what she felt like. "You think it broke you? Imagine how much it broke her."

I grabbed the comforter with a tight fist just so I had something to hold on to, frayed threads and embroidered flowers crumpled in my palms. I was overwhelmed, and I was still angry. But most of all I was sad. I was just . . . so sad. A sister who wouldn't even come into my room. A brother who kept spinning in circles because he'd never learned how to sit still and feel something. And me, huddled on my bed like it was a life raft.

This wasn't how our family was supposed to be.

"Do you remember the one time we went to the beach together?" Liam asked after a few moments had passed. He was spinning in the chair again, though slower than before. More deliberate. "I was like . . . eight? I know Freddie had just turned sixteen. Hattie, I guess you were ten. And Mom was doing a workshop during the summer in North Carolina, so we all drove down and went to the beach." I still didn't feel like I could speak, but I nodded, stared at the faded stripes on my pillowcase. Freddie must have nodded, too, since Liam kept going. "We spent the entire day in the water, basically. All five of us. And Mom kept saying that she needed to get back to work, and Dad would tell her to just stay a little longer, and she would. And at the end of the day, we were all exhausted. But I remember Mom smiling at Dad and saying she was glad she had him. Because otherwise she would have missed a wonderful day."

Liam got up from his chair, came over to the bed, and sat beside me. I leaned my head on his shoulder, felt him breathe. Felt him find his stillness once we were connected.

"Everything's been off-balance since Dad died. I think maybe Mom is the most off-balance of all of us, though."

"Yeah, but she's our mom." I was wiping away tears, even though I was barely conscious of crying. "She's supposed to be the one to take care of us."

"You don't magically get a road map for being a perfect person once you grow up." Freddie was still in the doorway. I wanted to tell her she could come in, that she could be part of this if she wanted to be, but I didn't know how. "As convenient as that would be. Trust me."

I didn't know, honestly, if I'd ever thought of my mom as a person. She was more like . . . an idea. Dr. Tilney, Headmistress, destroyer of worlds. I'd blown her up into a god over the last three years, turned her into a cartoon villain over the last three months. The person who was keeping me from being happy. The one who was ignoring Dad's legacy, his memory. It seemed like she was happy to forget Dad, to move on like he'd never existed.

But hadn't I rejected his legacy, too? Our shared love for the unusual, his curiosity about the world. I'd rejected it just as thoroughly as Mom had, and I knew how much I was still grieving.

Maybe I could allow for the possibility that she was, too.

"It's too late, though," I said finally, my head still on Liam's shoulder. "Everything's broken. Isn't it better to just give up?"

"You're getting *better* confused with *easier*," Freddie said. "They're not the same thing."

I did, for the record, hate the idea that Freddie was maybe right.

But Freddie *was* maybe right.

"Did you really not apply to any colleges?" Liam asked, his voice vibrating through me. He sounded more like a grown-up than my little brother these days, and that sent an extra pang through me. "That's wild."

"I *did* apply to Udolpho. And I really thought I was going to get in, so I didn't apply for any backup options right away, and then I just . . . didn't. It's been a weird few months, Leems." I sighed as I sat up, rubbing the back of my neck. "Maybe college isn't in the cards for me."

"Come on." Freddie rolled her eyes. "Hattie Tilney, giving up? There are plenty of people that college isn't the right choice for. I'm still figuring out if I count among their number. But you're not saying that because it's actually a choice you're making. You're saying that because it would be easier to stop. And if you could get through the last three years, you can push a little further."

"And I can help you!" Liam chimed in. "Freddie, too. We can do some super-speed research about what schools would be good for you, and help you organize the applications. Most schools' deadlines are the end of the year, right? That's still, like, more than a week away. We can do this."

"Kit tried that." I shook my head. "It didn't work."

"Kit's not your family." Liam held his hand out toward the doorway, and after a second, Freddie came in properly, sat down at the very edge of my bed along with us. *That's Liam*, I thought. Able to bridge the gaps I didn't think could be bridged. "I'll help you."

"Me, too." Freddie reached out and patted me on the knee once, before she drew her hand back fast; and even though I knew my sister and I had a lot to work out, a lot more than could be resolved in a single conversation, I nodded. Maybe I needed to learn to just . . . take the help, sometimes.

"Freddie? Liam?"

My head shot up, and my heart dropped to the bottom of my chest when I saw Mom in the doorway, in Freddie's just vacated spot, looking . . . . nervous. It wasn't a look I'd ever seen on my mother before.

"Do you mind if I talk to your sister?"

"I'll get to work on that research." Liam gave me a quick, tight hug, a brief glimpse into the kid I knew was still at the heart of my quickly turning into a (semi) mature adult person brother. As he turned and left the room, Freddie followed him out, though not without a glance back over her shoulder at me. I offered her my best attempt at a smile. It wasn't quite understanding, it wasn't quite respect, but it was . . . something. And something was better than whatever we'd had before.

Chapter Thirty-Five

If talking to Liam and Freddie had been uncomfortable, it was just the warm-up routine for the conversation I was facing down now.

"Hi." It was, as usual, the coward's move, but I kept my gaze tilted down toward the floor. I didn't think I was ready to face my mom head-on yet.

"Hi." She came into the room and closed the door behind her, sitting down at my desk like Liam had, albeit with a lot less spinning. I was glad she didn't try to come over to the bed. "We need to talk about what happened."

"I didn't mean to—"

"No." My mom held up a hand as I looked up, surprising me. "I should have clarified. *I* need to talk about what happened. And what's been happening. You can ask any questions you'd like at the end, but I need to simply . . . say my piece. Is that acceptable to you?"

"Okay?" I didn't know where this was going—honestly, no

matter what Freddie and Liam had said, it still felt distinctly possible that Mom would toss me out on the street for being a disappointment—but I was ready, at least, to listen. My pillow was back in my lap, held tightly against my chest. With a quick nod, she began.

"There were things I never understood about your father." I breathed in sharply, but didn't interrupt. She kept going, looking past me. "Even with as long as we were together. That's how it is with some relationships, I think. You can love a person deeply and still not understand them fully. I've always been . . . I've made it clear, I think, how important my ambitions are." A small smile played on the edge of her lips. "I've always wanted to make my mark on the world. Education spoke to me; I loved to learn, growing up, and I knew it was a world I'd thrive in. So I had grand plans for that world. I would be the dean of a major university. Work in education policy, perhaps. Something big enough for me."

Her eyes were glazed over, distant.

"When I met your father, I told him about my dreams, and he wanted me to have all of them. To do anything, with his full support. Even when we got pregnant with Freddie, he made it clear that he'd do anything to make my dreams a reality. And while I loved that . . . I didn't understand it. Because I couldn't see myself doing the same thing for another person." She took a deep breath, a shuddering inhale. "If your father had ambitions like mine, I don't know what we would have done."

"But he didn't." I knew she'd said not to interrupt, but the words came out of me without warning. She glanced over at me, like she was remembering I was there. Then she kept going, her hands still as death on the arms of my desk chair.

"You're right. He didn't. And that's the part I didn't understand. As our lives went on, as our family grew, he was just . . . content. And I never was. Not because I didn't love what we had. But because something inside of me always wants more, Hattie. I'm determined to push. I'll admit I pushed Derek, sometimes." It was the first time in years I'd heard her say his name. "I like to think he didn't mind it. I don't know. It's one of the things I regret most—that I didn't spend more time appreciating the happiness he found in our everyday lives. He was so good at that, wasn't he?" Although she'd said not to speak, it was a question that seemed to require an answer, so I nodded. Held my pillow closer.

"I've never been so lost as I was when he died. All of these plans, everything I'd worked for . . . undone in an instant. Of course I still had my work, I'd just gotten the position here at Northanger, but it seemed like none of that mattered with Derek gone."

"You had us." Another necessary interruption. Mom sighed.

"I know. And I regret how I've handled that, too. You all just . . . you loved your father so much. You especially, Hattie. You were so close. He did all of the parenting. Did everything a mother is supposed to do." She laughed, short and sharp. "Someone said that to me, after the funeral. 'At least they didn't lose their mother.' Can you even imagine—well. No, you can't. But that was the worst I'd ever felt. The idea that as your mother, I was somehow more valuable to the family than a father. And, Hattie, I know I'm not."

Part of me thought I should protest, but Mom wouldn't like me lying.

"I was supposed to be strong for the family." Mom shrugged, an unfamiliar gesture on her. It showed uncertainty, an emotion I'd never seen her express. "And yet I had my career, and even if I wanted to give that up, I couldn't. I needed it more than ever to support us. And it's not easy, Hattie, to be a woman in my position. I would love if that came as a surprise to you, because it would indicate times were changing, but I'm sure it doesn't. I'm an authority figure. I can't show weakness. If I did, it would be proof that I couldn't handle my responsibilities. Did you know I'm the first female head of Northanger in twenty-three years? And I have a responsibility there, too. To show that I'm capable. That my ambitions weren't for nothing. And it turned out," another sigh, "it turned out that I couldn't do both. My body didn't have the capacity to properly grieve and to be successful in my work at the same time. I felt like the life was being sucked out of me every time I went into school and put on my stern authoritarian demeanor without Derek there to bring out the lightness in me. I felt like I was turning to stone. At home, here . . . I didn't know how to talk to you, and to Liam and to Freddie. I didn't know how to show you the compassion you needed without breaking down completely. And, Hattie, I'm so sorry for that."

Her gaze returned to me, and even though her voice was choked, her eyes were dry. But I didn't hold that against her. I'd gotten pretty good at pushing back the tears, too. I thought of the story of the nuns in the abbey. Scrubbing and scrubbing until their bodies fell away, reduced only to their work, just like Mom.

"The world doesn't see a woman in pain as strong." She pushed one of the loose curls that had fallen out of her bun back behind her ear, a gesture that looked just like Freddie, just like me, in a way that made me ache. "So I had to ignore my pain to be strong instead. It's not an excuse. I know that. But I want . . . I want to try and do better. I want to figure out a way for us to come together as a family again. I've pushed you three away for too long, just because it hurt to have you close. That's cowardice. And do we stand for cowardice in this house?"

It was something she used to ask when we were little, when we were avoiding a task we didn't want to do. Despite myself, I smiled. Shook my head. Maybe with my family on my side, I could relearn what it meant to be brave.

The road to forgiving my mom would be even longer than my road to forgiving Freddie, I knew. But she was my mom, and she was hurting. I was hurting, too. Maybe things would be better if we let ourselves hurt together.

"I'm sorry about Dad," I whispered, my throat tight. "I'm sorry you lost him."

Mom nodded slowly.

"I think if he were here," she said, "he would tell you that he's not lost. That was what he loved about the paranormal, wasn't it? That people could find their way back to each other."

"But he didn't." My voice was so small. "He never found his way back to me."

Mom paused for a long time.

"Ah," she said finally. "That's why you left that business behind."

"See?" I held my pillow even tighter into my chest, pressing the fabric into my shirt. "And you say you don't know me."

Mom shifted in her chair, as if she was considering coming toward me. In the end, she didn't. Just spoke again.

"I made you Mr. Morland's ambassador because I remembered how much you loved working on that sort of thing with your father, you know." My head shot up, fast. "I couldn't figure out why you'd abandoned it so thoroughly. I thought perhaps Kit would help you. Help you be happy in a way I knew that I couldn't. I suppose I misread that particular dynamic."

"No, he . . . he did help me." It pained me to admit it, especially since it was possible that I was the one who'd ruined everything with him. Yes, he'd pushed me too hard sometimes. But with the way I was drowning, I couldn't blame someone for trying to pull me to shore. "You maybe got one thing kind of right."

"Goodness," Mom intoned, her eyes wide in feigned shock. "One whole thing in seventeen years of being your mother. They should give me some kind of award." A laugh escaped me, and she smiled. "Do you want to go to college, Hattie?" The subject change caught me off guard. "I know I've applied all of my ambition to you since your father died. You've just been so capable. So helpful. I wanted you to have everything you could possibly achieve. But I never asked what you wanted. So I'm asking now. Is that what you want?"

I took a moment, considered. I could hear the heater buzzing in the wall behind me, pumping warm air into the small room. Enveloping Mom and me.

"I think so," I said finally, releasing my grip on my pillow and placing it carefully to the side. "I don't know what I want to do there. But I want to go and find out. But, Mom"—anxiety crept into my voice—"I don't know that there's time. Even with everyone helping me."

"That is absolute nonsense, Hattie." She stood up and held her hand out to help me up, too. I took it, and her grip felt comfortingly familiar. "We're the Tilneys. And anything we want to achieve, we achieve. Do you understand?"

"Yes," I said, and Mom nodded, satisfied. Then, so fast that I barely saw it coming, she reached forward and hugged me, her arms around my shoulders for half a second before she dropped them again, stood in front of me with her shoulders straight.

It wasn't a lot. But it was something.

"Then let's get to work," she said, and I followed her downstairs, where Liam and Freddie were waiting. Where maybe my life wasn't quite as over as I'd thought.

Chapter Thirty-Six

The next week passed in a frantic haze of applications. We stopped briefly to celebrate Christmas—and, yes, my heart did want to break into a million pieces when I saw Liam shoving a box labeled for Kit back into his closet—but then it was right back to work, the whole family sitting around the dining room table together, typing furiously and occasionally calling out to each other.

Liam and Mom stayed up all night doing research—insisting, after the first hour in which we'd made our game plan, that I get some sleep—and in the morning presented me with a list of schools that didn't seem overwhelming and had flexible requirements for incoming freshmen. Nothing that would set me on a firm track, but places that encouraged students to explore their options for a year or two, while still maintaining some of the structure that I admitted to liking. I was starting to realize that it was okay to like having a plan and following it, as long as it wasn't, you know, incredibly self-destructive.

Once we had made our list—five different schools, each

with an application deadline of January 1—we buckled down. Mom pulled all my transcripts and test scores; Freddie organized them and scanned in everything I'd need. Liam worked with me on brainstorming application answers and essay topics—with five applications to do in less than a week, we needed to pick one theme and stick with it. We looked over my application for Udolpho, since Mom suggested it might be worth pulling from, but in rereading my essay I could see, now, how dry it was, how completely devoid of life. It was no wonder I didn't get in.

In the end, we went with a topic Liam had suggested.

Ghosts.

I'd been hesitant at first, but he reminded me how much I loved the storytelling aspects of all my research with Dad. The videos I'd loved making, even the podcast we'd dreamed of doing together. Why not let myself love it again?

So even though I was determined to go into freshman year with my major undeclared, I focused my essay on my love of history, on the stories that bound us all together, and how I'd always found ghost stories a fascinating lens through which to view the past.

I wrote in a haze of caffeine and Bagel Bites, with Freddie occasionally reading over my shoulder and offering (unhelpful) suggestions. Once I was finished, I emailed the essay to Mom, who went into her office and closed her door with a soft click. While she was in there, I made finishing touches on the few short answers I had to submit while Liam and I sat in the living room and pretended we weren't waiting with bated breath.

After half an hour, the door to the office opened, and Mom

came out. In the fading light of the late afternoon, I thought maybe her eyes were red, but it was hard to tell. She gestured toward my computer.

"I emailed it back to you. It's . . . it's really something, Hattie."

"No notes?" I asked hopefully, and Mom laughed.

"*Some* notes. But the core of it is perfect." Next to me, Liam raised his arms in the air in triumph, and I allowed myself a smile. It was December 30, and the common app was due at midnight tomorrow. I could handle some notes before then.

"I can't believe we're going to pull this off," Liam said as Mom headed back into her office, and I opened my email to download the updated file she'd sent. "You know you have to come back from college for my senior year winter break now, right? So that we can do this all over again?"

"Don't even joke about that," I muttered, skimming over my mom's notes. They were good. Constructive without being harsh. I supposed that this was, after all, her job—the whole guiding-her-students thing. It was nice to finally have it applied to me. "We're doing all of your applications this summer, so that we never have to go through this again."

"Right." Liam laughed and leaned back against the couch, texting. Only then did I look over at him. Consider the subject that had been on my mind these last few days, even as I did my best not to think about it. Some thoughts were impossible to ignore.

"You haven't talked to Kit, have you?" There. Just . . . ask it. Get it out in the open, and then when Liam inevitably said, *Yes, and he hates you now,* I could move on.

"A little." Liam didn't look up from his phone, and I resisted the urge to shake more of an answer out of him. He must have sensed my distress, though, since he added, "He's been asking about you."

"Has he?" I tried to make my voice sound casual, but I assumed I'd done a terrible job. Over in the kitchen, where Freddie was making more coffee, I heard a loud snort. Liam rolled his eyes.

"I don't even get what happened with you two."

"*I* happened." I sighed, flopping back against the couch cushions. "He . . . asked a lot from me. Not like that," I added with haste, as Liam made a gagging sound. "I just mean, like, in terms of what kind of person I was. He wanted me to be as adventurous and carefree as he is. And I just don't have that in me."

"Did he?" Liam looked over at me, his brow furrowed. "That doesn't sound like Kit."

"I don't know, Liam." I closed my eyes. "He wanted me to be brave. And I'm not. When he needed me to be, I wasn't. I guess it happened enough times that we just couldn't come back from it."

"But you miss him."

"Yeah." I opened my eyes, stared down at the Word document blinking up from my laptop. "That doesn't fix what was wrong with us, though."

"I don't know." Liam finally put down his phone. "I think what you're doing now, what you've done this week, is brave. Standing up to Mom was brave, and listening to her afterward . . . that was pretty brave, too. You're stronger than you give yourself credit for."

"Not strong enough for Kit Morland."

"How do you know, unless you try?" Liam got up, shoving his phone into his pocket and heading for the staircase. "And speaking of trying, I'm going to *try* and get some sleep."

"Right. Tell Erik hi." I waved, and Liam stuck his tongue out at me before running up the stairs, his phone already out of his pocket again. Ah, young love. I remembered when it felt as pure and full of hope for me as it did for Erik and Liam.

I felt deeply, immensely guilty for how things had gone down with Kit. It didn't matter if I'd yelled at my mom afterward—I should have stood up for Kit right away, in the moment. He deserved someone who would do that for him. Someone who would declare to the entire world how proud they were to be with him, how much they cared about him. Because Kit Morland was extraordinary, and he deserved extraordinary things.

Well. I couldn't think about that now. I returned to my mom's edits, to the slow work of salvaging my future.

And, after far too little sleep and many hours of staring at word choices later . . . it was done.

"Whoa." Liam sat back in his chair at the dining room table, where the whole family had gathered—even Freddie—for my final moments of work over lunch the next day. "I can't believe you pulled it off."

"*We* pulled it off." I grinned over at him. I felt briefly like I could do anything. Like this whole ridiculous ordeal was proof of my enduring resilience. I felt *good*. Across from us, Mom smiled, a little indulgent. Even Freddie looked pleased. "Thanks, everyone."

"That's what family is for," Mom said, her voice clipped, before indicating my computer. "But go on. I'll feel better once it's submitted."

"Right. Okay . . . *now* we're done." I waited for the little confirmation page to pop up, then closed my computer with a sigh of relief. "I need lunch. And three to four days of sleep."

"Speaking of." Freddie jumped to her feet, went into the kitchen, and returned with a pot of what looked like boxed macaroni and cheese and four bowls. "Dig in."

"You cooked?" I stared at my sister, slack-jawed.

She scoffed. "I'm not completely worthless, you know."

"I know. That's not what I . . . thanks." I nodded at Freddie, who gave me one in return. Progress, I guessed, at least for us. I would take progress, especially if that progress was accompanied by sweet, cheesy carbohydrates.

We spent most of our meal in a comfortable silence. While we ate, a new thought was percolating in my brain. And after lunch, as we were clearing our plates, I approached Mom in the kitchen, determined to be brave.

"I want to see Kit." I'd abandoned subtlety some time ago, apparently, and Mom was startled enough that she almost dropped the plate she was rinsing. "I know you thought he was a terrible influence on me, but I was going to influence myself either way. He just . . . happened to be there for it.

He's a good guy, and I messed everything up with him, so I want to see him. I owe him like a million apologies."

"We're speaking of the same boy who said all those disrespectful things about me, yes?" Her composure seemed recovered, which was good, because if it hadn't, I would have been really worried. I was worried enough about this as it was. "The one who I kicked out of the house?"

"That's the one." I leaned back against the counter, drummed my fingers against it. "He's not a bad person, Mom. He just wants me to be happy. He doesn't want anything to get in the way of that."

"Like me."

"Yeah." God, this was uncomfortable, but I was starting to suspect that getting older, growing up, was about more than just graduating with good grades and going to college or whatever. It was about knowing how to have the conversations that sucked. "He was looking out for me. Don't you want people to do that?"

Mom didn't respond, just kept rinsing the dishes and loading them into the open dishwasher without looking at me. I held my breath. If she said no . . . I was going to see him anyway.

Finally, she sighed. "Do you remember when we read *Little Women* together, when you were younger?"

"Kind of." It was a blurry, faint memory. Mom coming into my room before bed, reading to me as I fell asleep.

"The mother in it—Marmee—she says that she's angry nearly every day of her life." Mom shook her head. "And I'm sad nearly every day of my life, Hattie. Not all the time—not a great, all-consuming sadness, not anymore. It's not as bad as it used to be. Or at least, it's different than it used to be. But it's still always there. And I've been terrible about searching out the things to counteract that. When I was in New York that weekend? I was still sad every day. But I got to be happy, too." She put down her last dish, closed the dishwasher door, and turned to me. "I want you to go after the things that make you happy. And if this Kit is part of that . . . then you should see him."

"Really?" I jumped away from the counter, nearly throwing myself into Mom's arms before I stopped at the last moment. She smiled at me, took my hand and gave it a squeeze, then left the room. And that was okay, I reminded myself. We didn't need to have some Hallmark movie version of a mother-daughter relationship for our relationship to have value. As long as we loved and respected each other, that was enough.

I tore out of the kitchen, up the stairs, and into Liam's room, giving only a perfunctory knock before bursting in.

"Where is he?" I half asked, half yelled at my brother, who was lying back on his bed and texting with a smile on his face. When he saw me, he shot up right away, dropping the phone. "Where's Kit?"

"Why?" He looked suspicious. I didn't blame him.

"Because." Is this what being brave always felt like? I felt like I was flying. "I need to make a grand declaration of love to show him that I'm sorry, and I need to know if that's going to involve flying to Florida. Are you going to help me or not?"

Liam's face erupted with joy.

"Oh, *hell* yes." He punched his fist in the air, already shoving his feet into the sneakers that he'd abandoned partially across the room. "He's not far—Jolie's got a bunch of the Ghost Brigade at their house, some farm in the middle of nowhere. He took the bus, but I don't know if it'll be running today, with it being New Year's Eve. Or if it is, it'll be full of drunk idiots. We should get Freddie to drive us so we can take her car."

"She wouldn't." My heart sank. We hadn't even left the house yet, and already there was a complication. I really was not having any luck with plans this year. "Crap."

"What wouldn't I do?" Freddie had appeared in the doorway, leaning against the frame in her familiar way. Liam leapt toward her before I could stop him.

"We need you to drive us on an epic quest for love and romance!" He grabbed Freddie by the shoulders for support, probably because he only had half a shoe on and was in danger of falling completely over at any point. "Hattie needs to see Kit, and he's only a couple of hours away. Please will you drive us?"

Freddie looked over at me, her face expressionless.

Here we were, at another opportunity for me to shut down, back out, give up.

"We really need your help," I said, even as the words pained me. "Please?"

After what felt like an eternity, Freddie nodded. Liam audibly whooped. I should have gotten him a lot more YA romances for Christmas, since grand romantic gestures were apparently all he cared about. But for now, I was just grateful.

Time to face my fears.

Chapter Thirty-Seven

We were about an hour into the drive, Liam asking me a million questions about what I was going to do when I saw Kit while I sat quietly and tried not to throw up from nerves, when Freddie made a sudden turn onto a side road, and I had to grab the door to keep from flying directly into her.

"What the hell?" I asked as I righted myself. Behind me, Liam scrambled for his phone on the floor, where it had been tossed from his hands. "Drive much?"

"Didn't want to miss our turn." Freddie smirked, tossing her head so her curls settled behind her shoulders. "You're fine."

"Why are we turning?" I looked at the narrow, winding road, surrounded by leafless winter branches that stretched overhead. "Liam said it was farther away than this."

"Kit is, sure." Freddie's eyes were on the road, but I didn't love the expression I saw in the rearview mirror. A little too much determination for my taste. "But Kit isn't the only one you need to apologize to."

"What do you—Oh, no." Because as we emerged into one of those small, middle-of-nowhere New York towns that was basically a main street and nothing else, I knew exactly where we were. "Freddie. We are not doing this."

"I'm not letting you decide that a *boy* is the only person worth making amends with." Freddie's voice was determined as she made another left turn, a little fast for my comfort. "He wasn't entirely blameless, but you decided to forgive him anyway, because you care about him or some crap. That's what you're going to do here, too."

"Sorry, where are we?" Liam asked from the back seat, but we both ignored him. My heart was pounding, my palms sweating. I'd never been to this town before, but I'd seen pictures of the church we were passing, of the diner on the corner, all tacked up around Izzy's side of her and Priya's room. This was the town where her mom lived, where she was spending winter break this year.

"Izzy was a complete asshole to me and to Kit," I protested as my sister turned off the main road (if you could call it that) and meandered our way down a side street. "I don't have anything to say to her."

"I didn't realize we were expecting perfection out of our friends now." Freddie checked her side mirror before turning. "Every time Izzy hung around during cross-county practice, you know what she would do? Spend the entire time asking about you."

"Yeah, so she could manipulate me."

"Because she *cares* about you." I could hear the frustration in Freddie's voice that time. "Liam told me what went down

at Cry Fest." I shot Liam a look of betrayal over my shoulder.
I didn't even know *he* fully knew what went down at Cry Fest,
but the Northanger rumor mill was very effective. "She pulled
a dick move, for sure. But she and Priya talked about you all the
time during practice, about how you'd ditched them for Kit.
You were best friends for three years and then you turned into
a totally different person that completely abandoned them, by
their telling. Maybe you're not entirely blameless in this, either."

"I didn't . . . I'm not a totally different person." My voice
sounded feeble, weak. They were *worried* about me? I'd assumed that was impossible. Izzy only needed me to keep her
dad off her back. Priya only hung out with me by association.
"I'm just trying to be who I actually am. That's not the person
Izzy and Priya want to be friends with."

"Well, I think you owe them the chance to make that decision for themselves." Freddie's gaze was steely as she pulled
over finally in front of a medium-sized green-and-white house
with two cars parked in the driveway. I recognized the one
that belonged to Izzy's mom, with its Northanger Abbey
bumper stickers. And Priya, I knew, would be there, too, staying with Izzy and her mom for the last weekend of break.
It was something she'd mentioned excitedly one of the last
times we'd chatted properly, weeks ago. *Weeks ago.* The thought
echoed uncomfortably in my head. "Besides, I already texted
Priya and told her we were coming, and *she* already told Izzy."

"You *what?*"

"She texted me first." Freddie shrugged. "They miss you,
Hattie."

Oh, God. Growing up and taking responsibility for your

actions was the worst. Freddie was watching me, waiting for me to get out of the car, and when I looked into the back seat via the rearview mirror, Liam caught my eye and shrugged.

"New year, new you?"

"It's December thirty-first."

"Well." Liam returned to his texting. "Old year, new you. Whatever. Freddie's not going to leave until you go in, and my phone battery's getting low."

I *really* didn't want to do this. The person I was with Izzy and Priya—all about achievement, all about our transactional friendship—was the worst version of myself. And, yeah, I hadn't exactly been a good friend to either of them, but the cowardly parts of me felt like it would be easier to just wipe the slate clean. Move on.

But we're not being cowardly anymore, I reminded myself. The only way out was through, or whatever. So I took a deep breath, opened the car door into the bracing winter air, and walked up the driveway toward the house.

When I rang the doorbell, I'd expected Mrs. Thorpe to answer. To lead me into the living room, where I could compose myself and figure out what exactly I was going to say to my so-called friends.

When Izzy was the one who answered, all of that went out the window.

"Hey." She seemed as surprised to see me as I was to see her. "You're— I didn't think you'd really come."

"Freddie was the one driving." I shrugged. Home Izzy looked a lot more vulnerable than School Izzy—wearing leggings and a Northanger Student Council shirt, her hair pulled back in a loose French braid, no makeup. "I didn't have much of a choice."

"You could have refused to get out of the car." She stepped aside, let me come into the hallway, and closed the door behind me as I took off my shoes. "I did that to my dad once. Right after he and Mom split up, and they were still doing the every-other-weekend thing. I was tired of getting bounced around between them."

"You told me that." We stood awkwardly in the hallway, stark white and modern, decorated with just a few posed photos of Izzy above the staircase. "Where's Priya?"

"She went out for a run. You literally can't get the sneakers off that girl." Izzy tossed her braid over her shoulder, the gesture deeply familiar. "Look. I'm sorry I wrote that post, okay? It was stupid and petty and not even very good journalism. I took it down and sent out a retraction, which I'm guessing you didn't see."

I shook my head. "I've been kind of distracted."

"Yeah. I just . . ." She sighed, looked at the pictures on the wall instead of at me. "Things were way easier last year, when it was just the three of us looking out for one another. And then this year started and you ditched us for Kit, like, immediately, and my dad was on my back all the time about following in his footsteps and being more responsible and I just . . . I snapped. But the three of us were supposed to crush senior year together, you know? And then you just decided you didn't want that anymore." She still wouldn't look at me. "That sucked, Hattie."

"You can't be mad at me for becoming friends with someone new." There were no pictures of her entire family any-

where on the wall, I noticed. And thinking about it, Izzy didn't
have any in her room, either. All the pictures of her mom and
her dad were separate. "Especially someone who didn't want
anything from me. You've made it plenty clear over the years,
Izzy, that the main reason we were friends was because of my
mom. And that was fine because I needed you, too, to find
a place at Northanger. But Kit just *liked* me." He might not
anymore, but he had, at least. "Can you really blame me for
running toward that?"

"Do you really think our friendship didn't mean anything?"
Izzy took a deep, raggedy breath, and if I didn't know her
better, I'd say she was getting choked up. "Yeah, the stuff with
your mom was super convenient, and it might have started
out that way . . . but we were friends, Hattie. Real friends. Or
as least as close as we could get, considering that you literally never let your guard down around me or Priya. That felt
great, by the way. When I realized you were closer to Kit in
five minutes than you'd ever let me get in three years."

It was possible, it was very gently possible, that Izzy may
have had a point.

"I didn't know you wanted that from me. And I'm sorry I
didn't just tell you I couldn't get you a recommendation from
my mom." I sighed, leaned back against the wall of the hallway. "Maybe we could just . . . I don't want to go back to the
way things were. We can't, anyway. But we can try to start
over. If you want."

"That could be cool. I guess." Izzy allowed herself a small
smile, and I felt a rush of affection for her, my deeply misguided
friend, who had nevertheless protected me at Northanger until

I got up the courage to take care of myself. "Does that mean I have to hang out with Ghost Boy, too?" The nickname didn't feel mean, not like it had before.

"I don't know yet." I shrugged. "I kind of ruined things with him. That's where we're going now, to try and, like, big gesture him or whatever. See if he'll forgive me."

"He will." Izzy's smile had a certainty I wished I could borrow. "He's obviously completely in love with you. It's gross, honestly."

"You could come with us, if you want?" I surprised myself with the question, but it was time to stop pretending Izzy wasn't important to me. Making mistakes didn't make her a bad person, not when she was willing to learn from them. "Liam and Freddie wouldn't mind the company, I bet."

"Thanks." Izzy let out a long breath, tucked a loose strand of hair behind her ear. "I think . . . I don't think I should. But I appreciate the offer. And let's plan to all hang out when we get back on campus, okay? Even Ghost Boy."

"That sounds good," I said. The awkward standing continued, both of us shifting from foot to foot. Then, finally, Izzy reached forward and wrapped me in a quick and awkward hug.

It lasted about half a second, but as far as half-a-second hugs went, it was a good one. At least, it was the start of a good one. And with Izzy, I would take the start of something good. That was all we needed.

Priya got back from her run right as Izzy's mom was loading me up with road trip snacks, racing over as soon as she saw me.

"Hattie!" She came to a gasping halt at the side of the car, just as I was passing Liam a full case of Capri Sun. "I'm so glad you're here. I'm sorry, okay? I should have stood up to Izzy for you back at the festival. I just didn't know that she was doing the post, and then I had to, like, process it, you know? But I should have said something right away. And, like, I should have done that a million times over the last three years. The whole first day I got here, I barely talked to her at all, just to teach her a lesson."

"It's okay, Pree." I reached out and put a hand on her elbow to stop her, if only because I was worried she'd hyperventilate from talking so quickly after a run. "It's something I need to be better about, too. But I'm down to keep trying if you are."

"Yeah." Priya nodded fast, then sipped at her water bottle. "That sounds great. Where are you guys going? That's . . . so many snacks."

"Hattie's going to declare her love for Kit!" Liam called out as he was carrying a case of Girl Scout cookies out of the garage, courtesy of Izzy's mom. "It's a road trip!"

"I kind of messed everything up with him," I added at Priya's perplexed expression. "So now we're grand gesturing."

"Really?" Priya's eyes widened with joy. "Can I come?"

"You want to?" I asked, a little skeptical. Although, to be fair, we had a *lot* of snacks. "Izzy's not coming."

This time, Priya was the one who squeezed my arm. "I want to come anyway."

So after an extra twenty-minute delay while Priya showered and threw on fresh clothes, Liam ran inside to use the bathroom, and Izzy's mom announced she had to get a picture of all of us, we were finally all in the car, as Izzy waved to us from the front steps and Priya and I shouted out the window that we would text her what happened. Then we were on the road, Liam in the front with Freddie this time, me squeezed into the back seat with a billion snacks and one of the girls I was hoping to call a friend again, on our way to try and save my relationship.

This wasn't how I'd expected my winter break to go, but you know what? I couldn't have planned it any better.

Chapter Thirty-Eight

As we got closer to Jolie's house, where a select few members of the Ghost Brigade, plus Kit, had gathered for New Year's Eve, I started to feel like I was going to either throw up or pass out. Maybe some fun new combination of the two. It was fully dark by now, Liam was stuffed full of the snacks provided by Izzy's mother, and every time I thought about what I was about to do, I wanted to reach forward, yank the wheel out of Freddie's hands, and turn this whole car around.

Priya's constant questions—*Do you know what you're going to say? Do you think he'll forgive you? Why exactly did your mom kick him out of the house?*—weren't helping, either.

Eventually, we reached the sign for Woodston Farm (Jolie's family's home), and pulled into the long, snow-dusted driveway. Fields stretched out behind the house, bordered by woods; Liam said that was where everyone was hanging out for the night, stargazing their way into the new year. It was freezing and kind of overcast, but I didn't need to understand the choice to acknowledge the romance of it. The Ghost Brigade knew how to create an atmosphere.

An atmosphere I was about to ruin.

"I don't know," I said suddenly, just as Freddie turned off the engine. "Is this a terrible idea?"

"Oh my God." Freddie turned around to face me as soon as she'd unbuckled her seat belt. "Henrietta Tilney. Wouldn't you like, for once in your whole goddamn life, to actually go after the things you want?"

Well. When she put it like that.

"Yes?" I offered, and then Priya launched herself out of the back seat, pulled me out of the car, and pointed me in the direction of the back of the house, where, over the roof, I could just barely make out the wisps of smoke from a bonfire. "Wait." I turned around to see her jump back into the car, shivering. "Are you guys not coming with me?"

"You don't need us." Priya reached out to squeeze my hand, then closed the door behind her, shouting her last words of encouragement through the closed window. "You've got this."

I've got this, I told myself. No matter what happened— because, it seemed important to remember, this might go terribly—just the going after something I wanted was the important part. If I managed to grab hold of it . . . great. If not, then just the trying was still good. Still worthwhile.

It would feel a hell of a lot better if it worked, though.

And by the time I made it to the bonfire, saw a ring of cars backed up against the flames with half a dozen kids I recognized curled up on their roofs, Kit's head visible above all the others, I at least knew what I wanted to say.

"Who's the— Oh, shit." Jolie was the first one to notice me, their face lit garishly from underneath by the roaring fire. The rest of the brigade sat up and stared, their eyes glowing with the fire's reflection. Kit, naturally, seemed to be the last one to turn, but he was too far away for me to make out his expression. "Hattie? What are you doing here?"

"Hey, everyone," I said, getting some hesitant waves in return. I mean, fair. Kit had probably told them why he'd ended up here. "I'm, um. I'm here to see Kit."

"And you think he'd want to see you after—"

"Jolie." Kit hopped off a truck bed and stepped into the light of the fire, where I could finally see his face. He mostly looked . . . tired, honestly. "It's okay. What's up, Hattie?"

"I, um . . . how are you?" I squeaked, because when I'd planned my speech in the car, I hadn't been expecting so many curious faces staring up at me.

Kit shrugged. "Bad? Since I ruined everything?"

"You—what?" I had to do a literal double take with that one. "Kit, you didn't. I was the one who messed up." I stepped forward toward the fire, so that it was the only thing left between us, and even though the giant dancing flames were a formidable obstacle, I was just glad not to have to look at anyone else. "I should have stood up for you. Time and time again, I should have stood up for you, but the last time . . . that was when I needed to do it the most, and I completely failed."

"No." He shook his head, his hair falling over his face.

"I got too swept up in being, like, your white knight or whatever, and I pushed you too far. I was trying to tell you what I wanted, instead of asking what you wanted. I mean, yeah, you probably could have stood up for me more." A corner of his mouth quirked up into a flash of a smile. "But I'm the one who dug up all your ghosts."

"They needed to be dug up." I took a deep breath. Again, this would have been easier without the entire brigade watching with bated breath, but I needed to prove to Kit I could love him in front of an audience, anyway. "Kit, I—I talked to my mom. About everything. Yelled at her about it, if I'm being honest." I laughed at the way his eyes widened. "And she's— she's not a monster. She's just hurting. Like me." That was one thing I definitely *didn't* want to go into further in front of everyone, but from the way Kit nodded, it was clear he understood. "And we spent the whole week getting my applications ready—the whole family. So you didn't, like, ruin my future, if that's what you were thinking."

Kit let out a long exhale. "I'll admit, it did cross my mind." He shoved his hands deep in his pockets. He was wearing a dark gray peacoat and his favorite slouchy beanie, and he looked so much like the hero of a romance set in the English countryside that it was taking all of my willpower not to throw myself into his arms. *Forgive me*, I willed internally, hoping against hope. *Trust me*. "But I still don't know that we were a good idea, Hattie. I feel like I kind of broke you."

"Please," I scoffed. "That's giving yourself a little too much credit, isn't it?" Across the fire, Kit's eyes danced. "Trust me.

I was broken long before you got to Northanger Abbey, Kit
Morland. And I'm not here because I think you'll fix me. I'm
here because I'm ready to try and fix myself, and I want you
with me for the journey."

"Do you really think that's possible?" He ran his hand
through his hair, knocking the beanie askew. "That I could
even . . . Honestly, Hattie. It's one thing to say it. But do you
really believe it?"

There it was. I took a deep breath, straightened my shoulders.

"I used to be terrible at believing in things," I said as Kit
stood across the fire from me, as the Ghost Brigade looked on,
as a hundred yards away a car filled with my friend and family
hoped in my direction. "And then I met you, and you're so
good at belief. I didn't know how that was possible. But someone told me—hint," I added with a grin, "that someone was
you—that you only need two people to believe in something
to make it true. And, Kit, when you believe in something as
hard as you do, it's infectious. It got me to believe in things,
too. Like myself. And I know that's, like, the corniest thing I've
ever said," I added hastily, "but it's true. You didn't break me,
and you didn't fix me, but you showed me the path toward
fixing myself. And now, yes, I believe that I can follow it. I
believe that we can do it together. I believe in *us*. It only takes
two people believing something to make it true, Kit." I took
a deep breath. "So will you make this true with me? Do you
want to believe in us, too?"

The next ten seconds were the longest of my entire life.
They were Christmas morning and waiting for exam results

all rolled into one; they were sneaking out past curfew and expecting something to jump out from the dark and seeing if you'd gotten what you'd really wanted.

For those ten seconds, I watched Kit through the flames, and I watched him consider. Watched him rock back and forth on the balls of his feet, watched him breathe out frosty air that covered his features in smoky white so that for a second, he was the ghost.

And then he grinned, and he started to close the distance between us around the fire. And I was running, too, so that we met in the middle, crashing into each other, a tangle of arms and legs and hands and hips and then lips and tongues. And when Kit kissed me, I kissed him back with everything I knew, with everything I didn't know yet but was willing to believe in. Around us, the Ghost Brigade burst into cheers, and from the sounds of pounding feet and yelling coming toward us, I suspected that my family had poured out of the car, too, to join in the jubilation.

"We still have to finish our project," Kit whispered in my ear as he pulled me against him, his breath warm against my skin. "We didn't get the chance before I left."

"Don't worry." I pulled his mouth down to mine again, let my hands weave through his long, dark hair. "I think we can figure out a way to work on it together."

Take care of them, Henrietta. That was what my dad had said. But taking care of the people I loved started with taking care of myself. And as Kit and I finally broke apart, his hands tangled in my hair, mine wrapped around his waist, I felt a sudden and tremendous lightness. It was like . . . like being happy.

Like letting go of a few of my ghosts. They weren't leaving me—I knew they never would, knew that grief never fully left—but they didn't have me in a stranglehold anymore.

So what the hell. I pulled Kit in to kiss him again, because I was worth happiness.

I was worth everything.

The morning of my graduation from Northanger Abbey was hot, sticky, and perfect.

Freddie made waffles, and Mom even managed to stop in and eat half of one, though this was one of her busiest days of the year, and she had to be on campus hours before I did. That was okay. It gave me a little extra time with my siblings before I headed up to school, to joke and laugh and let Freddie style my hair while Liam watched and offered unhelpful suggestions. They even drove me up to campus when it was time, so I wouldn't have to walk the forest path in my heels, even though Kit had very valiantly offered to carry me as far as I needed. I had declined, as romantic as it sounded. I didn't want to go into graduation with anyone carrying me.

After today, the classmates who had defined the last four years of my life would be scattered to the winds. Priya and Izzy were both working this summer before they left for school— Priya to Sarah Lawrence, and Izzy to Northwestern, who'd accepted her even without the ghost piece in her portfolio. We were talking about a trip together before we all left, a weekend in the city or something, and while I didn't know if we'd make it happen, I was glad we were all still open to the possibility.

And even though Northanger would still be here—along with my family, and Kit, who was getting an enormous head already at the prospect of being a senior—I'd be gone, too. I'd committed to the University of Delaware for the fall semester, a school that was large enough that it had everything I needed but with small enough programs that I could get some of the intimacy of a cozier school. Liam and Freddie had bought an enormous inflatable blue hen mascot and put it up on our front lawn, and if nothing else, I had to admit that it deterred the worst of the rogue ghost hunters.

I was excited, even if I was sad to be leaving Northanger. To be leaving my family, my friends. Kit. But it would be good for me. Good to see who I could be on my own.

And besides, I was reminded as Kit crashed into me from behind, just before the ceremony when everyone was supposed to be lining up, it wasn't like I'd *really* be alone.

"What are you doing here?" I straightened my mortarboard, knocked askew by Kit's hug. "This area is graduates only, I'm pretty sure. Don't you need to go sit with the other high schoolers?"

"You're still a high schooler for another hour." Kit bent down to kiss me, and I didn't protest, let myself play with the ends of his hair before he pulled back. "So it's chill. Hey, I found something awesome for us to do this summer."

"You did?" I did my best to fluff my curls back out, slightly crushed by Kit's embrace. "What is it?" Kit was staying with us for all of July, an invitation my mom had extended to go along with the whole sorry-I-kicked-you-out-of-my-house thing. Liam was thrilled; he wasn't the only one.

"Hear me out, okay?" His eyes sparkled, as they always did when he had a new idea; and even though teachers were starting to line us up, and I really needed to go, I nodded. "Ghost hunting podcast! We can spend the whole summer investigating in town, maybe get Freddie to drive us out into the country a little—there's an abandoned sawmill forty-five minutes from here that had some *very* interesting evidence of paranormal activity pop up recently. And then even when you're in school, we can keep it up, right? I mean, I know you'll be busy, but I can handle the editing, and then it'll give us an extra excuse to hang out and . . ."

I kissed him. Stood up on my toes and pulled him toward me by the collar of his button-down shirt, felt his exhale of surprise against my mouth that turned into a smile. Just like it always did with Kit.

"Hey." I tucked a piece of hair behind his ear. "I love you. You know that?"

What had been a regular-sized smile before grew into a megawatt glow, brighter than the sun.

"I'd suspected. I love you, too." He kissed me again, and I felt a thousand futures in it, a world of possibilities, each one better with Kit Morland by my side. "Now go graduate."

"You got it." I waved goodbye and fell in line, became one of a mass of black robes that marched out onto the field of Northanger Abbey, to a crowd of cheering parents and friends and family. And maybe Kit and my dad were right. Maybe this school—maybe this field, hell, maybe the very podium where my mom was now speaking, as we all took our seats, as she pointed me out in the crowd of graduates, and my classmates all hooted and hollered while I blushed furiously—maybe it was all haunted.

But I wasn't. Not anymore.

Acknowledgments

Ever since I read *Northanger Abbey* back in college, I loved it. From the gothic in-jokes to the adventures around Bath, from the "horrors" lurking within the abbey to the always magnificent Mr. Tilney, it's an absolute dream of a novel. But adapting a beloved story is never easy, and I wouldn't have been able to do it without the help of an amazing group of people I'm lucky enough to have on my team.

First of all, thanks to Moe Ferrara and the entire team at BookEnds, who have always had my back for the many (many!!!) years we've been working together now. Moe, in your honor, I won't make fun of the Penguins *once* for the remainder of these acknowledgments.

A million thanks goes out to my amazing editor, Sarah Grill, my publishing soul sister—thank you for always finding the best Taylor Swift lyric for every situation we find ourselves in. The entire team at Wednesday Books continues to be a dream to work with, and I owe a world of thanks to Rivka Holler, Sarah Bonamino, Meghan Harrington, Diane Dilluvio, Eric

Meyer, Michelle McMillian, Carla Benton, Martha Schwartz, and Christina MacDonald.

If a picture is worth a thousand words, then a brilliant jacket design and cover illustration must be worth even more—thank you to Kerri Resnick and Amelia Flower, who captured the characters and the vibe of this book so perfectly.

As a person who gets nightmares from the *trailers* for scary movies, I was a little worried when I set out to write a gothic and paranormal-inspired novel—but luckily I have the world's best critique partner and beta reader in Ann Fraistat, horror writer extraordinaire. Ann, thank you for everything you've done for this book, and for me.

Writing books can be a super weird and isolating job, but it's a lot better when you have amazing industry friends by your side. Thank you to Erin Hahn, Jenny Howe, Serena Kaylor, Amie Kaufman, Samantha Markum, JC Peterson, Tiffany Schmidt, Ashley Schumacher, Jessica Spotswood, Stephanie Kate Strohm, and Andrea Tang, for the endless support and occasional tomfoolery.

I'm lucky to be a part of the best bookstore family in the world at One More Page Books. Thanks to Eileen McGervey, Lelia Nebeker, Rebecca Speas, Rosie Dauval, Sam White, Amber Taylor (honorarily), Anna Bright, Lauren Wengrowitz, and the rest of the team.

Working for an indie bookstore means you're a part of a large and wonderful community, and the support that the indie bookstore community has given me since my debut has been amazing to behold. No matter where in the country I go, there's an indie bookstore where I'll be welcomed with open arms, and I'm eternally grateful for it. Special thanks to Riverstone Books, East City Bookshop, Bethany Beach Books, Fountain Bookstore, Penguin Bookshop, White Whale Bookstore, Parnassus Books, and the many other wonderful indies I've gotten support from over the last year and beyond. A shout-out as well to the many Barnes and Noble booksellers who have been so kind when I wander into your stores with an overenthusiastic smile and a Sharpie—thank you.

I'm also incredibly thankful to the many librarians who have made sure that my books make their way into the hands of readers who need them, as well as the Bookstagrammers, TikTokers, and bloggers who have helped shout about them. And for my amazing readers themselves—thank you as well. You can spend hours pre-debut wondering what it's going to feel like when people are actually reading your book in the world for the first time, but nothing can prepare you for how amazing it feels when people reach out and tell you how much your words meant to them. Thank you, thank you, thank you.

To my amazing friends, in DC, Pittsburgh, and everywhere else, thank you for sharing in all of this excitement with me. Special shout-out to Carly Britton, who let me read the most devastating passages of this book out loud to her just to see if they were effectively heartbreaking; Max Klefstad and Lindy Bathurst, who continue to be the most supportive friends a girl could ask for (with the most comfortable couch); and Dan Connolly and Elizabeth McDonald, who helped make an extremely scary move to an entirely new city into something manageable—I hope you can recognize the seeds of our rambling philosophical conversations in this book. And to my Numenera gang—Dan, Andrew, Tom, Dustin—I couldn't let a six-year campaign come to an end without a printed thank-you to all of you for being amazing collaborators who have kept my storytelling skills sharp for all of these years.

I keep writing books about families because I have, in my not so humble opinion, the very best one out there. To my extended family, Quain and Wockenfuss alike, thank you for buying copies of my books for your unsuspecting friends and book clubs—it means the world. To my grandfather Frank Wockenfuss especially, who I have to assume has single-handedly doubled my book sales by pitching my books to every dental hygienist, waiter, and neighbor he talks to—thank you. To my in-laws, Virginia and Randy Tiedemann, who have shared my book from coastal Virginia to Brazil—I'm so grateful. And to Ben, Erica, and Avery Blaschke—thanks for letting me flood your house with more picture books than was previously thought possible. I have no plans to stop.

To my parents, Bill and Jeanne Quain, who didn't even blink when I told them I wanted to pursue a creative career, and who showed me that this kind of life was even possible—thank you. And to my sister, Kathleen Quain, the queen of cat voices and perfect presents—thank you for always reading right alongside of me. I love you all so much.

To Jane Austen, for the amazing worlds I get to play in. Thank you.

To Jenny, who still hasn't learned how to read, because she's a cat—you're my number-one girl.

And to Dustin Tiedemann, my amazing husband. There are no words to describe everything you've done for me, so I'll offer you this instead—I love you, I love you, I love you.